Charity Begins with Murder

Annie McDowall

First published 2011

ISBN 978-1-4709-9929-2

Beanstalk Publications

Thank you....

Joe Britto, Lois Graessle, Chris Bolton, Mary Rollinson, Anthony Joseph – my critical readers, who gave encouragement and constructive criticism and told me when I'd lost the plot.

Leone Ross, inspirational and challenging creative writing tutor, who gave ruthless instruction on murdering little darlings.

VG Lee for generous support and encouragement right from the first workshop in York.

The City Lit, Arvon Foundation, and Morley College – tutors and fellow students.

Mary Salinsky, for guidance on SatNav

Gina Smith for technical advice

This book is for everyone working in the voluntary sector, and especially for those who regularly suffer curly-edged sandwiches at tedious committee meetings in the name of trying to make the world a better place.

Chapter 1

Before the murder was the Job Centre. I wouldn't have got caught up in all this mess had my personal adviser not been so keen to meet her targets. When I went to sign on, Chantelle was all in black. She'd had her nails done since I saw her two weeks ago. They must have been two inches long, curving inwards like talons. They were painted scarlet with an intricate design traced in gold over the surface. Her left hand nails tapped a brisk rhythm as her right hand moved a mouse up and down the current vacancies list on her PC. I was in my usual khaki Dockers and T-shirt. Short nails – nothing to get in the way of whatever my hands were doing – and red Kickers that I'd had for nearly a decade.

"There's a job on the meat counter at Tesco's," she said.

"I'm vegetarian."

"You need a job."

She was getting mean.

"You mean you need to get me off your books."

"Getting a job will be really good for your self esteem, Nikki. You just need to get a foot in the door…"

"Arbeit macht frei," I said and then felt ashamed at comparing the Department for Work and Pensions, represented by Chantelle, with a nazi death camp.

"What?"

"Nothing. Look, I'm not working with dead animals, ok?"

"You'll lose your benefit."

"I can refuse on moral and religious grounds."

"What's your religion then?"

"I've Buddhist leanings. Isn't there something else?"

She tapped her fingers harder, war drum nervy rhythm.

"Admin worker stroke receptionist. Small charity with big dreams."

"I type with two fingers and I'm allergic to filing."

"You can pick up a phone, open the door. You could be quite personable if you tried; and this one can't be against your religion – it's a charity!"

"Won't they want someone with nails like yours?"

"Look Nikki. Either we make the call, I get you an interview and you give them your best smile…. or you lose your benefits. Simple as that." Ten nails tapped a snare drum warning on the birch effect desk.

"Well, when you put it like that…"

"So what did you say?"

"I said I didn't know. I didn't think so."

That evening I'd met up with Carla. We'd known each other since 1990, worked together in a crisis house for women and children. Stayed friends, soul sisters, as what had remained of the women's movement disintegrated around us, crisis houses turning into war zones, lipstick and fetish gear emerging as the ultimate victors. Right now we were trying to untangle my love life.

"Are you in love with her?"

"I don't know."

We sat quietly then for a moment or two while the bar around us filled with noise and smoke.

"Shall we have another bottle? Celebrate your almost becoming one of the working population?"

"Haven't had the interview yet. They might turn me down, and then I'd have to go back to Chantelle. God! How can you do anything with nails like that? I kind of like her, though. I'll miss her, miss our fortnightly battles."

"And Ruth?"

"Ruth. Ruth….she's…oh shit, let's get that other bottle."

Tanners Lane was a back street that wound parallel to the main road. There was a KFC box in the gutter, dog shit, grey blobs of hardened chewing gum, and grease stains on the pavement. Mean little workers' cottages, that looked as if they'd been squatted, faced buildings that could have been small factories or warehouses, all barricaded behind high metal gates. There was a kebab shop on the corner, from which oozed the reek of rancid sheep fat. I looked again at the directions Chantelle had given me. "*Action in Caring*" was supposed to be at number 39b. The cottages were all even numbered, the industrial buildings anonymous, like gangsters hiding their faces behind shades. I walked the length of the road and then back again. No-one else was around. I'd have to ask the lone worker in the kebab shop.

"Hi. I'm looking for number 39b. D'you know where it is? I've been up and down the street, just can't seem to find it."

His chef's tunic was stained yellowy grey. The hairs on the backs of his hands glistened with grease. He scratched at his nose.

"I think it's a kind of community centre, something like that," I added.

"It's few doors down, behind blue gates, innit." He pointed out of the door to the right.

"Thanks," I said, "I've got a job interview."

"They bit funny, that lot," he said. I stopped, turned back to him.

"What sort of funny?"

He scratched his nose again, frowned, ran a greasy hand through greasier hair.

"No-one stays long, innit. Except for lady boss, she been there long time. You get job, you come for kebab. Free, innit. On house."

Maybe he'd make me falafel.

"Hi Carla? I'm standing outside a kebab shop. Me. In a place where they spin reconstituted sheep around an electric bar heater. I wish you'd pick up. Listen, I've got a funny feeling about this place. The area feels all wrong and the bloke in the

kebab shop said there was something funny about Action in Caring. What do you think I....shit! Your ansaphone's hung up on me again!"

I found the blue gates. They led on to a forecourt. There was a grey door covered with a metal grille. Above the door, a sign read, *c on i C r ng*. I pressed the bell and the door clicked open with a low buzz. I found myself in a reception area. There was an indoor palm in a red pot next to the door. No-one had remembered to water it. A slight black woman sat behind the reception desk.

"Hello, can I help you?"

"Hi. I'm Nikki Elliot, and I've come about the receptionist job."

"Oh! Good to see you. Can you take a seat for a minute? I'll be right with you."

The orange moulded plastic chair had seen better days. Somebody won immortality – or at least fame and fortune – for designing these. The woman was sifting through a pile of papers. She looked harassed. She'd pulled her hair back tightly, but coils of black and silver were escaping the confines of the red elastic and sticking up around her head. It was hot, and her skin was shiny. Square rimmed glasses slipped down her nose. She was painfully thin, as if she worried too much and forgot to eat. I wondered what it would be like to work with her. I had a feeling that she was ok, and I needed to be around someone, anyone, who felt ok. She finished her sifting and moved the pile to one side. She turned to me and smiled.

"Hi. Sorry about that. I'm Geraldine. Geri. Can I get you some tea? Coffee? Cold drink?"

"Water, please."

"No problem."

She flew through a door behind the reception desk and came back a few seconds later, handing me a glass of water. It was dangerously full, water dancing around a less than clean rim. I thanked her, and she darted off again to answer the ringing phone. As she picked up the receiver, a large white woman in oddly mismatched clothes barged through the door at the back of reception. Small grey eyes disappeared into a frown that contorted her pasty face.

"Has that girl from the Jobcentre arrived yet? Oh." She glanced in my direction. "Come through, please."

I rose from the orange chair with a mixture of relief and trepidation and followed the woman past a small kitchen and into a dimly lit office. The walls were lined with bookshelves, and the shelves themselves were a mess of slouching rows of magazines, dishevelled piles of papers, and random books. The trade directories were eight years out of date; *Who's Who 1997*; and an ancient looking series of Open University text books.

"I'm Veronica Stein," she said, seating herself behind a cluttered desk. "You must be…"

"Nikki Elliot," I said. My legs felt shaky, so I crossed them tightly. Stupid! I'm not really the nervous type. Get a grip!

"So, Nikki. What do you think you have to offer Action in Caring?"

"Well…..I can be quite personable, I can answer the phone, open the door…I think I'd be an ideal receptionist." Chantelle had schooled me well. My hands were hot and sweaty and I tucked them under my legs. Veronica glanced through the CV that Chantelle had sent through. My life story in three sides of A4.

"I see you worked for *Life's for Living*."

"Yes."

"Isn't that where that man…."

"Yes, it's the hospice where Brent Woodcraft killed himself."

"I see." She'd raised her eyebrows, but didn't look me in the eye. "And did you…"

"Yes, I knew him. He was my boss. I was the one who found him."

There was a cold heavy silence. I guessed that she was wondering how to get me out of the door. No-one wants to associate with someone who's been that close to violent death; but instead, she asked me,

"How are your administration skills?"

"I can file – I'm a graduate so I had to organise all my own research – *not that my former polytechnic exacted very high standards.* And I'm fairly computer literate" *I can bash out a word-processed article, as long as you don't want fancy formatting.* "And I'm really interested in what Action in Caring is all about," I finished with a flourish.

"Action in Caring is about revitalising our community. It's about giving people hope. We have lunch clubs for the elderly, a youth club for teenagers, young offenders group, and a mother and toddler group that meets on a Wednesday. Yoga classes, various arts groups. It's busy and you never know who might turn up on the doorstep. Are you good with people?"

No, I'm an anti-social psychopath.

"Yes, I'd consider myself to be truly a people person," I said. Well, it wasn't a complete lie. I did get on with people I liked.

"The hours are eight forty-five to five o'clock, with an hour for lunch. You get four weeks holiday and the pay is £16,500. The contract is temporary for six months."

"I see." I couldn't believe it. This strange, slightly sour-smelling woman in clothes that had hardly made it to the charity shop was offering me a job.

"We'll need references and there's a probationary period."

"Well…that's great. I mean, thank you. I can start…well, any time. Tomorrow, if you like….although Thursday would be better." I had people to see, daytime soaps to say goodbye to.

"Thursday will suit us very well. I'll see you then."

She rose, the green Paisley print skirt sticking to her thighs, revealing chunky stockinged knees.

"Thursday, then. By the way," she glanced at my polo shirt and then down my body all the way to the Kickers, "the dress code is smart casual."

I was dismissed. It was as easy as that.

"They're good roughage, pears," said my mother, deftly slicing away the stalk from a particularly plump one.

"As long as you eat them with the skin on." She cut it down the middle and then dissected each half. Watching her sculpting out the seedy core with precision, I thought my mother could have been a surgeon.

"As good as All Bran," she added, and I pondered her preoccupation with the elimination of toxins from her body.

"I've got a job, Mum."

"Great. What is it? Not that research post you were after?"

"No, nothing quite as grand. Just a reception job. For a charity. Not too far from home – I can cycle there."

"Good. You've been sitting on your bum way too long. I do think you let that business at the last place get to you too much. And I'm glad you won't be travelling on the tube. That always worried me, even before they started blowing it up."

"It's only been bombed once." But I knew what she meant. The fact that I could cycle or take the bus to *Action in Caring* was quite a bonus. I too worried about the people I loved moving around our great city. Carla, Ruth…but I couldn't let myself think about Ruth. Not with my mother talking roughage and a new job to worry about.

"What do you think I should wear?"

"You're asking me?" She laughed. Mum was a perennial hippy. She'd conceived me at the Isle of Wight pop festival in 1969, and her trump card whenever we were arguing was that if it hadn't been for me she'd have heard the whole of Dylan's set and not just the last half. I'd felt guilty about it for years, until I figured that she and my dad had to take responsibility for getting into each other just before the big man's set. "What were the others wearing?"

"One of the women was wearing quite a smart black skirt and blouse – but you won't catch me dead in a skirt; and the boss was wearing a ghastly green Paisley print skirt and thick stockings."

My mother frowned and fingered the large amber beads around her neck.

"What about those grey trousers and the peach shirt I bought you for your birthday? And darling, I know they're your favourites, but maybe not red shoes with peach."

I went home to iron the long forgotten peach shirt and polish my black interview shoes.

Home. A top floor bedsit in a rambling Edwardian town house not far from Streatham High Road. Shells and pebbles, crystals and sheets of tree bark decorated my window sill. Purple curtains made out of Indian bedspreads some twenty years ago hung around the bay window. A turquoise throw disguised the holes and stains of the ancient sofa that I'd inherited with the flat. Snuggled into a corner was my bed, my roomy, soft but not too soft double bed with its lilac, green, turquoise scatter cushions. Next to it, the bedside table that I had rescued from a skip and lovingly restored, rubbing the ugly white paint from its delicate wood grain. In a weird way, I identified with that bedside table. I wished someone would rescue me from the skip. A Georgia O'Keefe print hung on the wall facing the window. I'd spent the best part of the winter sheltering in this room, living on benefits and occasional off-the-cards earnings. I'd got hooked on daytime soaps and hardly noticed the seeping away of my confidence, my ability to function in the world outside. The government's determination to see everyone of working age in a job – any job – and Chantelle's corresponding targets were forcing me to leave this safe place. I looked around wistfully. On Thursday I would be starting again. In two days' time I would meet people with whom I would spend large parts of the day five days a week for the foreseeable future. There was a trembling uneasiness in my gut. I drew the curtains, poured a large whisky and went to bed. Suspended from the ceiling, the delicate dream-catcher that my niece Ruby had made me swung softly in the breeze. *Keep the nightmares away,* I prayed silently.

Chapter 2

Thursday morning. Seven thirty, and I was almost ready to go. I'd skipped supper and my guts were too tightly knotted for me to think about breakfast. I felt light headed. Mum had been right to suggest the peach shirt. I looked professional, somehow more grown up than I had done for months. The hem was coming down on my left trouser leg. I took the trousers off, rummaged around in my drawer until I found a glue stick. It would do until I could mend it properly. I stuck the folded material together, put the trousers back on, and squeezed my feet into black shoes with a small heel. I went to get my bike out of the communal cupboard under the stairs. It felt heavier than usual as I wheeled it out. Shit! The back tyre was completely flat. The back one! That meant getting the wheel off, trying not to mess up the complicated gear system – and I was wearing my only decent work clothes and was hopeless at fixing bikes anyway. I considered my options. I could take the bus, there was still plenty of time. Or I could borrow my friend and neighbour Benjamin Rosenthal's bike, a machine smarter and sleeker than mine that tempted me from the back of the cupboard. I squeezed its tyres. They were hard as a gym junkie's biceps. Benjamin wouldn't mind. He didn't use it every day and besides, he owed me. His party last week had kept me awake for most of the night. I reached in my shoulder bag for a note pad and pen. *Hi B - Emergency. Borrowed your bike. You can use mine if you can find a pump. Gone to work* (he'd have to read that part twice) *See you later. N.* I took the lock off my own bike, put the note on my saddle, and shoved it back into the cupboard. I was out of the door by seven forty-five and heading for my new life.

Benjamin's bike was light and fast. I wove in and out of the stagnant lines of traffic on the South Circular and then crossed onto Clapham Common, that vast green south London playground that helps to make city life bearable. It was a crisp spring morning and the trees were in bud. The grass glistened with dew. Groups of dog owners stopped to talk, sipping from steaming thermos flasks, while their charges leaped around, sniffed each other's bottoms and did the sort of things that dogs do. I've often thought that coming back as a dog would be a pretty good way to be reincarnated, but the bum sniffing puts me off. I swerved to avoid a manic border collie and then cycled down towards the main road, heading for Tanners Lane. I was early. The kebab shop was closed, roof to pavement metal shutters protecting it from thieves, but not from the ubiquitous graffiti artists. I veered across the road and through the blue gates of *Action in Caring*. I chained Benjamin's bike to a drain pipe and rang the door bell. The door clicked open and I walked through. Geri was sitting behind the desk, talking to a tiny wrinkled woman wearing a grubby checked coat and trainers. When Geri saw me, she stood up and grinned.

"You turned up then! Welcome aboard. You won't believe how pleased I am to see you! Oh, and this is Dora. Dora Popp."

Dora looked at me and sniffed.

I nodded to Dora and smiled back at Geri. "Where do I start?"

"We start with coffee. Then I give you the health and safety briefing. Then we meet everyone. Then you get down to some serious work!"

"Sounds like a plan to me."

The door behind the reception desk opened and Veronica appeared. "I'm just going out for an appointment," she said, buttoning up a grey raincoat that was a size too small for her.

"See you later, then," said Geri, as Veronica propelled herself through the front door. "She thinks we don't know," said Geri, "but she's trying to stop smoking and get over her allergies. She goes off for a hypnosis session once a week."

"Is it working?"

"She hasn't had a cigarette for a couple of weeks, but sometimes I wish she would, she's so bad tempered! Anyway, let's get down to business." Geri opened the door that led us behind reception. I followed her into a small meeting room with a long table and more moulded plastic chairs. Pictures on the wall of young men fixing motorbikes, old people drinking tea, posing for the camera with a grinning mayor, and a circle of women and toddlers. On the wall near the door was a framed certificate showing that *Action in Caring* had been given an award for meeting quality standards in 1994. It was eleven years out of date.

"Make yourself comfortable. What can I get you?"

"Tea would be good. Not too milky, one sugar. Thanks."

"While I'm gone, have a read of this."

She laid a slim booklet on the table in front of me. On the cover, in bold text it said *Action in Caring: Staff Handbook*. I flicked through it. A set of company rules. Grievance and disciplinary procedures, holiday entitlement, how soon they cut your pay if you're off sick, warnings that using the computer system for personal e-mails or downloading pornography would lead to instant dismissal, and so on. What sort of dreary person sits down and writes this kind of manual? The introductory notes credited the booklet to Gordon Smedley, Finance and Administration Manager. I guessed I'd be meeting him on my imminent grand tour. I signed the back page to show that I'd read the book and agreed to abide by the rules. I felt like I was signing away part of my soul. Still…maybe this place wouldn't be too bad; and it had to be better than the meat counter in Tescos.

Geri came to rescue me after ten minutes, and I started my tour of the building. "These are the toilets. That's the games room over there. It's mostly used by the youth club. That room over there is for the mother and toddler groups – all the toys and things are in there. We've got a kitchen just through that door – you can bring your own lunch to heat up. We all help to keep it clean – well, that's the theory, anyway."

The building was bigger than I'd imagined. There were two floors. As we went to climb the stairs leading to the first floor, an elderly woman in a lavender jogging suit stopped Geri.

"Excuse me dear, I just wanted to tell you that someone's been using our coffee again. And I thought Dora was looking rather more dishevelled than usual."

"Joan, this is Nikki. She's starting work today. Nikki, meet Joan Moran, the leading light of the *AIC* Arts Group and Grannies for Peace, stalwart member of the management committee. Use our coffee for now, Joan. I'll have a word with Justin. Maybe we need to label the cupboards. I don't know what we can do about Dora."

Joan nodded and went down the corridor. She moved with some stiffness. From the back I could see the wispy grey hair falling out of a bun that was sculpted haphazardly and held temporarily in place by a dozen Kirby grips.

"Joan was quite a celebrity in her youth," said Geri

"What did she do?"

"She sculpted. Painted a bit too. Worked with some really famous people. I don't know much about art, but I think she worked down in Cornwall for many years. She worked closely with a woman called Barbara something. Sounds like an actress…can't remember her name, but she's really well known. Joan had to stop when the arthritis got too bad."

"What a shame. I'll look forward to getting to know her."

"She's one of the nicest people involved in this place. You'll like her. I offload to her all the time. Shouldn't really, but she's so easy to talk to."

"Who's Dora?"

"Dora Popp's a bit of a local character. She stops by when her pension's late arriving. We lend her the odd ten pounds, give her a cup of tea, listen to her rantings."

We'd turned a corner. The corridor here was narrower and the light seemed dimmer. Geri knocked on a door to the left. A nasal male voice responded, and she led the way into an office that was stark in its minimalism. The book shelves lining one wall held uniform Lever Arch files, each labelled with the same neat hand, each standing as if to attention in complete alignment with its neighbour. Gordon Smedley sat behind a modern desk. He wore rimless glasses, a grey suit, white shirt and navy tie. He looked out of place in this ramshackle community centre.

"Gordon, this is Nikki, our new admin worker."

He looked up and seemed to be appraising me with a coolness that I found unnerving.

"Good to meet you," he said. He rose from his chair and held out his hand. I stepped forward to shake it and touched cold, limp flesh. Just as he was sitting down, the door burst open and Veronica Stein stormed in.

"Geraldine, someone's left a bike chained to the drain pipe. See whose it is and get them to remove it. Health and safety. Clutters up the forecourt. If it happens again I'll have the machine taken away for scrap."

The thought of Benjamin's bike heading for the scrap yard alarmed me.

"It's my bike..I mean, it's my neighbour's. I put it there. Do you want me to put it somewhere else?"

Veronica looked at me. She frowned, as if trying to place me, then remembered she'd just hired me.

"Rule number one," she said, "Nothing is to be left in the forecourt apart from Gordon's and my cars. Get rid of the bike."

"Where should I leave it?"

"Out of sight."

I wondered how long I would be able to work with a woman who got apoplectic about the parking of bikes. Weren't people who worked for charity supposed to be charitable? And I thought hypnosis was supposed to leave you feeling relaxed. If this was how she behaved after a session, heaven help us when the effects wore off. Gordon Smedley sat quietly, manicured fingers resting on the desk. Geri looked down at the floor and clasped her hands behind her back.

"Is she always like that?" I asked Geri as we closed Gordon's door behind us. "And he's a bit of a cold fish, isn't he?" Geri didn't reply for a moment. She looked down at the floor, sucked in her lower lip. "Well….the bike….I'd better…."

"Yes, you'd better go and move it. Look, I'm sorry. I don't want to make things hard for you on your first day; but it can be quite difficult working here. I've got to sort some bookings. We'll talk later."

"But I haven't met…." but Geri was almost running down the corridor, running away from me. She called back,

"We'll do the rest of the tour this afternoon. You've met most of the people who are here."

Damn Chantelle and Tony Blair and their wretched targets. I could be safely at home, curled under my duvet or sat at my desk. I could be reading or writing or arguing with Richard and Judy, getting stoned with Benjamin, maybe even getting ready to have lunch with Carla, and instead, here I was in this strange place with its even stranger cast of characters. I went down the stairs and out to the front. I unlocked Benjamin's bike and brought it into the building. There seemed to be a space under the stairs, so I tucked it away in there and relocked it. Then I went to find Geri at the reception desk. She was arguing with someone on the phone.

"You made the bookings a year ago. You made block bookings. We could have let out the room…..yes, I know it's your right to go wherever you want, but……no, you listen…I could have let that room out. We're going to lose money, I won't be able to re-let at such short notice…we're a small community centre, we rely on bookings like yours…that's just not true…what evidence do you have? That's just malicious gossip…yes, ok you've made your decision. I really think you should talk to Veronica….I will have to look at the booking agreement…you'll certainly need to pay for next week's booking and probably the whole month's…well, do seek legal advice, then…Yes, I'm sorry too…bye."

She put the phone down with a sigh and raked her fingers through her hair.

"What was that all about?" I asked.

"Another cancellation. The youth club. Look, Nikki, we can't talk here. Let's go out for lunch. Can you hold reception for the next couple of hours?"

"Anything I should know? Like how the switchboard works?"

She showed me the system. It was so straightforward that even I couldn't get it wrong.

"What about if there are any calls like the last one you had?"

"There are hardly any bookings left to cancel, especially since the council pulled the funding for the lunch club. But if you get stuck, give me a call. I'll be in the office next to Veronica's.

I played Solitaire on the PC waiting for the phone to ring. It didn't. I didn't get a chance to practice my door-opening technique either. I tried ringing Carla on my mobile, got her message service.

Hey Carla, I'm at work. Managed to make it. Had to borrow Benjamin's bike – serves him right! Are you free…. My invitation to a boozy evening was cut off as her answering service kicked me off line yet again.

At twelve thirty, Geri came out of her office carrying a small shoulder bag.

"Let's go for lunch. We'll set the ansaphone. No-one's due into the building until this afternoon."

We walked to the other end of Tanners Lane, and Geri stopped outside a small café with tables outside on the pavement.

"Here ok?" she asked.

"Fine," I said. The day was pleasantly warm, so we chose an outside table. A skinny blonde waitress with an Eastern European accent brought two menus.

"You want drink to start?" she asked, and we ordered sparkling water.

"Special today is on board," she added, pointing to a blackboard over the counter inside.

"It's on me," said Geri. "Have what you want. The avocado and mozzarella salad is good."

That sounded fine to me. Geri ordered a Cajun chicken sandwich for herself.

"Sounded like there were some problems this morning," I ventured, remembering her stressful phone call.

"There are problems every morning. And every afternoon. And most evenings. Look, I don't want to put you off before you've even started, but you ought to know what you're getting yourself into."

"What do you mean?"

"Don't look so worried – no-one's died or anything like that. Hey, what did I say?"

My hand was shaking so much that I spilled most of my water down my peach silk shirt.

"Nothing….I'll tell you about it some time." She frowned slightly, and went on.

"It's just that working with Veronica is far from easy, and Gordon can be tricky. Everyone who works in the centre is just out to get the best for their project. There's no sense of teamwork, no vision of *AIC* being a *community* centre. Nobody thinks about how to make life easier for all of us, not just themselves. Except maybe Joan. And Veronica hasn't a clue about managing people or how to bring people together for the greater good."

"Sounds like normal office politics to me."

"Up to a point that's all it is; but we're losing business fast. The new resource centre in Kennington is taking a lot of our trade. They've had loads of European money pumped in and their manager's brilliant at marketing. And because they've been set up by some consortium of politicos and businessmen, they've no ethical values, no sense of us all being part of a community network. They're using the crudest trick in the book: undercutting the competition. They're so heavily subsidised they can afford to. We can't even afford to repair the roof, let alone brighten up the centre with a coat of paint. So we're losing customers. The young women's group has gone, and the youth club has just cancelled all its bookings. That was what you heard on the phone this morning. Two members of the management committee are involved in the new centre – its grand title is South London Community and Enterprise Centre. Felicity Balmforth, the yoga teacher who's been teaching a class at *AIC* for years, is making noises about going off there too. I think Joan's persuaded her not to, though, at least for the time being."

"There must be something you can do."

"Time's running out. If we're not selling space, we're not earning money. The maths is simple. But it gets worse."

"How?"

"Someone's spreading rumours about Gordon. About him being…well, about him liking young boys. Very young boys. That's the main reason we're losing the youth groups."

"Is it true?"

"He doesn't have a police record – we check everyone out through the Criminal Records Bureau; but that doesn't mean anything. Most paedophiles are clever enough to not get caught."

"What's going to happen?" I saw myself back at Chantelle's desk. *It wasn't my fault, honest, Chantelle! I did want to give the job a go, but they were already going bust!*

"There'll be a management committee meeting. The trustees will witter on for an hour or so, and nothing will happen. My guess is that *Action in Caring* will be history by Christmas. I'm applying for other jobs."

"Would it be such a bad thing for *AIC* to close?" I asked.

"It's one of the few really independent grass-roots organisations around."

I wasn't sure how much importance I'd put on that, but I'd only been there for a morning. It was the thought of having to go through all the hassle of signing on again that made me sigh. That, and thinking about psyching myself up for yet another new beginning so quickly. I didn't think I'd want to stay if Geri left.

"You want coffee?" asked the waitress. I looked at Geri.

"Let's just pay the bill and go back," I said. My appetite had vanished. While we waited for the bill, I said, "Tell me more about Gordon."

"What do you want me to say? He gets the job done – he's certainly improved the admin procedures. You'll have to make up your own mind about him."

"I get the feeling you don't like him much."

"He's Veronica's spy. He tells her things that make her doubt people's loyalty, that make it look like it's him and her against the rest of us. Sometimes he tells downright lies."

"Why would he do that?"

"Power. It's always about power, isn't it? Everywhere you go. I used to sing in this gospel choir. It was part of my mum's church and we were both involved. The choir was great and we were starting to be in demand for concerts and recordings; but then the rows started up. The church elders couldn't agree about the choir's programmes. It was like they were competing over who knew most about music, who had invested most in the choir, even who was closer to God; there was a great rift between the three best sopranos because they each felt they should get most of the solos and the girl who did was rumoured to be sleeping with the pastor; and it got so that going to rehearsal was a real pain. You could cut the atmosphere, it was that bad." She had cupped her chin in her hand and her eyes were focused way beyond me, seeing kaleidoscope images from the past. "I used to love singing in that choir, making the kind of sound that took you and everyone listening one step closer to heaven. But I hated the politics, the backstabbing, so I left. Mum did too. She found other ways of talking to God."

I didn't say anything for a while. What Geri was saying resonated with my own experience. Carla and I had gone through similar things with women's and environmental groups. We'd seen rape crisis groups fall apart as women bickered over ideological differences. And by the mid nineties, councils had gone off women's issues and didn't want to fund the work any more. When it got to one woman accusing another of inventing her own particular rape story, I had to leave.

"Gordon," I said. "You were telling me about Gordon."

"Oh. Well, be careful. Don't tell him anything about your personal life. Never bad-mouth other staff to him – he'll go straight to Veronica. And whatever you do, don't say anything negative to him about Veronica."

We walked back to Tanners Lane, silent for most of the way. As we neared the blue gates, Geri said,

"You haven't told me anything about you. What was your last job?"

"I worked for a hospice in west London."

"How did you cope with all that sadness and death?"

"It wasn't really like that. Sometimes, working there, I thought, people are never more alive than when they're dying. It was amazing. The art work that people made, the stories they wrote, and the love that people showed each other. It changed my life in a big way. For most of the time it was a really happy place to work."

"Most of the time?"

"Yeah, well, that's another story."

"What happened?"

We'd passed the kebab shop. The man with the kind eyes was slicing meat from the slowly turning column of mutton, and a group of school kids, shirts hanging over trousers, ties at half-mast, tapped at mobile phone keys as they waited for their dinner.

"My boss was really nice. He was the best boss I'd ever had. Fair, reasonable, friendly. He'd tell you when you'd done well, make sure you learned from mistakes, that sort of thing. He was decent."

"You're talking about him as if he's dead."

"He is."

Geri stopped and turned to look at me, eyebrows raised.

"How?"

"He…" I was about to tell Geri the story when we turned into the gates of *Action in Caring*. Veronica flung open the door just as we reached it, and almost knocked me flying. She had a thing about flinging and slamming doors, did Veronica.

"About time!" she shouted. "What do you think you're doing, leaving the reception desk unmanned? I'll speak to you later!"

The last comment was aimed at Geri who just looked away. Veronica pushed past us and we went back to our posts: me to the reception desk where so many exciting things happened, and Geri to the back office.

There was one phone call from a stationery company offering to undercut our current suppliers, and another from a Mrs Lester saying that she wasn't bringing her son to the mother and toddler group again, not after what she'd heard about goings on at the centre and a member of staff liking little boys. I told the stationery firm to call us back in six months and took Mrs Lester's details to pass on to Veronica. I got a text message from Benjamin asking where the fuck his bike was, but otherwise the afternoon passed quietly and slowly. I was looking forward to going home. I wasn't used to being chained to a desk doing nothing. Suddenly, I heard heavy feet stomping across the floor over my head. A door slammed and there were raised voices. I thought I heard a woman – Veronica, I guessed – shouting at someone, but I only caught odd words: *How…what…disaster…scandal…idiot…ruin.* Another voice, quieter, male, uttered responses that I couldn't hear. The door banged again, and angry feet marched in the opposite direction. There was a draught from the front door that was icing my right shoulder into a painful spasm. I wanted to go to the gym and get home in time for Eastenders. Make my peace with Benjamin. At a quarter to five, Veronica appeared.

"I need you to attend the management committee meeting tonight. I trust you can take minutes and type them up?"

"Well…yes…but I did have other…"

"Good. The meeting starts at six. It's an emergency meeting. It'll probably go on until nine. You need to organise some sandwiches and make sure they all get tea and coffee. Lawrence, the Chair, only drinks herbal tea so make sure we've got some."

"But…"

"And please tidy up this reception desk. It's a disgrace."

With that, she turned back to her office, leaving behind a whiff of unhealthy sweat. I really didn't like that woman. I went into the kitchen to see if there was the wherewithal to make sandwiches and check on the herbal tea situation. There was a loaf of sliced white in an enamel bread bin. The packet said that it should have been used two days ago, but only the top slice was showing any signs of mould. I binned that and smeared the rest with some fake butter that I found in the fridge. I sliced a lump of cheddar that was lurking on a grimy shelf, found a jar of Branston pickle and made a plate of cheese and pickle sandwiches. I didn't bother to cut the crusts off. There was a packet of ham in the fridge, but you wouldn't catch me doing stuff with bits of dead pig. I covered my handiwork with cling film, poured out a packet of peanuts I'd found in the pantry into a dish, laid a tray with mugs and plates and went back to the reception desk. I dug my mobile out of my bag. Benjamin had texted me again. I'd better phone him.

"Hi Ben, it's me."

"Yeah, I know it's you. Where the hell are you? And where's my bike?"

"I'm at work. I got a job."

"Well, that'll turn the national debt around. But where's my bike?

"Under the stairs."

"No, *your* bike's under the stairs with a flat fucking tyre!"

"Under the stairs here, at *Action in Caring*. Where I work." It felt funny saying that: I hadn't yet made friends with my new identity.

"So how am I supposed to get over to Camden tonight?"

"You can use mine. It's only got a puncture."

"It's a girl's bike! I've got a hot date and I'm not going on a girl's bike!"

"You mean you can't be arsed to fix the puncture!"

"I mean I'm not going to meet the potential love of my life, who happens to be a leading member of CycleOut, on a girl's bike!"

"What's CycleOut? Sounds like a club for menopausal women!"

"God, Nik, you're so ignorant! It's only *the* gay cycling club! And I can't turn up for my first ride with a new bloke on a girl's bike!"

"I've got to work tonight. There's a meeting."

"I'm coming for the bike. Where are you?"

"Tanners Lane. Just off the High Street. Ben, can you do me a favour?" There was a silence and then I heard him sigh.

"What?"

"Can you fix my tyre and bring my bike? We'll swap."

"What's it worth?"

"Dinner?"

"Not if you're cooking. Seeing as you're now one of the earning classes, you can take me to the new Japanese by the bus garage."

"Deal."

Chapter 3

"Did you manage to make the sandwiches?"

Geri had emerged from her office looking weary. Even more of her hair had frizzed itself out of the confines of the elastic band.

"Yes, I made a plate of cheese and pickle. Hope that's ok."

"Did Veronica tell you to do her a separate plate?"

"No."

"She won't eat cheese – she's got some food allergies; so I usually do her a plate of ham or tuna."

"I used all the bread."

"I'll run round to the corner shop and get a new loaf. Otherwise you'll be in even more trouble and it's still your first day!"

"She didn't say a thing!"

"That's Veronica for you. Don't worry, I'll sort it."

"There's ham in the fridge."

"That'll do, then."

Geri left the building. My feet felt pinched in their working shoes and the silk shirt wasn't warm enough for sitting still behind a draughty reception desk. Getting a job isn't all it's cracked up to be. Is this how it would be until I reached sixty five? Geri was back within five minutes bearing a loaf of Mighty White bread. I wouldn't eat it if you paid me. Just the name was enough to put me off, echoes of white supremacist nastiness.

"Want me to make them?" I asked. She looked so tired that I'd even consider handling dead pig.

"No, it's ok. I know how she likes them. Best to keep her as happy as we can!"

Geri scurried to the kitchen while I tidied up the reception desk. When she came back, she was carrying her coat and bag.

"I'm off, then. Good luck with the meeting. Sandwiches all cling-filmed and in the fridge. There are some biscuits and snacks in the cupboard too."

"See you tomorrow. And thanks for everything."

She smiled as she opened the door. Waved and went on her way.

I just about had time to run down to *Healthy Heaven* to buy some cereal for my breakfast tomorrow. Veronica grudgingly said I could go as long as I was back within ten minutes. When I got back, six trustees had already turned up for the management committee meeting. Five were sitting round the meeting room table. Veronica and a sixth committee member emerged from the kitchen and joined the others. Gordon was also there. I recognised Joan from my morning tour.

"Hello again," she said. "How has your first day been?"

"Interesting. Lots to learn." I said, which was the most diplomatic answer I could manage.

Veronica was talking to a man with a grubby looking beard. The shoulders of his jacket were salted with dandruff. There was a light crusty patch of something once edible on the front of his navy sweater. Gordon watched them from the other end of the table. He reminded me of something predatory. True, the things Geri had told me hadn't helped, and maybe I was affected by the rumours of his liking for young boys; but something deeper in my gut was stirring up a warning. I checked over the room. A slight young woman wearing a black hijab pored over the minutes of the last meeting. A thin, silver haired man wearing a tweed jacket sat next to Gordon and flicked through the pages of a small diary. I wondered if he was looking for something or just trying to keep his eyes and hands occupied. A very large white woman with short dyed red hair wearing chunky gold chains around her neck and wrists sat next to him. Her necklace told the world her name was RITA. A dapper looking man in a suit and tie placed his brief case on the table and took from it a neat package of papers and a flashy looking roller ball pen. He was the man who'd entered with Veronica. He closed up the case and placed it neatly by the side of his chair. Veronica shifted her attention from dandruff man and called to me.

"Where are the sandwiches Vicky?" I wondered whether she ever spoke civilly to anyone, or whether she only knew how to bark.

"It's Nikki. They're in the fridge. Shall I get them?"

"Yes of course. They should be on the table."

The plate of ham sandwiches was, as Geri had promised, in the fridge. I took it out and added it to the tray. I made a pot of tea and a mug of peppermint tea. I took the tray back into the meeting room. The large woman called Rita helped me to find a space and we unloaded the food and plates onto the table. I took Veronica's plate to her place. She ripped off the cling-film without thanking me. *I hope they choke you!* I thought to myself.

"Where would you like me to sit?" I asked Veronica.

"Next to Lawrence would be best," she said, nodding towards dandruff man. I hoped the meeting wouldn't be a long one as I sat before my blank pad of paper, pen poised to capture their words of wisdom. Joan came up to me.

"Have you done this before?" she asked.

"No. Well, not here. Not for a while." In fact, I hadn't taken minutes of a meeting since the Polly Marthaschild Refuge, which my mum had helped to set up, and for which Carla and I volunteered, got taken over by some amorphous housing association.

"I'll tell you who's here and who's not. "

"Thank you!"

Rita passed the plate of cheese sandwiches around and everyone except the young woman tucked in.

"This is Lawrence, our Chair," said Joan, indicating dandruff man.

"Rita you've met. That's Maryam," she continued, nodding towards the young woman with the hijab. The silver haired man was Bernard; the dapper man with the brief case Derek. Each smiled politely as Joan introduced them. I scribbled the list of names onto my pad. Added the date.

"Nikki's just started today," said Joan, completing the introductions.

"Let's get on, please," said Veronica. "We need to look at the financial situation, and then we have some governance issues to address. As you all know, the Charity Commission has certain regulations to which we have to adhere, and it has come to my attention that we may be in breach of them, which is the other reason for calling an emergency meeting."

Lawrence coughed, shuffled his papers and declared the meeting open. Veronica grabbed a Mighty White sandwich and stuffed it in her mouth. Lawrence asked whether the committee agreed with the minutes of the last meeting. There was a murmur, which sounded as if people agreed that they were correct, so I noted down that they were.

"On to Matters Arising, then," said Lawrence. His voice was surprisingly thin and high. "Derek, as treasurer, can you tell us whether there has been an improvement in the cash-flow situation?"

The dapper man started to reply.

"Well, Chair, I'm sorry to report…"

Just then there was a sound of gasping and rasping coughing. All eyes turned to Veronica. Her face had turned red and blotchy and she was clutching at her throat. Her chest was heaving. Her eyes were wide with fear. She struggled for breath, wheezing with the effort. An asthma attack, maybe, but worse than any I'd ever seen before.

"Does anyone have an inhaler?" I asked, but the management committee were glued to their chairs, watching the scene with paralysed horror. Veronica groped frantically in her handbag. She pulled out an object but dropped it, and it skittered onto the floor, rolling under the table towards Gordon. He and Derek both reached down and seemed to grope on the floor for whatever Veronica had dropped. Derek was the first to surface.

"Just a biro," he said, and placed a black ballpoint on the table. Veronica's eyes were wide with panic.

"Come on!" I yelled. "She's in trouble here! Doesn't anyone have any first aid training?" Rita leapt to the rescue.

"Maybe she's choking," she said and moved behind Veronica. She thumped her back hard, but Veronica's distress just intensified. Rita tried to clasp her arms around Veronica's middle, but Veronica was hunched over the table, contorted in pain and gaining a firm grip was difficult. I'd never seen anyone carry out the Heimlich manoeuvre and was impressed at Rita's rapid repertoire of anti-choking strategies. She managed to interweave her fingers somewhere under Veronica's bra line and sharply yanked her fists in and up. Veronica projected a spray of vomit across the table, narrowly missing Gordon. As her head turned to the side, she retched again, this time scoring a bull's eye on Lawrence's tacky jumper. He grimaced and stood, knocking his chair to the floor. Without a word, he stalked out of the door, presumably to clean off the stinking mess. The others moved their chairs back. Rita moved to see if she had successfully dislodged the obstacle, but Veronica was in even greater distress. Her eyes were rolling upwards, hands still clutching at her throat but feebly now, her strength having all but left her.

"Nuts!" she uttered in a strangled whisper.

I'd left my mobile at the reception desk.

"Someone call an ambulance," I cried. Maryam reached inside her bag for a phone and put in the nine nine nine call.

"Ambulance, please," she said to the operator. "Yes, it is an emergency. A woman is choking. She can't breathe. Yes, we've tried that. Um…her face is red. She vomited. Oh, she's just passed out."

"Tell them her pulse is racing like mad," called Joan who was holding Veronica's wrist and looking at her watch.

"She was eating a sandwich. No I don't know what was in it," said Maryam. "My colleague says her pulse is very fast."

"Ham," I said.

"Ham," relayed Maryam, with a slight grimace. By now, Veronica's hands had drooped to her sides and she was sliding off her chair. Rita tried to hold her in place, but staggered off balance as the weight of Veronica's unconscious body slumped to the floor.

"She's fallen off her chair," reported Maryam. "Yes, please hurry. Is there what? Hold on, let me ask." She covered the mouthpiece on the phone. "They said maybe it's an allergy. Has she got an epi-pen?"

I remembered Geri saying that she was allergic to all kinds of foods. "Have a look in her handbag," I said. The men had watched as helpless observers, but now Bernard reached for the fallen handbag and tipped its contents on the table. There were pens and tissues, a purse, a mobile phone, a pink comb with half its teeth missing, a notebook. Nothing that looked medicinal, not even a pack of aspirin.

"Nothing here," said Bernard.

"No," said Maryam. "Nothing in her bag like that."

Lawrence had returned and was hovering by the door. Now Bernard moved to place his coat under Veronica's head. Suddenly there was quiet. No sound of wheezing. Joan took Veronica's wrist in her fingers again. She turned pale. Moved her fingers up the arm, and then down towards the hand. Then she felt for a pulse in Veronica's neck.

"I can't find it," she said. "I can't find a pulse. Her heart's stopped beating!"

Rita knelt awkwardly beside the disheveled body. She started pounding on Veronica's chest. Her breasts bounced with the effort of trying to kick-start Veronica's heart, and the gold necklace swung from side to side. Rita was turning puce with the effort and her short hair was damp with sweat. Joan's hair had all but escaped its chignon. Maryam was clearing plates. Derek had stood up and was watching, his face showing impotence and fear. Gordon half stood, his hands on the table, beads of sweat dribbling from his forehead.

"Now try mouth to mouth," said Joan.

Rita stopped pounding on Veronica's chest, squeezed her nose with one hand and forced open her mouth with the other. She took in a deep breath and clamping her mouth to Veronica's blue lips, blew it out.

"Again!" cried Joan. Rita kept blowing. I thought it might help if I pounded on the chest.

"Good girl," said Joan.

The doorbell rang and Derek moved quickly. He came back moments later, two paramedics in green boiler suits following him.

"Make way," said a ginger haired man with a moustache. We moved back and he crouched down. Felt for Veronica's pulse, looked under her closed eyelids, lifted her blouse revealing a once pink bra, put his ear to her chest.

31

"Can anyone tell me what happened?"

Gordon spoke for the first time. "She seemed to choke on a sandwich. It was all very quick."

"She might have had an allergy," I added.

The paramedic opened his bag and took out a syringe. He stuck it into Veronica's thigh. Then he felt for a pulse at her throat. He looked under her eyelids again, and then sat up slowly.

"Let's get her to hospital. We'll fetch the stretcher. And let the police know. Afraid we have to do that when there's a sudden death."

Rita staggered to her feet and burst into tears. Joan put an arm around her.

"You did what you could, Rita," she said.

"It wasn't enough, though, was it?" snuffled Rita.

"It was more than the rest of us could do," I added.

The paramedics loaded Veronica's lifeless body onto the stretcher. Derek held the door open for them as they processed into the corridor. I watched numbly as my new boss's corpse disappeared into the ambulance. As they drove off, they almost knocked a cyclist to the ground and he swore loudly as he swerved into our forecourt. It was Benjamin.

"Here's your fucking bike!" he yelled thrusting it at me. "Trust you to have abnormal tyre valves! It's taken me half the afternoon!"

"Not now, Ben," I said quietly.

"Yeah, yeah, I know, you're working now, big deal, but I want my bike. *My* bike, not your poxy contraption."

"I'll get it, just calm down please, Ben. Someone's just died." I couldn't help it, I'd started to cry. This couldn't be happening to me again. There was a soft touch on my arm.

"Tea," said Maryam, handing me a mug with a cracked rim.

"Thanks," I said. It's a sign of Britishness, isn't it? Tea in any crisis. Benjamin's mouth was gaping.

"God, I'm sorry Nik. What happened?"

"Not sure. She went red, choked, wheezed, puked, passed out, and died. Cried out "Nuts!". That was her last word."

Benjamin sniffed, like he does when he's about to make a portentous announcement. "Sounds like anaphylactic shock to me," he said. Benjamin had completed one year's medical training before dropping out: a doctor who faints at the sight of blood is no good to anyone.

"Ana what?" I asked.

"An extreme allergic reaction," he said, pleased with himself for remembering this gem. "It's often nuts set it off, but other things can do it as well. Animal bites and stings do it for some people."

"She only had a ham sandwich and she wasn't allergic to that," I mused, "and there were no insects in the room. It was so quick!"

"They didn't have you make the sandwiches, did they? You know how lethal your cooking is!"

"Don't joke now, all right? I've just watched a woman die. No, I made them for everyone else, but she had a special plate. Geri made them." Maybe she wasn't really dead. Maybe they'd kick start her heart like they do on the medical soaps on the telly. Give her electric shocks until she returned from the great beyond a new and humble person. But that wasn't going to happen, was it? Maryam continued to hand around tea. Joan, pale and looking suddenly very small, sat on the same moulded chair that I'd waited on just a few days ago. I'd been hopeful, fearful, but never imagining that I would again be encountering a horrible and untimely death. Was this the universe's way of telling me that I wasn't cut out for working and I should just stay on the dole, defying Blair, Chantelle and the welfare to work fascists? That I should be focusing on paying my mother some attention, on meaningful lunches with Carla and Benjamin? That my energy would be better spent in pursuing Ruth?

Rita stood just outside the front door smoking, dragging on the Mayfair Kingsize as if her life depended on it.

"I keep trying to give up," she said apologetically, as Maryam handed her a mug of tea, "but then stuff keeps happening and I'm back to twenty a day."

"D'you need me to stay?" Benjamin asked. I remembered his hot date.

"No, it's ok. We'll have to wait for the police and then lock up. I'll get your bike for you."

I went to retrieve his bike from under the stairs. Shame. I'd really enjoyed riding it.

"Will you get home ok?" he asked.

"Yes, don't worry about me. I might ring Carla," I said.

"Do that. You shouldn't be alone. Are you sure you don't want me to…"

"No! You get away to your new man. I want to hear all about him and this cycling club. Come and see me when you get home. If you get home. I'll be fine." I was being brave, and he knew it, and the chances of my getting hold of Carla were remote; but he nodded, patted me on the back, swung his leg over the saddle and pedalled into the dusk. The power of the promise of new sex had won out over chivalry and loyalty to an old friend. He was just a pressure cooker bursting with testosterone.

A white car with flashing blue lights drew into the forecourt. *Here we go*, I thought and took a deep breath. The policewoman was probably in her late twenties. She had feathery short brown hair, splendid bone structure, a wide mouth. She wore no nonsense shoes. Sturdy. Gorgeous on top, well grounded below the hips. No way she'd be a pushover in any sense of the word. I thought I might have seen her somewhere before. Maybe it was at the Glass Bar, but I couldn't be sure. Her colleague was older, probably in his mid thirties. His body was long and thin, his hair was short and fine. His fingers were long and bony. The backs of his hands were dotted with light freckles. He reached for his radio. It crackled and he tapped it on his thigh a couple of times. It crackled again, more feebly, and then went quiet.

"Bloody thing," he muttered, as much to himself as to us. "Technology's supposed to get better, isn't it, but it just seems to get more useless every time they issue new kit."

The woman sighed in sympathy.

"A policeman's lot…not a happy one?" I said, but everyone glared at me. You didn't crack jokes just minutes after your dead boss had been carted away. I couldn't get the look on Lawrence's face as Veronica's vomit hit his jumper out of my head. It was the sort of moment that should be filmed and sent to a Saturday night six o'clock kind of programme to be screened with a sound track of canned laughter. I was dangerously close to hysteria. I hate it when this happens: everything in you says you need to sob in grief, or maybe fear, but you're overtaken by involuntary, helpless giggles. I feigned a coughing fit and headed for the kitchen and a glass of water.

"I'm Sergeant Wendy Baggott, this is PC Geoff Newsome. Who's in charge around here?" the woman was asking as I returned to the group, hysteria drowned for the present. She had a pleasant voice, a soft Scottish lilt. East coast.

"I'm the Finance and Administration Manager, I suppose it's me," said Gordon.

"I'm the Chair," said Lawrence.

I liked watching men trying to outrank each other, though these two made an unlikely pair of alpha males.

"So who can tell me what happened?" asked Sergeant Baggott. I loved her voice.

Lawrence and Gordon described what had happened, taking it in turns to augment each other's sentences.

"We'll need to interview each of you," said Sergeant Baggott.

They started with Gordon, and then moved onto everyone in turn, taking each of us into Geri's little office. Those of us who weren't being interviewed stood or sat, smoked or drank tea, or did both. No-one knew what to say except to rehearse the evening's shocking events and proclaim disbelief. After an hour, it was my turn to say what had happened. Wendy Baggott was sitting in Geri's office chair, Geoff Newsome in a typing chair that wobbled. I sat warily in a grey moulded chair, sister to the one by reception.

"Can you tell us your name?"

"Nikki Elliot."

"And what were you doing here tonight, Ms Elliot?"

"It's my first day working here. I'm the receptionist and do some admin. Veronica Stein asked me to take minutes for the management committee."

"I see," said Wendy Baggott, making notes in a little pad. "Can you tell us what happened?"

I went back over the evening, told them what I had seen. Then I remembered what Benjamin had said. "It might have been ana... some kind of shock," I said. "They told me she was allergic to all sorts of things, Geri said she was having hypnosis to stop smoking and get over her allergies. Her last word was "nuts"."

"Who made the sandwiches?" Wendy Baggott asked.

"I made the cheese ones," I said, "and a colleague made some especially for Veronica."

"Which colleague?"

"Geri. Geraldine. Sorry, I can't remember her surname – I only started today. But she knows what Veronica can and can't eat." Wendy Baggott gave me a long look and then returned to scribbling notes in her pad.

"Thank you, Ms Elliot, that'll be all."

Chapter 4

The police had finished their interviews. While they'd been interviewing us, a team of forensic officers had come to take samples and examine the meeting room. They'd bagged up the remaining sandwiches, put things in phials and plastic envelopes. One of them had taken photos.

"You can clean it up now," said the one who seemed to be in charge. Then they left.

A BMW drew up into the forecourt.

"It's my brother come to pick me up," said Maryam. "D'you need me to stay?" She looked from Lawrence, to me, and finally to Gordon.

"No, thanks for your help, but there's no need to stay." He'd been silent up until then. I'd forgotten he was there. He was, though, the most senior member of staff, and Lawrence was clearly going to be as useful as Brylcreem to a bald man.

"I'd like to take Rita home," said Joan, to no-one and everyone.

"I need to check that the kids are ok," said Derek.

"We might as well all go home," mumbled Lawrence.

Maryam's brother was tapping on the steering wheel impatiently. She gave Rita a sad smile, climbed into the car, and the BMW pulled away. Joan led Rita towards the bus stop. Bernard was standing alone and looked old and sad. I wondered if he had anyone waiting for him at home.

"Right, well, I'm sure we all want to get home," he said, as if reading my mind. "Anything you need me to do? Dreadful thing. Tragedy. Don't know what to say." He shuffled from one shiny brogue to the other.

"Will you be ok? I mean, going home?" I asked him. He was the sort of man it was easy to overlook. "Is there anyone at home for you?"

"Just the wife, just the wife. Better check that she's all right. Alzheimer's, you know."

"I'm sorry," I said. What else can you say?

"Oh don't be," he said. "We've had our time. Damn lucky, really. Cheerio." He turned out of the forecourt and headed into the night. Gordon locked up the building, then he, Derek and Lawrence made to go.

"You'll be ok?" asked Gordon. "Not the best way to start a new job."

"No. Yes, I'll be fine." I felt invisible and vulnerable. I stood in the forecourt with my bike and realised that I couldn't face going home and being alone. I sent a text to Carla, on the off chance that she might have her phone switched on. I needed company to obliterate the horrors of the day with copious amounts of alcohol. *Crap day. Need gd friend. U free? Xx.* I waited. Sighed. Mounted my bike, and then came the miracle of feeling my phone vibrate, hearing it sing out its tinny version of *Sweet Dreams are Made of This.*

"What's up Nik?"

"My boss just died. Ben thinks it was anasomething shock."

"Hang on, run that by me again. Who died?"

"Veronica Stein. My new boss. Well, ex-new boss."

"As in the boss of the place where you only started today? That new boss?"

"Uh-huh." I was starting to shake. Just telling Carla was making the shock hit home.

"Jesus! Were you there?"

"Yup."

"You want me to pick you up?"

"I've got the bike, thanks. Probably need the exercise."

"Sure?"

"Mm. *Sappho?*"

"I'll be there. Half an hour max. You be all right 'til then?"

"Yeah. Yeah, I'll be ok. I'll see you there. And Carla....thanks for being there. Here."

"Where else would I be?"

It was a quiet night at the women's bar near the Elephant and Castle. Carla was already there, sipping at a large glass of red wine and frowning over the Guardian crossword. She'd got us a sofa near the fire. When she saw me, she got up, arms open to pull me into one of the best hugs I know. None of this slight stiffening of arms, holding back, half hug with a touch of fear that some women give. Carla's were rich and fulsome. Safe at last, I could let the tears go. They soaked into my friend's soft cotton shirt and she rubbed my back gently, as if easing out the pain. After a while, I stopped shaking. I pulled away, wiped my face with my sleeve.

"Wine ok, or do you need something stronger?"

"Wouldn't say no to a whiskey," I said. "Jameson's if they've got it."

Carla nudged me towards the sofa and I sank into it. I could have curled up there and then and gone to sleep. Whiskey and sleep: my answer to most of life's crises. Carla came back from the bar with what looked like a double.

"Eva thought you looked in a bad way so she put in an extra measure, on the house."

I signed my thanks to the woman with the Afro behind the bar. *Sappho* was a haven for all kinds of women. Eva knew and cared for her customers and I hoped that we brought her enough business to keep the bar running. Carla settled beside me, folding her long legs underneath her. She picked up her wine glass with one hand, tucked her dark wavy hair behind her ears with the other.

"Ok, tell all," she said.

I sighed, and relayed the sorry story to Carla, introducing her to all the characters in my new workplace.

"I hope you didn't make the sandwiches!"

My complete lack of culinary competence was the butt of most of my friends' jokes. I sniffed.

"As it happens, I made the others, but not hers."

"How come?"

I explained about Geri and the Mighty White.

"What's she like, this Geri?"

"I like her. She feels…you know, decent. She was really kind and helpful when I started, made me feel welcome. We had lunch today and got on well."

"What was Veronica like?"

"Unpleasant. Didn't treat people with respect from what I could see. Really nasty to Geri – I thought she might have been a bit racist. Negative kind of energy about her. But the centre's under a lot of pressure. Maybe she was just stressed." I'd finished my whiskey. Eva came over and ruffled my hair.

"Rough day?"

"About as rough as they come."

"So what are you girls drinking?"

"A bottle of Merlot?" suggested Carla, and I nodded my agreement.

"Ruth was in last week," offered Eva, when she came back with the wine and two glasses.

"Oh." I tried to sound indifferent, but could feel a blush spreading from my suddenly tingling breasts up my neck and spilling out into my cheeks. Carla looked at me, and there was an irritating twitch at the corner of her mouth.

"How was she?" I sensed that I was supposed to say more than *oh*.

"Gorgeous," said Eva. "New haircut, good tan, a certain glow. Maybe there's someone new in her life."

No! Don't let someone else have her! I cried inwardly. "That'd be nice," I said, resisting Eva's tease. Carla made a strangled sound.

"Didn't stay long, though. You know your problem, girl," pronounced Eva.

"Yeah! I've just been railroaded into a job by the fucking Jobcentre and this evening I watched my new boss choke to death!" It was a heavy card to play, I know, but they were edging me somewhere I was too vulnerable to go. Ruth hadn't even told me that she was back in town.

"Hey, I'm sorry," said Eva, "but I was talking about you going for what you want, or who you want. Believing in yourself."

"Oh, that," I said, and gulped down half a glass of wine. "Well, I'll tackle that tomorrow."

Eva play-punched my arm and left us to go and talk to a couple who were sharing a joke at the bar. They looked cosy and settled. I always felt ambivalent about coupledom, more so now that people were starting to tie the knot in civil partnerships.

"You ok?" Carla slipped an arm around me.

"Mm. It was awful, you know?"

"Tell me."

"I didn't like her, but it looked so painful. She struggled not to die. I tried to help…"

"I know you would've."

"We tried mouth to mouth, heart massage, everything."

"What did Benjamin call it?"

"Anaphylactic shock. She was allergic to all sorts of stuff, and especially nuts. We looked to see if she carried any medication, but there was nothing in her bag."

"You said you had a bad vibe about the place."

"Mm. There are loads of problems – Geri told me; but this is a charity, a little community project, not some cut-throat city firm. How bad can it really be?"

"Nik, we've both seen the real world of charities, people consumed with ambition, bastards as ruthless as the worst city whizz-kid. Get real!"

I remembered Brent, the agony he went through. He may have officially taken his own life, but others had stolen it from him long before he snapped his neck.

"Drink up, I'm taking you home," ordered Carla.

"But my bike…."

"I'll stick it in the boot. I want to make sure that you're tucked up in bed."

She might almost never answer her phone, my mate Carla, but when it came to friends, she was the best.

Benjamin's windows were dark and his bike wasn't under the stairs. Carla helped me to put my bike away and then led me upstairs. I staggered, half asleep already, into the bathroom. Peed, showed my teeth their toothbrush.

"Tea?" called through Carla.

"Not for me. You have one," I mumbled, lunging into bed.

"Another time." She unbuttoned the peach shirt, pulled off the unfriendly work shoes, and slipped off my trousers. She was tender as a mother as she pulled the duvet over me and kissed me good night.

"Thanks," I whispered.

"For what?" she asked.

"For picking up my message."

She kissed my forehead. "Good night."

Chapter 5

I woke up at five-thirty. My head was throbbing and my mouth was foul and sticky. The room careered into focus, and I remembered yesterday's events. Maybe I could just not go into work. Forget I'd ever had anything to do with *Action in Caring*. Go back to the job centre: *Chantelle, it was all a big mistake. Is that job at Tesco's still an option?* God! I hated having to work! Why hadn't I married some city broker who spent most of the week in Brussels, so that I could spend mine flicking a duster at expensive ornaments and gossiping in some health spa with a group of pampered girlfriends? Well, I guess I knew the answer to that one. I staggered into the kitchen, poured myself a pint glass of water, threw in a fizzy extra strong multi-vit and drank it down. I decanted the last glassful of orange juice from an out of date carton in the fridge. I was in luck: it hadn't started to ferment. Clenching my teeth against rising nausea, I stuck a slice of wholemeal bread in the toaster. While it browned, I went into the bathroom, stood under a running shower, scrubbed myself with lemon zingy shower gel, and finished by turning off the hot tap and letting the cold water shock my system out of its sorry, hung-over state.

A breakfast of toast and Marmite later and I was almost human. I'd go into work and hand in my notice. I'd work until the end of the week and then hand it over to some other poor victim of the Department for Work and Pensions. Chantelle would score two hits for the price of one. I'd be helping her targets to look good. Geri would be disappointed, but she was looking to move on herself and we'd only known each other for a day.

I put on a pair of black jeans and a rust coloured corduroy shirt: they were clean enough and I didn't think anyone would mind if my clothes were rather more casual than smart. Not today, anyway. I put the black pumps at the back of the wardrobe where they belonged and slipped my feet into their old friends, the red Kickers. As I shut my front door, Benjamin clattered into our shared hallway with his bike. His cheeks were red and glowing from his ride in the crisp early morning – or maybe from something else.

"Hi Ben, how did it go?"

"Nik!" He looked startled to see me. "Oh…it was fantastic! He's

something else! Cutest arse you ever saw, great muscles, good mind. I'm so in love!"

I noticed he'd got his latest man's attributes in the right order. Right for a gay bloke, that is. Me, I'd go for the mind first and then the eyes. Then voice, then hands; or maybe hands, and then voice…or maybe the voice comes first…

"Nikki?"

"What?"

"I was asking about last night. What happened after I left? Are you ok?"

"Yeah, yeah I'm fine. Sort of. Cops interviewed us all, took some notes. I met up with Carla, got a bit pissed, she put me to bed. I woke up. Here I am."

"You going back, then?"

"Mm. I'll work until the end of the week, then see if Chantelle's got anything else, preferably somewhere that isn't about to go bust and where no-one dies."

"Sounds like a plan. S'pose I'd better get ready for work. See you later?"

"Yeah. I want to hear all about your menopausal cycling club."

"Cycle Out! And it's men only, so it can hardly be menopausal!"

He could be so pedantic, could Benjamin.

"Ok, ok, see you later." I pulled my bike out from under the stairs, and Benjamin shoved his in its place. I was early, so I cycled over to Tooting Common, got off the bike and sat on a bench watching the joggers and dog walkers, and those who were on their way to somewhere, and those who weren't. I wondered how Geri would take the news of my imminent departure. A lithe woman with long wavy hair strolled past holding the leashes of two sleek Afghan hounds. An elderly man, small and lean as a ferret, paused as his Jack Russell peed against a plane tree. The fresh air was clearing my head. I got back on the bike, rode across to Clapham Common, swung into Tanners Lane. I let myself in with the key that Geri had given me yesterday. One of my jobs was to open up in the morning. Everything in me screamed against going back into that building, but I stepped through the door, breathing in, holding, and breathing out, holding. It felt as if death were lingering, as if nasty jagged fragments of Veronica were suspended in the air. Too much imagination. Too many scary films. There was the dead plant in its red pot. There were the mugs, some still holding tea, now cold and filmy. The meeting room would need cleaning up and I didn't think that that unpleasant task would fall to anyone other than me. I'd need coffee first, so I headed for the kitchen and filled the kettle. Geri came in as I was stirring in my sugar.

"You're early," she said. "How'd it go last night?"

She seemed so innocent and I was about to wreck her day with my account. I stalled.

"Coffee?"

"No thanks, I've brought in a smoothie from *Healthy Heaven*."

"Look, Geri," I began.

"What is it? Don't tell me: Lawrence lost the plot and Veronica made Joan cry?"

"Worse. Much worse."

"Really?" She looked curious. I took a deep breath.

"Veronica's dead."

"Nikki, that's not funny."

"It's true. Veronica died last night at the committee meeting. They took her to hospital, but she was already dead."

"Veronica? Dead?" She was shaking her head in bewilderment. To herself, she said,

"It can't be. No, not possible." To me, she said,

"What happened?"

I gave her the short version, told her that Wendy Baggott and Geoff Newsome were on the case, finished off with Benjamin's theory.

"But *I* made her sandwiches," she said. "I was careful. I always am. I know what she's allergic to and what she's not. There's no way anything on that plate could have harmed her!"

We both stood and reflected. I sipped at my coffee.

"What did you put in her sandwiches?"

"Her special dairy-free margarine. Ham. That's how she likes them. Nothing else."

"Maybe..." but I was interrupted by the doorbell ringing. I went to open it. It was too early for the Youth Offenders' Community Support Network, whose members, Geri had told me, rarely greeted the day before it was half over. The yoga class was booked in for the hour before the youth group. I hoped I hadn't overlooked another booking, because I'd yet to clean up the macabre meeting room. But it was Gordon, and close behind him was Lawrence. Gordon grunted some kind of greeting to me and moved to go towards his office. He was nursing a large Starbucks beaker oozing milk-scented steam. I hated people who went to Starbucks. Lawrence murmured something in his high, whiney voice. I was relieved to see he'd changed his jumper, but it wasn't much of an improvement.

"Come to make sure that everything's in order," he said.

"I was telling Geri about Veronica," I said.

"Terrible. Can't believe it," he said in the same tinny monotone.

Geri came through the door looking bemused. She was still trying to take it all in.

"So, what do we do now?" she said.

"Clean up the meeting room, I s'pose," I said. She must have seen the dread in my face, because she put an arm around my shoulder.

"We'll do it together," she said.

Lawrence wiped his sleeve across his nose.

"I'll go and talk with Gordon," he said. "We need to decide what to do next. This won't help us. It won't help us at all."

Such compassion. I liked the man less and less each time he opened his malodorous mouth. Leave the girls to clear up the mess, go off and talk men's talk. They were the top brass, Geri and I the poor bloody infantry. I turned back towards the kitchen, filled a bucket with hot water and disinfectant. Geri found a dustpan and brush. We headed off to the meeting room. I felt shaky as I opened the door. A stale smell of old sandwiches and dried vomit hit me as I stepped into the chaotic scene. Geri held back, rigid with the realisation of what had happened in this room so recently. I started to pick up fallen chairs.

"God! What a mess!" whispered Geri. She crept into the room, stood for a moment and then started to gather the teacups and plates in slow motion. I swept the dry debris of crumbs into the dustpan. Then, Geri having finished clearing the table, I washed it down with the hot water. The ancient quality certificates seemed to mock us from their frames.

"I'm going to leave," I said, washing down the chair from which Veronica had tumbled into her next life.

"You can't!" she cried. "You've only just started! You can't leave me with all this." She looked at me with a furrowed face full of fear and pain.

"I have to. Last night was awful. I just need to get away. The last job was bad enough, I don't want more of the same.

Don't need it." I squeezed out my cloth in the bucket. "Anyway, you're looking to move. You'll get another job really easily. Me, I'll have to go back to the Jobcentre."

"They'll all think I did it," she said, and I saw tears in her eyes.

"But you didn't, did you?" I said.

"No, of course not; but she probably died from a food allergy. I made her sandwiches."

"We don't know for sure that she died of an allergy. That's just Ben's conjecture. He dropped out of med school after the first year. Maybe he got it wrong. What if she had a heart attack? She was over fifty, overweight, stressed. It happens."

"Did she say anything before she…you know, before she…"

"Died?"

"Yes."

"She clutched her throat and said "nuts"," I said.

Geri looked at me, I looked back. It was almost funny, but neither of us dared laugh. Instead we got cleaning. So intent were we on soaping away last night's horror, that neither of us heard Gordon enter the room.

"Haven't you finished yet?"

"Oh! Hello Gordon," said Geri. "Sorry. We're doing our best."

He just glared at us. "Just get this mess cleared up. There's work to do." He turned and left, the door swishing closed behind him. After a while, Geri said,

"We need to know if we're staying open because if we're not we have to ring people to cancel their sessions. And I bet Gordon and Lawrence haven't thought of the PR angle. Letting the papers know, that sort of thing."

"Will you go and ask them?" I asked.

"Yeah, I'd better. You know, this could finish *Action in Caring*."

"Or it could be the saving of it if we get someone who's a bit more of a people person in charge," I said.

"Maybe. I'll go and brave Gordon."

I opened the window to air the room. Secretly I saw myself ushering Veronica's spirit out of the building and into the atmosphere. I thought about last night, paused to text Carla. *Thanx 4 lst nite. U a star. Luv u. xx.*

I took my place at the reception desk and waited for Geri to tell me if we were open for business. The phone was silent. I felt edgy, longed for the safety of my room, my other life. I'd written the first sentence of my resignation letter when I heard a door bang, and shouting in the corridor above me. Men's voices, raised and angry. Geri came through looking worried.

"What's going on?" I asked.

"Don't know. Sounds like Gordon and Lawrence are having a row or something," she said. Lawrence swept through, face frowning and jaw set hard. He was muttering under his breath, and ignored Geri and me as he flung open the front door and stomped out, banging it behind him.

"Wonder what that's all about!" I said.

"More than a lovers' tiff, that's for sure," said Geri.

"Gordon give you any idea of what we should do next?" I asked.

"He's writing an obituary of Veronica to send to the local paper. I'm writing to the Council and the Lottery who've funded our work. Could you do a phone round to all the user groups?"

"You want me to ring them and tell them that Veronica's dead?"

"Yeah. I think we should tell them it's business as usual, while we plan what to do next. Tell them that Gordon's in charge for now."

"That'll inspire their confidence!" She just gave me a long stare in response. I wondered if there was history between Gordon and Geri. They seemed an unlikely pair, but you never could tell…

I heard the doorbell ring as I settled into my chair. I checked the monitor and saw Wendy Baggott and Geoff Newsome standing outside. I pressed the button that opened the door with an electronic buzz.

"Hello," I said. "Can I help you?"

"We've come to talk to Geraldine," said Wendy Baggott. "Is she in?"

"Yes. I'll go and get her," I said. I slipped through the door towards Geri's office. "Police want to talk with you," I said.

"I thought they would," she said. "Can you show them in?"

"Yeah. You need anything?"

"No, I'll be fine." But she looked anxious and a pulse in her temple was visibly throbbing.

I'd just settled back behind my desk when the doorbell rang again. No wonder they needed a receptionist in this place. I looked up at the monitor. Little Dora Popp was standing outside, shuffling from one foot to another. I buzzed the door open and she came in. She was like a grubby little bird.

"Who are you?" she asked, squinting at me."

"Nikki. I've just started working here," I said. " We met yesterday. And you're Dora."

"How'd you know? Who's been talking about me?"

"Just Geri. When she introduced us."

"Where's the fat one?"

"Pardon?"

"The fat one. The one what's in charge."

"Veronica?"

"Where is she?"

"Look, Dora, I don't know how to say this; but…well, Veronica…"

"I want to see her. I've got some money for her. Pension came today."

"I'm really sorry to tell you this, but Veronica isn't in. She won't be coming in. She…er…"

"She on holiday again?"

"No. No, she's not on holiday. She…well, you see, she died."

"Who killed her?"

"I'm sorry?"

"Who killed her?"

"I don't know that anyone killed her. She died at the meeting last night."

"How?"

"I don't know. Maybe a heart attack. Maybe an allergic reaction."

"They killed her. I knew it would happen. You can't do things like that and not be killed."

"Things like what?"

"Like what she did. They always get you in the end."

Dora Popp was beginning to frighten me, with her sharp little eyes, the grey greasy hair, rancid breath and cold, cryptic words. Just as I was about to ask her what Veronica had been doing, Geri came out with the police officers.

"You here again, Dora?" she asked.

"You take it," said Dora, holding out a crumpled bank note. "If she's not here to take it, you'd better. I don't want to owe nobody nothing."

"Thanks," said Geri, reaching for the money. "Just hang about while I see these people out and get you a receipt." To the police she said, "I'm sorry I can't tell you anything else."

"You've been very helpful," said Wendy Baggott. "If we've any more questions we'll be in touch." She and Geoff Newsome nodded their goodbyes and strode out of the door.

"How'd you get on?" I asked.

"I told them what I could. Which wasn't much," said Geri. She turned to Dora Popp. "Do you want some tea?"

"No. Business to see to." Dora scurried out of the door, minus her receipt, before I had a chance to ask her to explain more about what Veronica had been doing that might have got her killed.

"What was Dora on about?" I asked Geri.

"What did she say?"

I told her what Dora had said. "What do you think it means?"

"You don't want to take too much notice of Dora. She spent years in hospital. She's borderline paranoid most of the time."

"I read that within every paranoid fantasy there's a grain of truth," I said.

I rang the yoga teacher. Felicity Balmforth expressed her shock at the news.

"I did feel that there was something rather negative about her aura," she said, "but this is terrible news. Very bad karma. Most unfortunate for the building"

"I'm sorry? The building?"

"Disrupts the harmony. Contaminates the atmosphere. We'll need to rebalance the energy."

"Yes, that would be very helpful," I said. "We've cleaned up and I opened the window."

"Jolly good. I'll be along in an hour or so to get the room ready," she promised.

"You'll go ahead with today's class, then?"

"Oh yes. Veronica may have spiralled to a different plane, but there's still work for us to do here."

I didn't think I'd want to do yoga in a room that had so recently seen someone die in it. I hoped that Ms Balmforth would arrive with extra strong aura cleansing detergent and a sturdy pair of spook-proof Marigolds.

The phone rang. This was a first! I picked it up.

"Good morning. *Action in Caring*. Nikki speaking. Can I….."

"Yeah, yeah, I know. Look, what's going on over there?" I heard Aussie accent, male, very flustered.

"I beg your pardon?"

"Just heard about the manager. Odd woman. Heard she'd snuffed it."

"And you are…?"

"Yeah. Sorry, sorry. All a bit of a shock. Sorry mate. Justin. Young offenders' outreach. You new?"

"Yeah, I just started this week. Nikki."

"Oh, well, g'day Nikki. So what's the story?"

I gave him the short version.

"Fuck!" he said. "Any idea what happened?"

"Looks like an accident. She had a lot of allergies apparently."

"So none of my lads in the frame for murder?"

"I don't think so."

"Phew!" He gave a little whistle of relief.

"So will you be coming in then?"

"Yeah, guess so. Too late to ring everyone up."

"Ok, so we'll see you later." I thought about reassuring him that Felicity Balmforth would have cleared away the negative vibes by the time he and his lads arrived, but decided to leave that as a nice surprise.

Felicity Balmforth must have been six feet tall. She was thin and her hair was a mass of auburn bubbles that tumbled down her long neck, stopping short before her narrow shoulders. Amethyst and silver earrings dangled from pendulous ear lobes She was wearing amber coloured loose cotton trousers and an orange tunic. A vibrant yellow and orange scarf wrapped her upper body and her arms jangled with bangles. Her wide, hazel eyes swept me up and down.

"You must be Nikki," she said. Her voice was rich and strong.

"Yes," I said. "Felicity?" The rolled up mat was a bit of a giveaway, not to mention a subtle waft of patchouli. "We've cleaned up the room," I said.

"Wonderful. I'll go and sense the vibes and see off any remaining pain."

She sounded like she ran classes in rooms where people died every day. She'd only been gone for five minutes and the musky smell of nag champa incense sweetened the air. I heard a monotone vibration, a clear sound that insinuated itself in my head. What was she doing? Curiosity took over, and I slipped away from my reception desk to go and investigate. Felicity had pushed the board table to one end of the room and had stacked the chairs. She was standing in the middle of the room rubbing a brass bowl with a wooden baton. Her eyes were closed, and the sound just carried on, mingling with the incense to give the room an altogether different feel. Had I imagined the dreadful scenes of last night? Felicity slowed down her rubbing around the bowl, and then broke the contact between bowl and baton. She opened her eyes and saw me watching her.

"Nearly done," she said cheerily.

"What's that sound?" I asked.

"Tibetan singing bowl," she said. "You know, this wasn't an accident."

"What wasn't?"

"Veronica's passing. I don't sense accident in this room."

"What do you sense?" I wondered if the woman was slightly mad.

"Murder," she said. "I sense violent death. Malevolence. Murder."

Chapter 6

It was good to be home. I picked up my post as I closed the front door behind me. A credit card bill and the latest bank statement. A copy of the free Streatham Guardian that had got ripped being forced through the letter box. Headlines showed a photo of a young black man killed on a fifty-nine bus for his mobile phone. A teacher was quoted as saying that he was quiet but popular, a talented artist, and had had a great future. His auntie said he was with the angels and God would punish his killers. His mother was under sedation. He'd been fifteen but looked younger. The grainy photo showed a boy with a shy smile and kind eyes. Easy prey. They'd shut the school for a day and teenage girls had left garage forecourt flowers and teddies by the gates. I wondered if they'd taken any notice of him while he'd been alive. I chucked the paper into the recycling box, threw the bank statement onto a pile of unopened junk mail and stuffed the credit card bill under the telephone. What a day! And I still hadn't managed to finish my letter of resignation, let alone hand it in. I poured a glass of fair trade Chilean red wine and put on my favourite John Martyn cd. *No Little Boy*. Carla had given it to me three years ago, and I still loved it. Me and Ian Rankin's Rebus. After the weirdness of Felicity's singing bowl, I needed to hear about Solid Air. Clear the vibes in my own way. The yoga class had chanted *Om* for the best part of the hour that they were there. The boardroom was probably pure enough to be a temple by now. Felicity's words were still echoing in my mind. Had she really picked up something or was she just barking? Gordon had gone out at lunchtime and hadn't come back. Geri had drafted the press release and talked to the funders and local worthies. People had made the right sounds and said they were very sorry.

"But I don't think anyone really *liked* her," Geri had mused. "She was quite isolated – you know, none of the networking and joint working that other community workers do. It was as if she didn't really trust anyone."

"Paranoid?"

"Insecure. She got on ok with a couple of the management committee people – Derek and Lawrence, mainly. And she was pretty tight with Gordon." She sighed and shrugged. "Too late to do anything about any of it now."

We'd closed the centre at four thirty. The young offenders had slouched in and slumped out. Justin had said,

"Smells like a bloody ashram!" as he arranged the chairs in the newly balanced meeting room. He was tall, built like a fit rugby player. Fair, gelled hair.

"Felicity Balmforth cleansed the aura," I'd said, and he'd snorted.

"Load of bloody hippy dippy rubbish!" but he'd been very good-natured about it. I'd been grateful to finish early. I was still wiped out from the previous night. I prowled my little flat as John Martyn slurred out the familiar songs. *I don't wanna know 'bout evil, I only wanna know 'bout love.* You're not the only one, John. I thought how good it would be to see Ruth, but it wasn't going to happen. She'd probably gone back to some godforsaken war zone anyway. I hadn't had an e-mail for over a month, and she hadn't even rung to say she was in town.

Look, Nikki, take me as I am. I'm old and tired and angry. And don't expect post-cards from Gaza, she'd said one night when I'd dared to say I'd missed her.

Fuck Blair, and fuck Bush, she'd said between clenched teeth, hurling my remote control at the TV one night when we were watching the news. She'd missed the telly, but I was shaken by the immensity of her anger. How could whatever there was between her and me not be affected by the misery and injustice that she witnessed day after desperate day?

"Where do I fit in?" I'd ventured, the last time I'd seen her. "I mean, what can I do to support you?" I couldn't read her face.

"You just go on doing what you can," she'd said, and I'd had an unpleasant feeling, which later I named as feeling patronised. Still, I worried about her, watched the news religiously, sent e-mails to presidents and prime ministers urging humanitarian compassion, cessation of the arms trade, little things like that. But I'd never been on the front line, and that created a chasm between us. I had been a port in the storm that raged within her between Kandahar, where she'd been supporting clandestine schools for girls, and Gaza, that sorry strip of sand that had become a gulag of misery. A breeding ground for nihilists prepared to gamble that the next world would be better – how could it be worse? - by strapping explosives to themselves and blowing up buses, shops, night clubs and restaurants. Places where people, whatever troubles they faced, had at least some autonomy, some hope. I was helpless. I hadn't been there, so apart from giving her the hottest sex she'd ever known, I was an irrelevance. A ten month long sabbatical. A breathing space between one real life nightmare and the next. Me, I was smitten. Bedazzled. Missed her every hour, every day. And at the same time was angry with her. I had helped to soothe the pain that she'd brought back from Afghanistan, cool the rage that made her want to unveil every burkha'd illiterate woman she'd met there and wipe out most of the men. I'd eased out the knots of grief; but where was she when Brent killed himself? Who did I have to come home to when I needed holding? Not Ruth, that was for sure. It was Carla who'd come up with the goods, Carla who'd shown me what friendship is at its best. And Benjamin, self-centred, vain Benjamin, he had made me laugh, shared midnight spliffs, distracted me with his own outrageous adventures. Now Ruth didn't even contact me when she was back in London.

Enough. It was time to go to the gym, work off some of my miserable dross, sweat out all the stress of the day in the sauna. I belonged to Gunn's Health and Fitness Club. The equipment was good, the company relaxed, it was reasonably clean, and had a state of the art sauna, replete with twinkly fairy lights in the ceiling. I was in good shape from cycling everywhere, but I needed the buzz that you get from hard work with weights. Most of all, I wanted to stretch out in that hot, dark sauna, breathe in the scent of scorching wood and clean women. I gathered my work-out gear and pulled my bike out from under the stairs. Pedalled down Streatham High Road, weaving in and out of stagnant lines of homebound commuters stuck and sighing in their cars. The receptionist at Gunn's looked pleased to see me.

"How're you? All right?" she said.

"Yeah, not too bad," I said. I hadn't been for a couple of weeks. Not a lot had changed. The running machine that hadn't worked still didn't. No-one had replaced the ripped and worn covering on the abdominal crunch bench. There were some new balancing balls, though, and some new members. I warmed up, burned off five hundred calories running and stepping, and eased back into my weight-training programme. It felt good to push my body to its limits and to see a few familiar faces. There were gym buddies that I only ever saw at Gunns. Sometimes we knew each other's names, sometimes not, but we often knew the most intimate and extraordinary things about each other. It was like being in a soap opera. You'd tune in two or three times a week to catch up on Josie's no good man, Julie's quest to find a cure for her IBS, Linda's noisy neighbours and Shoba's monstrous boss. After I'd tested every muscle in my body, I sprinted downstairs, stowed away my contact lenses, showered away the sweat, headed for the sauna.

The sauna is the hottest place in the health club. It's not just the physical heat, but it's where you get the hottest gossip and where fierce debates rage. Some nights it's like a meeting of the UN, and if the collection of women in that little wooden cabin had the power, we'd sort out most of the world's problems. My flip-flops made a sucking sound on the wet floor. A welcome blast of heat enveloped me as I opened the door. Almost blind in the gloom and without my contacts, I groped my way to a spare place in the corner of the top shelf. There were women on all the shelves, their bodies naked, oiled and shining. They were chatting and laughing, and I quickly grasped the theme of tonight's debate.

"I tried to get a triangle, but I took too much off this side."

"Let's see….looks ok to me. A bit dark down there!" An explosion of laughter.

"I put mousse all over mine. Couldn't see what I was doing, so I just shaved away and then I was just left with this tiny patch. Think I got carried away!"

"Oh, let me look…no, hon, it doesn't look too bad."

"It's grown back now. Itches like mad!"

"Was it like a Mohican?"

"Yeah, just this tufty bit down the middle." I wondered whether men discussed the coiffeur of their pubes in their sauna cabin.

"Don't fancy having a Mohican, me. I'd rather have a neat lickle triangle. It's more natural, innit?"

"Natural, yeah, but with all these high-cut swimsuits and things, I've just had to take more and more off, you know?"

Someone was tapping their fingernails on the bench.

"So how 'bout you, bush baby? What you got?" More laughter.

"Me, I don't bother too much. Just shave along the top, like that."

"You gotta go in the direction of the hair."

"I know! It goes this way…"

"Hair doesn't grow that way!"

"Mine does!" More laughter and a few legs kicking in the air. Someone threw some Olbas oil at the heater.

"Why we bother with all this?" The voice sounded familiar, but I couldn't place it.

"'Cos we like bein' pretty down there, innit?"

"Feel cleaner. Don't you feel cleaner?"

"Yeah, definitely cleaner when there's not so much." I sneaked a look at my own haywire bush and felt guilty of self-neglect. Not pretty.

"Me, I just want to feel good down there. Don't want to put on no beauty show!"

"Hey girls, it's HOT in here! I'm going to shower off." Suddenly I remembered where I'd heard that irritating tapping, and whose voice it was I was hearing. It was Chantelle! I froze. Hunkered as far into my corner as I could, wrapped my towel around me. It was like some kind of panicky nightmare, finding yourself standing naked before the inquisitor, or in my case, my personal adviser at the job centre. Thank God she hadn't noticed me! But then the door opened again.

"Forgot my towel! Oh…sorry…er, Nikki?" Chantelle was reaching for the towel that had been drying on the hot slats next to me.

"Hi Chantelle. Fancy meeting you here!"

"Yeah." She sounded as embarrassed as I felt. "How's the job going?"

"Well, I need to talk to you about that. Don't think I'll be there much longer."

"Not now, Nikki. I'm trying to relax. But I'm disappointed. I'd expected more from you."

"Hey, don't be so quick to judge! You don't know what it's been like!"

"Yeah, yeah, I hear it all the time. Some people just don't want to work."

"That's not fair! How would you feel if your boss had just died?"

"That was a year ago. Get over it girl!"

"Not that one. Not Brent. Veronica. The director of *Action in Caring*." She'd frozen. I couldn't help noticing the neat triangle that told me she wasn't the woman with the Mohican.

"You're joking me!"

"Last night. At the management committee meeting. I was taking the minutes. She ate a sandwich and died. It wasn't very nice. So I was going to hand in my notice and see if you had anything else going."

Chantelle, what you doing? We going to this party or what?

"Yeah, coming. Look, Nikki, I'm sorry. Make an appointment. Jesus, maybe what they said about that place was right."

"What do you mean?"

"Nothing really, just rumours…."

Chantelle! You not cooked yet?

"Coming!"

"What rumours?"

"Just something I heard…"

Chantelle!

"Yeah, I'm coming." She turned to open the door.

"Hey, what do you mean? What rumours?"

"Look, I gotta go. Meet me for lunch on Monday. Noodle bar on the High Road. Ok?"

Chantelle! I'm warning you…

"Ok. See you then." I let out a big sigh as she closed the door behind her. She'd just undone all the good I'd done through my work-out. There was nothing for it. I'd have to head for the Jacuzzi.

Chapter 7

I got home and threw my gym bag on top of the recycling box. The Jacuzzi had helped, but I was troubled by my encounter with Chantelle. I'd just poured a glass of wine when there was a knock on the door. Immediately my thoughts turned to Ruth, an absurd surge of hope flaring in my mind, only to fizzle as I heard Benjamin's voice.

"Nik, you in?" he called as he knocked again.

"Coming! Keep your hair on!" That was a bit of a joke, because Benjamin didn't have much hair. He'd shaved it off because he was a fashion victim, and he looked a bit like Ben Kingsley in *Gandhi* . His mum had practically disowned him.

"Like something out of the camps, he looks, my son! That he should be home-oh-sexual is enough punishment for a mother, but to do that to his hair...Oi!" Ben had done an excellent impression of his fretting, never-happy mother and hummed a rendition of *My Yiddishe Mama* to wrap it up.

I opened the door.

"Great! You've got some wine on the go!" he said, depositing a light kiss on my cheek as he pushed his way into the flat. I sighed and poured him a glass. My meditative evening and early night were fast disappearing into a mist. He gulped down half the glass.

"You ready for tomorrow, then?" There was an evil glint in his eye.

"What do you mean? What's happening tomorrow?"

"You haven't forgotten?

"What?"

"We're doing that day on facing your fears."

"Shit! I'd forgotten all about it!" Now my quiet weekend pottering amongst my window boxes and catching up with my reading was disappearing too.

"Nik, you can't let me down on this one. You owe me!"

"What for?"

"Fixing your bike, for one."

"You said I could take you out to the Japanese place."

"Well, what about bringing your wretched bone shaker to that community centre you claim to be working in?"

"You wanted your bike back so you could impress Mr Lycra Pants!"

"You need this workshop."

"I do?"

"You do. Your bosses are dying with worrying regularity and your love life's shot to pieces. Pass the bottle." I was rapidly losing control of my life.

The workshop had been Carla's idea:

"You're getting so you're almost frightened of your own shadow, Nik. I don't know what's happened to you. Why don't you try this workshop – *Face your fears and laugh at them*?"

Benjamin found out about it through his Kabbalah 101 study group. One of the members had casually slipped a flier into his hand at the end of the meeting.

"Hey Ben, thought you might be interested in this," he'd said and then vanished. Benjamin had been indignant when he told me about it.

"Honestly, anyone would think I had problems!" he'd cried as he scurried around in his kitchen looking for a bottle opener.

"Well, Benjamin, you do sometimes seem a little…I don't know, a little…*timid* about …well, about …life…and your parents…"

"What about my parents? Of course I have issues with my parents. They're Jewish, for Christ's sake!"

"Yeah, I know. So are you. Makes for quite an intense kind of relationship, doesn't it? Look… how about we both do this workshop? It sounds interesting and Carla thinks I should do it."

"Why?"

"Because even non Jews have issues, Benjamin. I too need to sort out my life. Especially my love life. And I'm terrified."

"You are?"

"Yes."

"Ok, let's do it."

So here he was to remind me of our pact. We watched a re-run of *Will and Grace* and finished the wine.

"Now go," I said, ushering him towards the door. "I need my beauty sleep, so do you." He grunted, but left, agreeing to meet at eight thirty the next morning.

I got dressed in jeans and a comfy purple jumper that had seen better days. I locked my front door and went to call for Benjamin. He, of course, was dressed to impress: off-white chinos and pink shirt. We clashed alarmingly. It was a dull morning with a threat of drizzle in the air, and I'd rather by far have stayed curled up in bed. We walked to the High Road and took the bus to Brixton.

"You read about that kid that died on the fifty nine?" I asked Benjamin

"Yeah."

"Think it's time to move out of the big city?"

"No." Ben wasn't at his most eloquent in the mornings.

"I've been thinking about it."

"Oh."

I gave up and opened up the Ian Rankin. I was hooked by the end of the first paragraph.

Brixton on a Saturday morning has a particular atmosphere. Dossers are still snoring in their soaked blankets in grimy doorways. Clubbers who've just emerged from *The Fridge* are dazed by daylight as they grope towards the nearest coffee-selling outlet. Some sit in

McDonalds, their moods plummeting as the uppers wear off and they realise that they have to brave public transport in their party gear. Girls in trousers so low cut that their cracks are on display despair over having to face the world in stale, streaked make-up. Boys in baggy trousers grow sullen at the realisation that, yet again, they've failed to pull. A wasted looking guy with matted hair tried to sell us a travel card.

"Only three quid, love," he said, thrusting a crumpled ticket at me.

"It's yesterday's," I pointed out.

"Oh," he said, and shrugged.

The African selling incense was setting up his stall. The flower man hadn't arrived. I used to buy Ruth flowers from him: they were always fresh.

We took the Victoria line to Euston and then changed onto the Northern line. We got off at Hampstead and walked the short distance to the therapy centre, following the e-mailed instructions that I'd carefully printed out. It was as if we had travelled to another land, not simply to another part of London. Chic patisseries nudged boutiques with colour co-ordinated window displays. None of the clothes showed price tags. Parents pushed fashion plate tots around in buggies the infant equivalent of Chelsea tractors.

The therapy centre was in a converted attic. There were nine of us in the group. The facilitator, Ro, was sallow, underweight and dressed in black and red. She scared me before she said anything. We were a miserable, fearful group of three men, including Ben, and six women of various sizes and ages. Everyone had to say what frightened them. People talked about spiders and snakes, babies and flying, being blown up on the tube. When it got to me, I took a deep breath.

"Death," I said. "I'm frightened of death."

"Uh-huh," said Ro, and everyone nodded.

"My last two bosses have died violent and unnecessary deaths," I offered. "The first killed himself because he couldn't cope any more with being bullied. He was gay. The second only happened this week. She seemed to die from an allergic reaction to sandwiches." There was a silence and everyone was looking at me with even more fear in their eyes. I was much scarier than getting on a jumbo full of spiders and babies or braving the post seven/seven tube. "So, I'm…well, I have this fear, and I know it's irrational and the deaths were nothing to do with me, but I'm pretty scared about what might happen in my next job. And I find violent death pretty scary, having seen it close-up. So I worry more about the people I care about."

"I hear what you're saying," said Ro, nodding. "Love and death are the big ones. But we're here today to *laugh* at our fears. How can we help you to see these deaths as just another of life's little quirks?

"Umm…"

"I think maybe we could use drama here. Act out the scary stuff. Put it out there. What do you think?"

"I'm not sure that that's entirely appropriate, to be honest," I said. "Brent hanged himself and Veronica had an explosive reaction to a ham sandwich. Don't think I'm quite ready to turn it all into a musical."

"You have to change what you think in order to change how you feel about it," said Ro. "And drama's a great way to do it!"

I didn't think so, somehow.

"Ro, I don't think I can work with this woman in the room," whined a skinny whey-faced woman with lank dirty blonde hair who was afraid of babies. "She's really freaking me out."

"Me too. I'm really not ok about Nikki's aura. I feel like she's brought death with her and that's very distressing to me." This supportive statement was from a short man with a pot belly who'd been sitting in a lotus position looking superior. His thing was flying.

"Well, can we put all these fears in a big salad bowl and act them out?" asked Ro. The looks on everyone's faces told me we couldn't.

Ben and I left the workshop at lunch time. We both hated everyone in the group except each other.

"Have you ever come across such a group of whinging heads up arses?" asked Benjamin as he lit a fag running down the stairs. "Why can't we just face our fears and live with them? Why, all of a sudden, has everyone become obsessed with being fearless? It's a pretty scary world and it seems to me that being fearful is a normal kind of reaction to have."

"And that Ro!" I'd added, slamming the door to the chi-chi therapy centre. "What planet was she on? I swear I smelled vodka on her breath."

"You can't smell vodka, that's the point."

"Oh yes you can."

We went back to Benjamin's flat. He rolled a spliff and we sat and smoked it without talking for a while. It was good weed and I felt my body loosening, my brain getting clearer and fuzzier at the same time. The weed paradox. Someone should write a book about it.

"So what do you fear most?" I asked

"Women," he replied.

"Me too," I said and giggled.

Suddenly we found ourselves helpless with giggles as we realised how ridiculous the day had been so far. How ridiculous we both were. Benjamin was the first to utter a coherent sentence.

"You ever done it with a bloke, Nik?"

"Mmm. Long time ago. Found I definitely preferred women. You?"

"All the time."

We shrieked some more and kicked our legs in glee as I realised what I'd said.

"No, I mean, have you ever done it with a woman?"

"Well…sort of. Not really."

"What do you mean?"

He lit up a new spliff, inhaled deeply, held it, exhaled.

"Christ, Nik, you don't want the details, do you?"

"'Course I do. Let's face our fears, Ben. Let's you and I do together what we went to Hampstead for. Let's have a bit of self-help therapy."

"I couldn't do it."

"Yes you can, it's me, your friend and neighbour."

"No, I mean I couldn't do it. Couldn't do it to Etty Goldblum"

"Etty Goldblum? How the hell did you nearly do it with – and Ben, as a feminist I have to tell you it's *with* and not *to* – a girl called Etty Goldblum?"

"Long story. We met at Hebrew class. I was nineteen. She asked me to her eighteenth birthday party at her parents' house. We'd had champagne. She took me to her room."

"What was it like?"

"Pink. Really girly – lots of frills around the bed, that sort of thing. Not very tidy."

"No! Not her room! Having sex with her!"

"Oh. Well, she just started taking off her clothes and looking at me in this weird way, like she'd been watching sex scenes on telly, only she hadn't quite got the look or the moves right."

"And?"

"And I wished she wouldn't. Or that she'd turn into Colin Firth. But she didn't."

"Turning into Colin Firth was a bit much to ask."

"I know. And then she said, *Benjamin, I need you to make love to me. It's my birthday and I'm the only eighteen year old virgin I know and I really like you, Benjamin, so please make love to me.*"

"What did you do?"

"I thought, how the fuck do I get out of here? By then she was down to her bra and knickers and then she bounded towards me, and she said, *Benjy, do you want to take my bra off?* And I said, *No, Etty, not really* but she just kept coming and muttered something about me being shy and made a grab for my trousers."

"How did you feel?"

"Sick."

"And then?"

"So she's tugging at my trousers and all of a sudden she's got her hand in my fly, and because she's touching me, something starts to happen, you know?"

"What sort of something?"

"Christ, Nik, use your imagination!"

"So did you deflower Etty Goldblum?"

"She led me to her single princess bed. Pulled down my trousers and pants, lay down, pulled me on top of her. She's tugging away and trying to get me inside her but the sound of the Klezmer band downstairs was really putting me off – I hate that manic clarinet-on-speed stuff. And I was shit scared that her father would find us, and I realised that I didn't even like Etty very much."

"Then?"

"She really wanted to, and it was her birthday, and I'd been brought up to be nice to girls, so I closed my eyes, thought of Colin Firth with a wet shirt; thought of Marlon Brando in *On the Waterfront*; but at the end of the day, it was Etty Goldblum pushing her funny little body up to mine, making funny girly sounds, smelling of something sweet and synthetic. Her breasts scared me. Everything else was tucked away. I couldn't see where anything was."

"You could have gone down on her."

"I especially didn't want to go there!"

"So Colin and Marlon weren't working?"

"Nope. I was limp as a carrot that had got forgotten at the back of the fridge."

"That's beautiful. I'm going to use it when I write my book. Then what?"

"Etty sat up, asked me what was wrong. She said, *Benjamin, are you gay or something?* And I said, *you know what, Etty, I just might be. I'm really sorry.* I put my clothes on and legged it. The Klezmer band had worked itself up into a demented frenzy by then. It was doing my head in. I threw up in Etty Goldblum's front garden over a rather lovely rose bush."

"No wonder you've got issues with women!"

"I haven't. I'm just gay."

"But are you? Are any of us?

"Are any of us what?"

"Gay, straight. If we weren't obsessed by which box we fitted in, couldn't we just have sex with people we liked?"

"Some people do. They're called bisexuals."

"We like each other."

"Nik, wherever you're going with this, don't."

"Yeah, you're right." I was suddenly overwhelmed by a feeling, by the most powerful drive on earth, the need that is common to every life form. I was hungry. I'd got the munchies, and I'd got them bad. Smoking weed always did that to me. Made me want food and sex with equal urgency. Food usually won out and was a lot less complicated.

"You got anything to eat, Ben? I'm starving!"

"I thought we were getting into something there." I heard relief in his voice.

"Are you crazy? I'm starving! I'd give anything for a great big bar of chocolate. Something really sweet and milky."

"Me too," he sighed, and pulled himself up from the floor. He headed for the kitchen and I followed him.

"What've you got then?"

He opened the fridge. There was a carton of juice and a jar of pickled cucumbers (kosher, of course). It was the most minimalist fridge I had ever seen. There's such a thing as taking style too far.

"What about the cupboards?" I asked hopefully. He opened a door into pristine emptiness. I had never seen a kitchen cupboard that held nothing at all. He opened another and reached deep inside.

"Aha!" he exclaimed with triumph, as he pulled out a small glass jar. I wasn't hopeful.

"What is it?"

"You'll like it! It's chocolate."

"In a jar?"

"Body paint. It's the chocolate body paint that Josh gave me before we split up."

My face must have been showing distress, because he said,

"It's chocolate, Nik! You melt it a bit and then paint it on someone you fancy and then you lick it all off. It's sex and chocolate all at the same time. Isn't that just what you always wanted?"

I was stoned, but not that stoned. No way was I was up to licking melted chocolate off Benjamin. I was desperate, though. I needed food and I needed chocolate most of all, and it was either the body paint or the pickled cucumbers. There was no competition. Benjamin unscrewed the lid of the jar and put it in the microwave.

"Mustn't leave it in for too long, or we'll get scalded," he said.

"We're not really going to…I mean, I don't think …"

"Eat it off each other?" he asked, looking mischievous.

"I'd rather do it with a spoon," I said.

He slid open a white-fronted drawer. "One for you, one for me," he said. "Ladies first."

I scooped out melted chocolate, and my mouth closed over the spoon, devouring the sticky bittersweet stuff. I closed my eyes and the world swayed.

"Better than sex," I said.

Benjamin grabbed the jar from me and stuck in his own spoon. "Almost," he said. Later, after we'd eaten the whole jar, he said, "Wanna crash in the spare room?"

"Yeah, that'd be nice."

I followed him into a cool white room furnished only with a bed, chest of drawers, and wardrobe. No knick-knacks to clutter the space. A tall, stylish standard lamp in the corner, black curtains with a silver vertical stripe. It was all very manly. He folded back the white bedspread to reveal black sheets. I'd never seen black sheets before. I slipped between them and felt the curious day slip away. But my last thought before sleep was, what could Chantelle possibly have to tell me?

Chapter 8

The next morning, I awoke to find myself in Benjamin's spare bed and the smell of freshly brewed coffee tempting me from the kitchen. There was a bathrobe hanging on the door so I wrapped it around myself. I padded out to the bathroom and slipped into the shower. Then I dried myself and put on yesterday's clothes. I went to join Ben in the kitchen.

"Good morning, oh chocolate fiend!"

"Good morning yourself," I replied. "Did you sleep ok?"

"Fine. Only I dreamt I was being chased by Etty Goldblum and a posse of alarming little people and all the girls were like miniature versions of Etty and all the boys were miniatures of me. Scary!"

He must have been out to the nearby patisserie, because there were croissants on the table. I was impressed.

"D'you treat your boyfriends like this?" I asked.

"If I'm lucky enough to get them to come this far," he said.

"So what are you planning for this splendid Sunday?" The sun was bright and it was the kind of morning that just urged you to go outside.

"I'm meeting Dan for lunch and a ride around Hyde Park."

"Dan?"

"Cycle Out. Leader of the pack."

"Oh! Getting serious then?"

"I live in hope. How about you?"

"Not sure. To be honest, I'm troubled about *Action in Caring*. There was something very off about Veronica. Gordon, the second in command is kind of cold and creepy. Geri's on the verge of a nervous breakdown. And Chantelle hinted at there being a bit of history. So I think I'm going to do some snooping around, web search, touch base with Suresh."

"Your mate on the South London Press?"

"The very same." I drained the coffee cup and picked up the last of the croissant crumbs with my finger.

"Thanks, Ben," I said. "You're great, you know? But I'd better go."

"Yeah, it was a laugh in the end, wasn't it?"

We hugged goodbye, and I went up to my flat. Put on Stevie Wonder while I tidied around and did my weekly clean. Then turned on the PC and clicked onto Google.

First I checked my e-mails. Two offers of penis enlargements, one tempting offer of a fake Rolex, some veiled attempts to sell me Viagra, nothing from Ruth. I logged off and went back to Google. I typed in *Action in Caring* and scored three hits. The first linked to the Council's website, listing the charity as a community resource centre. The second took me to a paper that someone had written about lack of investment in youth services leading to greater delinquency, citing the young offenders' scheme that we ran as an example of rare good practice. The third took me to minutes from a council meeting held two months ago. Reading them, I gathered that this was a meeting to set budgets and agree which services our elected representatives deemed worthy of continued funding, and which they planned to cut. A councillor called Nigel Bentley said that *Action in Caring* had failed to meet certain quality standards and there were questions over its most recent accounts. Add into that allegations that had been made about Gordon Smedley and a predilection for young boys, and Councillor Bentley felt that there could be no justification in keeping the charity open. Cynthia Hope, for the opposition, argued that the allegations against Gordon had been investigated and found to be without substance, and that the auditors had worked with the management committee to improve the accounting system. Given the centre's record on preventing re-offending amongst young people, and the valuable activities it provided to older people, and the general cost-effectiveness of its services, Cynthia felt that to close *Action in Caring* would be calamitous and lead to poverty, rather than regeneration, within the community. Chandrika Patel, speaking for the Lib Dems, said that she thought an interim grant should be made to *AiC* with the proviso that the charity make certain improvements within prescribed timescales. I thought back to the out of date certificates on the wall, to the feeling that *AiC* needed more than a face-lift. Councillor Patel had a point. Nigel Bentley said that with the new South London Community and Enterprise Centre opening, there could be no justification for maintaining *AiC*. He said that most of *AiC's* regular activities had transferred, or were about to transfer, to SoLCEC, where the facilities were first rate, and the funding came from Europe rather than our hard-up council. Cynthia said that the new centre was too intimidating for some groups. Chandrika said that she thought an evaluation was needed, with the views of current and former *AiC* users canvassed. Nigel Bentley said that a final decision would be made in cabinet. That sounded a bit grand to me, but then local nobodies love to give themselves airs and graces.

There was nothing else, apart from a six-year-old reference to a jumble sale. I printed off the committee minutes and closed down the PC. It was Sunday. I doubted that I'd get hold of Suresh until tomorrow. I was at a loose end. Carla would be busy with her own weekend stuff. I had the keys to *AiC*. No-one else would be there. I could have a look at the files, dig around Veronica's office, see what I could find. Crazy. But the more I thought about it, the more I felt drawn to doing a little bit of quiet investigation. We'd heard nothing from Wendy Baggott or her sidekick since their initial visit, and I doubted that they were working overtime to solve the mystery of Veronica's untimely death. And I was curious.

I glanced around me. Tanners Lane was deserted. I crept across the forecourt and stealthily turned the key in the lock. The alarm started to buzz and I had a sudden panic: what was the code? And then I remembered, keyed in the numbers, and shut down the noise. Daylight warmed the building. It was utterly silent. I headed for Veronica's office. Something didn't feel right. I paused, and then realised what it was. The office was tidy. The unruly piles on my former boss's desk were no longer there. Even the bookshelves had been tidied into orderly rows. There was a clean smell of polish and the floor had been vacuumed. As far as I knew, Geri hadn't been in this room since Veronica's death, and neither had I, so who would have gone to such lengths to clear it? And why?

I moved to the other side of the desk. There were three desk drawers. I opened the top one. Paperclips, staples, biros, post-its, treasury tags, a solitary drawing pin. The next drawer contained stationery: letterhead paper, compliments slips, envelopes of various sizes. Nothing of any interest. The third drawer yielded a box of tissues; a Bic lighter; an ancient Boots Number Seven lipstick in a vile coral colour; a pair of tights in a packet – American Tan, twenty denier, Woolworth's special offer; some antihistamines; a half empty packet of Rennies; and a small green notebook. Maybe it was her diary. There was only one way to find out. No-one would know...and so I opened it. Even if it told of tawdry secrets, I didn't have to tell anyone and Veronica was beyond caring. It was indeed a diary. I flicked through January and February until I got to the middle of March. It looked as if Veronica had a regular appointment on Thursday mornings. She'd pencilled in the initials DR. Doctor? Maybe she was having some kind of medical treatment. Then I remembered my first day, and Geri telling me that she was getting treatment to stop smoking and cure her allergies. Sure enough, there on 7th April she'd written *DR 9.45.* I glanced further up the page. Against 6th April, she'd written *dentist 8.30. NB 7.15.* Did that mean *note bene*, make sure you don't forget, something you have to do at seven fifteen? Why hadn't she written down what it was she was doing at seven fifteen? I turned the page, hoping to find the answer. The only other entries were two birthdays – someone called Pauline on September 10th and Dad on November 2nd. She hadn't written in any more DR appointments. Either she'd anticipated being cured by 7th April, or she made them week by week. I put the notebook back and shut the drawer.

Suddenly I heard the sound of a door opening and closing, footsteps. I froze in cold panic. Who else would be here on a Sunday morning? The footsteps had gone upstairs and I could hear them above me. They had to be in Gordon's office. If it were a burglar, it would be my responsibility to call the police; but how would I explain my own presence? And if it were Gordon, how would he react to finding the new receptionist snooping around the deceased director's office? I heard a chair being scraped across the floor. Then there were voices. Raised voices.

"That stupid new girl forgot to set the alarm."

"I didn't think it would come to this."

"What did you think would happen?"

"I don't know. But not this."

"Don't tell me you're getting cold feet!"

I tried to place the voices. I strained to hear the words, and the voices were too muffled to be easily recognisable.

"'course I'm not. But I thought we'd agreed, no…"

A siren screeched past outside, drowning out their voices. It acted like a wake-up call. I had to get out. Self-preservation was winning out over curiosity. I opened the office door a crack. I'd creep into the meeting room, hide there until the coast was clear. I closed Veronica's door noiselessly behind me and slipped into the meeting room. There was a crash from upstairs, the sound of angry men shouting at each other. I hunkered down in the far corner, praying that they wouldn't carry their argument down here. There was something shiny under a stack of chairs. It glinted out from a cloud of fluff. This was a corner that the cleaner never reached, forensics had overlooked, and Geri and I had missed when we'd cleaned up the room. I reached for it. It was a slender, plastic tube, and it contained a syringe. So one of Justin's boys was using. There was a pharmacist's label wrapped around it. The product was called Ana-Guard. In smaller print, I read that it contained epinephrine. Suddenly I remembered Rosie Lingwood in my class at junior school. She had a peanut allergy and the teacher always had to have the antidote to hand. An epi-pen, they called it. "It's got this stuff called epinephrine in it," Rosie had told me proudly one day. "It's to stop me dying when I get an allergy." And then I saw Veronica. My memory replayed that terrible night, watched her groping desperately in her handbag. The object she dropped. Derek and Gordon groping under the table and emerging, not with an epi-pen, but with a ball-point pen. But it must have been this syringe that she had been seeking. This pristine life-saver that had eluded her. I slipped it into my pocket. I'd need to pass it to the police. The men were still shouting. I hoped they hadn't noticed my bike under the stairs. Wheeling it noiselessly out, I tiptoed to the front door. I slipped out, mounted my bike and headed for home, heart pounding, my head red inside with fear and anxiety. I don't think I breathed until I'd reached the common. Two football teams were warming up. A woman jogger ran in time to her iPOD soundtrack. Five kids in hooded sweatshirts sat on felled logs smoking. I got off my bike and sat on a bench. I rang Carla. Of course her ansaphone took my call.

Carla, it's me. I went snooping around the office this morning. I know it's crazy, but I had to and, um, there were men arguing. Two of them. In Gordon's office. And I found something. An epi-pen that could have saved her … The ansaphone cut me off. I rang her back.

Ring me, Carla. This is getting freaky.

Someone said, "Nikki?"

I looked up. It was Rita, accompanied by five bouncing dogs of various breeds. Great! That was all I needed: another reminder of the shitty situation that was getting more sinister by the day.

"Hi Rita. What are you doing here?"

"Walking Prudence and some dogs I'm looking after. I'm a dog walker."

"Oh! So… that means…"

"Walking dogs for people who are too lazy to do it themselves or who go on holiday. Prudence is mine, though." She indicated a mongrel with more than its fair share of wire-haired terrier. Prudence wagged her tail, gazed at me with adoring brown eyes and then sat herself at my feet. If only human love were that simple. I patted her wiry head and received a lick in return. Maybe it was true what they said about stroking animals calming you down. I was shaking less.

"She likes you," said Rita, approvingly. "You got animals?"

"Nah. I had a hamster when I was nine, but he died."

"They do," she said.

"You were really great the other night," I said. "How are you doing?"

"Still can't believe it. One minute she was being her usual bossy self, the next, dead. Can't believe it. Never liked the woman, but she didn't deserve that."

"Why didn't you like her?"

"Dunno. She was, you know, cold. Bossy. To be honest, I don't think she wanted me on the management committee."

"How did you get to be on it?"

"Young offenders. My Scott was one. They all go through it, these lads. He had a bad couple of years. Dropped out of school – mind you, I don't blame him for that. Got into some dodgy stuff. Got caught. But that project at *Action in Caring* turned him round. They got him into college, got him onto an apprenticeship scheme, and now he's making a bomb as a plumber. People always need plumbers, don't they?"

"Yes." I hadn't really given it much thought, being a dab hand with a plunger. "I s'pose they do."

"So I'd got my boy back and I wanted to give something to the people who'd helped him. They wanted people for the management committee, so I put myself forward. And here I am!"

The dogs were sniffing around, getting restless and tugging at leashes, all except for Prudence who was just lying quietly on my feet.

"You all right?" she asked. "It was your first day, wasn't it? Bloody awful way to start a new job!"

"Yeah. I'm ok. Just stunned, I s'pose. And wondering how it could have happened."

"One of those things, I expect. Just a horrible accident."

"D'you think so?" I looked at her.

"What else?"

I didn't answer.

"Better get this lot off on their walkies. Come on Prudence, leave Nikki's shoelaces." Prudence had been sucking at the lace on my left Kicker. She gave my hand a last lick and they all trotted off, Rita almost carried along by the leaping, tail-wagging mutts.

Chapter 9

Carla hadn't rung back. I went to the gym. Might as well keep up the good work. After burning off some of the week's weirdness, I relaxed for a few minutes in the sauna. It was quiet, just me and a woman I didn't know. I finished with an icy shower and got dressed. I didn't feel like being at home on my own. They were showing a new French movie that I wanted to see at the Ritzy, so I passed the evening puzzling over voyeurism as a metaphor of our times. I snuck in a can of Guinness and a large bar of Galaxy chocolate and snuggled into the darkness. Afterwards I went home, read another chapter of the Ian Rankin (wonder if he's ever actually seen a dead body?), listened to a couple of favourite Ferron tracks, and then crashed into bed.

On Monday morning, I dressed for work and headed off for Tanners Lane. Geri was already in.

"I think we might have had a break-in at the weekend," she said. I remembered my Sunday exploits with a guilty jolt.

"Oh?"

"The alarm wasn't set. Some chairs had got knocked over. It looks as if someone was in Veronica's office. Gordon's is a real mess too, papers all over the place, everything on his desk whipped onto the floor."

"Maybe Gordon came in." I couldn't tell her I'd been snooping.

"He wouldn't have left his office like that. It's odd, he's not in yet and he's usually one of the first, checking up to make sure that no-one's running late."

"Is anything missing?"

"Not that I can see. The safe was locked and it doesn't look as if anyone's tried to break into it. The computers are still here."

I had to tell her. But would she think me mad? Would I just add to her anxiety?

"How was your weekend?" she asked.

"Oh…you know…did a north London thing with my friend Ben on Saturday. Then…well, that was Saturday. Saw a film, went to the gym on Sunday. Same old, same old. You?" *Coward!*

"Went shopping on Saturday. Didn't find anything, though. Wasn't in the mood. Sang in this group I go to on Sunday. Saw my mum. That was it. The weekends go by so fast!"

"Yeah. I'm going to make coffee." Why couldn't I bring myself to tell her what had happened on Sunday? I could trust Geri, I was sure I could. The doorbell rang before I'd got halfway to the kitchen. I ran back to answer it. Rita was there with Prudence.

"Hi Rita," I said. "You ok?" Prudence had leapt up at me as if I were her long lost lover. Her tongue was hanging out, her tail was wagging, and her front paws were leaving muddy splodges on my Ben Sherman shirt and chinos.

"Down, girl," I said, patting her head. But even a dog's affection was welcome these days.

"Hello Rita," said Geri, sounding surprised to see her. "How are you doing? Sounds like the meeting last week was a total nightmare."

"You could say that. Nikki and me was talking about it yesterday, wasn't we?" Geri looked puzzled.

"Yesterday?"

"Yeah. We met on the Common, Rita and me," I said quickly. "She's a dog walker." I don't know why I added that last bit. I was sure I looked like someone with something to hide.

"What were you doing on the Common?" asked Geri.

"Oh, you know, just….riding my bike….enjoying the morning…Rita, can I make you some coffee? Tea?"

"Tea please, love. Two sugars if that's all right."

"'course." I scurried off to the kitchen. Geri followed.

"What are you hiding?" she demanded.

"What do you mean? I'm not hiding anything," I said, planting the kettle in its base.

82

"Yes you are. You're all pink and you sound like someone with a secret. And what were you doing on the Common with Rita?"

"I just bumped into her. Honestly! She was walking five dogs, and Prudence, who's hers, that's Prudence out there, took a shine to me."

"And?" She stood with her arms folded around her skinny middle.   "And …I came to *AiC* to snoop around. There's something not right about this place, Geri, or about the way Veronica died. So I came in because I thought no-one else would be here. Someone had tidied up her office. I read her diary but it didn't give much away. Then there were men arguing, so I hid. I found an epi-pen. I think Veronica was trying to reach it as she died. I didn't set the alarm, because the men were still here. I don't know who they were, but one of them must have been Gordon. Please don't tell him! I don't think they know I was here."

"God, Nikki! What were you thinking of?"

"What do you mean?"

"Look, what if you'd been caught? What if one of the men …You've got to tell the police!"

"Yeah, well. I'd been onto Google, and there was some stuff in the council minutes, and I thought, if I have a quiet look, maybe I'll find a clue as to what happened."

"Knock, knock!" We'd both forgotten Rita.

"Oh, Rita…tea's just coming," I said. Prudence hadn't read the health and safety manual that banned dogs from kitchens and was reacquainting herself with my shoelace. I wondered how much Rita had overheard.

"I thought you might need a hand," said Rita.

"No, I think we're ok. Everything's under control," said Geri, trying for brightness."

"Only, if there's anything you want done…"

"You're our woman!" I said, adding breezy to Geri's bright.

"Did you see Joan over the weekend?" asked Geri. "D'you know how she is?"

"She's gone to her sister's," said Rita. "I went round to hers the day after Veronica…you know, the day after it…"

"Yeah, yeah," we both said. Prudence gave a little yap and put her paw on my knee. This dog had a serious crush on me. It was getting to be mutual. Something about big brown eyes. Ruth's are cool and grey. Cool and grey always spells trouble for me. I should keep going for the brown.

"She was really shaken. I'd never seen her look like that. She was scared. Whole thing just freaked her out. She looked white and old. And she's tougher than she looks, is Joan, but this had really got to her."

"Did she say anything?" I asked.

"Like what?"

"Well, you know, like…how did it happen?"

"You mean did she ask if it was an accident?"

"Yeah, that sort of thing," I said. Geri looked at me, frowning

"She kept saying, *unbelievable* and *I can't believe that it has come to this*. She seemed…well, I s'pose she was in shock. She'd seen Veronica…you know…"

"Yeah," we both said.

"Well, she'd seen her…choke. Die. We did try, you know."

"You were brilliant. Both of you. You couldn't have done more," I said, to reassure her.

"But what with all that stuff going on in the council, and the SoLCEC mob's dirty tricks…"

"Dirty tricks?" we both said at once. "What do you mean?"

"Well, who do you think started the rumour about Gordon?"

Geri and I just looked at each other. "Who?" we said in chorus.

"Joan thinks it was Lawrence," pronounced Rita.

"Why?" asked Geri.

"Well, he's very tight with one or two councillors," said Rita.

"He is?" I asked, wondering how anyone could be tight with Lawrence.

"But why would he want to damage *Action in Caring?*" asked Geri.

"Bigger fish to fry. The new SoLCEC centre has kudos. And money, of course."

"Which councillors?" I asked.

"Leader of the Council for one, Nigel Bentley," said Rita.

"But surely the SoLCEC people wouldn't want a loser like Lawrence on their committee?" I said. "Won't they want guys in suits who can talk to the Lottery, that sort of thing?"

"Oh yes," said Rita, "but they need some authentic pillars of the community to add credibility. And they want yes men like Lawrence, not people like me and Joan who might ask awkward questions."

We were all quiet for a minute or two. Rita and I sipped at our drinks. Geri gnawed a hangnail.

"So you don't think Veronica died by accident?" I said.

"Looked fishy to me," said Rita. "I mean, who made her sandwiches?"

"I did," said Geri.

"And how long have you been making her sandwiches?"

"I don't know. A couple of years, maybe."

"So you know what she can and can't eat, right?"

"Yes. I'm always very careful."

"There you go, then."

"So you think someone doctored the sandwiches?" asked Geri.

"Well, you've got to wonder. And after I'd talked with Joan, I thought, yes, that's the only thing that makes sense, unless she'd accidentally dipped into the bowl with the nuts, and I can't see her doing that."

"I didn't see her go near the bowl of nuts," I said, "but I was busy trying to take notes. We need to talk to the police." I needed to tell

Wendy Baggott about the epi-pen. I could suggest the spiked sandwich theory while I was at it.

"And say what? Excuse me, Ms Plod, but we think Veronica was poisoned by a sandwich spiked with nuts – or cheese, or whatever it was what did for her. Don't make me laugh! Anyway, they'd try and pin it on Geri."

Geri looked pale and her brow was so furrowed that her eyebrows were almost meeting in the middle. I decided to come clean.

"Look, I might as well tell both of you…"

"It wasn't you, love, was it?" chipped in Rita.

"No! Of course not! I'd only just met the woman!"

"Go on," said Geri, knowing part of what was coming next.

"Rita, you know when I met you and the dogs on Sunday?"

"On the common?"

"Yes. Well, I'd been snooping around this place."

"You never!"

"Yeah. I was curious. We all think it wasn't an accident, right?"

"Right," they both said.

"So I thought I'd have a look and see if there were any clues in Veronica's office. Only someone had got there first."

"Well, I never!" exclaimed Rita.

I described the voices I'd heard raised, the escalating argument, my discovery amongst the dust bunnies, my quiet escape.

"I thought you was a bit funny when I bumped into you," said Rita. "No wonder!"

"And when I came in today, it looked like there'd been a fight or scuffle," added Geri.

Just then the phone rang. I went to the reception desk to answer it.

"Good morning, *Action in…*" but the caller interrupted before I'd finished my well-rehearsed spiel.

"Yes, yes, it's Gordon here," said Gordon. "I won't be in today. Please let Geraldine know, and be so kind as to rearrange my appointment with the bank this afternoon. That's all." He'd rung off before I had time to ask which bank, or when we could expect him in. I relayed the message to Geri.

"Odd," she said. "He seldom misses a day, and it's not like him to cancel the bank. I'd better phone them."

"Have we got much else on today?" I asked.

"Just Felicity's yoga for expectant mums this afternoon. Joan would normally have her art group, but as she's away with her sister…"

"They'll probably get on without her," said Rita. "I don't mind lending a hand with getting the room ready and the pencils out."

"I'm meeting someone for lunch. Is that ok with you?" I asked Geri.

"Fine. Look, where do we go with this? We're all thinking that something dodgy's going on."

"I'll call Wendy Baggott," I said. "And maybe we could do a bit of quiet snooping while Gordon's not here?"

"Wonder what he's doing. Where he is," mused Geri.

"Planning what to do with the money when he gets Veronica's job, I shouldn't wonder," said Rita.

"You think he's in line for her job?" I couldn't see him rescuing and running a sinking community centre. It was strange enough to find him in the position he'd got.

"Oh yes," said Rita, as if nothing had been more obvious. "He's been after that job since he got here. He's always thought that he was the brains behind this place, that without him, it would go under."

"A bit like Gordon Brown and the Labour Party, then," I said.

"Exactly!" said Rita. "Veronica and Gordon, they was just like Tony Blair and the other Gordon. Not a pretty sight."

"I thought they were really tight?" I was getting confused. I looked at Geri.

"Yes, up to a point they were; but I think Rita's right. He was always looking for his chance. You should never tell him stuff. It'd get back to Veronica in the way *he* wanted it to, which isn't necessarily the way you'd meant it. He likes to mix it."

"So much for working for charity!" I said.

"This your first time?" asked Rita, looking sympathetic.

"No. No, it's not," I said. "I worked at a hospice…and I did some voluntary work in women's hostels, but you kind of hope that things aren't as desperate in the voluntary sector as you know they sometimes are."

"I'll see if I can find anything," said Geri. "I've got an excuse. It's my job to sort things out, have a tidy up, make sure that everything's done that needs to be."

"I'll get back to reception, then," I said.

"I'll get the art class ready," said Rita. "I do think that you should be careful, you two. Don't be here on your own. Not for a bit, anyway. Not until we know what's what."

I called the number that Wendy Baggott had left for us. Someone at a general switchboard answered. Apparently Sergeant Baggott was off duty until tomorrow. Did I want to speak to anyone else? Or leave a message? I opted to leave a message. I'd rather update Wendy Baggott than start the whole story again with someone new.

"I'll give her the message," said the switchboard operator, and rang off.

Chapter 10

Chantelle was already in the noodle bar when I got there. I nearly asked after her pubes but thought better of it.

"Hi Chantelle. How's it going?"

"Crazy. They're making all these cuts everywhere, but we're still supposed to make sure that eighty percent of the population is in work."

"What, even the pensioners?"

"No. But it probably won't be long before we have to set up silver job clubs. If you ask me, that's what all this age discrimination is about, it's not about people's rights at all. Anyway, at least *you're* off my books."

"For now."

"Don't even think about making yourself unemployed again."

"I think I could argue extenuating circumstances," I rallied. "After all, most people going into a new job don't find themselves watching their new boss die on their first day."

"No excuse."

"You're hard," I protested.

"Just doing my job." She was tapping her fingernails on the table. She'd changed the colour. The talons were painted purple with little gold stars and a white stripe across the middle. She ordered prawn and vegetable noodles and I went for agedashi tofu. The food came quickly. After we'd finished eating, we got down to business.

"So what do you know about *Action in Caring* that you didn't tell me?"

"Nothing much, Nikki, not really; look, promise me this conversation stays between us."

"Ok," I shrugged

"If my boss knew I was telling you this stuff, I'd lose my job." I didn't think it would be such a bad thing, and maybe Chantelle would get a life and get in touch with her softer, more human self; but I was ready to pander to her paranoia.

"So this is just between you and me. What's the big secret?"

"It's just that I've sent a couple of decent workers there and none have stayed longer than a month. They said the managers were always fighting and one said she wasn't prepared to be treated like a skivvy."

"Yeah, well, I can see why they'd say that," I said.

"And Tanya – she was the last one – said that she thought that Mrs Stein and the finance manager were on the fiddle. She said she'd done a course in accountancy, and one day, when she was sorting the post, she came across a bank statement. Loads of money had gone out of the account in one go, and she didn't recognise the payee name."

"What's *loads*?" I asked. "One thousand? Ten?"

"Fifty."

"Fifty pounds?"

"Fifty thousand."

"God! "

"And then Tanya said that the finance bloke – what's his name?"

"Gordon Smedley."

"Yes. Gordon. Well, he saw her looking at the statement and freaked. She said that he snatched it away from her and seemed very angry."

"Then what happened?"

"She asked if the bank had made a mistake, said it was a lot of money to be going out in one go. He said it had been transferred to a higher interest account, and she should keep her nose out of *AIC* management stuff."

"And then?"

"They sacked her. Said the placement wasn't working out, that Tanya didn't have the skills they needed."

"Did she?"

"Yes, as it happens. She'd got the accountancy qualifications and her last job had been working in a council neighbourhood housing centre. Good admin skills, plus she could get on with people."

"Where is she now?"

"I don't know. She didn't sign on again. Last I heard, she was going up north for an interview. Said Manchester had more to offer than London these days."

I could see the attraction. Sort of. "Did you do anything with what she'd told you?"

"Not my place to do anything. And she was off my books. Funny, though. She wrote to tell me about Manchester. Look, Nikki…I just wanted to say…" she paused.

"What?"

"Well…I'm sorry. Sorry it isn't working out for you. Sorry I sent you somewhere with, well, you know, problems."

"That's one way of putting it!"

"It's just that…well, we've got all these targets to meet…"

"And you thought I had my head up my arse and you wanted to teach me a lesson. You tried the meat counter, and when I wouldn't go for that, you thought you'd send me somewhere with a resident psychopath. Thanks, Bushbaby."

"Hey! That's not…what did you just call me?"

"Or are you the *pretty lickle triangle*? Well, next time, try not to be so judgemental, all right? And seeing as I haven't been paid yet, I'll leave you with the bill." Her mouth was open and she'd clasped her hands over her throat. I stormed out. I was shaking with fury. A white light was flashing inside my head. How dare she mess with people like that? How dare she mess with me? I'd chained my bike up nearby, and mercifully (for Streatham is no longer the nice safe place it once was) it was still there. I unlocked it and raced back to work.

"How'd you get on?" asked Geri as I stowed my bike under the stairs.

"Don't ask!" I snapped. "I feel like I've been set up. Why didn't you tell me about all those others who didn't stay?"

"You didn't ask," she said.

"Yeah, well, you still might've told me."

"It's not the kind of job people stick for long," she reasoned. "I warned you that it wasn't easy working here. I was getting round to telling you about Gordon, and I would've done what I could to protect you from Veronica."

"Hmm," I grunted. I knew none of it was her fault, but all the stress of the past few days was erupting in my head and I was in a foul mood. I took my place behind the reception desk.

"Look, I'll just go on and see what I can find in Gordon's office," she said, retreating from my barrage of bad vibes. The doorbell rang. I buzzed in Felicity Balmforth, today dressed in vivid mauves.

"Oh dear, what's happened to you?" she said by way of greeting. "Your aura feels very agitated."

"So would yours if you had to work here," I retorted.

"I do work here," she said. "Would a little massage help? I've got time before the class arrives." Why is it that when you're out of sorts, the nicer people are, the more you want to hit them? I took a deep breath. *Get a grip, Nikki,* I told myself. *You're not angry with her. Nor with Geri. You just feel out of control.*

"Come on, let me help you to balance your energies."

"Well…ok. That would be nice." Not that I had a clue what she meant. Two minutes later, I was lying on my front on a cushioned yoga mat, Felicity's hands moving over me with mysterious skill. Whatever she was doing it felt good. It was as if she was pulling all my stress and anger out of me. I was sinking, then floating. I gave in to her healing touch.

"How's that, then?" she asked, aeons later.

"Mmm," I mumbled.

"Good," she said. "You're much more balanced now."

"Mmm."

"I need to get ready for the class."

"Mmm." I didn't want to move, but I knew I had to get back to work. And I still hadn't called Suresh.

"Get up nice and slowly." I did as I was told, stood for a moment. The ground felt steadier under my feet and my head was calmer and clearer.

"You're a witch!"

"Nothing wrong with a bit of magic."

Eight women with bulging bellies trooped through the door clutching mats and blankets. Something about their blatant fecundity stirred me. Occasionally I had disturbing urges to do my bit for procreation and produce a brood of babes. Or at least one. Maybe I should get a dog. I'd probably cope better with a pooper-scooper than I would with nappies. I thought about Prudence and her unquestioning, simple adoration. You wouldn't get terrible twos or teenage horrors with a dog. Mind you, at least babies eventually grow out of nappies. Once the mums to be were settled into their class with Felicity, it was quiet. Only a waft of incense told me that there was serious serenity building going on in the room behind me. I looked up Suresh's number in my address book and picked up the phone.

"Hi Nikki! Long time no hear! How's tricks?"

"Good to hear you, Suresh. Well, I've got a job, but there are some problems. Any chance of meeting up to pick your brains?"

"Can you be more specific?"

"*Action in Caring*. Community centre in Clapham. The director died in strange circumstances last week, I want to know more about the local politics. Run a few names by you."

"Is there a story in it?"

"I'm not sure. That's why I want to talk to you."

"You talking with anyone else?" He was keen, was Suresh. Determined to scoop the story that would land him a job with the Guardian (the national one, not the local freebie) or the Independent.

"No. If there's a story in it, it's yours. Exclusive."

"Cool! You free this evening?"

"I can be."

"Can you get to Battersea Arts Centre? The café?"

"Sounds good. Six o'clock?"

"Great."

I went to make my peace with Geri.

"Sorry," I said. "I was a bitch earlier."

"Felicity sort you out?"

"She's good."

"Mmm. Well, I haven't come up with much, but looking at Gordon's diary, he seems to have had a lot of meetings with Nigel Bentley, the councillor."

"Have you looked at the finances?"

"Not yet. I was just getting to that."

"Chantelle said that Tanya told her that there'd been a payment to someone of fifty grand."

"What!"

"That's what I thought. Any idea what that would have been about?"

"God, no! That's a helluva lot of money! And if it got through without my knowing about it, that's really worrying."

"I'm meeting a friend of mine tonight. He works on the South London Press. I thought he might have some inside info on the council."

"Good idea."

"Did Rita go?"

"Yes. She had dogs to walk."

I rang Carla again. It was unlike her to take so long to return a call. I left a message: *hey, u ok? let me know. Xx Nik.*

I found Suresh poring over an open reporter's pad nursing a mug of coffee at the Arts Centre. His hairline had receded an inch since I'd last seen him.

"D'you need another?" I asked.

"No, I'm good. Get you one?"

"I'll sort it." I went to the bar and ordered a cranberry juice. This was the sort of place that made you go all trendy despite your best efforts.

"So, what's been going on then?" he asked, pen poised above the notepad.

I told Suresh about Veronica's sudden death.

"You didn't make the sandwiches, did you?" I glared at him in silence. My ex-flat mate from our East London Uni days never missed a chance to have a dig about my culinary incompetence. "Ok, ok, only joking!"

"Yeah, well, I think my sense of humour just took flight," I said. "Anyway, there's more."

"Go on,"

"There's something not right about the finance manager, Gordon Smedley."

"Don't know the name."

"I think he may have deliberately stopped Veronica getting to her Epi-pen, you know, the antidote to allergic shock. And my predecessors left with indecent haste, most of them not lasting more than a month. And there's a dodgy money transfer. Fifty grand to another account. Gordon Smedley said it was to a higher interest account."

"So not a lot going on then? No, but seriously, Nik, are the police involved?"

"They came on the night Veronica died. There didn't seem anything suspicious about it at the time. It was like some horrible accident. But now I'm not sure. I've left a message with them to call me about the Epi-pen. I found it yesterday." I wasn't going to tell him the whole story of hiding out in the building and sneaking around at the weekend.

"Well, they'll pick up on anything iffy. And you know, moving money to a higher interest account is not that crazy."

"But the administrator didn't know about it, and all transactions should be logged by her. And the centre's being run down. The new SoLCEC centre is being pumped full of Euros and stealing all the business. And there are rumours about Smedley and young boys."

"Where does Nigel Bentley come into all this?"

"Smedley has been having meetings with him." Suddenly I remembered Veronica's diary. NB. *Note bene* or Nigel Bentley? "Veronica might have had a meeting planned with him too. What do you know about him?"

"He made a fortune in property during the eighties, but he keeps that pretty quiet. Bought up several ex-council flats during the Thatcher years for next to nothing. Rented them out. Sold them on and made a killing when the market soared. Known as a wheeler-dealer. What he wants he usually gets. Ambitious. Looking for his main chance in national politics, but he's too old to make it now. Has to make do with his south London power base."

"Why would he be interested in *Action in Caring?*"

"I don't know." His mobile rang, a no-nonsense bleep. He flipped it open.

"Hi love…no, not long…Battersea…with Nikki. Remember Nikki Elliot? Flat mate? Uni? Yeah, that one. Story. Mysterious death in a new job…no, she didn't kill anyone. What time? Oh, ok, I'd forgotten…yeah, I know…yeah, should've put it in my Blackberry…no, won't be long. Bye. Bye."

"Trouble?"

"What man isn't always in trouble?" he grinned. "Meena's sister's just rung to say she's coming round tonight for supper. I'm needed at home. Look, it was good to see you and I'll see what I can dig up. Touch base next week?"

"That'd be great. And I'll let you know if I uncover anything at this end." Suresh shoved his notepad into a compact backpack, swigged the last of his coffee, waved and ran. I sipped at my cranberry juice and pondered. A lot had happened in less than a week. I needed a quiet evening in to reflect on things. When I got outside, someone had nicked the front wheel of my bike. As I swore loudly, my phone rang. It was Carla.

"Hi Nik. It's me."

"You ok?"

"Can you come round?"

"Yeah. Give me half an hour – someone's nicked my front wheel. What's wrong?"

"Nothing too bad, I just had a bit of an accident."

"Are you hurt?" Concern about my bike vanished in worry about my friend.

"Only a bit. Tell you when I see you."

"I'm on my way."

Chapter 11

Carla's arm was tucked into a sling. She stood aside and let me in, closing her front door behind us.

"What happened?"

"Bloody bus," she said. "I was on the top floor, started to come down the stairs and the driver did one of those stop-start tricks. They must have this game, London bus drivers: how many of the bastards can we kill or maim today? Anyway, it threw me forward and I fell. Found myself on my back on the ground floor with a bone sticking out of my arm."

"Jesus, Carla," I said, furious that someone had done this to my friend. "Did anyone help you? Did the driver stop?"

"Young bloke with a hoodie helped to pick me up, driver couldn't have cared less. The other passengers just curled themselves into their Metros and London Lites. I took myself to A and E at Kings. Why do we do it, Nik?"

"What? Travel on buses?"

"Live in London."

"Because nobody here doesn't fit in somewhere."

"Come again?"

"Cities are where you can be yourself, whatever that is. We're used to being around people who are all different. It makes us feel safer."

"I think I'd feel safer somewhere leafy and green and quiet where there weren't homicidal bus drivers."

"And where everyone has provincial blinkered thinking and most of them have never met, let alone talked to a black person, and they think all gays have AIDS and they've never heard of falafel …get real, Carla. You know you'd be miserable as sin in most of those safe little towns and villages."

"You're probably right. Still, it does get me down, the grime and the crush and the misery."

"Hebden Bridge is supposed to be cool. Tea?"

"You know where stuff is. Sorry, I'm not much good…"

"..but at least you're 'armless!" She hurled a cushion at me with her good arm. Anyway, I'd drawn a smile from her. I went into her neat little kitchen and yelled at Ginger, the black and white cat who was lounging defiantly on the working surface. He was seventeen, smelly, periodically incontinent, and threw up with grim regularity; but he'd been part of Carla's life for almost as many years as I had. He slithered down, giving me a disdainful glare. I brewed two cups of Rooibos and vanilla tea and went back to join Carla on her sofa.

"How's work?" she asked.

"Can't wait to leave. But I'm puzzled. Something's going on there and I want to know what. I feel like I can't leave until I know why Veronica died."

"Any closer to finding out?" I explained about meeting up with Suresh and my fraught lunch with Chantelle.

"You left her with the bill? That was a bit much, Nik!"

"I was pissed off with her. She'd set me up."

"Still, she was only doing her job."

"That's what the concentration camp guards said."

"Will you stop with this Nazi thing? Not everyone is a fascist whose mission is to wipe all traces of Nikki Elliot from the face of the earth!"

"I only meant…"

"I know what you meant, Nik, but you need to keep a sense of proportion. You know, you could just walk away. Look in the Grauniad like any other leftie, find a nice normal job. Get your life back."

"Hmm."

"And don't you dare sulk or I'll set Ginger onto you!"

"It's all right for you. You didn't find your last boss hanged and watch the next one choke to death!"

"Brent died a year ago. It's time to let go, Nik. Let him be. He'd want you to be getting on with your life, the last thing he'd want would be for you to be holding yourself back. Brent did some good things. He'd want you to be out there making a difference too, like in the old days, like you and I did. We changed the world, Nik. Just a bit, I know, but we did it. And there's more work to do. And this woman, this Veronica. She meant nothing to you. You didn't even like her!"

"I didn't. And I don't like Gordon Smedley. But I do like Geri, and Felicity and Rita. S'pose I want to see it through, find out what happened, for them, as much as for me." I sipped at the red, healing tea. "You think I'm clinging on to the past?"

"You know I do."

"Time to get a life?"

"Yup."

"I'll think about it." She grinned and wrapped her unbroken arm around me.

"Help me write a letter to the bus company?"

"Yeah."

After we'd written the letter and printed off photos of Carla looking miserable in her sling, we had a glass of wine.

"You staying the night?"

"You want me to?"

"You could help me have a shower. It's kind of difficult with this bloody plaster on my arm!"

I got as wet as her, but at least she felt clean. I blow dried her hair for her, settled her into bed.

"Sheets are clean in the spare room," she said. "There's a new toothbrush under the bathroom sink. Anything else you need?"

"No, that'll do. Lend me a pair of knickers for tomorrow?"

"What are friends for?"

I tucked her in and settled myself in the bed I slept in from time to time, but which wasn't mine and felt strange. My mind wouldn't settle. Why had Veronica died? Who had a hand in her death? Should I get a dog? Would I ever stop thinking about Ruth? Was it really time to get my life back on track? I fell asleep before I had any of the answers.

The next morning, I showered and took a cup of tea into Carla. She groaned as she tried to turn over.

"Sleep ok?" I asked.

"Not really. Every time I try to turn over, this thing gets in the way. Think I'll have a duvet day. Can you ring work for me?"

It wasn't like Carla to miss work: she must be feeling rough.

"Sure. Who do you want me to speak to?"

"Try Andrée, she'll know what and who to cancel for me." Carla was a manager for a housing association, and she mostly worked with people with learning difficulties. She loved it. I made the call. Andrée made sympathetic noises and told me to tell Carla not to worry.

"Knickers?"

"Top drawer." I selected a pair of black M and S briefs.

"Giving the red thongs a miss, then?" she teased.

"Thongs! What is it with thongs? Why do women wear strings up their arses? Give me a pair of sexy black hipsters any day!"

"All in the cause of ridding ourselves of VPL," she said

"What?"

"Visible panty line."

"Don't have to worry about that with chinos."

"You're such a dyke!"

"And you're not?"

"Well…sometimes…"

"You're just a lipstick lesbian, that's what you are, Carla Jennings!"

"Away with you! Go solve a murder and do some work for a change."

"Anything you want before I go?"

"No, I'm ok. Ring me later."

"See you."

I walked my wheel-depleted bike to Clancy's Hub and Spoke bicycle shop and sighed at the quote the man gave me for a replacement wheel.

"When d'you want it?" asked Clancy.

"Tomorrow?"

"Sure. Want a clean and oil at the same time? I'll not charge you extra."

"Yeah, why not." I walked the rest of the way to work. It was a fine morning, puffy white clouds scudding across a blue spring sky. The air was as fresh as it gets in London. When I got to work, Geri was already there. She looked smarter than usual. A sea-green skinny rib top replaced the dull colours I'd seen her in up to now, and a jazzy pendant swung above her breasts. She'd had extensions woven into her hair and she looked younger, brighter.

"Hi Nikki. You ok?"

"Yeah. You look great. What's on today?"

"Young Offenders group with the lovely Justin," she rolled her eyes, "and Joan's art class, if she's back from her sister's. Not much else."

"Did you find anything else while you were rooting around?"

"It's odd, you know. The money just doesn't tally. By my reckoning, over a hundred grand's gone missing. I just don't understand it."

"D'you think Gordon'll be in today?"

"Who knows? He doesn't usually miss a day. Look, Nikki, I ought to tell you, I'm going to take a couple of hours out at lunch time. I've got an interview." So that was why she was all dressed up. I wasn't surprised she'd made it to interview. I'd known Geri for less than a week, but she seemed like a good worker: honest, reliable, warm. The sort of person you'd pick for your team.

"What's the job?"

"Operations manager for LOTUS: Lambeth Opportunities for Training and Upskilling Supersisters."

"If you're a supersister, why do you need training and upskilling?"

"Don't ask. All I know is, they've been around a while, the director has a good name in the area, place seemed friendly, I could do the job pretty easily, and the pay's good."

"Hmm. Do they need a receptionist?"

"You could aim higher than that. Check out their website. In fact, check out everyone's websites. You know what, Nikki? You need to get back in the swing. Stop hiding. Whatever happened before, get over it."

"Thanks." Someone else thought I needed to get a life. I realised that I still hadn't told her about Brent and *Life is for Living*. Another time. As I took my seat behind the reception desk, there was a confident ring of the bell. Funny how you can tell if the person ringing is confident or diffident or angry, just by how they press the bell. I buzzed the door open.

"G'day! How's it going, mate?" Justin breezed in with a huge, muscle-bound presence.

"Hi! We're cool. Can't wait for your kids to bounce in and inspire us a little," I said.

"Hey, no need for that! Those kids're ok," he countered.

"Didn't say they weren't, did I?" He glared at me, and swept through leaving a trail of masculine shower product aroma behind him. He probably worked out for a couple of hours each morning before coming to work.

"I'm going to rummage some more," said Geri.

"Ok, I'll let you know if Gordon shows up," I said. By eleven o'clock, Gordon still hadn't appeared and Justin's crew had started to slope in, their sullen faces hidden by hoodies, baggy trousers slouching down their slender bodies to rest on skinny haunches, revealing at best faux Calvin Kleins their mums had picked up in the market, and at worst bare bum cracks. I pondered the wisdom of national service and boot camps, and then my more liberal self wondered whether they wouldn't get more out of a car maintenance workshop. Geri came down at midday.

"Any message from Gordon?" she asked.

"Not a thing. Had he booked holiday or anything?"

"No. This is very odd. He's supposed to be running the pay-roll today. He's never missed that before. And it means you and I won't get paid." I grimaced: this month I'd be liable for my rent. Plus Chantelle would have made sure that my benefits payments stopped. I'd be in trouble. And I'd used up any good will my bank might have shown me years ago.

"Should we call him?"

"Yeah. I've got his home number. I'll do it now." She turned back to go to her office. The reception desk phone rang. I picked up.

"Hello, *Action in Caring*, Nikki speaking. How can I help?"

"Oh, hello. This is Councillor Cynthia Hope. I'd like to speak to Ms Stein, please."

"Councillor Hope, I'm really sorry. I thought everyone knew. Veronica died last Thursday." I remembered that this was the councillor who was really batting for *AiC*.

"Died? What happened?"

"We think it was an allergy. I know you were a keen supporter of *Action in Caring*. Can I put you through to anyone else? I can get Geraldine Francis for you."

"Geraldine? Oh… look, I think I'll come by, if that's all right."

"Well, of course. But at the moment there's only Geraldine and myself here, and I'm new, but you're very welcome."

"Is Mr Smedley not there?"

"No. We're not too sure where he is."

"I think I'll bring one of the other councillors, Chandrika Patel." I remembered that name too. I noticed she wasn't talking about bringing Nigel Bentley.

"We'll do our best to help."

I went into Geri's office. She was staring at the phone looking perplexed, wearing that eyebrow-knitting face of hers.

"Problem?"

"He's not answering. This is weird, Nikki. He's only worked here for a couple of years, but he's one for routine, and now he's not even answering his phone. You know what, Nik? I'm really worried."

"Well there's not much time for that. We've got two council cabinet members about to descend on us."

"Oh no! Not Nigel Bentley!"

"No. Cynthia Hope and Chandrika Patel."

"Well at least Cynthia's on our side. Chandrika's ok. What do they want?"

"I don't know. Cynthia wanted to speak to Veronica. I told her she'd died. She hadn't heard."

"You know what? We can't be expected to handle all this. I'm going to my interview no matter what. I think we should call Lawrence."

"You're joking!"

"He's the Chair. This is crazy! Veronica's dead, Gordon's gone AWOL, there's not a committee member in sight – well apart from Rita last week – and you've only just started work here. I know Lawrence is a nightmare, but he offered himself as Chair." She looked over the top of her glasses at a list of phone numbers on the wall, punched out some numbers, paused while the phone rang at the other end. Paused some more. I watched her take a deep breath before speaking.

"Hello Lawrence. This is Geri at *Action in Caring*. Gordon hasn't been seen at work this week, and we're about to be visited by Cynthia Hope and Chandrika Patel. We need you to be here, please. Nikki will be on her own this afternoon. Please let us know that you've got this message."

"Ansaphone?"

"Yup."

"What about Rita? Or that man who's the treasurer?"

"Derek? That's not a bad idea. I'll try him. And of course Joan should be here for the art class. Look, Nikki, I'm getting really nervous. I should have left ten minutes ago. Can I leave it with you? I'll be back as soon as I can."

"Yeah. You go. I'll be fine. Use my Irish charm to keep the wolves at bay!"

"You're Irish?"

"No. Well, I might be. A bit. A long lost great great grandparent. Who knows?" She laughed. "Look, just go," I said. "It'll be fine. Go! And good luck."

"I owe you." She grabbed her handbag and fled the building. I was alone with Justin and his delightful hoodlums. I went back to my post on the reception desk and was just in time to hear my mobile ringing. It was Benjamin.

"Nik? That you?"

"Yup, the one and only. What's up?"

"He's got someone else."

"Who's got someone else?"

"Dan. The bastard! How could he?"

"Lycra man?"

"CycleOut. He's the co-ordinator of CycleOut."

"But you've only just met!"

"I thought he was The One!" wailed Benjamin, not for the first time.

"That's so sad," I said, wondering what else to say. "Is there any hope?"

"He said that monogamy is passé," said Ben

"Don't you think that too?" I asked.

"Not if he's The One!" cried Benjamin. At that point, there was a ring on the doorbell. I peered into the CCTV screen and saw two women standing there, one of them white, middle-aged, with short wavy hair, the other taller long hair tied back, Asian. Shit! It was the councillors, and here I was on my own.

"Ben, I gotta go. Look, I'll see you later. We'll do dinner. I owe you."

"I won't be able to eat. I may drive down to Beachy Head."

"You don't have a car and you're too geographically challenged to know which county Beachy Head is in, let alone get yourself there. Hang on in there, I'll come down with a bottle of wine. I've got to go."

"But…" God! Why are men such wimps at times like this?

"Bye Ben. See you around six." I buzzed open the door.

"Councillor Hope? Councillor Patel? I'm Nikki Elliot." The women introduced themselves.

"I'm not sure if I can help," I said. "I'm new, Geri's had to go out, and we haven't seen Gordon. We've put in a call to Lawrence, our Chair, but he hasn't got back to us. I'm really sorry. I'll do what I can."

"Thank you, I'm sure you will," said Cynthia Hope. Just then there was a crash of falling furniture from the back room.

"I'll fucking stick you with this, cunt!" screamed a male voice.

"Hey, cool it!" I heard Justin reply. "Just put the knife away, Dwayne."

Shit! Today was turning out to be bad. Really bad. The two councillors looked at each other and both had turned pale.

"I'd better go and see if I can help," I said as more furniture crashed behind me. "Um – would you like some tea? Coffee?" I tried to smile brightly, terrified of what violence was erupting in Justin's group.

"No, thank you. Shouldn't you call the police?" Chandrika sounded nervous. I wondered what she did for her day job.

"Just give me a sec," I said and turned to head for the meeting room. I collided with a six foot two hoodie slamming his way towards the front door muttering about Aussie cunts, murder in his eyes.

"Hey! Watch where you're going," I said.

"Cunt," he spat as he pushed past and kicked open the front door. The two councillors were huddled into the corner near the dead palm. I had to see if Justin was ok. I ran towards the meeting room, held my breath as I opened the door. The boys were sitting in a sullen circle. Justin was standing, breathing hard, his face flushed, one fist clenched, the other raking through his hair. No-one seemed to have been hurt or killed. Two chairs lay on their sides and the picture of the oldies having tea with the mayor had been knocked off centre.

"What's going on?" I asked.

"Just Dwayne kicking off," said Justin as if this happened every day.

"I heard him threaten you with a knife," I said.

"Yeah," said Justin.

"Well, shouldn't we call the police? He's going to hurt someone!" I said.

"Leave it with me. If we call the cops, they'll arrest him and this time he'll get sent down."

"Yeah, well, maybe he needs to get sent down! Put somewhere where he can't "stick" anyone!"

"Man, he jus' crazy, innit," said one of the lads who reminded me of Kenny from South Park with his orange parka.

"Look, no-one got hurt," said Justin. "Just leave it for now. He'll be back tomorrow and we'll deal with it then."

"Great! Look, we can't have people running around this centre with knives!" I protested.

"I've got the blade," said Justin, pointing to an evil looking weapon on the table.

"So he'll just go off and get another one, or beat up his mum, or rape a woman," I said. "What is it exactly that you're trying to do here, Justin?" I'd had more than my fair share of violent men in my time, what with working in women's refuges.

"These kids've got problems, right? That's why they're here. Last chance for some of them." A few trainers scuffed the manky carpet in discomfort at hearing this truth. "Look love, leave it with me. I'll put in the calls. Do what I have to. You just cool it, ok?"

"Don't call me *love*, and don't you dare, ever, patronise me. You got that? And for your information, there are two councillors in reception who have the power to close us down. So you get your act together, you hear?" I stormed out of the room before he could answer. I could see the boys staring after me, but I didn't care. I just wanted to get out, to leave *Action in Caring* way behind me; but someone had to baby-sit the councillors. I paused outside the room, inhaled deeply. As I took measured steps back to the reception desk, I heard my mobile ring.

"Excuse me," I smiled at Councillors Hope and Patel who were still and silent in their corner. "Be with you in just one minute." I picked up the phone without looking to see who was calling. "Hi, Nikki here," I said.

"Nikki? It's Ruth. Um, I know it's been a while, but I wondered if...er...well I wondered if we could meet."

Chapter 12

"Bad news?" Cynthia Hope broke into my shocked silence. With a start, I realised I was staring at my phone, holding it away from me as if I'd just discovered that it was radioactive.

"No. Er, no. Just...a call I wasn't expecting, that's all. Sorry." The connection was still live, Ruth was waiting for me to say something. I could hear her saying *hello? Hello?* My pulses were playing ping pong with each other. I tried to sound cool, but my voice had risen half an octave.

"Oh, Ruth. Couldn't think who you were for a minute. Sorry. Look, this is a really bad time. I'm at work. Call me later. Ok?" but I didn't wait for her reply. I pressed the "end" key, locked the keypad and rammed the phone into my back pocket. I thought I might pass out. The doorbell rang. There on the monitor screen was Dora Popp. Could today get any worse? I needed whiskey and Carla in that order, but for now I had to attend to Cynthia and Chandrika and a crazy old lady who was shuffling through the door, today sporting red Wellington boots. On my own, while Justin held together a group of dangerous delinquents. Where the hell were Gordon and Lawrence? Not that Lawrence would be much help. The doorbell rang again. I looked at the CCTV monitor. There is a god after all! Rita stood there, splendid in a scarlet velour tracksuit. Prudence was by her side. I buzzed open the door.

"Hi Rita!" I cried. "Fantastic timing. Councillors Hope and Patel have come to see us and I'm here on my own. And I'm sure Dora would like a cup of tea."

Prudence leapt up at me with a joyful yelp. When I looked at Rita, her face looked strained, but she tried for a smile and turned to the councillors.

"Hello," she said. "Nice to see you. Anything wrong? Anything I can help with?" Cynthia Hope gave a little cough, and ventured a couple of steps out of the corner.

"We'd heard about Veronica Stein's death," she said. "We were concerned. Both Councillor Patel and I have been doing what we can to stop the withdrawal of your grant; but... well, I have to say, this afternoon has been rather..."

"Unusual," I chipped in. "Yes, it's been extremely unusual. Honestly, I don't think there's ever been trouble with the young offenders' group before, has there Rita?" My eyes pleaded with Rita to back me up.

"Always trouble," muttered Dora.

"Trouble? Oh dear, I'm sorry to hear that," said Rita. "That's one of our success stories, the young offenders' group. Well, you know all about that, Councillor Hope, don't you? You said some very positive things about us in council not that far back."

"I haven't visited for some time," said Cynthia, sounding as if she was having strong misgivings about having ever backed up *AiC*. "I have to say, what I've seen today hasn't inspired me with confidence."

"Oh?" said Rita, "Why's that then?"

"The centre is clearly under-staffed with just one junior person left to run the whole place; you've got a group of young men who are out of control, one of whom was carrying an offensive weapon; you don't know where the senior manager is…need I go on?"

"That's the voluntary sector for you!" said Rita, and I couldn't tell whether she was sounding cheerful or just defiant. "Good at managing on a shoestring, that's us."

"Where's my tea?" asked Dora.

"But," Chandrika had stepped bravely out of her corner to join in, "But what about health and safety? Surely it's not safe to leave one person in charge? What if someone had been hurt?" I was sure she had a point, but all I could think about was Ruth phoning me. Ruth had phoned. Me. She'd phoned me. Ruth. Ruth….

"Nikki? You all right?" Rita was waving a chubby hand in front of my face.

"Oh, er, yeah. Yeah, I'm fine. Sorry, I was just thinking about…tea. Let me get everyone some tea. Dora needs tea. Councillor Hope?"

"Well, I do need to be going quite soon – community services review meeting – but tea would be nice. Thank you."

"Councillor Patel?"

"Yes. Thank you, I'd like tea too." I heard a murmur of conversation from the meeting room and then the door opened and the lads, looking more subdued than I'd seen them, sloped out, hands in pockets or twiddling with MP3 players. A couple of them looked at me as they passed. One said "see ya," and another mumbled "'spect".

"Why don't you sit yourselves down in here?" said Rita, steering the councillors towards Geri's little office. I headed for the kitchen to brew up. As I was waiting for the kettle to boil, Justin came in. He looked almost sheepish.

"Sorry 'bout all that," he said.

"So you bloody well should be," I countered.

"Took me by surprise. Wasn't ready for him."

"Well you should've been, shouldn't you?" I snarled. Why was I being so nasty? It probably hadn't been Justin's fault. I'd been in groups where someone had just blown, and no-one had seen it coming. "Ok, I'm sorry. I shouldn't have said that. These things happen. You ok? Other lads ok?"

"Yeah, yeah, we're all cool. I'll have to report him to his probation officer. Bummer. Hate it when that happens. Hey, are we mates again? Wanna go for a tube after work?"

"Look, Justin, we just work in the same building, ok? And thanks for the offer, but I'm seeing someone tonight."

"Lucky bloke!" I doubted that Justin would understand the subtle strangeness of my relationship with Benjamin.

"That's what I keep telling him," I said. I wondered why I was so snappy with Justin. Waspish. He hadn't done anything wrong, he was just a bit too big and bouncy for my liking. Tigger. Did that make me Piglet? "Sorry if I let rip in front of the boys," I said by way of an apology. "Maybe a drink when things aren't so crazy around here?"

"Cool," he said, and then high fived me and bounded out. "See ya."

I found some half decent cups and saucers in a cupboard, made tea in an ancient aluminium pot, found a jug with only a slight chip on the rim for the milk, and poured some sugar into a cereal bowl. I assembled it all on a tray and went to join Rita and the councillors. I passed Dora, who was sitting in the orange chair at reception.

"I've wet meself," she said.

"Oh," I said. "Well, a cup of tea should help." I poured her a cup.

"Four sugars."

I spooned in the white stuff and handed her the cup. She started to slurp at it without thanking me. I carried on towards Geri's office.

Prudence's ears stiffened and she hung out her tongue in greeting. The women were sitting in a close circle and Rita made room for me to pull up a chair to join them. I gave everyone their tea.

"Rita was telling us about what happened at the management committee meeting," said Cynthia. "It sounds dreadful."

"It was," I agreed. "Pretty scary, to tell you the truth. Rita was brilliant, though."

"So were you, love," said Rita.

"I have to tell you both, we're very concerned about what's happening here," said Cynthia going from the obligatory sympathy to management seriousness.

"Yes, I'm afraid this afternoon has rather shocked us," added Chandrika.

"This afternoon has been very unusual," I said. "I'm sorry you got caught up with all that stuff going on in Justin's group; but he sorted it, and he's going to make all the right calls."

"But where is everyone? Where is Mr Smedley?" asked Cynthia, sounding increasingly agitated.

"We wish we knew." Geri had come back without us hearing her. I turned to look at her. Sent thought waves in her direction: *should we be saying this in front of councillors?*

"We thought that maybe he'd been called away on urgent private business," I tried lamely.

"At a time like this? And without letting you know?" exclaimed Chandrika. "Surely not! And if he did, it's the most unprofessional behaviour I've ever come across."

"We've tried to contact him, but he's not returning calls. We've left a message with our Chair. We're trying to keep things going here." Geri almost seemed to be pleading for help.

"One of our trustees has gone missing too," said Rita. We all looked at her in surprise.

"Who?" I asked.

"Joan," said Rita. "That's why I came round. Her sister said she'd left after just one night, but she hadn't rung to say she'd got home. It's not like her."

"Did she come in to do the art class?" Geri asked me. I'd been so caught up with foul-mouthed would-be assassins and Ruth calling that I'd forgotten about Joan's art class.

"No. I haven't seen her, and she hasn't rung." I saw Cynthia and Chandrika exchange glances. Didn't they have a council meeting to get to?

"Her students would have been due around now," said Geri, "and Joan is always in an hour or so ahead of time to set things up."

"I'm dead worried," said Rita.

"Have you tried her mobile?" I asked.

"Don't be daft! Our Joan with a mobile? She thinks they give you cancer! No, Joan is ahead of her time in lots of ways, but she's never got the hang of gadgets."

"Maybe she went away for more than a weekend," I suggested, trying to sound hopeful.

"I hope you're right," said Rita.

"How long have you worked here?" Cynthia turned to me.

"Me? Oh, this is my first week. I'm still the new girl."

"She's great, though, is Nikki," said Rita with warmth. "Don't know what we'd have done without her!"

"This is just not tenable," said Cynthia. "If you can't get hold of your Chair, and your senior manager has vanished, I really think you should close the centre. Just until things get back to normal."

"We can't afford to," said Geri. "If we close the centre, all our remaining users – and there are precious few – will migrate over to the new SoLCEC centre, and that'll be the end of *Action in Caring*. I don't want that: do you?"

"Well...n..n.. .no, of course not," stuttered Cynthia.

"No, no, we wouldn't want that," added Chandrika, quickly.

"So we have to try to keep on running," surmised Geri, "and that's what we're trying to do."

"I'm around to give a hand," offered Rita, "and I'll try to get the other trustees in for a meeting tonight or tomorrow." I heard Geri mutter *good luck* under her breath. I didn't hold out a lot of hope for her getting the trustees together before next week. And I certainly wasn't going to give up my evening: there was Ben to take care of, Carla to check on, and of course – my churning stomach wouldn't let me forget – there was Ruth.

"Can I have more tea?" Dora's tiny figure appeared in the doorway.

"Of course," said Geri. I noticed the unmistakable stink of urine emanating from Dora.

"They done it," said Dora.

"Who done what?" I asked.

"Them. They done it." She grabbed the cup from Geri and scuttled back towards reception.

After the councillors had gone, I turned to Geri. "What are we going to do?" I asked. Rita was still there.

"I think that Rita should convene a meeting of the management committee. I think we should try to make sure we're both around and that life goes on. Did you manage to get hold of Sergeant Baggott?"

115

"I left her a message. Has she rung back yet?"

"Don't think so."

"I'll try again."

"I just don't know what to do about Gordon," sighed Geri. As I was formulating a complicated answer that included search parties and last known addresses, my mobile rang. Oh God, suppose it was Ruth again? What would I say? I wanted to see her more than anything, but I was afraid. Afraid of…falling further, of getting back onto that roller coaster of hope and despair. But it wasn't Ruth. It was Benjamin.

"Hi Ben, what's up?"

"Nik, I don't think I can cope."

"You can cope until six. Then I'll rescue you with a bottle of wine. Maybe a spliff. If you're really lucky, a toasted cheese and onion sandwich."

"Don't tease, Nik. This is dreadful! I'm going to die!"

"You're not going to die, Ben, and I'm at work. Look, why don't you go for a good work-out or a cycle round the common to work off some stress?"

"I'll never get on a bike again!"

"Good. I can have yours, then."

"Nik, don't be cruel," he pleaded. Men!

"I'm not. Look, hang in there. I'll have to pop in on Carla, and Ruth rang. But I'll be with you by six. Promise."

"Cheese and onion?"

"With pickle."

"I'll *try* and hold on." It occurred to me, perhaps unkindly, that Etty Goldblum had had a fortunate escape where Benjamin was concerned.

Meanwhile, Geri was looking after reception and had opened the door to several people, most of them over sixty, with keen and eager faces who'd come for the life drawing class. She bustled into the kitchen, her new extensions swinging.

116

"Crisis!" she exclaimed, with a kind of hysterical gaiety.

"Another one?"

"No model. A class full of eager artists, and no model. No teacher either. I don't suppose..."

"No!" There were limits to what I'd do to keep *AiC* open. "Why don't you do it?"

"You're joking! No way. I don't take my kit off for no-one!" She was so South London when she got upset or angry over something. Just then, Justin breezed past.

"Hey girls. Forgot my mobile. Wow! Geri! Beaut hair-do. Fancy a tube after work?"

"That's really sweet, Justin," she said, back in grammar school voice, "but I've got a hot date tonight. There is something you can do for me, though." I swear she was batting her eyelashes. Straight girls are so good at playing men.

"Anything for you, mate," said Justin.

"Well, you know Joan's life drawing class?"

"Sure."

"Well, there's no Joan to teach, and no model to pose, but all these lovely people have schlepped across London to get here. I'd hate to disappoint them."

"Hey, I'm no Rolf Harris! Can't paint to save me life! No, sorry, teaching art's not what I do."

"I wasn't going to ask you to teach the class," said Geri.

"You want me to cover for you while you model?" he asked, looking hopeful.

"Oh no, not me. I thought...well, you have such a...muscular body, you're so well toned..."

"Nah! You won't get me taking me clobber off!"

"But they're really good. And they love having a man for a change." She had missed her vocation in sales. "And you're so good looking, and think of those portraits you'll be able to send home to your folks…" Flattery goes a long way. He'd started, ever so subtly, to flex his biceps, stand a little taller.

"You think?" He raked his fingers through dark blonde, gelled hair.

"I don't think, I *know*!"

"Now?"

"Mm hm."

"Well…"

"You'll get paid. It's £12.50 per hour. Just for standing or lying around looking gorgeous."

"You know what? You're on."

"Fantastic! You're a life saver, Justin. So just go up to room seven, Rita will show you what to do." Rita had perked up at the thought of helping Justin begin his new role as life model. As nude model. Seeing Justin in the buff would be better than Baywatch any day. The two jogged off to rescue one of our few remaining classes. I turned to Geri.

"You're very good, you know! Can you get people to do anything?"

"I wish! But Justin's easy. Like most blokes. Most women too, really. You just need to appeal to their vanity."

I returned to the reception desk. What was I to do about Ruth's call? I pulled out my mobile and clicked onto her number. Took a deep breath and punched the call button. Waited. It rang five times. Then she answered.

"Hi Nikki," said the horribly beautifully familiar voice. "Thanks for ringing me back."

"Yeah. So. How are you?"

"Oh, I'm fine. Back from Palestine."

"Yeah, I heard. Eva at *Sappho* was telling Carla and me she'd seen you."

"Yes, I got back a couple of weeks ago. Feels strange."

"Guess there aren't too many lezzie bars in Gaza, then?"

118

"Uh..no. No, I don't expect so." She gave a strange sort of laugh. Then there was silence. I didn't know what to say. How many days and nights had I ached to hear her voice, and now here it was, here she was, and I was lost for words.

"I've got a job," I offered.

"That's great. What is it?"

"Community centre. Sort of administrator, receptionist."

"Sounds interesting," she said, and I could tell that she thought it sounded boring as hell.

"You could say that."

"What happens there?" She was trying, I'd give her that.

"Oh, all sorts. Delinquent boys with knives. Directors who drop down dead at management committee meetings. Finance managers that go AWOL along with trustees who once were famous artists. Missing thousands…right now it's quiet. There's just a naked muscle-bound Australian posing for a bunch of pensioners who think they've died and gone to heaven…" I was rambling, I knew it, I just couldn't stop."

"Sounds interesting," she said, and I knew she hadn't heard a word.

"So why did you call?" I asked, feeling a distance stretch between us.

"I thought it would be good to meet up."

"Oh?"

"Well, only if you want to."

"Yeah. Well, why not. How long are you in town?"

"I don't know. Could be a while." That was unusual. I wondered what was happening for her.

"Actually, there was something I wanted to…well, to run by you. If you've got time." This was unlike Ruth. What could she possibly want to run by me? An old wise grandmother voice inside me said *no, make your excuses politely, but don't meet her.* And another voice said, *maybe she'll tell you*

she's always loved you, only you, and can she please move into your bed and your life.
My internal siren. The grandmother didn't stand a chance.

"Not tonight," I said. "I have to see Benjamin, and Carla's injured."

"Oh." Did she sound disappointed or was I imagining it? "How are you fixed for tomorrow?" I wanted time to do my washing, make sure my favourite chinos were clean and ironed, along with the purple silk blouse. No, tomorrow was too soon.

"No, sorry, can't do tomorrow. Thursday? *Sappho?*"

"No. D'you know the Bedford? Balham?"

"Yeah." I was surprised. I knew the place, but wondered why she'd choose to meet there. Seems more like a hang-out for straight Balham trendies. But their chips were to die for.

"Fine. Let's meet there, then. Seven-thirty ok for you?"

"Make it eight." I was reclaiming my power.

I heard movement from upstairs. The art class trooped down the stairs for their tea break. The old women had a certain glow about them. One or two were giggling together like schoolgirls.

"How's the life drawing?" I asked as I helped them to make tea.

"Never been better!" exclaimed a smart woman in her seventies with softly waved hair. A short tubby woman with round cheeks burst out laughing and elbowed her.

"You can say that again!" she chortled.

"Ooh, he's gorgeous!" said a woman in a dusky pink Damart sweatshirt and baggy matching trousers.

"The ones at Morley College are all scrawny," added a tall woman sporting a spray-on tan. "This one...well, I could certainly fancy *him!*" She was game, I'd give her that, but she'd have to dream on as far as Justin was concerned. There was one poor man in this group of drooling ladies, and I felt sorry for him. He seemed to hang back from the crowd and looked slightly puzzled, as if he couldn't work out what the fuss was all about. Rita appeared, Prudence wagging a cheery tail behind her.

"How's it going?" I asked her quietly.

"I think we've found the key to keeping the centre open!" she whispered excitedly. Her cheeks were also several shades pinker than they had been earlier. "They love him! Mind you, I can see why! I tell you Nik, I can't remember when I last saw a bloke hung like that..."

"Enough!" I said. Justin was bad enough fully clothed, but the thought of him basking naked and stirring up all these fantasies was just too much. But maybe Rita had a point: what Justin had, we could bottle and sell.

"Time to go back ladies. Oh, and Brian, of course, " said spray-on tan, nodding to the bemused little man. Off they tripped, suddenly light-footed, primping their hair. Damart woman was squinting into a compact mirror, powdering her face. The tubby one was slapping on crimson lipstick. They'd probably all go on diets from this evening. Brian shuffled up behind the eager ladies. He gave me a look that was almost conspiratorial in its bewilderment. I shrugged at him and smiled. It was time to see whether Geri had managed to contact anyone. I went into her office. She was sitting staring at the telephone, chin in hand.

"Any luck?" I asked. "Art class is going well! Justin's a hit."

"Mmm. Still no Gordon. No Lawrence either. I did manage to get hold of Bernard, though. He's worried about Joan. Said he'd come in for a meeting if he could get someone to watch over his wife."

"She's got Alzheimer's."

"Yes. He said something odd."

"Oh?"

"He said, it wouldn't be the first time someone had disappeared with the family silver. I said, but we're just a small group. He said, rich pickings."

"Bernard said *rich pickings*?"

"His exact words. So, I guess we'd better put a freeze on the bank accounts, try the police again, call a committee meeting."

"Want me to do the bank?"

"No, they're used to me. You arrange the meeting. And can you call the police?"

"Yes."

I wrote an emergency meeting notification, printed off six copies and stuffed them into envelopes to post to the trustees. I was about to ring the police when Geri came out looking pale and shaken.

"Problem?"

"We're virtually cleaned out. All the money's gone. Except for around four grand. Our little stash of reserves. The money we need for running costs. It's all gone."

"Shit."

"We're finished."

The art class trooped down the stairs, chattering loudly. Phrases like *coming again next week* and *wish we could do this every day!* and *ooh, I feel twenty years younger* floated past with them.

"No," I said. "We're not finished. Not yet."

Chapter 13

The doorbell rang, startling Geri and me out of our shocked state. I went to open it. Saw with pleasure that it was Joan.

"Joan! We were worried when you didn't show up! Are you ok?"

"Yes. Why wouldn't I be?" She looked surprised, dishevelled, the silver hair almost a halo in the bright setting sun. She looked smaller than I'd remembered. Fragile.

"Well, no-one knew where you were. Rita was really concerned. She said your sister didn't know where you were."

"Oh dear! I'm so sorry. I just needed to get away. You know… You look lovely dear!" She aimed this last comment at Geri. I realised that I'd been holding the door open, Geri right behind me, but not letting her pass.

"Sorry! Do you want tea or anything?" I stepped aside and she entered.

"Tea would be nice. I so hate missing my classes, letting people down, but the train was late and I couldn't let you know. Maybe I should get one of those mobile phone things. Did they come? Were they terribly annoyed with me?" Her voice had acquired a slight tremor.

"Yes, they came. The class was fine. Look, let me tell Rita you're here."

Rita had been clearing up in the kitchen. "Joan's back," I said.

"Where's the silly old bag been?"

"You'll have to ask her."

"Does she look ok?"

"Yeah. Said she had to get away." Rita followed me to Geri's office, where Joan was now sitting and smiling, looking somewhat embarrassed.

"Joan! Where've you been?"

"I just needed to go back to Cornwall for a few days. Recharge the batteries."

"Cornwall?" Rita repeated as if amazed that anyone would disappear to Cornwall for a rest.

"St Ives. It's still home, really. And I wanted to see Barbara's work. I missed it."

"Who's Barbara?" Geri and I chorused.

"Barbara Hepworth. The sculptor. If you ask me, the greatest. Though of course, I love Brancusi. And Henry's work has its own charm. But Barbara, just being near her work gives me light and strength, helps me to see things for what they are."

"Oh," we said, not really any the wiser.

"The fire was a great tragedy. Such a loss. She taught me everything I know. So, when things get difficult, that's where I go. You've never been? The garden is extraordinary."

"Garden?" Rita was also losing Joan's plot.

"So, what's been happening?"

Where to start? Gordon going missing? The visitation of the councillors? Justin's new career as life model?

"Things aren't looking good," said Rita, "Gordon's disappeared."

" So has all the money," said Geri. Rita's mouth dropped open.

"What!" Joan looked aghast.

"We've not seen Lawrence either," added Geri.

"And I'm not sure what Councillors Patel and Hope made of us this afternoon," I added. "One of Justin's lads kicked off with some colourful threats, and there was just me here until Rita came, and I think they thought we should just be closed down."

"Not a very promising first week, then," commented Joan, looking at me and I realised how little time I'd spent at *Action in Caring* and yet how closely I identified with it already.

"We think there needs to be an urgent committee meeting," said Geri. "We've written to everyone asking them to come in tomorrow. Maybe you could chair it, Joan?"

"Well, I don't know…I'm not really…"

"Of course you should!" butted in Rita. "You'll keep everyone on track."

"Did you get through to the police?" Geri asked me.

"No. I was just about to ring when Joan came back. I'll go now." I headed back to my work station. As I was about to pick up the phone, there was a ring at the door. I glanced up at the CCTV monitor. It was Maryam. We must almost have had a quorate gathering of management committee members. I went to open the door.

"Look!" she cried, brandishing a copy of the South London Press in my face. "Have you seen this? That filthy man! Well, I want nothing more, *nothing* more to do with this place. That's it. I quit! They'll have to find another token Asian."

"Hey, hang on Maryam. What are you talking about?"

"This!" and she flung the paper down on the reception counter. I picked it up. The face on the front page was coldly familiar. The headline read, *Beast of Battersea caged.* The article went on, *Gordon Smedley, Finance Manager at jinxed Clapham charity, Action in Caring, was arrested at his Battersea home on Monday morning. Smedley, 48, is suspected of being part of a ring of paedophiles. Metropolitan Police Commissioner, Donald Fairbanks, said, "Mr Smedley is currently helping us with our enquiries". Last week, Action in Caring's Director, Veronica Stein, died suddenly at a meeting of the management committee. Former centre user, Dawn Burton, said, "I stopped sending my boys there last year. I knew there was something not right about it. Now we know. These pervs should be locked up and never let out." Her friend Ron Cripps added, "Hanging's too good for them." Mr Smedley will appear before Lambeth magistrates on Friday morning. He is being held on remand.*

No wonder we hadn't seen him. The article was by Suresh. Cheeky bastard! He hadn't thought to let me know he'd got a scoop on *AiC.* And by the style of the piece, I'd say he was heading for the Star or the Sun, rather than the Guardian. I'd deal with Suresh in due course. For now, I had to tell the others what I knew. And Maryam was still fuming.

"So what kind of a place is this?" she cried.

"Well, I've only been here a week, but I'd say it's a community centre with problems and potential," I said.

"You're mad!" she said. "I'd get out while you can, if I were you," she advised. "My brothers won't let me have anything more to do with this place. I don't want to, either."

"Well, at least come to the committee meeting tomorrow," I begged.

"No, I don't think so," she said. "Not after last week, and now this."

"But the centre's not about Gordon Smedley," I argued. "It's about kids, and pregnant mums chilling with yoga, and bad boys getting a second chance. It's about pensioners finding out they're artists when they're seventy three." Where did all this passion come from? This was just a job, for God's sake. But something about *AiC* had got to me. I wanted there to be somewhere for Felicity and Joan to work their magic. Even for Justin to save a few delinquent souls. Maryam looked at me. She took a deep breath.

"Look," she said, "I'll come to the meeting tomorrow. But then, that's it. I'll say my goodbyes and move on."

"Ok," I said, hoping she wouldn't go just yet. We would need all the help we could get to survive all this. She left without taking the paper. I took it to share the latest instalment of our soap opera with Geri, Joan and Rita.

Five o'clock. Joan and Rita had left an hour ago, still stunned by the latest news. Geri and I looked at each other.

"Home time?" I asked.

"Definitely," she said. "Well, at least we know why Gordon's been out of touch."

"What'll happen next?"

"Up to the management committee. They've *got* to meet tomorrow now."

"I didn't ask you," I added. "How did the interview go?"

"Great. I think I did well. They said they'd let me know by Friday."

"Oh. Well, I suppose I hope you get it. Though I don't want you to go."

"I'm not sure I do, either. I really love this place. The people, anyway. Not Gordon, never Veronica; but the people who come in and out and make it their home. And before we had to make people redundant we had a good team. It was fun. Oh well, we'll see. Doing anything special?"

"Checking on Carla – she's got a broken arm. Comforting Benjamin. You know, the bloke whose bike I borrowed on my first day. The latest love of his life turned out not to be The One. You?"

"Book club. Talking about the new Zadie Smith."

"Any good?"

"In places. Well, let's lock up."

I headed for Carla's. Siobhan opened the door.

"So, Nikki," she said. "Long time no see." I hadn't seen Siobhan for over six months. She and Carla had once been lovers and were still firm friends. I was pleased to see her.

"You're looking good," I said, giving her a hug. She'd put on a little weight, and her chestnut curls had grown so that they tumbled around her shoulders. There had always been something wholesome about Siobhan.

"So do you," she said, squeezing my hand. When she smiled, the corners of her mouth melted into dimples. "I hear you've abandoned the ranks of the unemployed and joined those of us who toil for a pittance!" She was one of the few who had been quietly supportive after Brent died.

"For my sins," I said. "So, how's the patient?" I looked beyond her to seek out Carla.

"I'm ok," said Carla, emerging from the kitchen. "Just fed up with not being able to do things. Making a cup of tea one handed is a whole new experience. Want one?"

"No, I've got to go and minister to Benjamin if you're ok," I said. "Just wanted to see how you were doing."

"Siobhan's going to cook," she said. "Then we're going out to the pictures." I wondered whether there was a chance that they'd get back together again. I hoped so. I never quite understood why they'd split up.

"What are you going to see?"

"Something weird and French at the Ritzy."

"Close your eyes at the second kitchen scene," I said, remembering my recent solo trip to the cinema. "It's good, though," I added, not wanting to put them off.

"I'll catch up with you tomorrow," said Carla. "Any developments at work?"

"Loads. The finance man's been arrested for allegedly being part of a paedophile ring. All the money's gone."

"Bloody hell, Nik! It just goes from bad to worse!"

"Tell me about it! On the plus side, Justin the youth worker's just found his calling as a life model. But I'll tell you the details tomorrow. Have a great evening." I gave Carla a careful hug, kissed her cheek. Gave Siobhan another hug for luck, waved as I exited. It was time to save Benjamin from himself.

He opened the door almost before I'd finished knocking.

"Oh. It's you, Nik," he said, as if I was the biggest disappointment this century.

"Well who did you think it would be? Marlon Brando?"

"No, no…I just thought…maybe…"

"Did he even know where you lived?" It was depressing to think that I'd been more intimate with Benjamin's bed linen than had lycra Dan.

"Yes! Of course! Well, he knew it was Streatham…"

"Come on upstairs with me," I said, putting an arm around him. "There's wine, and I said I'd make you a toastie."

"I'm not much company," he said.

"I know. Want to watch *The Producers*?" It was our favourite cheer-up film.

"I think I'm too far gone."

"Well, see how you are after the toastie."

Benjamin settled on my sofa while I poured wine and prepared cheese and onion toasties with extra pickle. There was a defeated look about him that I hadn't seen since Josh left. The toasties sizzled in the sandwich maker. A spicy smell of pickle wafted up. The cheese smelled cheesy and the onion smelled sweet. I handed Ben a glass of red wine.

"Thanks." He gulped at the wine miserably.

"So what happened?" I asked.

"He's got someone else."

"Someone serious?"

"Serious enough. A bloke with a hot job in finance who spends half his life travelling the world first class."

"Leaving lycra Dan to get all lonely?"

"Pathetic, isn't it?"

"Yeah." I skipped into the kitchen to fetch the toasties. I didn't know what to say to Ben. He'd just have to get over Dan in his own time. I could distract him, though.

"Want to hear the latest from *Action in Caring*?" I asked, handing him his plate.

"No, not really."

"Oh. Well, let's put the movie on, then." He sighed and took a big bite out of his sandwich. That was a good sign: he wasn't intending to waste away from unrequited passion. I fumbled around my video and DVD collection until I found *The Producers*. Popped the disc in the slot. Sat back to enjoy the show. I only had to hear the opening bars of *Springtime for Hitler* to crack up. There was Zero Mostel and his simpering widows with their *chequies*. There was Gene Wilder cowering in terror with his comfort rag. The traumas of my day didn't get a look in. I glanced across at Benjamin. He still looked glum. This was bad.

"Hey Ben, your favourite bit's coming up," I said.

"Is it?"

"Yeah. Look, they're on the roof. Here it comes. The scene where they meet Franz Liebkind. You love this bit…" and as the demented Nazi made his appearance, sure enough, a tiny smile appeared on Benjamin's face. By the time it got to the rehearsal of *Springtime for Hitler*, we both had tears running down our faces, and we joined in singing raucously.

"Thanks, Nik," said Benjamin, after the closing credits. "You're a real friend."

"So are you," I said, giving him a hug.

"I really thought…" he began.

"He was the one?"

"Yeah. There was …I don't know, a kind of…chemistry."

" Hm. Know what you mean." I'd felt that way with Ruth. Like Ben, I'd got it wrong. Or had I?

"And I'll have to quit CycleOut, and I've only just joined. Quite fancied some of those trips."

"Why should you quit? You hang in there! You've as much right as lycra Dan!"

"I don't know. I'm not sure I could bear seeing him. And I'm the new boy, he pretty much runs it."

"Give it a week or two. Anyway, you might meet someone else."

"I think I'm giving up on men. But maybe you're right. I should give it another go."

"Ruth rang me today."

"Oh? What for?"

"She wanted to meet up. I'm seeing her on Thursday."

"Well, I hope you have better luck than me."

"I don't know."

"What do you mean? You've been pining after her for months!"

130

"Yeah, but I'm not sure she's good for me. And I don't know why she wants to meet me. Why now? She's been in town for a few weeks. God, but I've missed her."

"Need armed back-up?"

"No! But how about we watch an old *Cagney and Lacey*?"

"Why not?"

"I'll open another bottle of wine." We watched the eighties re-run that now looked impossibly dated. I still fancied Christine Cagney, though, and Ben lusted after Mary Beth's Harv. I was sleepy, and knew that tomorrow would be demanding in all sorts of ways.

"I need to sleep now," I said. "Will you be all right?"

"Yeah. I've just got a bruised ego and an empty bed."

"Well, we can fix both of those in time."

"You think?"

"I know."

"You didn't tell me about work. What's up?"

"Not now. I'll tell you tomorrow. Sleep tight."

"Thanks Nik." He gave me a big hug and went down to his own pristine flat, leaving me to clear up the debris and fall into bed. Ruby's dream-catcher swayed in a breeze from my open fanlight. I'd fixed a lot of things today. I'd helped my friend. I'd kept things going at work. Maybe I wasn't completely useless.

Chapter 14

My dreams tumbled one into the other and involved police car chases, an art class that was so full there wasn't room for me to erect my easel; and a sparkly show, girls with feathers, men with top hats, that disappeared down a hole in the stage. I woke up at half past seven, having forgotten to set my alarm clock. Shit! I'd have to miss breakfast, just shower and go. I wanted to be in early. I needed to chase up Suresh, find out what else he knew, bawl him out about going to press with his story without telling me first. And I needed to put my best jeans on to wash so that I'd be ready to meet Ruth, not to mention hand washing my purple shirt. I showered and put on yesterday's chinos and a black sweatshirt that had seen better days. The trusty Kickers went on over socks with soles so threadbare it was hardly worth wearing them. When – if - I got paid, I'd have to pay some attention to my wardrobe. I stuffed my Dockers and assorted dirty washing into the ancient washing machine and set it to work. It rumbled into life. I washed my shirt in the sink and hung it to dry over my kitchen chair. My bike was still with Clancy, so I'd have to take the bus to work, unless Benjamin was serious about never cycling again. I decided not to wake him to ask that question. It was a crisp, sunny morning, so I jogged to the bus stop, caught a bus to Clapham Common, and jogged the rest of the way to *Action in Caring*.

Geri was already there.

"So, what's on today?" I asked as I slung my denim jacket over the back of my chair.

"Felicity's got a class. Justin's back with his crew. Joan should be teaching a water colour class. That's about it."

"Apart from finding out where that money's gone and what Suresh thinks he's playing at!" I added. "And chasing up the police!"

"And there's the management committee this evening," Geri said.

"You know, it's been nearly a week since Veronica died, and we've heard nothing from the family, nothing about a funeral or anything," I said.

"Yeah, that's odd. She wasn't married, and I don't think she had kids or a partner; but you'd have thought someone would have been in touch. Did you give the police her next of kin details?"

" Gordon had already done it. How long had she worked here?"

"About five years, I think. Maybe longer. I'll go and check." Geri went into her office and I heard her open the drawer to a filing cabinet. No-one else would arrive for an hour, so I rang Suresh.

"Hi Nikki. Like the piece?"

"Oh yeah, great journalism. Cutting edge stuff. Think it'll get you a nice little post at the Guardian. The Streatham Guardian, that is."

"Hey! Don't be like that!"

"Well! What do you expect? I gave you the lead into *Action in Caring*. You could at least have let me know that they'd arrested Gordon!"

"No time. Up against deadlines. You know how it is in this business."

"No, actually, I don't. Whatever strange and sometimes iffy jobs I've had, they've never involved scavenging in gutters and screwing my friends."

"Ok, I'm sorry. It's just, what with Meena's sister coming, and the babies going down with chicken pox, I just forgot. Sorry Nik."

"Yeah, well, you can just start to make amends."

"What do you mean?"

"I want to know everything. What you found out, who your sources are, what you know but didn't publish, everything, Suresh. And I want it this side of lunchtime. In fact, tell you what, you can take me to lunch."

"Er…"

"And if you're thinking of wriggling out, remember I know stuff about you that you'd rather Meena didn't know."

"Hey! That's blackmail!"

"No, it's being assertive."

"But you'd never tell Meena…"

"Yes, I'd tell Meena all about…"

133

"...Ok. Lunch. Eco?" Eco is the best pizza place in London, if you ask me. Probably the best this side of Palermo. You could easily miss it on Clapham High Street, sandwiched as it is between all sorts of other enticing eateries and the Abbey National. Its interior is utilitarian, and it doesn't seduce with linen tablecloths or vases of flowers or even interesting arrangements of tables and chairs. It was vaguely trendy around fifteen years ago. But the food is wonderful, and that's what counts.

"Eco. One o'clock. Don't be late. I only have an hour."

"I'll be there."

Felicity arrived at nine thirty looking vibrant. Her chosen colour for today was orange. She beamed at me.

"Nikki! How are you?" she asked and, to my surprise, leaned over to give me a hug. We did the continental kissing thing that everyone in London seems to do these days.

"We're just about keeping things together here," I said. "How about you?"

"Looking forward to my class today. It's the Reclaim Your Serenity group for people who've had a lot of stress, depression, things like that. I love seeing people build themselves back up, find the key to keeping themselves sane. Well, relatively sane, of course."

"Sounds brilliant. Wish I'd had that a year ago."

"Join us!"

"No. Thanks, Felicity, I'd love to, but I've got work to do. Did you hear about Gordon?"

"Yes, I saw the item in the paper. I never did like that man. And of course there was all that carry on at his last place."

"What carry on?" I was intrigued.

"Well, he worked for the Guild for London Amateur Drama before coming here."

"Never heard of it!"

"No, and you won't in the future. It doesn't exist any more."

"What happened?"

"About a year after Gordon joined as Director, the organisation went into administration. Folded."

"Did Gordon have anything to do with it?"

"He'd negotiated a pretty hefty pay rise soon after joining. Sacked half the staff who, naturally, took him to employment tribunal for unfair dismissal."

"Who won?"

"They did. The Guild had to pay out in excess of fifty thousand pounds. People who'd supported them moved away, didn't like what they saw. And the big London grant givers withdrew funding on the grounds that the organisation was a lousy employer and had breached equal opportunities in pretty much every area since Gordon had taken over a the helm."

"So was there a management committee? What did they do?"

"They were too stupid to see what was going on. They'd backed Gordon when they should have backed their staff. In the end, they gave him a huge pay off to go quietly."

"So he never had to answer to anyone for what he'd done?"

"Only to the employment tribunal – but he omitted to submit the appropriate paper work, so it was an automatic find in favour of the ex-staff. He didn't even turn up to the hearing."

"How do you know so much about this, Felicity?" She gave a wry smile.

"My partner Leo was the Development Officer. He was one of the people shafted by Gordon."

"You don't think it was deliberate, do you? A set up?"

"I never wanted to believe that, but it was hard to accept that it was all some dreadful management cock-up."

"My God! How could you bear to work for the same organisation as him?"

"I've been running classes at *AiC* for years: long before Gordon Smedley came here to work. I thought Veronica was courting disaster in appointing him, but my opinion didn't really count. Our paths don't cross often."

"So were you surprised about the paedophile stuff?"

"Well, I have to say that did surprise me. There'd never been rumours of that nature before, and he didn't show any interest in the young people here. Now, enough of all this. I've a class to prepare for!" She swept off, brown curls bouncing off orange tunic. I wondered what other secrets were lurking behind the scenes at *AiC*. Had Veronica simply been unpleasant, or did she too have a past? Felicity's class began to arrive. They were a mixed bunch of people: a skinny young woman with worry lines etched across her brow, a man in his thirties with straggly hair wearing a duffel coat, a couple of older looking women carrying shopping bags, a young bloke with a crew-cut who smelled of stale tobacco. They nodded their greetings and signed in before heading for the meeting room. I decided I could leave my post for a few minutes and went to find Geri. I filled her in on Felicity's news.

"God! How come I never knew about that?" she said.

"Guess it isn't the sort of thing that Gordon would boast about," I answered. "Have you found anything in Veronica's file?"

"She's been here for five years. Had been here for five years. Before that, she was Chief Officer for something called SOS IBS."

"Sounds fun. Irritable Bowel Syndrome?"

"Hang on. I'll Google it." Geri turned to the PC and tapped at the keyboard. "Here we go. Nothing coming up…oh, here it is." She clicked with the mouse, opening up a website. "SOS IBS…advice and information for people with irritable bowel syndrome…no current services due to lack of funding. Website last updated in two thousand."

"So it didn't survive long after Veronica's departure."

"Looks that way."

"Any other references?" She scrolled down the Google list.

"No. Nothing here."

136

"What did she do before that?"

"Her CV lists her as working as head of administration for Allergy Emergency. She was there for a couple of years."

"*AiC* must have been light relief after her last two jobs!"

"Let's see if that's still going…" she tapped at the keyboard again, moved the mouse. "Nothing on the first page. Nor the second."

"Any mileage in looking them up on the Charity Commission website?" Geri interrogated Google again.

"Last accounts filed 1997."

"Another failed charity, then. Let's hope *AiC* doesn't go the same way. What about Gordon? What did he do before GfLAD?"

"Let's have a look." Geri stood up and went to the filing cabinet. She sifted through the files.

"That's odd," she said.

"What?"

"His file's missing." She went through the drawer again, lifting each of the files to check the name on the tab. "No, it's not here. I wouldn't have moved it. What could have happened to it?"

"Does anyone else have access to the personnel files?"

"Only me. And of course, Veronica did. I don't think Gordon had a key, but he might have known where Veronica kept hers. I keep mine on a bunch of keys. I'd know if they'd gone missing." She looked perplexed. "I just don't understand. I'm really careful about keeping this cabinet locked."

"Could Veronica have been working on it before she died?"

"But why? And where's the file now? We've both looked in her office. It's not there, is it?"

"Not that I could see. Maybe she took it home."

"But why would she do that?"

"Maybe she wanted to check something out? Maybe something about Gordon was troubling her?"

"Those two were pretty thick together. It always seemed to be them against the rest of us."

"You know what, Geri, we might never know."

"But what if…now, I know this sounds crazy, Nikki, but what if she found out something about him – something about his past – and was going to do something about it? Maybe sack him?"

"Ok, here's another thought: what if she found out about the Guild for London Amateur Drama and the missing money here, put two and two together, and figured that Gordon was trying to bankrupt *AiC?*"

"But why would he do that? He didn't stand to gain anything."

"We still don't know where that money's gone."

"You mean he could have siphoned it into his own account, and she found out, and he killed her?"

"Well…"

"That's just too crazy, isn't it? She'd have to notice that the money was missing. She couldn't have failed to. She must have been checking the bank accounts. Yeah, she and Gordon used to meet with Derek the treasurer every month to look at the finances. Derek's a cheque signatory, so he's in and out a couple of times each month to sign cheques and have a look at the bank statements. She'd have to know. So would Derek. There must be a rational explanation. He must have been putting the money into a higher interest account or something."

"Funny that Tanya lost her job as soon as she picked up on the transfers, though."

"I think he just felt threatened by anyone who knew anything about financial management. And she wanted to move out of London."

"And no-one's heard of her since."

Felicity's class emerged looking lighter and brighter. The skinny woman was smiling and chatting with the man who smelled of tobacco. The two women with shopping were trying to decide where to go for lunch. The man with the duffel coat was talking to Felicity. Felicity waved at us as she passed the office door.

138

"See you on Friday," she called.

The doorbell rang. I went back to my perch at reception to open the door to Justin and his lads. Dwayne wasn't amongst them.

"You ok?" I said to Justin.

"Beaut," he said. "Hey, when's the next art class?"

"Joan's due in today," I said, "but the next life class is on Tuesday. You up for it?"

"Sure! I really enjoyed it."

"Good. I'll let Joan know that you're happy to model for a few weeks."

"Cool," he said. The boys in their hoodies slithered into the meeting room.

"Have fun!" I said, wondering what Justin had in store for his posse today. It was nearly half past twelve. I was due to meet Suresh in half an hour.

"Geri, I've got a lunch date," I said. "Can you hold the fort?"

"Yes. You get off. Anyone special?"

"Suresh. I want to see what he's dug up. Think I'll ask him to dig a bit deeper into our friend Gordon."

I walked briskly across the Common to Clapham High Street. Eco was buzzing with hungry lunchtime punters. The smell of wood smoke, garlic and bubbling cheese was almost too much to bear. Suresh was already there, and had taken a table in the quietest part of the restaurant. It still echoed with orders being called, pans being clattered, and the noisy chatter of happy eaters. Suresh was oblivious to the hubbub and was doing something that took a lot of concentration with a tiny stylus and his Blackberry. He was wearing jeans and a black sweatshirt.

"I want avocado tricolor to start," I said, plonking down opposite him and making him jump. "And then I want pizza with aubergines and spinach and extra mushrooms and a rocket side salad. And then I want tiramisu for pudding. And I might have a large glass of wine. And you're paying."

"Hi Nik," he said. "Good to see you too. I'm fine, thank you for asking. Kids miserable as sin with chicken pox. How about you?"

"I'll be better when I've eaten and stopped being pissed off with you," I said. He sighed.

"Ok," he said, "I should have phoned you. Or at least dropped you an e-mail. I'm sorry. I just got caught up in it all, and there were two other hot stories running at the same time."

"We might be back on speaking terms once I know food's on its way," I said. The waitress came and took our order.

"Any drinks?"

I decided I'd better give the wine a miss: never had been a lunch time drinker. We both asked for freshly squeezed orange juice.

"And some olives, please," I added. She bustled off. "So, what have you got for me?" I asked Suresh.

"Well, your man's accused of kiddy fiddling. But you know that. His work history's interesting. Before *Action in Caring* he headed up GfLAD - Guild for London Amateur Drama."

"Yeah, yeah, I know all that," I interrupted. "Tell me something new." Suresh looked surprised. I hoped that wasn't all he had to tell me.

"He'd been Director of Finance for an outfit called All London Blind Action Group," he said. "Seems like something similar happened there. According to my sources, he got a hefty pay rise pretty early on, and within a year, the organisation had folded."

"Was any action taken against him?"

"No. Not that I could find, anyway. Looks like he made a quiet exit after nine months. ALBAG struggled on for another three months, and then the administrators were called in. Their Chief Officer left suddenly to take a post in Yorkshire, and that was the end of ALBAG."

"So he makes a career of bankrupting charities?"

"Looks like it."

"Anything on his personal life? Finances, that sort of thing?"

"He's got a flat in a new riverside development in Battersea. They don't come cheap. You're talking about half a million for a two bedroomed place. Hard to see how someone working in the voluntary sector could afford something like that."

"Unless he had private means?"

"I couldn't find anything. Looks like he was a local boy. Went to school in Croydon, grew up in Crystal Palace. Doesn't sound like the kind of background for an heir to a fortune."

"One of the councillors, Nigel Bentley, got into property in the eighties. They were tight by all accounts. Any link there?" Suresh looked impressed.

"You should write crime fiction, Nikki," he said, "or go into investigative journalism."

Our first course arrived. The mozzarella was soft and fresh, the avocado perfectly ripe.

"I should do anything other than what I'm doing," I said, "but your friend Tony Blair's determined to get us all paying tax and ticking boxes…" I couldn't resist a dig at New Labour, especially as Suresh had stood for parliament in '97. He'd found it hard to ditch his fantasy that the Labour party would give us all the good life and wash away the sins of Thatcherism at a stroke. The fact that they'd been even more draconian in so many areas had been tough for Suresh, especially their approach to asylum seekers and refugees. He'd been an active law centre volunteer not so long ago, had helped many people fleeing from torture to negotiate their way through our Alice in Wonderland immigration system.

"He's not my friend," said Suresh, crunching down hard on his bruschetta.

"Gordon Smedley. Money. Links," I said, laying down my knife and fork.

"Bentley's rumoured to be bent," said Suresh. "I'll dig a bit deeper. See what my sources on the Council come up with."

"Look into Gordon's employer before ALBAG, too," I said. "While you're at it, have a look into SOS IBS and Allergy Emergency.

Veronica worked for them both, and it seems they didn't survive her departure for long."

Our pizzas arrived, huge, crisp, and steaming, shining with tomato and olive oil, too tantalizing to talk over. We ate in silence.

Back at *Action in Caring*, full of pizza and tiramisu, I updated Geri with what I'd managed to glean over lunch with Suresh. Then I went back to reception desk to await the next visitor – if indeed there was to be one.

"Wendy Baggott returned your call," said Geri. "I said you'd call her back."

I rang the number that Wendy Baggott had given me and finally got through.

"Hello, it's Nikki Elliot, *Action in Caring* here," I started.

"Ah, hi there Nikki. I'm glad you rang back. I'm sorry I missed your call. What was it you wanted to tell me?"

"Well…I think I have some new information. I think someone may have tried to kill her, or at least they stopped her from reaching the antidote she needed."

"And what makes you think that?"

"I found an epi-pen under the table. I think she dropped it out of her bag, and she tried to reach it, but someone knocked it out of the way and gave her a ball point instead, and now he's been arrested for molesting kids…"

"Ok, ok. Sounds like I'd better get someone out to you. Have you got the epi pen?"

"Yes."

"Touch it as little as possible and put it somewhere safe. We'll get a detective to come and see you. Thanks for letting us know."

The phone rang, and I answered it.

"Hello. My name is Pauline Stein," said a quiet, tremulous voice. "I'm Veronica's sister. I just wondered…"

142

"Ms Stein! Veronica's sister? We were wondering when someone from her family would be in touch. Look, I'm sorry about Veronica, Ms Stein. This must be a really hard time for you," I said. What else was there to say?

"I still can't believe that Veronica's…that she's…" I could hear her working hard to hold back the tears. So, someone had cared about Veronica.

"Is there anything I can do to help?"

"Well, I just wondered…"

"Yes?"

"Were there any…personal effects?" She blew her nose and I moved the phone away from my ear.

"Not many, I'm afraid, but you're very welcome to come and take the few things that she left here," I thought about the little diary that I'd file somewhere else before Pauline arrived. She'd be welcome to the Rennies and American Tan tights. "When would you like to come?"

"I'll be in London tomorrow. Would that be convenient? Say in the morning?"

"It'll be fine. We'll see you then."

"Thank you. It's all such a shock. I still can't believe…"

"No, we can't either."

"Were you…I mean, did you…?"

"Was I there?"

"Yes."

"Yes, I was. It was my first day at work. I didn't know your sister well, I'm afraid."

"Did she…I mean, was it…?"

"Was she in pain?"

"Yes."

"Not for very long. It was over very quickly."

"Oh. Good. I suppose. Well, tomorrow, then."

"Yes. I'll see you tomorrow."

After that, it was quiet, so I focused on beating myself at Solitaire on the PC. My mobile rang, making me jump. I didn't recognise the number that came up on the screen.

"Hi, this is Nikki," I said.

"Nikki, it's Chantelle. From the Job Centre," said a voice that sounded anxious. She was probably ringing to tell me that I'd forgotten to fill in some vital piece of paperwork.

"What's up?" I asked moving the jack of diamonds onto the queen of clubs with my mouse.

"We need to talk," she said.

"What've I done now?"

"Nothing. It's not you. It's Tanya. She's dead, Nikki. We need to talk."

The hand holding the phone started to shake. I felt cold and sick.

"Nikki? You there?"

"Yeah. Yeah, I'm here."

"Can you meet me after work?"

"Um…yes." But then I remembered: "No. No, I can't. There's a management committee meeting tonight."

"Now, then. Can you get away and come to the Job Centre?"

"Ok. Give me half an hour."

"Be careful." There was no background tapping of fingernails. Just the silent sound of fear rippling across the space between our phones, and the tachycardic pulsing of my heart in my ears.

Chapter 15

"Geri, can you hold the fort?"

"Hey, what's up? You've gone white."

"Tanya's dead."

"What? Tanya who worked here?"

"I don't know of any other Tanya."

"My Lord! What happened?"

"I don't know. Chantelle wants me to go to the Job Centre. Geri, I'm scared. This is all getting too crazy for me."

"Maybe she had an accident. An asthma attack. Could be anything."

"Or it could be tied up with whatever's going on here." Geri just stared at me. We both knew that something bad had happened to Tanya. We both sensed danger.

"I'll take care of things here. See what Chantelle has to say. I'll do the sandwiches for tonight, just get back in time for the meeting."

"Don't poison anyone," I said, and then wished I hadn't. "Sorry," I said. "Just my way of…"

"Yeah, I know."

"Look, if the police come, I've locked the epi-pen in the desk drawer."

"Ok."

I grabbed my coat from the back of my chair, retrieved my rucksack from under the desk and made my exit. I'd go via Clancy and pick up my bike.

Clancy had put on a new wheel and serviced my bike for no extra charge. I owed him. But the new wheel had cost me over forty pounds. I'd better be paid soon.

"Drive safely," he said, wiping oil-blackened fingers down his coveralls. "You got a helmet? We're doing a special."

"Might come back for one. Gotta get up to Streatham now. Thanks, Clancy."

"You take care, now," he said and waved me off. The bike was smoother and faster, and the effort I put into cycling uphill to Streatham helped to disperse some of my adrenaline. The Job Centre was down a side street that led to a loading bay for a struggling supermarket. I wasn't taking a chance on leaving my bike outside. I pushed it through the doors that said *staff only*.

"Customer entrance is round the corner," said a man with dreadlocks idling behind a makeshift security desk.

"I'm here to see Chantelle," I said. "Look, I know this is a really big favour, but can I leave the bike here?"

"Dunno 'bout that," he said.

"I've only just had the front wheel replaced – someone nicked the old one – and I've got a job, but they haven't paid me yet, and I just can't afford any more repairs…" I gave him my best pathetic, lopsided smile. He weighed up his options. To be nice…not to be nice, that was the question.

"How long you will be?"

"Not long. Only about ten minutes."

"You a friend of Chantelle's?"

"Yeah. Yeah, I'm a good friend of hers," I lied.

"Ok. Put it there in the corner. Today's your lucky day."

"Thanks, mate. You're a star. I owe you."

He picked up a phone and pressed a series of numbers on a mini switchboard.

"Hey Chantelle. Friend here to see you. What's your name?"

"Nikki," I said. "Just tell her Nikki's here."

"Says her name's Nikki. Ok ." He replaced the handset.

"Go on up," he said. "Take the lift to the second floor, she'll meet you. Ten minutes, mind."

"Thanks," I said. I pressed the button for the lift. Inside I pressed the button that read two. After an age, the doors closed and the lift told me we were going up. It stopped with a slight judder and the doors opened. The lift told me we were at the second floor. I love it that lifts speak to you these days. Chantelle was standing there. The sassiness was gone. She almost hauled me out of the lift, pulled me towards a set of double doors.

"We'll go into one of the interview rooms. If anyone asks, it's a review meeting to see how the job's going." She seemed almost furtive as she opened a door to a small windowless room and nudged me in. I sat in one of the low chairs that are meant to make you feel comfortable but actually make you feel powerless to escape. Chantelle was carrying a tote bag. She reached inside it and pulled out a newspaper. She sat down opposite me and flung the paper on the coffee table between us.

"Look," she said. "Here it is." The paper was Monday's *Manchester Evening News* and she'd folded it open at page two. Bold headlines read *Girl Crushed in Tragic Tram Trip*. There was a grainy photo of a young woman with a dark bob. She was half smiling, the way you do for passport photos.

Tanya Middleton was killed in a tragic tram accident on Saturday. The twenty seven year old was hit by the tram near the G-Mex at the junction of Windmill Street and Lower Moseley Street. She was taken to the Manchester Royal Infirmary, but pronounced dead on arrival. One eyewitness said that Tanya, who worked for the Co-operative Bank, had tripped and fallen in front of the Metrolink tram. Another said that it looked as if she had been pushed. Police are investigating reports that a man in a dark raincoat was seen leaving the scene. Tanya's father, Raymond, who lives in Bristol, said that the family was "devastated". Tanya moved to Altringham from London less than a month ago.

"So what do you think?" asked Chantelle.

"Guess it depends on the police reports. She could have just fallen. It could have been an accident."

"Seems like too much of a coincidence to me," said Chantelle.

"But why would anyone kill her?" I asked. "I mean, ok, suppose she'd found out that Gordon was on the fiddle. That still wouldn't be enough to make him want to kill her, would it? As far as we know, he's a dirty little child abuser, which, disgusting as it is, doesn't make him a killer."

"Do you still think there's something odd about the way Veronica died?"

"Oh God, Chantelle, I don't know. Yeah, ok, it looks as if someone spiked her sandwiches. Maybe they just wanted to give her a fright. And the police are going to look into how an epi-pen found its way into a forest of dust bunnies when it could have saved her life. Look, I've got to go. There's a management committee meeting tonight. And your man won't guard my bike forever. Let me know if you hear anything. By the way, how did you come by a copy of the *Manchester Evening News?*"

"I was up there for a Welfare to Work meeting. Picked up the paper on the train coming back. My cousin lives up there, though, so I'll get her to keep an eye on developments."

"Cool. Ok, I'm going."

"Thanks for coming, Nikki. Take care." I could almost imagine that Chantelle liked me.

"Yeah. You too. Maybe see you at the gym." The chatty lift talked me down the two flights to the ground floor. I thanked the man on the desk and retrieved my bike from the corner.

"Should wear a helmet with that," he said. Nice that two people today thought my brain worth protecting. "They're dangerous, them roads," he added.

"I'm going to buy one when I get paid."

"You do that," he said and waved me out. The truth was, I hated wearing cycle helmets. I hated their heaviness and the itchy strap beneath my chin. Sweaty hair in summer, cold ears in winter. The thing about riding a bike is it gives you freedom, and freedom to me includes taking risks and feeling the wind in my hair. And I'd heard that helmets only protected you for falls from one metre, so wearing one was futile. I mounted the bike, a fleeting memory of being seven years old and pretending my two-wheeler was a horse, making me smile. Being cut up by a giant jeep with a bull bar drove out my reverie and made me reconsider the whole helmet thing.

I could hear the commotion at *AiC* before I opened the door. I flung it open to see Justin being pinned to the wall by Dwayne, the rest of the young offenders group huddled around in shuffling silence, Geri trying to separate the two men and using her best school teacher tone.

"Enough now! Dwayne, back off," she shouted.

"I'll get this fucking cunt," yelled Dwayne, pulling back his right arm as if to swing a punch.

"You just try it, mate," gasped Justin, "and I'll have you sent down, I swear."

I leapt in and grabbed at Dwayne's arm, spinning him off balance.

"You don't want to do this," I said, edging now between them. "Cool it. We'll sort it out. What's he done now?" I looked Dwayne straight in the eye and met dull hatred masking fear. "What's it all about, Dwayne?"

"He been chattin' shit about me, man," said Dwayne. "Ain't no-one chats 'bout me. No-one." Justin had wriggled free and was retreating to a safe space.

"Tha's right, bro," added a skinny white lad with an overactive Adam's apple.

"Stay out of it," warned Geri.

"Aussie twat," muttered the boy in the orange parka who reminded me of Kenny from South Park.

"Fun's over," I announced. "Justin – go and tidy up the room. We've got a meeting tonight. You lot," I added, addressing the boys, "go home. Just sod off, all of you. We'll sort this tomorrow. Dwayne, you're banned until Geri says you can come back. Maybe your probation officer can find you a nice little holiday retreat like Feltham." They shuffled out. Dwayne kicked the door as he left.

"Bloody hell," I said. "Can't leave this place for a minute without one of those guys losing it. You ok?" Geri nodded.

"Nowhere else will have them, you know," she said. They pay way over the usual fee for their space here. They're a large part of what keeps us going."

"Maybe they need a different worker. Maybe Justin would be better off sticking to modelling," I said. "He doesn't seem to have much control over those lads."

"They're the post-*Neighbours* generation. Coming from the same continent as Kylie Minogue doesn't command the respect it did ten years ago. Nowadays it's all about "respect"."

"Haven't they thought about needing to earn respect?"

"That's not how it works, Nikki, you know that."

"Yeah, I do. But I hate it. I hate their swaggering bully boy ways."

"The girls aren't much better."

"At least they don't go around shooting each other or pulling knives just because someone's accidentally trodden on their toes or strayed onto their housing estate."

"Wanna bet?"

Justin appeared looking tired and stressed.

"Sorry girls," he said. "He just kicked off. I couldn't stop him."

"You need to report him," Geri said.

"And we've banned him," I added. "Look, Justin, are you getting any support?"

"Yeah. I mean, you guys are triff."

"That's not what I meant. Who do you report to?"

"Oh, some girl called Lizzie, but she's been off sick for five weeks."

"What with?" asked Geri.

"Dunno. Stress, I think they said," replied Justin.

"You've got to report Dwayne," I said. "I saw that look in his eyes. He's going to hurt someone."

"Yeah, that's what his mum said."

"His mum said that?"

"Yeah. He's beaten up on her a couple of times."

"He can't come back here, you know that don't you?"

"I hear you, but if the courts say he has to attend this group, there's not much I can do. Anyway, no-one got hurt."

"Only 'cos I pulled him off you!" I exclaimed.

"Yeah. Look, I'll talk to the boss. See what he says." He walked towards the door.

"You do that. And make sure you get debriefed. That's two threatening incidents you've had in the same week," I called after him.

"The police came while you were out," said Geri. "Took notes, I gave them the epi-pen. Told them about what had been going on. Guess we just have to wait and see."

"Was it Wendy Baggott came?"

"No, a couple of detectives. Plain clothes. The management committee meeting's due to start in less than an hour," said Geri. "We'd better get the room set up."

"Want me to make sandwiches, or did you do them?" I asked.

"I've just bought in some packets from M and S," said Geri. "Seemed the safest option. Don't suppose you got round to typing up the minutes from the last meeting, did you?"

"No! No, to be honest, I didn't give it a thought!" I said. I filled Geri in on the conversation with Veronica's sister. Then I retrieved my notepad from under a pile of junk mail by my computer. I turned to the pages with the notes. There was the list of everyone who was present, there were the apologies. I'd stopped taking notes at the point when Derek was about to give the financial report. It wouldn't take me long to type them up. I settled to the PC, opened up Word and copied out my notes into a new document. I saved it and printed off seven copies. Just as I was logging off, the doorbell rang. Rita and Joan were outside, so I buzzed them in. Joan looked more windswept than ever, and Rita gave me a friendly hug. She smelled of Imperial Leather soap with a homely trace of sweat and dog.

"No Prudence?" I asked.

"No, love. I've left her at home this evening. Anyone else here?"

"Not yet. You're the first."

"We'll make the tea, then, shall we?"

"Yes, I think so," said Joan, and the two trotted into the kitchen.

Maryam arrived next, looking uncomfortable. "I really don't know why I've come," she said. "Still, this will definitely be my last meeting."

"Fair enough," I said, not knowing what else to say. Bernard and Derek arrived together, and now the only person missing was Lawrence, our esteemed Chair. The meeting was due to start at five thirty and it was now five thirty five. The rest of the committee had drifted into the meeting room. Rita was handing out teas and coffees. I went to help Geri with the sandwiches and biscuits.

"What do you think we should do?" I asked. "Can we have the meeting without Lawrence?"

"I don't know. It's up to the rest of them. I wonder where he's got to?" We took the food into the meeting room.

"No sign of Lawrence?" asked Rita.

"No. He hasn't rung either," I said.

"Well, maybe we should just get on with things," said Bernard. He was wearing a green and cream checked shirt and a green and red striped tie with a little pin. "Joan, you're the vice chair. Why don't you start us off?"

"Well, if you think…" said Joan.

"Yes, let's just get on with it," said Maryam, clearly keen to be away.

"Derek?" asked Joan. The treasurer cleared his throat. He was wearing a dark suit and white shirt and had opened his laptop in preparation for something. Maybe he was going to give the report he'd been prevented from giving when Veronica had her reaction to the sandwiches.

"Yes. Yes, I think we should start," he said, sounding nervous. "Joan, if you're happy to take the chair…"

"In that case, I declare this meeting open," said Joan. "Now, given the circumstances, we don't have our usual agenda. I suggest we look at our financial situation and focus on where we go from here."

"We've got a dead director and a finance manager who's been molesting young boys," said Maryam. "What exactly is there to discuss? Surely we can't keep this place open?"

"Veronica's passing is tragic and Gordon's arrest unfortunate; but we don't know that he's guilty, yet," said Bernard. "Shouldn't we see what we can do to keep the centre open?"

"I'm not sure we can do anything useful here tonight ," said Derek.

"We can't let *Action in Caring* close!" added Rita. "We've got to find a way to keep going, for all those people who depend on us! What about the art classes, and those poor young men who are getting a second chance with us?" I wondered if she would be as enthusiastic about the young offenders if she'd eyeballed Dwayne.

"The management accounts…" started Derek.

"Yes. Let's start with the money," said Joan. "Derek, can you talk us through the accounts?"

Derek handed round a sheaf of papers. Each trustee received a bundle of about seven sheets. Each sheet was covered in columns of numbers, and the typeface was miniscule. I watched Bernard frown at the papers, flick through them, turn back to the front. The others appeared equally mystified. "Ok. Can you all see the figures?"

"Well, I'm not sure I understand…" began Bernard.

"Couldn't we just have a simple income and expenditure report?" asked Maryam.

"I'm afraid the system doesn't really lend itself to that, and I thought we needed some extra detail."

"But we've said before, we don't understand the accounts when you present them like this," said Maryam. "I'm far from stupid and I'm part qualified in accountancy, but these figures just don't make sense."

"Is there a cash flow report?" asked Bernard. "Something to tell us what we've got in the bank and what we're expecting to get in and pay out?"

"It's all here if you look at the figures," said Derek. "But I'll try to explain in simple terms. Well, first of all, we're running at a serious deficit. During the last quarter, we earned ten thousand pounds, give or take, but we spent over seventeen thousand. There are one or two anomalies in the accounts, and the most recent bank statement shows that we only have four thousand pounds left in the bank account. I tried to speak with Gordon about this, but then Veronica passed away and Gordon was arrested. I have to say, this is not a happy situation."

"Could it be a cash flow problem?" asked Bernard.

"I couldn't really tell you without talking to Gordon," said Derek.

"Have we paid all the bills?" asked Maryam.

"I don't know without looking at the administration," said Derek. "Geraldine, would you be able to shed any light on this?"

"I'm responsible for processing the invoices, and I pass them to Gordon, who should raise the cheques and countersign them with Veronica," said Geri. "I don't know if they've all been paid, but I do know that over one hundred thousand pounds seems to have been moved out of our main account. A former member of staff noticed a big transfer of fifty thousand pounds a couple of months ago. Gordon said that he'd moved it into a higher interest account. Our latest statement showed we'd got nothing in our main account. And neither Nikki nor I have been paid, and we can't pay our sessional staff like Felicity. But Derek, you kept a pretty close watch on the money. Wouldn't you have noticed if…"

I couldn't keep quiet any longer. "And that member of staff who saw the statement saying that fifty thousand had been moved has just been killed in a tram accident in Manchester," I said. You could hear the proverbial pin drop.

"So Gordon fiddles charitable money as well as kids?" said Maryam, her cheeks a high colour framed by her beige hijab.

"We don't know that yet," said Bernard.

"Have we heard anything more about Veronica? Like when the funeral's due to take place?" asked Rita. She was answered with silence.

"Her sister phoned earlier," I said after a while. "She's coming in tomorrow. Maybe she'll be able to tell us about the funeral and what's happening."

Derek fiddled with his laptop, Bernard with his fountain pen. Maryam tapped impatiently on the table. I thought about my unpaid rent bill, a dead young woman, and someone deeply unlikeable who had met a gruesome and untimely end by eating the wrong thing.

"Look, I know it's probably not my place," I said, "but we need to sort out quite a bit tonight. First of all, who's running this place? Geri and I have been holding it together, but there's only the two of us and there are health and safety issues, and neither of us are managers. Secondly, are you going to make sure we get paid? I can't afford to work here for free. I'll be evicted if I don't pay the rent. And what are you going to do about the situation with Gordon? I mean, you could suspend him on grounds of gross misconduct, couldn't you? Then we could bring in someone else. And we still don't know what really happened to Veronica. Or poor Tanya, come to that. And we've got a potentially risky situation with the young offenders' group – some of those kids are seriously disturbed. And you're the management committee. What are you going to do?" They all stared at me. Geri was the first to speak.

"Nikki's right. You've got to make some decisions tonight, otherwise we'll just have to close down the centre. We've already got the councillors breathing down our necks – they'll withdraw our funding if we can't convince them that we're still viable. And there is, as Nikki said, the small matter of paying us."

The stunned silence was interrupted by the ringing of the doorbell. I got up to answer it. I looked up at the CCTV screen. There was Lawrence, looking scruffier than ever. I buzzed him in. At least it was a different dandruff spangled jumper. This one had once been yellow.

"We thought you'd vanished," I said. "The meeting's started. Joan's chairing."

"I've not been well," he mumbled. "Had to have a few days in hospital," he added.

"Anything serious?"

"I suffer from chronic anxiety," he said, "and I needed help with my OCD."

"OCD?"

"Obsessive compulsive disorder," he said, looking at me like I was some kind of moron. Privately, I wished he had the kind of obsessive compulsive disorder that led to excessive cleanliness.

"We're through here," I said, leading the way into the meeting room. All eyes turned to look at him. Joan was the first to speak.

"Hello Lawrence. Come and join us. Do you want to take over as Chair? We've only just started."

"No, no, you carry on. I'm still…you know. Not quite…"

"No. Of course. Well, if you're sure…" Joan said. Lawrence shuffled into a vacant chair and reached across the table for a sandwich.

"So, to recap," said Joan, peering through half moon glasses at her notes, "our financial situation is dire and there are questions to be answered about where large amounts of money have gone. Geri and Nikki are concerned about being paid. Gordon is in custody. Our centre has never been more vulnerable. And the question is, what do we do now?" No-one answered her. No-one had an appetite for the sandwiches apart from Lawrence.

"What happens to us as trustees?" he finally asked.

"You're the Chair. What do you think happens?" retorted Maryam, who was feistier than I could have imagined at first meeting.

"Maybe we should be getting some legal advice," offered Bernard. "Talk to a solicitor, perhaps?"

"Go to the police, more like," said Maryam. "I mean, am I the only one who thinks there's been fraud here? Where has all that money gone? And if they're already looking into Veronica's death, aren't we withholding evidence by not telling them?"

"I don't think we should call in the police yet. I need better access to the accounts," said Derek. "I'm sure there's an explanation and I'd like to do some more work with the figures. Gordon had said something about moving funds to a higher interest account. Maybe that's all that's happened."

"Maybe one of you should visit Gordon in the nick," I threw in.

"Yes, Nikki's right," said Rita. "He's the key to this. He's the only one who will know what happened to the money."

"I could talk to the bank," added Derek.

"But if someone's been fiddling the books, alerting the bank at this point is the last thing we want to do," countered Rita.

"Why?" asked Bernard.

"They'll close us down, won't they? Bring in the cops. If we can find a simple answer..."

"Not likely, is it?" said Maryam. "I mean, that there's a simple answer." Silently I agreed with her.

"We need to know if we'll be personally liable," rejoined Lawrence, spluttering a stray morsel of cheese across the table. "I mean, we could all be bankrupted by this. That'd finish me." Derek threw him an odd look. Lawrence already seemed pretty finished to me, and his self-absorption made me want to shake him. I wished Brent were still alive. He'd have known what to do. I thought the committee probably needed to at least talk to the Charity Commission, the cumbersome quango that regulated our weird and wonderful voluntary sector. And I thought talking to Gordon would be a good first step. If Veronica's office hadn't been cleared up, would she have left a note somewhere? Would there be any clues in her computer files? In his? We hadn't begun to look there. I decided to speak up.

"Look, Geri and I have searched for paper records relating to Veronica and Gordon," I said, "and we haven't found anything." For some reason I didn't mention that Gordon's personnel file had gone missing. After all, I still didn't know who had been in the centre arguing at the weekend. I didn't know whom here I could trust – or at least, whom I couldn't. "But we haven't looked in the computer files. Maybe there's a note somewhere to explain what happened to the money. It could all be in a high interest account, as Derek said."

"Then we need to peruse the statements," said Derek. He had a point. "I meant to ask these questions at the last meeting, but then Veronica…"

"Yes," said Joan. "And then Veronica…"

I was feeling antsy and wished they'd come to at least one decision. Rita must have read my mind.

"I'll see if I can track down Gordon," she said. "I know a couple of the lads down the nick. They'll tell me where he's being held. Then how about I ask him what's happened to the money?"

"Good idea," said Joan. "Everyone agreed?" They all nodded.

"Not that it'll do us much good!" spat Maryam

"If it's likely to lessen our personal risk," Lawrence muttered.

"Only way to move us on," said Bernard, the agreeable pragmatist. I noted down the decision – the first this meeting – before they could change their minds.

"If we've got four thousand in the bank, can I suggest you pay us?" I asked boldly. "And Felicity?"

"Yes, I think we can do that," said Joan, looking at Derek for approval.

"Problem is, Veronica and Gordon are cheque signatories," said Derek. I can countersign, but it needs one of them to sign unless we go to the bank, and then we'll have to tell them what's happening…"

"I'll take the cheques with me, then," said Rita. We had a second decision.

"So do you want us to carry on? And what help will you give us?" I asked.

"Might be safer to freeze everything and stop all activities until everything is sorted out," said Lawrence.

"If we do that, it'll be curtains for *Action in Caring*," said Rita. "We'll lose the remaining trade to SoLCEC and we'll never open again. I say we keep open. And if it's any help, I'll give Geri and Nikki some back-up." I could have hugged her – although maybe it would be in my best interests for the centre to close. Then Chantelle and I could start over again....

"Is that acceptable to everyone?" asked Joan. There was a muttering that sounded more positive than negative – although only just.

"Well, that's agreed then," she said. "Is there any other business?"

"I only came to tender my resignation," said Maryam.

"Well, that's a shame," said Rita.

"You'll have to get yourself another token Asian," added Maryam

"You were never a token," said Joan. "We'll be sad to lose you. But if there's nothing else?" There was silence. "Then I declare this meeting closed," she said.

Chapter 16

I rang Carla, got her voicemail. *Hi Carla, it's me…how's the arm? You in? Thought I'd pop over…weird day…you'd never believe…* but my time to leave a message had run out, and I was kicked off line. I might as well go over anyway. Just as I was mounting my bike, my mobile vibrated and the Eurythmics sang out their tinny song.

"Hi Nikki?"

"Hey Carla. How're you doing?"

"Not so bad. Can you bring something to eat? Pizza would be good…"

"Fiorentina with extra mushrooms?"

"What else! And cheese cake. I'm depressed. I need something sweet."

"Give me half an hour."

Pizza Express lived up to their name, and within thirty minutes I was ringing Carla's door bell, bearing pizza for her, salad for me, and two cheese cakes. I'd picked up a bottle of Chianti on the way too. Carla let me in.

"How's the arm?"

"Still hurts. Over five more weeks of being in plaster. I'm fed up already," she said. Carla was one of those fit, active people who hated being ill or incapacitated.

"How'd it go with Siobhan?" I asked.

"Great. Really good to hook up with her again. You know, Nik, I just don't understand why we broke up."

"I never understood that either. You getting back together then?"

"Maybe. She's coming over at the weekend."

"I've always liked Siobhan. I think she's good for you."

"Is that a vote of confidence?"

"Yeah, I s'pose it is. And if you guys get hitched and do the civil partnership thing…"

"Don't call it marriage!"

"I didn't. But if you do it, promise me I'll be there as a witness."

"As long as you promise not to cry."

"I'll try to keep the snivelling *sotto voce*."

"Deal. Now will you please get on and cut up that pizza for me?" I did. Carla fumbled with the stereo and put on an old Annie Lennox CD that we both loved: *Diva*. We ate quietly, while Annie asked *Why?*.and then walked on broken glass. I was surprised at how hungry I was, despite my big lunch with Suresh. Ginger crept in and tried to steal some cheese from Carla's plate.

"Bugger off, you flea ridden moggy," I shouted at him. He ignored me, like he always does. I could say anything to that cat and he'd carry on in his own smelly way. "You've got to do something about his manners," I said to Carla.

"Tried. Failed. He's geriatric now. Probably got the cat equivalent of Alzheimer's. I've given up. So should you."

"Hmm," I grunted.

"So, what's the latest at *Action in Caring*?" asked Carla. I filled her in on the day's events.

"I can't say I'm surprised that Suresh held out on you," she said.

"Really?"

"I've never trusted him. He's ambitious. A journo. What do you expect?"

"Well…he's also a mate. We lived together, for Christ's sake!"

"Student flat shares don't count."

"This one does."

"Whatever. But that thing with Chantelle. That's creepy. D'you think Tanya's death was an accident?"

"I don't know what to believe. It could have been an accident. Other people have died in accidents with trams. But then it seems to be

161

too much of a coincidence. She sees something iffy with the bank statement, is sacked, goes up to Manchester, is dead within a month. As is her former boss. It feels like something very bad is going on, and I don't know what or why." We'd finished the Chianti. "Got any more wine?"

"In the cupboard next to the fridge."

"At least I should get paid," I said, returning to Carla's living room bearing a new bottle. Her cream coloured carpet needed a hoover and the glass coffee table was smudged with fingerprints. I'd offer before I left. Carla liked her flat to be clean and tidy.

"You still meeting Ruth tomorrow?" My stomach lurched at the jolt to my memory.

"Yeah. At least, she hasn't cancelled," I said.

"What do you think she wants?"

"Me?" We both laughed. That was the least likely reason why Ruth had called. But then again...

"Nik, you need to protect yourself," said Carla.

"What, you mean safe sex? That sort of thing?"

"You know what I mean. That woman hurt you. She'll hurt you again if you don't take care."

"I'm older now, wiser..."

"You're sweet and soft and a sucker for anyone who shows you a bit of affection," said Carla. Damn! She was so right.

"So d'you think I should cancel?"

"Well, that's one option, but I know you won't take it. For what it's worth, I think you should think about putting a time boundary on the evening. Have something you have to go on to. Me, for example. So it's clear from the beginning that you're there to hear what she has to say, but you have to get to my place by nine."

"It's a plan," I admitted.

"And I'm a friend in need," she grinned. "Where's the cheese cake, then?"

"I'll get it."

Thursday morning. What weirdness would today throw my way? Geri was already at work when I arrived. So were a dozen angry people with placards reading *No nonces* and *Death to perverts*. I felt like I was battling through a picket line as I pushed through the crowd towards the door. News of Gordon's arrest had clearly got around.

"What kind of place is this?" screamed a young woman with ratty hair. She grabbed at my sleeve, but I pulled away. "We thought our kids was safe here, but they wasn't, was they?"

"And you bastards must have known!" bellowed a man with a shaven head whose body was taut with anger, fists clenched. "You did fuck all."

"I'm sorry," I said. "I'm new. We didn't know."

"Yeah, that's what they all say," spat the woman.

"Great! Just what we need!" I grimaced as Geri secured the door behind me.

"You can't blame them," she said.

"I know."

"Maybe we should talk with them," said Geri.

"D'you think they're in the mood to listen?"

"It's either that or we have to call the police, and I'd rather not do that."

"Want me to have a go?" She nodded. I took a deep breath, opened the door again. I heard a click and saw a large camera pointed in my direction. The day just kept on getting better: now the press were involved.

"Hello," I tried. The crowd was chanting *Close the centre, kill the pervs.*

"Hey," I shouted. "Please just give me a moment. Please listen."

"Why should we?" bawled the loud man.

"Because we're on your side," I yelled back. The crowd quietened. "Look, we're as angry about this as you are. Do you think we want to work somewhere where kids are at risk? We're here, Geri and me, because we care about people and especially about kids."

"Yeah, you say that now, but you let 'im get away with it," said the woman with ratty hair. "You didn't do nuffink to protect our kids."

"The man who's been accused of child abuse isn't here. He's in prison," I reasoned. "And we don't know if he's guilty or the victim of rumours. We're trying to keep this centre open for you, your kids, the old folk, the community." There was a murmuring. Geri stepped up to my side.

"We're doing what we can to keep the centre safe and decent," she said. "Please, work with us."

"How many kids did he molest, love?" shouted the man with the camera. Press. You can rely on them to turn up just when you don't want them. I might have to call in a favour or two from Suresh.

"We're confident he didn't harm any young person at this centre," said Geri. "He was an administrator. He didn't have direct contact with the young people coming here. And we're none of us alone with kids, anyway. The point is, if what they're saying is true, and we don't know that it is, he still shouldn't have worked anywhere near young people. But we have good child protection procedures. No-one got hurt."

"Yeah, you would say that!" cried ratty haired woman.

"No, Jade, she might have a point," said an older woman.

"If anything bad did happen, it'll come out and there'll be an investigation," I said. "Just work with us to keep this centre open – as a safe place for you and your kids."

"What do you mean, work with you?" asked the older woman.

"We need volunteers. Good people to keep this place alive," I said.

"If you come in now, we'll make some tea and we can sit down and decide what to do next," said Geri. There was silence. Even the reporter had let his camera drop by his side. The crowd shuffled. I noticed a couple of people sloping off towards the kebab shop. Jade stood with her hands on her hips. She looked at the older woman, who nodded.

"Ok," said Jade, tucking her hair behind her ears. "We'll talk." The angry man unclenched his fists and flexed his fingers.

"But it better be good," he growled.

After tea, the protestors left. We'd reached an agreement. Jade, the angry man, whose name was Pete, and the older woman, whose name was Iris, would come in to back us up for a day a week each. Geri and I looked at each other.

"Girl, we're good," she said. "Where'd you learn to do that?"

"What?"

"Conflict resolution. Whatever it was. Magic."

"Seemed like the right thing to do," I said. "Just seemed like getting into a fight with them wouldn't get anyone anywhere. Anyway, it was your idea to have tea. What made you think of that?"

"I thought about what my gran would have done. She'd have put the kettle on."

The doorbell rang. A tall woman with light brown hair in a dark suit stood next to a shorter man, also suited, blowing his nose on a cotton hanky.

"Hi," said Geri, as if she knew them.

"Ms Francis. We've just come to take a few more details. And this is….?"

"Nikki. Nikki Elliot. She started work last week and she was with Veronica Stein when she…you know…when she…"

"Died?" said the woman.

"Yes," said Geri. These, then, were the detectives. The woman turned to me.

"Ginny Lancaster," she said, holding out her hand. "DCI Ginny Lancaster." A light dusting of freckles made her face look somehow wholesome, healthy, yet there was a sharpness about it. "And this is Sergeant Darren Lowe."

"So you're looking into Veronica's death?"

"Was it you who found the epi-pen?" Her accent was Essex. East of Ilford.

"Yeah. I found it in the meeting room. It'd got hidden under a chair."

"So how did you come to find it?" Shit! What would she think about my Sunday prowling around? Would I be making myself look guilty – or at the very least, dodgy, by admitting sneaking around the building over the weekend?

"I, uh, I…had come into the building on Sunday. I'd left something here. A book. I needed to come back for it." She looked at me quizzically. I wasn't sure she believed the bit about the book. "And…I heard voices. Angry voices upstairs. Men arguing over something – I couldn't catch what – and I was scared, so I hid. I know it's daft and it sounds crazy, but I was still pretty spooked by Veronica's dying, and I just dived into the meeting room and squatted down by the curtains. That's where I found the epi-pen."

"Did you find your book?"

"Yes. Yes, I found my book."

"What was it?"

"Sorry?"

"The book. What was it called?"

"Oh." I had to think quickly. What was I reading? "Jackie Kay," I said. "It was by Jackie Kay. Short stories. The first was about a woman in a supermarket who talks a lot." Darren Lowe hadn't said a word, but he was writing everything down, and he kept glancing up at me. Ginny Lancaster gave me a long look and then nodded.

"Ok," she said. "We may need to ask you more questions later on."

"That's fine," I said. "There's something I think you should know, though."

"Oh?"

"There was a woman who worked here. Tanya Middleton. She had my job. She'd got sent here by the Jobcentre, like me. Sounds like she was bright, knew her stuff."

"And?"

"Well…she's dead. She thought there was something dodgy going on with the money, and she said something and they sacked her. So she went to Manchester, and then she got run down by a tram, only she might have been pushed, and now she's dead." I paused for breath. My heart was beating too fast. Just talking about Tanya made her death more real, more scary.

"I see." Ginny Lancaster turned towards the door and Darren Lowe stopped writing.

"Is that it?" I asked. With all that was going on, I'd expected a bit more questioning.

"For now," said Ginny, with a small smile. And then they were gone.

No sooner had they gone than the doorbell rang again. I glanced up at the monitor and saw a short, dumpy woman clutching an oversized shopping bag that looked empty. I buzzed open the door.

"Pauline?"

"Yes. Hello." She shifted uncomfortably from one leg to the other. She looked as if she were weighted down with cares.

"I'm Nikki. We spoke on the phone."

"Yes."

"You've come for Veronica's things?"

"Yes. I've come for my sister's…" A tear rolled down her face. She was grey with misery.

"Would you like a cup of tea?"

"If it's not too much…I'm sorry…" the tears were falling fast. "Such a shock…"

Geri came out from her office. "This is Pauline, Veronica's sister," I said.

Geri stretched out a hand towards the woman. "I'm really sorry," she said.

"I'll go and make some tea," I said. "Maybe you could…"

"I'll take you to Veronica's office," said Geri.

"Thank you," said Pauline.

Geri led the way to Veronica's office and I busied myself in the kitchen. I made three mugs of tea and took them into Geri's little room. After five minutes they came to join me there. Pauline's shopping bag held the sad contents of Veronica's drawer.

"Well, I suppose that's it, then," she said.

"Were you close?" I asked.

"She was my big sister. She's – was – four years older than me. She was good to our parents as they got older. After her marriage broke up, she became their carer. Then when our mother died, and soon after our father, we saw less of each other. She'd had a few different jobs, and she came to work here, and that seemed to take up most of her time. I think she was happy here. I hope so, anyway."

"Did she have many friends?" I asked.

"I don't know. She belonged to an amateur dramatic group for a time. She didn't mention friends. She must have had some."

I wondered: maybe you could go through life without the kind of friends that I took for granted. I suddenly felt lucky to be alive, lucky to have people like Carla and Benjamin in my life, people I could rely on, as much to enjoy the fun times as those when things got tough. "Was she worried about anything?" I asked. Geri gave me a dark look.

"Not that I know of. But then she probably wouldn't have told me. She never said much about the problems in her marriage, but then she and Des divorced. I think she had some money worries, but she never said much about it." She sniffed and then blew her nose into a grubby tissue. "Anyway, you've both been very kind. I'd best be off." She stood up, put on her coat, picked up the shopping bag.

"Will you let us know about the funeral?" asked Geri.

"Yes. Yes, I'll do that," said Pauline.

We walked her to the front door and watched her stooped figure trudge away.

With the drama of the morning over, my mind turned to my meeting that evening with Ruth. Much more scary than facing a bunch of hurt and angry parents or a very self-controlled detective. I tried to bring my focus back to work.

"What's on for today, then?" I asked.

"Joan's art class. Not much else," said Geri.

"Maybe we should carry on with tying up loose ends," I said. "See whether those invoices were ever passed and signed. See if we can find anything else to shed light on Veronica or Gordon."

"That's what I thought."

" So, you tackle the personnel files while I sort through the rest of the admin?" I suggested.

"Cool."

Joan arrived in time to set up her class. Shortly after, Justin arrived, minus his usual crowd of delinquents.

"G'day, ladies," he said, sounding sprightly. "I'm here for the ...what do you call it? Life drawing?"

"So you're our model for today," said Joan, trying to hide her amusement.

"Sure am," said our own antipodean Adonis. The artists started arriving, looking more glamorous than usual, as if they were going on an outing rather than attending their weekly art class. Well, whatever turns you on...

I started ploughing through the mounds of administrative paperwork, looking for anything that would shed light on how Veronica met her end and anything connecting Tanya to recent events. There were committee papers from the Council, which told me what I already knew: that the new SoLCEC was the rising star, that money was being redirected there from community resources including *Action in Caring*. There was nothing new. Could it all have been a terrible accident? Anyway, my mind was on the evening. How would it be, seeing Ruth after all this time? And what was it she wanted? Fantasies of happy ever after jostled against scenes of sad farewells, partings of the way. Not that, please. Not yet.

By lunchtime, the art class had finished and a dozen women had giggled their way out of the building. There'd been some new faces, so at least Justin was proving good for business. The man himself swaggered past.

"Laters," he'd said, waving as he sauntered out of the door. For once he sounded more Streatham than Sydney. Geri asked if I was going to have lunch.

"No, think I'll skip it today," I said. "Had a big breakfast," which was a lie. As I was considering asking Geri if I could leave early, the doorbell rang. Rita stepped in, looking flushed. Prudence was panting at her side.

"God, it's hot out there!" she exclaimed.

"Tea?" I asked.

"Ooh, yes. You're a love."

"No problem." I went out to the kitchen and made her a mug of strong tea. I filled a bowl with water for Prudence.

"Geri's office," Rita said. I followed her. Prudence followed me, tongue hanging out, whether for me – her latest crush – or for the water, it was hard to tell. Only when I put the bowl down on the floor, it was clear to see that I was no competition for fresh water on a warm spring day.

"Call Geri," Rita said. I went to find Geri, who was still trawling through personnel files in Veronica's office.

"So you've seen Gordon?" said Geri.

"I've seen Gordon," Rita confirmed. Prudence, sated by the water, flopped onto my feet and idly chewed at a Kicker lace.

"And?" I said.

"And he's signed the pay cheques," said Rita.

"Great!" Geri and I chorused. We'd get paid. I didn't have to face homelessness. Not yet.

"And?" said Geri.

"And he says there's another account. Says there's nothing iffy about the money, that he's put it in a high interest account."

"Did he say where?" asked Geri.

"Said it's in the HSBC and if you looked in the finance files, you'd find all the info," said Rita. "Said he'd meant to tell Derek but didn't get a chance."

"So he's on the level?" I asked, and I must have sounded incredulous.

"I wouldn't go that far," said Rita.

"I'll go and look," said Geri.

We didn't speak while she was away. So much hung on what she found. When she came back, she was holding a file and looking puzzled. "It's here," she said. "The missing money is in another account, like he said. And it's in *AiC's* name ok. But why didn't he tell me? Or Derek?" I flashed back to that Sunday afternoon, hiding in Veronica's office, an argument raging above me. What had that all been about? I was sure one of the men had been Gordon, but who was the other one?

"Maybe he'd been planning to siphon it off, but hadn't got around to it," suggested Rita. It sounded likely.

"Look at the signatories," said Geri, handing Rita a sheet of paper.

"Gordon Smedley and Lewis Fairclough," read Rita. "Who's Lewis Fairclough?"

"Who knows? He's no-one who works here and he's not a trustee," said Geri.

"He *was* going to fiddle the books!" cried Rita. "Looks like we got there just in time."

"Main thing is it's here, and we're not broke," I said.

"You've done really well. Thanks," said Geri, grinning at Rita. "We'll need to let Ginny Lancaster know. I'll ring her in a sec."

"What else did he say? Anything about the kids?"

"Just that it was all lies and he'd never hurt a kid," said Rita.

"Paedophiles always argue that kids love it and what they're doing isn't abuse," I said. "Still, innocent 'til proven guilty, and all that."

"We'd better let people know about the money," said Geri. "I'll e-mail the management committee."

"I'd better pick up my other charges and walk them round the common," said Rita. At the magic word, Prudence bounced up, relinquishing my shoelace. "I'll pop in tomorrow," said Rita, as she headed for the door.

"D'you think Veronica knew? That she found out, and that's why she died?" asked Geri.

"It gets worse, doesn't it? Just doesn't seem real." I hated how things were turning out. The latent nastiness lurking behind even the most benign seeming organisation.

"I'll try to get hold of Ginny Lancaster."

"Look, this may not be the best time, but do you mind if I slip away a bit early?" I asked Geri.

"Hot date?"

"Probably not."

"Well, good luck. See you tomorrow."

I chained my bike to the railings outside the Bedford. A train rumbled by, clanking to a halt at Balham station. I could go home. Forget I ever had this arrangement with Ruth. Claim that something had come up at work. I could do that, chicken out. I had the feeling that nothing would be the same again if I went through the door into the pub.

But sometimes choice is just an illusion. I had to see this through. I took a deep breath in and puffed it out. The evening air was chilly. I thought I could smell daffodils mixed up with the heady city stench of exhaust fumes and tyre dust. I pushed through the double doors. I didn't see her at first and didn't know whether to feel relief or gloom. Then I saw her curled in a chair by the fire. She was watching me. When she saw that I'd seen her, she gave a small wave. I moved towards her, not sure what to do with my face.

"You're here," I said.

"You're late," she said.

"I'm not. I'm on time."

"Near enough, for you," she conceded. For a woman who spends most of her time in places where time is at best stretchy, she was ridiculously picky about punctuality. Ruth looked great. Black jeans, denim jacket over white linen shirt. She'd grown her hair, and it swung in a feathery bob below her jaw. Months in a hot climate had lightened it to pale blonde. She wore silver spiral earrings, and a large pendant of silver and shell at the base of her throat. When times were bad, her eyes were grey and clouded. Tonight they were blue and clear. God, she was beautiful.

"What are you drinking?" I asked

"Juice," she said. "Pineapple. Thanks." Strange. She was usually a sauvignon blanc type of woman. I went to the bar and ordered her juice and a pint of Guinness.

"Extra cold or normal?" asked the barman. Another Aussie. They were getting everywhere.

"Don't care. Whatever comes," I said.

"Well which do you want? We've got both."

"I don't know." He gave me a look that said *why can't women ever make up their bloody minds?* And stood, each hand poised over a different pump.

"Cold, then. Extra cold."

"Cool." I took the glasses back to Ruth and lowered myself into the armchair at right angles to hers.

"So how are you?"

"I'm good. I've just been feeling bad about not being in touch. So how about you? You're looking well. Have you really got a job?"

"Well I had to do something while you were out saving the world."

"I'm glad. You needed to get back into the swing of things."

"Thanks. Great that I've got your approval." She'd missed the sarcasm and just smiled. She was only partly here.

"So…what's happening? You've not been writing and I didn't know you were in London." *And how can I decide whether I'm in love with you if I never see or hear from you?*

"Mm. I'm sorry, Nikki, but I've had a lot going on, and we didn't part on the best of terms, did we?"

"It would've been nice to know that you were back. You know, safe and well, that sort of thing." *And I've missed you. I've missed you a lot.*

"Like I said, Nikki, lots going on, and I needed some time on my own. It's good to see you, though. I've always really cared about you." She hadn't missed me, I could tell. This was a meeting that she had to get through. I was a chore, maybe unfinished business. She was here because she had to be, out of some sense of duty, not because she wanted to spend time with me.

"I've only got an hour," I said. "I'm going over to Carla's. She's making a special meal. We arranged it weeks ago."

"Give her my love, then. Look, Nikki, I wanted to see you because there's something I need to tell you. Well, *want* to tell you."

"Oh?" I watched her pick at an invisible thread on her knee. "You've made Aid Worker of the Year and we're going to the ball?"

"Oh, Nik, you don't change, do you?"

"What's that supposed to mean?"

174

"Nothing. Just…Oh God, there's no easy way to say this." I felt cold. Whatever was coming, I wasn't going to like it. *Stay cool, Nikki.* I took a long drink of the Guinness that was already tepid from being too close to the fire. Ruth looked down at the floor and then up at me with those killer eyes.

"I'm getting married."

"Oh. I see. What's her name?" This was worse than I could have dreamt. I could just leave here and now. But I had to know. I'd come this far.

"Not her. Him. I mean, *really* getting married. Not the civil partnership thing."

"Him?"

"We met in Gaza."

"Him? You're marrying a man?"

"Tawfiq. His name's Tawfiq."

"But a *man*? How can you marry a man?"

"It just happened. I was never like you, Nikki. You knew I was more bisexual, that I might fall for a man again. I never hid that from you."

"Yeah, well, sorry if I got the wrong idea, Ruth, but you seemed pretty gay when we were in bed together."

"Nikki, it was great. Really great. You're a brilliant person and I really do care for you, that's why I needed to see you tonight; but I need to do this."

"So, what we had…"

"Was special. Really special. Great. You're a special person, really special…"

"Look, will you stop saying *really*? Because none of this feels at all real to me."

"I'm sorry, Nikki. I'd hoped you'd wish us well…"

"You're marrying some Arab and you want…"

"Palestinian. He's Palestinian. His family lost everything."

"Oh! I get it! You're on a rescue mission! Fuck an Arab – sorry, Palestinian – and make the world a better place!"

"I'm pregnant."

"What?"

"Our baby's due in October."

"Jesus, Ruth! Are you nuts?"

"I'm three months gone. I really want this baby. And I love Tawfiq."

"So…you and me…what was that all about? You said you loved me! You knew *I* loved you."

"I'm sorry, Nik. Really sorry." If I didn't leave there and then I'd be sick or pass out or do something even more embarrassing like cry. I stood up.

"Bye Ruth. Good luck."

"Nikki…" but I had turned away. I couldn't ever look into those eyes again. To glance back at her would be fatal. Lady of Shallot stuff. I strode to the door. Yanked it open, stepped into the cold spring night. My bike was still there and intact. My hands shook as I unlocked it. Ten minutes to Carla's. That was all. I shoved the chain and padlock into my back-pack. Ten minutes to safety. Then something crashed into the back of my head and what consciousness I still had after Ruth's bombshell spiralled dizzily away.

Chapter 17

There were voices. A too loud chatter of voices. *She's coming round* someone said. I could taste metal and smell my own fear. There was pain. Pain in my head, pain gripping my neck. A deep, deep sickness in my belly. I tried to move and couldn't. *Don't try to move* said a woman's voice. *Oh my God it's Nikki!* Said another, one that sounded familiar only I couldn't place the name. *What's happened to her? Make way please. I'm a friend.* Someone I used to know. I wanted my mum. I wanted her more than ever before. I had to call her. I tried to sit up, to reach for my phone, but my arms felt paralysed. I would die here. Where was here? I was going to Balham, but I couldn't remember why. Something to do with an Arab. A baby. And then I heard the voice again and remembered whose it was. Ruth. Ruth was here, even though she was out of my life. Pregnant. She'd told me she was pregnant. The sickness in my belly twisted and rose, escaping in a stinking spurt of Guinness and bile. I didn't want anyone to see me like this. Someone was holding my hand.

"The ambulance is here, Nikki. I'll come with you. You'll be ok."

Hearing Ruth's voice was unbearable. "Fuck off Ruth," I muttered as another swirl of nausea vortexed into the pain. *She drunk or what?* I heard a man ask.

"She's not drunk, she's been attacked," said Ruth.

"Can you tell us your name, love?" asked a loud man's voice.

"She's Nikki Elliot," I heard Ruth say.

"Can you tell us what happened, love?" asked the man.

"Carla," I said. "Call Carla."

"Do you remember what happened?" persisted the man.

"Head hurts."

"Police are here," said a woman. "Don't try to move," she added. "We'll soon have you safe and in hospital."

"What happened?" asked someone else, a woman, a voice that sounded faintly familiar. Scottish. East coast, not Glasgow.

"Dunno," said the man, who was feeling my pulse with latex gloved fingers. "Looks like she was attacked. Bag's still there, though. Don't look like they took anything. Nasty bang on the head." I felt him gently feel behind my head and wrap something sturdy around my neck. I tried to move my head and couldn't.

"Don't try to move, love," said the paramedic. "You've got a neck brace on. Just in case."

"Do we know who she is?" asked the woman. Where had I heard that voice? I tried to open my eyes.

"She's Nikki Elliot. We were having a drink. She left. I left a minute or two later, and there she was, on the ground." *Fuck off, Ruth and let me die in peace. I wasn't meant to see you again. Ever.*

"Nikki Elliot? I know that name." And I knew that voice.

"She work for Action in Caring?"

"Um…not sure. I just know she's got a new job," said Ruth.

"Nikki, can you tell me what happened?" Wendy Baggott. It was Sergeant Wendy Baggott. I'd be all right with Wendy in charge. Wendy to the rescue. Delicious Sergeant Wendy. So long Ruth.

"We're ready to take her to the hospital," said the paramedic. "You coming, Sergeant?"

"Och, why not? Nothing like a Thursday night in George's A and E."

"Could be worse. Could be Friday. Or Saturday," he said. Capable arms lifted me gently onto a stretcher.

"I'll come too," said Ruth.

"No," I said. "I don't want you. Call Carla. I'll be ok with Wendy. Sergeant Baggott."

"It *is* you!" said Wendy. "Not having much luck right now, are you?"

"No," I said, and passed out.

When I woke up, Wendy Baggott was by my side. There was a drip taped into my arm. I wasn't in pain and the nausea had subsided.

"What happened?" I asked, as a tiny nurse felt my pulse.

"I was hoping you'd tell me," said Wendy. "Someone bashed you on the head by the look of it. Can you remember anything?"

"Have I seen you at the Glass Bar?" I asked.

"Maybe," she said, and I could hear, rather than see her smile. "But I need to know what happened to you. D'you remember anything? See anyone?"

"No." It was all coming back to me. Ruth. The fire. Warm extra cold Guinness – someone should write a poem about it. Me. I felt lovely. All warm and safe and numb. So numb.

"Can you try?"

"Mm. She's pregnant."

"Who's pregnant?"

"Ruth. She's marrying an Arab called Toffee or Tofu or something." I didn't care. Wasn't bothered. Not bovvered.

"Is that why you were attacked?"

"No! He's in Gaza and she's gone. Out of my life. Poofff!"

"Is she delirious?" Wendy asked the nurse.

"Is the morphine. For pain." And she scuttled away on tiny light feet.

"Nikki, try to focus. Is anything missing from your bag?"

"Dunno. What's in it?" Just then I heard the familiar Eurythmics song that announced my phone ringing.

"That your phone?" asked Wendy, reaching into my bag. "Says it's Carla. You shouldn't really have a phone switched on in hospital."

"Please answer it. Carla'll wonder where I am. I'm supposed to be there, looking after her." I giggled at the irony. Wendy spoke into the phone.

"Hello? This is Sergeant Wendy Baggott. That's right. Yes, Nikki's here, but I'm afraid she's had a wee accident. No, nothing serious. Yes, she'll be ok. Hospital. St George's. Checking for concussion. What? Oh. No, someone hit her. Attacked her. Nasty bang on the head. Yeah, that's right. I'm sure she would. Let me hand you over." Wendy handed me the phone.

"Nik! What's happened? Are you ok?"

"Hey Carla! I'm cool. I'm in hospital. With Wendy Baggott. I like Wendy. She's looking after me."

"Are you drunk?"

"No! I didn't finish my pint. It's good, this hospital. Nice bed. Not too soft. Ruth's a cow."

"Who did this to you, Nikki?"

"Who did what?"

"I'm coming over."

"You've got a broken arm."

"I'm getting a cab."

I drifted in and out of sleep. Every time I woke up, Wendy was there. There was something I'd been meaning to say to her. What was it? Then Carla arrived. She looked tired and worried.

"Nikki, what happened?"

"Dunno. Someone hit me."

"You must be Carla," said Wendy Baggott.

"And you must be Sergeant Wendy Baggott," said Carla. "Have we met before?"

"Maybe."

"Thanks for looking after her. She sounded so out of it!"

"Pretty strong analgesic. Kills the pain and keeps her happy," said Wendy. "And just call me Wendy. Carla, can you do something for me? Can you look in her bag and tell me if anything's missing?"

180

"I'll try," said Carla. "You ever looked at the amount of junk that Nikki carries around?" Wendy didn't answer. I heard Carla rummaging around with her good arm.

"Her phone's here. Well, obviously, I called her on it. And here's her purse." I heard the rip of Velcro opening. "There's money. And her bankcard. And there's a credit card, and her Ritzy cinema membership card. Her bike chain and padlock. Looks like it's all there."

"Anything else? Anything missingl?" asked Wendy. I heard Carla rummage some more, and then the crackle of a sheet of paper.

"What's this? Oh my God! Listen to this!" Carla cried. "*This is a warning, cunt. Stop asking questions or your dead.* And they can't even get the right *you're*!"

"I'll take that as evidence," said Wendy, grimly. "Nikki, why would someone be warning you off? What are you involved in?"

"Don't ask me, Wendy," I said. "But I talked to Ginny Lancaster about the epi-pen. Tanya died. She was the receptionist before me. Found out stuff. Went to Manchester and got run down by a tram. Chantelle thinks it wasn't an accident."

"Who's Chantelle?"

"Long nails. Jobcentre. Wendy, will you go out with me?"

"Not tonight, Nikki." So there was hope. I slipped back into some technicolour dreamworld where Ruth's eyes were bright as sapphires and babies were coming out of her mouth and Wendy was naked and in my kitchen making toast.

When I next woke, Wendy and Carla had gone. In their place sat my mother, who was leafing through a new-age magazine. My head hurt and my mouth tasted of old vomit and blood. I tried to sit up. The pain in my head oozed down my neck and into my shoulders. But the good news was that I didn't feel sick or dizzy any more.

"Hi mum," I said.

She stood up to give me a hug.

"Ouch!"

"Sorry, sorry darling."

"You been here long?"

"Carla called me last night. I came then, but you were out of it. They said you were stable, so I went home and then came back this morning."

"What's the time?"

"Nearly midday. You've been asleep for almost twelve hours. Can you remember what happened?"

"I was in the Bedford. Ruth gave me the big kiss-off. I left, and someone hit me on the head. Oh, and Wendy Baggott. I remember Wendy Baggott."

"She'll be along this afternoon."

"Did she say anything? Like who hit me?"

"Just that there was a warning note in your bag. Nikki, what's going on?" She looked so worried.

"I got a job. Just like everyone said I should."

"Ruby's worried. She wants to come and see you." I loved my niece, but I didn't want her to see me like this.

"Tell her we'll go out next week."

I heard footsteps marching down the corridor. Every other step was punctuated by a squeak. Benjamin's face peered anxiously around my cubicle.

"Hey Nikki, how're you doing?"

"Oh, you know. Big headache. Bit worried that someone might have it in for me."

"What've you got yourself into?" I wished people would stop asking me that. I'd been perfectly happy signing on, doing the odd bit of off the cards bar work, being a good friend and watching enough daytime TV to write a PhD on Aussie small town soaps. Then Tony Blair and co got it into their heads that everyone should Get A Job, so off I went. As far as I was concerned, I hadn't got myself into anything: I'd followed Big Brother's instructions and shit had happened. Big time.

"Ben, can you rescue my bike for me? It's outside the Bedford. I think I'd unlocked it."

"Umm…ok. Yeah, I'll go and see if it's still there."

"It better be. I paid Clancy £40 for a new front wheel."

"Do you want to come home? Just for a few days?" asked Mum.

"No, it's ok. I just want to get back to the flat. Sort things out," I said. Once you've left home, you really don't want to go back.

"I'm worried about you being on your own."

"I won't be. Ben's downstairs, and Carla will come round. Anyway, I'm nearly ok." Ben gave me a look I couldn't read.

"Well…if you're sure…"

"Yeah. Thanks, Mum."

"How did it go with Ruth?" asked Ben.

"Tell you later," I said.

They discharged me from hospital after lunch and I took a cab home. The car was an old, but stately, Nissan. Half of the gee-gaws ever manufactured in China seemed to be dangling in front of the windscreen.

"Where to?" the driver asked, glancing at me in his mirror. I must have looked a sight, because he added, "You been in wars, innit?"

"Kind of," I said, and gave him my address.

"Your boyfriend do that to you?" he asked.

"No. I don't know who did it," I said.

"Too much violence. London, Birmingham, Glasgow, everywhere too much violence. Me, I've had enough. I'm saving up, then I'll take the missus and the kids away. Somewhere nice, innit. America. Or Germany."

"Where are you from?"

"Afghanistan, innit."

I struggled up the stairs to my flat. I just wanted to sleep and mend. I was still reacting to the heavy-duty painkillers. I picked up the mail. There was a letter from the bank with a first class stamp, which probably meant I was in trouble. I shoved it under the phone with last week's credit card bill. I checked the ansaphone. There was a message from Ruth: *I'm really sorry, Nikki, hope you're feeling better. Call me.* And one from Geri: *Hi Nikki, you haven't turned up for work. Just wondered if you were ok.* And one from Detective Chief Inspector Ginny Lancaster: *Ms Elliot, I'd like to talk with you this evening. I'll come round at around six. Please let me know if that's a problem.* I'd be pleased to speak to Ginny Lancaster. Maybe she could start putting all these pieces together. There was one final message: *That was just a warning, cunt. You mess with us, you're dead, you hear?* I felt sick. I knew the voice. Where had I heard it before? I knew it, but couldn't place it. Male. Young. Cold. Someone was trying to scare me off. Someone wanted me out of the way. Was it the same person who'd wanted Tanya out of the way? I shivered. He had my phone number. Did he know where I lived? I limped over to the front door. I never usually used the chain, but now I slid it into place. Better safe than sorry. Better alive than dead. As the painkillers wore off, the fear kicked in. Someone had hurt me and there could be worse to come.

I rang Geri, and told her what had happened. "So, I won't be in today," I said.

"My God, Nikki! You could've been killed!"

"Yeah," I said, and heard the tremor in my voice. "Ginny Lancaster's coming over to ask some questions later on," I said. "You know what, though?"

"What?"

"That voice on my ansaphone. I recognised it, but I just can't picture his face."

"Nikki...."

"What?"

"You take care now."

"I'll try." We said our goodbyes and I put the phone down. The doorbell rang and my pulse started to race.

"Who is it?" I stood close to the front door, but didn't move to open it.

"It's me," said Ben. "Open up Nik." I was so relieved to hear his voice that I nearly cried. I pulled back the chain and opened the door.

"What's with the chain?" asked Ben as he stepped in. I told him about the threatening phone message.

"Jesus, Nik! What's going on?"

"I wish I knew, Ben," I said, easing myself onto the sofa.

"I've brought wine," he said.

"Good. I could do with a glass. Do you mind doing the honours?" He smiled and started rummaging around in my messy kitchen drawer.

"Corkscrew?"

"Somewhere in there. Keep looking." There was more clanking of cutlery.

"Aha!" I heard, and knew he'd found it. "You sure you should drink after that bang on the head?"

"One can't hurt." He came back with two glasses of red wine.

"It's all too weird," he said. "Did you meet Ruth?"

"Yeah. And I kind of wish I hadn't."

"Why?" I told him about Ruth and her Gaza man and the baby. Ben whistled when I got to the bit about her getting married.

"Shit, Nik. What's the universe trying to tell you?"

"Fuck knows." I finished off the glass of wine. Suddenly I felt very weary. "Ben, if you don't mind, I'm going to bed now."

"Want me to go?"

"Yeah. And I want to put the chain on the door."

"I don't like this."

"Me neither. Did you get my bike?"

"'fraid not. No bike, not even the chain." I remembered undoing the lock before everything went dark. I couldn't afford a new bike, and I was fond of that one. What else was going to go wrong?

Chapter 18

The doorbell woke me from dreams set in a landscape peopled with faceless hoodies and men in chequered kafirs. I was paralysed as they advanced towards me, my screams drowned out by the roar of high speed trains. My head hurt and I felt groggy, but it was a relief to be awake. My bedside clock told me it was five past six. I had slept all afternoon. I remembered that Ginny Lancaster had said she'd be coming. I stumbled out of bed and pulled on my jeans and a sweatshirt. The doorbell rang again.

"Who is it?" I called.

"DCI Lancaster." I pulled back the chain and opened the door.

"Come on in." Her suit was light grey and fitted her perfectly. She wore a tailored light pink shirt underneath the jacket.

"Thanks. Feeling any better?"

"I'll live. I'm just scared. There was a threatening phone message on my machine when I got home this afternoon." She followed me into the flat. "Can I get you a drink?"

"Coffee, please."

"Black or white?"

"White, no sugar. Thanks." She walked over to my bookshelf as I went to make the coffee. I found a packet of chocolate digestives in the cupboard and put them on a plate.

"By the way, we've got your bike," she called through. "Your friend said it was yours as the ambulance was taking you to hospital. It's down at the station when you want to collect it."

"That's the best news I've heard in a while!" I said as I brought through the coffee and biscuits. "I thought someone had taken it, and there's no way I can buy a new one."

"So, what did you make of the Jackie Kay?" she asked.

"Pardon?"

"Jackie Kay. The book you went back to the centre to look for on Sunday. How was it?"

"Oh. I loved it. She's…you know…"

"Only it's not on your shelf, so I guess you're still reading it?"

"Yeah. Yeah, still reading it."

"By your bedside, is it?" My mind raced. What was this? Interrogation over my reading matter? And what *was* by my bed? I still hadn't finished the Ian Rankin. There was a pile. Ian Rankin was on the top.

"Probably. I dip in and out. Always got a few on the go at a time."

"Mmm." What did that mean?

"So…er…what are you reading?"

"Oh, I read all sorts. Not crime, though. Too close to home."

"Yeah, well, it would be." My head was starting to throb again. "So, have you found out anything?" I needed to know why she was here.

"About the assault on you or Mrs Stein's death?"

"How about we start with Veronica – Mrs Stein – and then move on to me?"

"The coroner's report was interesting," she offered. "Mrs Stein died of anaphylactic shock." So Benjamin had been right.

"An allergic reaction?"

"So it seems. There were traces of nut in her stomach."

"But she was allergic to nuts. They all knew that. I mean, we all knew that."

"Tell me again about the sandwiches." I went back over that first day. Told her about making the cheese and pickle plate, and then Geri coming in and saying that Veronica wouldn't eat cheese.

"So Geraldine Francis made Mrs Stein's sandwiches?"

"Yes. She went out especially for more bread. I told her there was ham in the fridge. She knew what spread to use and not to use butter."

"How would you describe the relationship between Mrs Stein and Ms Francis?" I had to think carefully how I responded.

"Veronica was rude to Geri. Demanding. But they'd worked together for a while and Geri knew – knows – how to do her job. I think she just wanted to do it well. She was worried about the centre losing business."

"How do you think she felt about Mrs Stein?"

"I don't know. It was my first day. Geri was stressed and she had a lot to do. She seemed to just do what she was asked, and quite a lot more, come to think of it."

"Did she like Mrs Stein?"

"I think they had a professional relationship. There were nuts on the table. Maybe Veronica took one by mistake."

"We're not ruling anything out."

"Geri wouldn't have done anything to hurt Veronica."

"You seem very sure. How long have you known Ms Francis?"

"Just over a week."

"I see. Now, about this phone message that you mentioned earlier, and the note in your bag?"

"Yeah. I'm trying not to be too freaked out about it all."

"Do you still have them?"

"Sergeant Baggott took the note. I can replay you the ansaphone message. It's digital so there's no tape." I realised I couldn't bear to hear it again. "Look, Ginny, could you maybe listen to it while I go to the loo?"

"Ok." I showed her to the phone and went to my bathroom. I could hear the voice through the door as I peed, but it was too muffled to be a real threat. I emerged when everything went quiet.

"Nasty," she said. "Any idea who would do this?"

"No, but I recognise the voice. Just can't place him."

"Let me know if you do." She reached for the door handle. "Thanks Nikki. That'll be all for now." And she was gone. I put the chain on the door. I hadn't asked her about Tanya. It would wait until tomorrow.

I was still tired, but too restless to go to bed. I was too scared to go out. I couldn't settle to watch TV. I wondered what Ginny Lancaster would have looked like in uniform. What was happening to me? I could return Ruth's message, but I didn't want to. I could ring Carla. Just as I was reaching for the phone, it rang. My belly twisted in fear that it would be my malevolent assailant, but the number flashing up was Ruby's.

"Hey Ruby. What's up?"

"Hi Auntie Nik. Nan told me about your accident. Sounds really awful. What happened?"

"Someone doesn't like me, and they decided to let me know."

"God, that's really random."

"No, it was me he was after." Random?

"Whatever. Want me to come round?"

"You not busy?"

"No. It'd be good to see you."

"Ok. It'd be good to catch up with you too." Ruby was nineteen years old and in her first year at university. I was proud of her. She'd worked hard at school, got three good A levels, and was studying psychology at Goldsmiths. Of course, she knew it all. More than me, certainly more than her parents, and usually more than my mum. But isn't that what being nineteen's all about? She earned her keep by waitressing at TGI Friday's.

"It's great," she'd said when I last saw her. "You see the whole spectrum of human behaviour. I'm going to do my dissertation on the inter-relationship between gender stereotypes and alcohol consumption in social situations." She'd got it all worked out.

Half an hour after her call, the doorbell rang. Ruby was wearing a fuchsia coloured tie-dyed cotton smock over a black T-shirt, over ripped bell-bottoms. Fashion fusion. I loved it. Her blonde hair frizzed out of an orange bandana.

"Hey, you look gorgeous!" I said, hugging her as she came in. "We'd better shut the door." I closed the door firmly and slid the chain into place.

"What's with the chain, Auntie Nik?" she asked. I gave her the short version of my recent escapades.

"What are the police doing about it?"

"Well, they're trying to work out what happened to Veronica – the woman who ran the centre where I work – and who's threatening me."

"Is there a connection?"

"I don't know."

"Shit. You could come and doss on my floor if you'd feel safer," she offered.

"Thanks. But I think I'll be ok here. Benjamin's downstairs." She gave me a look that said something like *and you think he's going to protect you from the heavies? Get real!*

"Whatever. So what's your new job like?"

"Not boring, that's for sure." I thought about all the people who came and went from *Action in Caring*. "There are art classes, yoga classes, grannies for peace, a young offenders' group." Suddenly I saw Dwayne's angry face, his cold eyes. "Shit! That's it!" I cried.

"What?"

"Dwayne. One of the young offenders. I'm sure it's his voice I heard on my ansaphone."

"The one who left the threatening message?"

"And probably knocked me over the head."

"Why would he do that?"

191

"He's a nasty piece of work. He's gone for Justin, the youth worker, twice since I've been there. He's been violent to his mum."

"But why you? Why would he threaten you?"

"I don't know. I separated him and Justin from a bust-up. Sent him packing. But I don't know how he'd know my phone number or why he'd threaten me, or why he'd attack me in that way. I'd expect him to lash out without thinking, but all this feels more planned."

"Could someone have put him up to it?"

"Maybe. Look, I'd better ring Ginny Lancaster, tell her that I've remembered whose voice it was. Want to get yourself a drink?"

"Got any diet Coke?"

"No."

"I'll pass, then." I found the piece of paper with Ginny's number and punched it in. She answered after two rings.

"DCI Lancaster," she said.

"Ginny? It's Nikki Elliot. Listen, I think I know who left that message for me. And maybe who attacked me."

"Go on,"

"One of the kids in the young offenders' group. His name's Dwayne. I don't know his last name. I recognised his voice. He's trouble." I told her about Dwayne's attack on Justin, and about his kicking off in the group. "Apparently he's violent to his mother, too."

"Any idea why he might be after you?"

"No. I'd have thought he'd be more likely to go for Justin, maybe even Geri."

"How sure are you it was his voice?"

"Very sure. And the way he said…well, the way he used the "C" word…" I'd always hated that word, and bad as my language could get, I'd never used it in anger.

"Ok, I'll check in the records, see if we can find out where he is. He'll be under the Youth Offending Team. In the meantime, don't go out alone and let me know if he makes contact."

"Thanks. By the way, Ginny, are you looking into Tanya Middleton's death?"

"Yeah, we've been talking to the officers who handled the case in Manchester. They'd got it down as an accidental death, but now they're re-opening the case."

"Good."

I was reassured that they were looking into Tanya's death. Somehow, it just had to be connected to whatever was going on. I looked at the clock. It was nearly eight o'clock, so I doubted that they'd make much headway before Monday.

"You want to eat?" I asked Ruby, who was texting someone on her mobile.

"No, that's cool thanks Auntie Nik. I'm meeting some mates in Brixton."

"How's the course going?"

"Ace. Listen, I gotta go. I hope everything works out, Auntie Nik." She stood up and hoisted her large patchwork bag over her shoulder.

"Me too. You take care. And thanks for coming." We hugged before she left, bouncing down the stairs. I wondered if anyone had ever looked at Tanya with the kind of love I now felt for Ruby. What would it be like to lose someone that precious? Someone young and fresh with peach bloom skin and eyes wide and bright with hope. Unbearable. As the front door clicked shut behind her, Benjamin's opened.

"How's the invalid?"

"Not too bad, thanks. And I think I know who attacked me." I told him about the latest developments. "How about you? Hot date tonight?"

"Nah. Thought I'd go into town, see what's happening."

"Have fun." Whatever Ruby thought, I felt secure knowing he was downstairs, and I felt vulnerable knowing he was going out; but I wasn't going to tell him that. As I shut the door behind me, my phone rang. I checked the number on the display and saw with relief it was Carla.

"Hey girlfriend. How you doing?" She sounded brighter.

"I'm getting there. How about you?"

"Mastering one-handed wizardry with impressive speed. I can now wash my hair and have almost managed to hang out the washing. Can't wash up, though. That's a two handed job. What's happening your end?" I filled her in on my afternoon and evening.

"Need some company?"

"Wouldn't say no!"

"I'm on my way."

I decided to have a bath. I'd got some rose scented bath oil that Carla had given me for my birthday. I took the Ian Rankin and a glass of wine with me into the bathroom. The hot, rosy bath helped to melt away some of the stress of the week. When, eventually, I got out, I watched the water swirling down the plughole. There goes Ruth, I thought with a pang. There goes Dwayne. Only it would take more than a bath to stop me hurting every time I thought of Ruth, and Dwayne scared me big time. I dressed in loose jeans and a sweatshirt. It was good to feel clean. Carla arrived just before nine thirty. She gave me the warmest hug a one-armed woman could manage.

"So what happened with Ruth?" I gave her the short version.

"Shit! Marrying some bloke from Gaza?"

"Yup."

"She must be mad!"

"I couldn't have seen it coming. Or maybe I just wasn't looking."

"You can't blame yourself."

"I'm still kind of numb. Can't quite believe it. I mean, it's not like I thought we'd end up setting up home and living happily ever after. But I thought we had something. I thought there was something special there. But there's all this stuff going on with work, and the threats from

Dwayne, and I don't know where to start to get it all sorted. Just over a week ago, my life was so simple. What's happening to me, Carla?"

"Fuck knows. Look, Nikki, why don't you come and stay with me for the weekend? Siobhan's coming tomorrow night. If you're up to it, we could go out. There's a karaoke night at *Sappho*. Sunday we could do something daft. Go to the zoo, go up to Camden Lock. I just think you need to get away for a couple of days."

"I don't want to be a gooseberry if Siobhan's coming over."

"You won't be. We could ask Caro to come out with us if it bothers you." I was tempted. I needed to get away. I needed not to have a heart attack every time the phone rang."

"You sure?"

"Of course. Go pack a bag."

I packed my rucksack with knickers, toothbrush, two clean T-shirts and the Ian Rankin. I checked that the windows were shut. I left a note for Benjamin so that he wouldn't worry. Double locked the front door.

We took the short bus ride to Carla's flat and I settled myself in her spare room. Ginger looked at me menacingly.

"I'm here for the weekend, so get used to it. You're going to have to behave for two whole days," I told him. He glared at me and then scratched behind his ear as if to say, *I'll just drop some fleas on your bed so you don't get too comfortable.* Carla and I settled on the sofa with a bottle of wine and she put on the Sandi Thom album that we both loved.

"So what do you think's going on at *Action in Caring*?"

"I've been trying to figure that out. Who tidied Veronica's office? Who is Lewis Fairclough, the signatory to the bank account that Gordon set up? Why is Gordon's personnel file missing, and who took it? And how did peanuts get into Veronica's system? And where does Dwayne fit into all of this?"

"Has Suresh come back to you?"

"Not yet. He's doing some digging – at least, I hope he is."

"Are the police taking it all seriously?"

"I think so. Ginny Lancaster seems ok." Sandi was singing about time. We'd finished the wine. I felt sleepy and safe here in my friend's home. "I think it's time for bed," I said.

"Give me a hand with the dishes?"

"Can't you just get Ginger to lick them all clean?" She gave me a horrified look. "Only joking!"

Chapter 19

On Saturday I cleaned Carla's flat and she did some Internet research on Gordon and Veronica. By the afternoon we didn't know anything we hadn't known on Friday, so we went for a walk to the police station and reclaimed my bike. We walked it back to Carla's via the common, where we sat for a while in the spring sunshine. Siobhan came over on Saturday night, and we met up with Caro, a friend of Carla's whom I'd adopted as one of my own. *Sappho* had been buzzing with women and a fair number of men and the karaoke was a hoot. After the second bottle of Merlot, Carla and Siobhan got up to sing *River Deep, Mountain High* with Caro and I harmonising loudly – and tunelessly – from the floor.

"Seen Ruth yet?" asked Eva.

"Yeah. Don't imagine we'll be seeing her in here any time soon," I said. Eva looked puzzled.

"She's gone straight. Got a man. Getting married, baby on the way." I shrugged, trying to look nonchalant, but I didn't fool Eva.

"Nik, I'm sorry," she said putting a warm arm around my shoulders.

"Me too," I said, and slurped some more wine. "But hey! Shit happens." Eva ruffled my hair. Carla and Siobhan tumbled back into their seats as a new couple stood up to sing *I will Survive*. I hadn't smoked in over ten years, well nothing other than the odd spliff; but I really fancied one then. Maybe I just needed another drink. I needed not to be thinking about Ruth, that was for sure. I stood up to go to the bar and then stopped. The woman leaning up against it and talking animatedly to a small woman with wild red curly hair looked very familiar. The light was too dim to see clearly. I peered more closely. Then I heard her laugh, heard her say something to the other woman, recognised her accent. Softly east coast Scottish. It was Wendy Baggott. I smiled to myself, and sauntered up to the bar.

"Hi Wendy," I said. She turned from the redhead and looked at me in surprise.

"Oh! Hi! Nikki Elliot. Well! Fancy seeing you here!" Her face burst into a grin.

"Small world," I said.

"Yeah! So, how are you?"

"I'm ok. Better now, thanks. Hardly any headache left. Oh, and thanks for making sure my bike was safe."

"No problem," she said. I loved her accent. I could go to bed with an accent like that. The red haired woman was looking at me with curiosity. Wendy introduced us.

"Jeannie, this is Nikki. She works at a community centre nearby. Nikki, this is Jeannie, an old college friend of mine, down in London for the weekend."

"Hi," said Jeannie. When she smiled, her nose crinkled.

I wondered if she and Wendy were more than college mates. "So, you guys going to have a go?" I nodded towards the stage.

"You've got to be joking!" exclaimed Wendy.

"Why not?" I said.

"Because when I open my mouth to sing, it clears the room quicker than an Asian guy walking in with a rucksack." I wasn't sure that it was ok to say things like that. Was Wendy being racist? Or was she just acknowledging the latent racism that the recent bombings had brought out of us all?

"Don't listen to her!" said Jeannie. "Voice of an angel, that one."

"Och, Jeannie, that was years ago," said Wendy, and I think she was blushing, though it was hard to tell in the low light.

"You don't have to sing well to do karaoke," I said. "I think the whole point is to sing as loudly and badly as you can." As if to prove my point, three women and a man clearly out of his depth belted out *Sex Bomb*. It was the least erotic performance I'd ever witnessed.

"Think I'll pass," said Wendy.

"Any developments around Veronica's death?" I asked.

"Isn't Ginny Lancaster working that case now?"

"Yeah, but I wondered if you had any inside information."

"I couldn't possibly comment!" she teased. "But Ginny's the best. If there's a puzzle to solve, she's your woman. And Darren Lowe may keep a low profile – ha ha! Low profile! Get it? No, seriously, he's pretty canny. Not a lot gets by him." Here was another side to Wendy. Pleasantly inebriated. Off duty and off guard. I liked her more and more.

"Thought I'd lost you!" said Carla, embracing me from behind. "Hey, it's Wendy, isn't it?" she said to Wendy.

"And you're Carla. We met at the hospital."

"That's right! Guess we've got our work cut out keeping this one out of trouble!"

"Too right. One thing after the other with her." Why did I feel that they were ganging up on me?

"Why was Nikki in hospital?" asked Jeannie.

"Long story," said Wendy. "Tell you later. What are you all drinking?"

Wendy brought the next round of drinks over to where we were sitting, and somehow we all ended up dancing, once the karaoke had given way to disco. They were playing soul, mostly from the seventies and eighties, and it felt good to shake away the week's traumas in time to Earth Wind and Fire and the Pointer Sisters. Then the lights got even dimmer, and suddenly I was in Wendy's arms moving to *Slow Hand*. She smelled clean and lemony. Her hair was soft. Her touch made me tingle deep inside.

"Is this allowed, Sergeant Baggott?"

"Only when I'm off duty."

"So, I'm not a suspect then?"

"Or maybe you are, and I'm trying to catch you out."

"You could be the honey trap."

"Oh, you've guessed!" As we turned, I saw Eva smirking from behind the bar. Wendy pulled me in closer and I didn't resist.

Carla brought in fresh coffee at ten o'clock the next morning. I woke with a strange flutter somewhere beyond my belly. As my brain made sense of the fragments flying fast and loose around my head, I remembered dancing with Wendy and the flutter shot up to my chest so that for a moment I could hardly breathe.

"Quite a night, then," said Carla.

"Mmm. Was I really dancing with Wendy Baggott?"

"Yup."

"Oh." I felt a sudden pang of disloyalty to Ruth, but where slow dancing was concerned, there was no competition. Wendy was delicious.

"So, you going to see her again?"

"I don't know. I think she said she'd ring me, but I didn't give her my mobile number."

"She'll have it already, won't she?"

"Oh yes. I hadn't thought of that. But wasn't she with Jeannie?"

"I think they were just old friends. Eva seemed to think you were in with a chance."

"Eva's always trying to pair people off."

"Only when she likes them and thinks they'll go together."

"Me and a policewoman?"

"Why not?"

"Because I was at Greenham when I was ten, and on the poll tax march and the march against the war in Iraq."

"Maybe Wendy was there too, maybe you share something."

"Only if her mum had been an activist like mine. And if we were both on the march against the war, we'd have been on different sides."

"Don't make assumptions."

"And if I go out with Wendy, I'll have to stop smoking spliffs with Benjamin."

"Well, would that be so big a sacrifice?" I thought of Wendy's fine bone structure, her hazel eyes, that siren like voice, and her lemony, woody scent. And I remembered how my body had responded to her touch.

"Maybe not."

"Anyway, remember Brian Paddick."

We ventured north to Camden Lock. Siobhan bought purple tie-dyed trousers, Carla bought incense, and I nearly bought a moonstone pendant for Ruth and then remembered that she was out of my life. Old habits die hard. I felt agitated. One minute my belly was contracting at the memory of seeing Ruth for the last time. The next I was melting at the thought of smooching with Wendy Baggott. And in between came the fear of what Dwayne might do next, and what nasty twists the *Action in Caring* saga would take.

"Fancy an Indian in Drummond Street?" asked Siobhan.

"Yeah! Haven't had a masala dosa for months!" said Carla. "Nikki?"

"I'm not really hungry," I said.

"That's not like you," said Carla. "I've never known you to pass on a Drummond Street Indian!"

"Lots going on," I said. "Look, you two go out to eat. I'll just walk for a while. Can I see you back at the flat a bit later?"

"You sure?"

"Yeah. Anyway, you and Siobhan need some quality time."

"No we don't," said Carla. But they did.

I walked south until I came to the river. I walked across the wibbly-wobbly bridge that links St Paul's Cathedral to Tate Modern, stopping to look west to the magic wheel that is the London Eye, watching the pleasure boats cruise towards me on their way to Greenwich. Sundays by the river are special. Couples and families, tourists and people who live here saunter and sit. The pace is completely different from working week London. At the weekend you can really appreciate the city in all its glory. I entered Tate Modern, walking down the broad slope into the Turbine Hall. There was some weird soundscape, speakers everywhere. Not my sort of thing, so I wandered through a couple of other rooms and then went back outside and walked towards Gabriel's Wharf. It was buzzing with people and there were queues waiting to go into the Gourmet Pizza restaurant. There was a festival of some sort on in the Bernie Spain Gardens, stalls selling gaudy pottery and organic snacks. An old black man played calypso on his guitar outside the National Film Theatre. I browsed amongst the bookstands, bought a copy of Wendy Cope's poems to cheer me up. Suddenly I just wanted to be at home. I could get a bus from Waterloo. I texted Carla. *Going home for a bit. Might come over later if it's ok.* She rang me.

"You sure it's safe, Nik?"

"I'll put the chain on the door. I just need to be in my own space for a bit. Ben's probably in." She made a sound that could have been a harrumph or could have been her swallowing some masala dosa.

"Come over later?"

"Ok."

No deranged thug was lurking outside my flat, ready to pounce. My flat was as I'd left it, and nobody had tried to break in. There was no sound from Benjamin's flat and his bike wasn't under the stairs. There was a postcard from someone I'd worked with at *Life is for Living* and a gas bill, which I stuck under the phone. There was quite a pile there now, and the phone looked decidedly lopsided. I'd have to deal with my paperwork. Not now, though. The ansaphone was flashing. I'd check it later. For now, I just wanted to curl up on my sofa with a cup of peppermint tea and the Ian Rankin. Rebus's trials made my problems seem trifling, and he had a drink problem to boot. Three hours later, I woke up. My tea was cold and Rebus was still in a fix. I'd been dreaming. I couldn't remember the details, but handcuffs figured strongly. What would my mum say if she knew I had the hots for a policewoman? *Nikki, it's one thing being gay, I don't have a problem with that, but there are limits…*I needed a shower to wake myself up. The smell of the lemon zingy shower gel reminded me of Wendy. Maybe she'd rung me. I'd better check my ansaphone. I dried myself and put on clean chinos and an orange T-shirt. I pushed the button to check my messages. The first caller had hung up without leaving a message. The second was from my bank: *Ms Elliot, we need to discuss your account. Could you please ring us at your earliest convenience?* I don't believe in this twenty four hour business, and ringing the bank would just have to wait until Monday. The third message was from Suresh: *Hi Nik. Wondered if you knew about the open day they're holding at the new SoLCEC Centre tomorrow. Thought you might want to have a sniff at the competition. Call me – I can get you in as press.* So, Suresh's guilty conscience was kicking in! And the last message was from Wendy Baggott. *Hi Nikki. Hope you're ok. Mm…well…I guess you're not in…I, uh, just wanted to say…I really enjoyed last night. Maybe…* but there'd been too many "ums" and pauses and my ansaphone had cut her off. What had she been going to say? My heart was racing and there was a tell-tale tingling in my breasts. I didn't know if I was in love – how could I be? I'd only officially split from Ruth two days ago – but my body was telling me that I was definitely in lust. I dialled 1471 and jotted down the number of the last caller. The phone rang. It was Carla.

"Hi Nik, where are you?"

"I'm here," I said.

"What are you doing there? You're supposed to be here. It's nearly nine o'clock. We've been worried."

"I fell asleep, and then I woke up and needed a shower. I didn't realise it was so late," I said, and realised that I didn't want to go out again. "Look, Carla, would you mind if I didn't come over?"

"D'you want us to come over to you?"

"No, no, I'm fine. No nasty messages or anything. One from Wendy, though! But I think I just need a quiet evening and an early night."

"Well, if you're sure…"

"Is Siobhan still with you?"

"Yes, she's staying until Tuesday."

"And are you two…"

"I think so."

"Good. Have a glass of wine for me."

"Sure you're ok?"

"Yeah, I'm sure." I rang Suresh.

"How are you doing?" he asked. I filled him in on the past few days.

"Bloody hell! Why is all this shit happening to you?"

"Dunno. But I'm definitely up for that trip to Kennington tomorrow."

"Ok. How about we meet outside the tube? Eleven thirty ok?"

"Cool. And thanks." I put the chain on the door and Sarah Jane Morris on the stereo. I could hear it starting to rain outside, and I was grateful to be inside, safe and cosy. By ten thirty, I'd finished the Ian Rankin, Rebus had scraped through yet again, and I was ready for sleep. *You haven't rung Wendy,* whispered a voice in my head. *I know,* I replied. *I'm saving her up for tomorrow.*

Chapter 20

The rain had stopped when I woke up on Monday morning.
I'd been dreaming about Ruth. A sick feeling, something way beyond
sadness, flooded my belly as I remembered, with the shock of the
newly bereaved, that she and I were not to be, that our connection was
severed. But then something was happening with Wendy. I didn't
know where it would go, but it felt good so far. I dreaded the thought
of going to work, but I didn't have much choice. By the end of this
week, I would have handed in my notice – although it wasn't at all
clear to whom I'd hand it. I cycled across the common. I had to push
through a strong breeze, and the effort helped to lift my spirits to a
point at which I could at least face the world. Geri was already there
when I arrived. She was showing Iris, the new volunteer, how the
phone system worked.

"Hi Nikki," she said giving me a little hug. "Should you be in?"

"Yeah, I'm ok. But I need a favour." I explained about Suresh's
proposition. "So I need to slip away around elevenish."

"No problem."

"I'll hold the fort," offered Iris. Her being here would make it
easier for me to quit.

"Thanks," I said. Geri and I still had papers to sort through. I
wondered what was on the computer system that might shed light on
what Gordon had been up to. "Can we get into the computer files?"

"I'm sure we can, but I don't know how," she said. "But I know
a woman who does…"

"You do?"

"Yes." She laughed. "My sister!"

"There are so many things we don't know," I said, after Geri
came back from ringing her sister.

"Gina's coming at lunchtime," said Geri. "Maybe she'll find
something on the system. Anyway, how was your hot date last week?"

I didn't feel that I could share all the details of my weekend with Geri, especially not the bit about dancing with Wendy Baggott. "Not so hot, and it ended with a bang on the head and a threatening phone message."

"Sorry. Stupid question!"

"That's ok. But do you know what's the worst?"

"What?"

"I think the caller was Dwayne."

"What, Dwayne from Justin's youth group?"

"Yeah. I've told Ginny Lancaster. He's under the youth offenders' team, so I guess they'll have hauled him in." Iris peeped round the door.

"There's a Councillor Hope on the phone," she said.

"Oh shit," I said.

"I'll take it," said Geri. She came back five minutes later. "Could be worse," she said. "They're freezing our grant, but they're not insisting we close down."

"Anyway, what about you? What happened about that job you went for?"

"It's going to second interview. They've called me back for Wednesday."

"Oh. Well, that's good, isn't it?"

"Yes. Yes, it's good. It'd be nice to have a change of scene. More money, too."

"Yeah, I s'pose it would. I'm thinking of moving on too. Just haven't got round to applying for anything else yet."

There was a banging on the door.

"Oh God, it's Dora again," sighed Geri.

"Why does she keep coming?"

"Because it's warmer inside than out, we don't abuse her, and if she's lucky she gets food and drink and a sub until pension day."

"Doesn't she have any family?"

"Doubt it. You ok if I go back to the papers?"

"Yeah."

I buzzed open the front door. "Hello Dora," I said, trying my best to sound friendly. She sniffed at me and wiped her nose with the back of her hand.

"They get you too, then?" she asked.

"What do you mean?"

"They get you? Beat you up? Worried you know too much, sneaking about on a Sunday like that? You oughta be more careful, you."

If she'd seen me on the Sunday, she must have seen who else was here. "Who are they, Dora?"

"They done it. I told you last week, they done it. I need a tenner. Where's that other woman, the coloured one?"

"What did you see, Dora?"

"I never seen nothing. Where's that coloured girl?"

"Will you tell me later?"

"Ain't nothing to tell. I need me money."

I sighed and went to call Geri.

By eleven twenty five, I was standing outside the tube at Kennington. Suresh arrived shortly after. He handed me a camera case.

"What's this?"

"You're my snapper for the morning," he said. "You do know how to take pictures?" He could be such a patronising git.

"'Course I do. I assume it's a point and click sort of thing?"

"It's digital. I don't think you can go too wrong with it." I wasn't so sure. I was happier with my trusty Canon Sure Shot and its nice little rolls of brown film; but this camera was clearly my passport into SoLCEC.

"Ready?" he said.

I hoisted the camera bag over my shoulder. "What are we waiting for?"

We set off down the road, turned a corner, and were soon standing in front of a shiny new centre with lots of windows and smart brickwork. The double doors opened automatically as we approached. How much had that cost? There was a reception desk ahead of us. The woman sitting behind it looked up at us.

"Can I help you?" She was my antithesis in every respect. She sat straight-backed in a tailored navy suit. She wore a pale pink blouse and little pearl earrings. Her black hair was straightened and pulled back tightly. There was a tiny silver cross at her throat.

"We're here for the opening," said Suresh. "South London Press."

"Name?" Her pen was poised over a neat computer printout.

"Shah. Suresh Shah."

"And you are…?"

"Nikki Elliot. Also with the South London Press. Photographer." I brandished my camera bag so that she could see I meant business.

"I don't have your name on the list…" she was frowning over the printout, moving her pen down the list of names. She was wearing that kind of glassily glossy lipstick that stays on for twelve hours. Or so the adverts say.

"You won't find her name," chipped in Suresh. "My regular camera man's gone down with 'flu. Nikki's covering for today." The woman looked sceptical. "Actually, Nikki's a better photographer than Mark. We're lucky to have her. I know she'll do you proud." He grinned at the ice queen. I smiled weakly, and the receptionist wasn't convinced, but by now there was a little queue behind us, and she waved us through towards a set of double doors.

"What now?" I whispered.

"Look cool. Take your camera out, hang it round your neck, check that there's a memory card in it. Look! There's Nigel Bentley!"

"Where?"

"Weasely man by the flower arrangement."

"In the loud shirt?"

"That's the one."

"Who's he talking with?"

"Simon Standing. Chair of the Chamber of Commerce."

"Is that a big deal?"

"Chamber of Commerce? No. But he thinks it is."

"Shall I take their picture?"

"Wait for me to make the introductions." We walked over to the two men. "Councillor Bentley," said Suresh heartily, holding out his hand. "This is a splendid occasion. Care to say a few words for the record?"

"I've prepared a statement. My secretary will give you a copy." He looked at Suresh as if he were sub-human. I didn't like him and we hadn't even been introduced.

"Nice photo of you and Mr Standing for the front page?" I asked, and before they could answer or arrange their faces, I'd started clicking away. "Thanks," I said and walked off.

"It would've helped if you'd have taken off the lens cover," said Suresh as we moved away from Bentley and Standing.

"Oh," I said, dismayed, and then saw that I had taken it off.

"Gotcha!" said Suresh, digging me in the side as if we were still eighteen.

"Bastard!"

"Told you this was a tough business," he said. The rows of chairs were filling up. The mayor was there in full regalia. There was a tall woman dressed in red with a shocking pink beret sitting near the front. I thought I'd seen her picture somewhere. I recognised someone else too. Derek, *Action in Caring's* treasurer was sitting in the middle, talking to a man with a goatee. What was he doing here? And then I remembered Geri telling me on that first day that two of the trustees were involved in

SoLCEC. I'd only known for sure that one was Lawrence. Derek was clearly the second. Maybe that's why he'd been lying low ever since Veronica's death. I'd try to talk with him later. In the meantime, I had a job to do.

"Ok, what do I need to do?" I whispered.

"Follow me." He walked towards the edge of the stage. A small group, which included the mayor and Nigel Bentley, was gathering behind a table spread with a blue drape decorated with the European flag symbol.

"Ok," said Suresh, "I'm going to take notes. You take some photos. I'm going to want one of the mayor speaking and you might as well see what you can get of the other speakers. If in doubt, flash away. Make sure the flash is turned on, by the way."

"Right." I checked that the camera was ready to go and took a seat in the middle of the front row. The speakers had all assembled on the stage now. Simon Standing had joined the mayor and Bentley. And there was Lawrence, looking shabbily out of place in corduroy trousers and a chequered jacket that was surely third hand. There was a woman in a lavender suit and a dull looking man in grey. Grey man stood up and tested the microphone. Lawrence wiped the back of his hand across his nose.

"Here we go," said Suresh. I raised the camera and looked like I was adjusting the focus or something equally technical.

"Can everyone hear me?" asked the man in the grey suit. There was a murmured assent from the audience.

"Good afternoon," he said. "For those who don't know me, I'm Gerald Goodman, Chief Executive of the Council." Suresh was scribbling so I clicked and flashed, which made Goodman blink. "It's a great pleasure to be here today at the official opening of the South London Community and Enterprise Centre. I'd like to welcome you all to this exciting project which marks the start of a new era in community provision." Nigel Bentley clapped and the others on the stage followed suit. There was a half-hearted echo of applause from the audience. "Today gives us an opportunity to share our vision and to invite you to find out about all the benefits that this European Union funded centre will bring to our south London community. And so, without further ado,

I hand you over to Nigel Bentley, Leader of the Council." There was muted applause again, and I flashed at Gerald and the rest of the panel. Nigel Bentley stood up holding his microphone and stroking his tie.

"Thank you Gerald," he said. "Ladies and gentlemen, this centre puts south London on the map at last!" He paused, as if expecting applause, but none came. "They laugh at us, north of the river," he went on. "They say that you know you're in north London by the number of blue plaques on the walls of houses, but you can tell you're in south London by the number of yellow signs calling for witnesses to crime." There was a murmur from the audience. The woman in lavender shook her head. "Well, there's a lot more to our community than gun crime and gangs, isn't there?" Lawrence nodded. The audience was quiet. "What about all the things they never write about in the paper?" said Bentley, casting a dark look towards Suresh. "What about enterprise? What about a thriving pluralist economy? We're no longer in the nineteen seventies and eighties. Times have changed, and people have changed. Ladies and gentlemen, it's all happening, and it's happening here. And the South London Community and Enterprise Centre will be the hub, the engine room, of all that is positive and growing in south London, from Lewisham to Wandsworth, from Sutton to Southwark. Here we have a new model for community and business partnership, for promoting the very best that our community in south London has to offer. Thank you." He sat down. There was hearty applause from the panel. A few people in the audience clapped. I had struggled to glean any substance from the rhetoric that sounded to me as meaningless and vacuous as any new Labour spiel. Maybe Suresh knew what Bentley had been on about. I took his photo anyway. The woman in lavender stood up.

"Good afternoon," she said. "I am delighted to be here representing London in Europe. I'd like to congratulate everyone who has brought this wonderful centre into being. It is a tremendous tribute to everything that the European Social Fund represents, and I am sure that it will transform our communities. We are going to see a flourishing of new enterprise and thriving small businesses, and no-one will be denied opportunities because of gender, race, disability, sexual orientation, age, or religion. And the South London Centre is, of course, working in close partnership with sister organisations in Portugal, Lithuania, and Germany, so that we can all learn from each other's experience. Thank you." There was a ripple of applause and I clicked my camera as lavender lady smoothed her skirt beneath her legs and sat down. Next up was Lawrence. He tapped his microphone. I could see specks of something old in his beard.

"Er...can you...er...can you hear me?" he asked, and then coughed. There was silence. "Er...this centre is just what we need in south London. There are great facilities and you can get here from anywhere in south London. It's great that finally there's a modern centre that caters for everyone. I'm proud to have been part of its creation and to be on the management committee. I'd just like to echo what Nigel, and the mayor, and Ms Naylor have said. There's lunch after question time, so I hope to have a chat to some of you later." I took his picture for posterity. Simon Standing waited to see if there was any applause, and when it was clear that there wouldn't be, he stood up.

"On behalf of the Chamber of Commerce," he began, "I'd like to thank everyone who's invested in the development of this splendid centre. There are over two thousand small businesses in this borough alone and it feels great to have a centre around which they can all congregate. Today's young people are the entrepreneurs of tomorrow, and this centre will show them new ways of developing their ideas and talents. The marketing suite will offer low cost facilities, including consultancy services, to local business people. And the programme of vocational courses is inspirational. And let's not forget that there's a nursery available at very low cost to all those mums who want to get back to business!" Three people clapped. Simon Standing sat down. Gerald Goodman stood up.

"So, without further delay, I'd like to ask the mayor, Councillor George Daniels, to officially open this centre." The mayor's chains clanked as he stood up. He looked weighed down by the heavy gilt.

"Well, what a pleasure to be opening this splendid community centre," he said. "Communities need places to gather around. Places that welcome mothers and youngsters, where youth clubs thrive and pensioners mount campaigns against councils, ha ha." No-one laughed. "No, but seriously, the South London Cultural Centre is just what south London needs, and I look forward to attending many multi-faith events here." Goodman leaned over and whispered to him. "Oh, sorry, wrong

212

centre! That was last week! So, I look forward to attending many exciting events at the South London Community and …er…Enterprise Centre. And I now declare this centre officially open." Everyone clapped. I could see beads of sweat erupting across the mayor's forehead. Gerald Goodman stood up.

"And so, ladies and gentlemen, are there any questions before we go off to enjoy the splendid lunch that's been put on for us?"

"Yes." I heard a strong female voice from behind me, and turned round. The woman with the pink beret stood up. "Here in south London we have some of the most deprived estates in the country. Gun crime is out of control and gangs hold whole communities to ransom. More kids refuse to go to school in this borough than anywhere else in the country. The number of children referred to child protection services is rising by the month, and only a fraction of them ever receive any help. The levels of abuse and poverty are leading to a generation in crisis. How do centres like this, with their focus on business and enterprise, help the kids and families and communities that so desperately need to be heard and need access to resources?" There was applause, and calls of agreement. I took her picture and hoped this would be the one to hit the front page. She sat down, folded her arms, and looked like she wouldn't go anywhere until she'd got a reply.

"Would you like to take that question, Nigel?" asked Gerald Goodman.

"Certainly," said Bentley. "As you know, Miss de Souza, there will be family activities based here at the centre, and much of the enterprise development will be aimed at disenfranchised groups within the community."

"What about the youth clubs? What about the young people's counselling project that your council withdrew funding from last March? What about the neighbourhood centres that can't survive because all the funding's coming to this place?" challenged the woman.

"You'll be aware of recent discussions between the council and some local businesses about a new approach to youth clubs."

"And the counselling? And the neighbourhood advice centres that families rely on? And the outreach teams that know the mums and dads and kids? And the projects that keep school refusers out of trouble?"

"I'm sure that you'll find, Miss de Souza, that new partnerships between business and council and police will benefit communities. That's what regeneration's all about. Any other questions?"

"Yes, I've got one!" A voice called from the back of the room. I spotted a slight man in a baseball cap. "The Transsexual Project that's been running from the Bankside Neighbourhood Centre is under threat because you've diverted the centre's funding to here. What are we supposed to do? Where can we go? We've got enough grief to deal with."

"I'm sure you'll be able to book some space here. Our rates are highly competitive," said Bentley. "Anyone else? No? Good! Let's go for lunch." And with that, everyone started to dismount the stage as if they couldn't wait to get away.

"Wait! I've got something to say!" A man in his mid-forties wearing a comfortable ribbed sweater stood up. The speakers paused and looked to see who had interrupted their exit.

"Mr Balmforth?" said Goodman. "Can you make it quick, please?"

"I'll take the time I need, thank you," said the man, who was quietly spoken but clear. "I just want to know why this council is systematically shutting down community centres. *Action in Caring* has just had its funding frozen. We've heard from Ms de Souza about neighbourhood centres and youth clubs that are being starved of resources. The infrastructure of our community buildings has been neglected for years. How much do you hope to raise from selling off the land on which these buildings sit? And how much is still owed towards this building?" He sat down, arms folded, back straight. Balmforth. Could he be Felicity's husband?

"Yeah, how much you planning on raising from selling our property?" called a young woman with a shaved head.

"It's all about profit for the fat cats, isn't it?" shouted a longhaired man in a green anorak.

"Our council taxes are just going into the pockets of the developers. You can't deny it! There's nothing left for our kids and old folk," added a silver haired woman in a patchwork jacket.

"And what about services for disabled people?" called out a young woman with a nose ring who had wheeled herself nearer the front of the hall. "We're losing what little independence we had because you're cutting back all the services."

"No land is being sold at present," said Goodman. "And I think you'd all do well to get your facts straight. This council spends more per head…"

"Yeah, yeah, we've heard it all before," said green anorak man. I tried to get photos of them all.

"I can't afford to have a council home help any more…"

"…prime property in Waterloo…"

"…pensioners' lunch clubs all closed…"

"…gays getting beaten up but there's no-one to help…"

"…hole in the roof so water gets into the electrics and it's not safe for the kids…" It was a cacophony now, and Gerald Goodman looked furious. I clicked away. There'd be some pictures he wouldn't want to add to his family album. Nigel Bentley ushered the speakers off the stage. Lavender lady tottered unsteadily on high heels.

"That's all for now, ladies and gentlemen," Bentley said. "Go and enjoy your lunch." Suresh was scribbling frantically. Little groups were forming around the main challengers. Most had gravitated towards the woman in red and pink, Ms de Souza. A few, including green anorak and the woman in the Quickie wheelchair were in earnest conversation with Mr Balmforth. I looked around for Derek, but he seemed to have gone. I flashed a few more pictures and then cut over to Suresh.

"Well, that was fun," I said, sitting down next to him.

"Went better than I'd expected," he said, finishing off an illegible scribble with a flourish. "Wonder if they'll start throwing the food at each other?" People were drifting in twos and threes, still talking with increasing animation, towards the room next door where, I assumed, the feast awaited them. "Make sure you snap any good bun-fights," he added.

"Is it true, then?" I asked. "Are they looking to close down all the neighbourhood centres and sell off the land?"

"I shouldn't be surprised," said Suresh. "They're strapped for cash, and the developers who built this place went two million over budget."

"Who's the woman in the pink beret?"

"Maria de Souza. Local community development worker. Ran some cutting edge mental health centres in the nineties. Set up a youth club for school refusers, she's something of a genius. God knows how, but she turned some of those kids around. I did an article last year on a girl who had a baby at thirteen and who had just got a first class law degree."

"Can I meet her?"

"Yeah, I'll introduce you, if she's still here. Come on then, let's see what's going down next door."

The group of speakers was clustered behind a table bearing plates of rich and gaudy gateaux. Others were standing around with paper plates heaped high with samosas, sandwiches and little fried nuggets of something. Maria de Souza held only a glass of water as she advanced towards the power club.

"So, Nigel, up to your old tricks again, I see?"

"Maria. Nice of you to come," said Bentley. "Cake?"

"I never eat with the enemy," replied Maria. Her voice was a rich, deep alto. "Leo Balmforth got it right, didn't he?" she continued. "It's all about selling off the land and making some dosh. This whole thing's just a smokescreen, isn't that right?" She swept her arms to take in the room

"Don't you think that you could be being just a touch paranoid?" asked Bentley.

"I think I know rather more about mental health conditions than you do, Nigel, and my own sanity is not in question. Yours, however..." She didn't finish the sentence, but raised the glass of water to her mouth. Her eyes didn't leave Bentley's as she drank.

"Now, be careful, Maria. Be very careful," said Bentley, and turned away. It sounded like a threat to me.

"Ms de Souza?" I said, as Bentley moved across the room. "I'm Nikki Elliot. I work at *Action in Caring*. I'm moonlighting as Suresh's photographer today. Is there really a systematic closing down of centres that might be worth more on the open property market?" She lowered her glass and turned towards me.

"Well, what do you think, Nikki?" I thought I was in over my head and I'd rather be tucked up at home watching daytime TV.

"Well, it seems like community groups are under a lot of pressure right now."

"And tell me, Nikki. What do you think this centre has to offer the young offenders that use *Action in Caring*?"

"Well…not a lot, if I'm honest. I can't see most of our kids getting past the woman on reception. And I can't really see our art class, or the yoga for people under stress, or the grannies for peace, although I haven't met them yet, fitting in here."

"Exactly."

"But is there some sort of conspiracy? Or should I just be moving with the times?"

"I see you two have met," said Suresh. "Hi, Maria. How's it going?"

"It doesn't get better, does it?" she answered. "How do you plan to cover this in the SLP?"

"I thought I'd explore the property angle," said Suresh.

"And to answer your question, Nikki, no, I don't think it's about moving with the times. It's all about money and power and big white men carving out niches for themselves and fucking over everyone else. How long have you worked there, then?"

"Oh, only a couple of…" but I didn't finish my sentence. There was a crash of crockery and a cry of rage. I wheeled round in time to see the man in the green anorak holding his fists to Nigel Bentley's face.

"You fucking arrogant bastard!" he cried.

217

"Camera, Nik," said Suresh. I was in time to snap green anorak man pulling back his right arm, a grimace of hate and frustration on his face, as Bentley cowered and ducked the blow. He didn't look very elegant.

"Now the fun begins," murmured Maria. But the woman in the patchwork jacket and Leo Balmforth each took one of green anorak's arms and pulled him gently but firmly back.

"Don't let the side down," I heard Balmforth say.

"He's not worth it," said patchwork woman.

"He's destroying us! He's wrecking everything we've ever worked for, everything our parents and brothers and sisters have struggled to achieve!"

"Hitting him won't do any good." Maria had moved across and had her hand on green anorak's back. Gentle but firm. "We'll find other ways. The press are here today. Let's use them." Bentley had retreated to the other side of the room. Lawrence was standing in the middle, his plate piled high with sausage rolls and egg sandwiches. He looked lost. He didn't move towards Bentley. Suresh and I moved towards Maria and the little group.

"I'd like an interview, but I think it's best if we go to the pub," said Suresh.

"Just make sure it's accessible," said the woman with the nose ring.

"What's the deal?" asked Maria.

"You give me your side. I get it past the editor," said Suresh.

"What's the angle?"

"Property dealing politician (probably bent) annihilates small community groups," said Suresh.

"What's in it for you?" asked green anorak man.

"It's my job," said Suresh. I could hear him thinking, *and I hate those smarmy Euro-bastards.*

We regrouped at a pub just a few minutes from the Costcutter supermarket. The floor was tacky. Suresh bought the drinks. Green anorak man, patchwork woman, Maria, Leo Balmforth, and the woman with the nose ring had come along. Leo was smoking furiously. I needed to take my photos and get back to *AIC*. I had a quiet word with Suresh.

"D'you need me for anything else?"

"No. You got what you wanted?"

"Well, just more questions, really. And does any of this have anything to do with Veronica's death, or Tanya's, for that matter, or Gordon meddling with the money?"

"I don't think you'll find the answers here, but it's probably worth setting up a meeting with Maria."

"Thanks. I gotta go," I said to the little group. Leo lit up another cigarette.

"It's about time all the corruption was exposed," he said.

"Think I've got some good pictures," I said. "Maria, can we meet up?"

"Yeah, if you and your pal here give us good coverage. Here's my card." Just what I wanted. Maybe this press and media game wasn't so difficult after all.

"Thanks. I'll be in touch. Good to meet you all." Fifteen minutes later, I was back at *Action in Caring*. Iris was in my place.

"Where's Geri?" I asked.

"They've arrested her," said Iris, looking grim.

219

Chapter 21

"What?" I cried.

"Two detectives came," said Iris. "Your friend had just shown the yoga group through, when the doorbell rang. They asked for Geri, and when she came out, they started reading her her rights. Said she was being questioned about the death of Veronica Stein."

"Oh my God! Did she call anyone?"

"Her sister was still here. She'd been doing something with the computers – I don't know what. She said she'd sort it out."

"Where've they taken her?"

"Down the nick, I s'pose. Didn't ask which one."

"Did her sister– did Gina leave a number?"

"No. I don't think so."

"Shit." I needed to rescue Geri, but I didn't know where to start. I could look up her next of kin details in her personnel file. I could ring Rita. I could wake up from this nightmare that my life was turning into. I decided to try the personnel files.

"You ok here if I go to the office for a few minutes?"

"Yeah, I'm fine." Iris had discovered solitaire on the PC. I left her with all the fives and no aces showing and headed towards Geri's office. There were files out on her desk and papers that she'd been in middle of processing. It was clear that she'd left in a hurry. Nothing on her desk gave me a clue as to who to contact for her. The personnel files were all stored in a locked cabinet. Where would she keep the keys? I looked in her desk drawer. It was neat and tidy, with paper clips, treasury tags and other stationery staples carefully divided into little compartments. There were no keys. I looked in the drawer beneath. There was a little lacquered box tucked into a corner at the back. I brought it out and opened it. There was a key inside. I tried it in the cabinet. It turned with ease. I was in. The files were clearly ordered, their labels printed in a strong, clear hand. I found Geri's and lifted it out. The front sheet had personal information such as address, phone number, medical conditions, and next of kin. I presumed it was her mother. Mrs Juliette Francis. Now all I had to do was to phone her. But there was an address, too. Maybe it would be better to pay her a visit in person. She lived in Franciscan Road, Tooting.

"Iris, can you hold the fort?"

"Going out again?"

"Yeah. Shouldn't be more than an hour." The meeting room door opened behind me, and Felicity tiptoed out. The room behind her was darkened and someone was snoring.

"I heard your voice," she said in a whisper. "I can't believe they've arrested Geri."

"They've taken her in for questioning," I said. "That's different from charging her. But it's still freaking me out. I think I met your partner today, by the way."

"Leo?"

"Yes. At the opening of SoLCEC."

"Ah! Yes, he said he had things to say in public about what the council's up to."

"He was very…" I tried to find the right word. "Eloquent," I finished.

"Good. Listen, I have to get back to the group to bring them out of their relaxation, but if there's anything I can do, just ring."

"Thanks." She crept back in and closed the door. I mounted my bike and sped down Tanner's Lane. The kebab shop was empty, except for the man with the kind eyes who was basting the meat spinning on its spit. I cut across Clapham Common and headed towards Balham and then on to Tooting. There'd once been an enormous Victorian asylum here, a building full of old terrors and tormented ghosts. Now there was a gated community. I turned into Franciscan Road and found the number that had been on Geri's file. It was a neat terraced house with a tidy front garden. I chained my bike to the nearby lamppost and pushed open the gate to the garden path. Spring flowers, crocus and daffodil, bordered the path. I pressed the doorbell. A slim woman with shiny, waved hair opened the door.

"Yes?" She looked younger than I'd imagined Geri's mother to be.

"I'm looking for Juliette Francis."

"That's me. Who are you?"

"I'm Nikki Elliot. I work with Geri."

"The police have taken my baby in for questioning about that woman's death. No way she could have done anything to harm anyone. No way."

"I know she didn't do it. That's why I'm here."

"You'd better come in." I followed Juliette through a clean, bright hall into a living room that throbbed with vibrant colours. The sofa and armchairs were broad and plump, covered with red, orange and purple throws and scatter cushions. Three of the walls were white and the fourth, around the fireplace, was warm crimson. There was an abstract picture on the wall in brilliant yellows, scarlets and umbers. The carpet was a rough Hessian weave, and there was a large purple and orange rug in front of the fireplace.

"Do you want tea?"

"Thank you. Yes, if that's ok," I said.

"Sit yourself down and I'll be right back." I wondered if this was the house in which Geri had grown up. It looked too smart to have nurtured children, but then Juliette didn't fit my stereotype of anyone's mother either. She came back with a steaming mug in each hand.

"Thank you," I said as she handed me mine. She sat down in the armchair opposite the sofa on which I'd perched.

"This situation is really crazy," she said. "My Geraldine wouldn't hurt a fly, let alone kill her boss."

"I know," I said. "I haven't worked with her for very long. Just a couple of weeks, in fact, but I know she didn't have anything to do with Veronica's dying. Not unless she's a brilliant actress."

"Her uncle is a lawyer. I've got him on the case."

"Is there anything I can do?"

"I don't know. They haven't charged her, so maybe they'll question her and let her go. Have they questioned anyone else?"

"They haven't taken anyone else to the station like that."

"So why Geraldine? Why not you, or that Smedley man, or one of the committee people?"

"I don't know. Maybe because Geri made the sandwiches for Veronica. And Gordon Smedley's in custody for something else."

"Or maybe because she was the only black person there." I didn't say anything. Juliette may have had a point.

"Mrs Francis, will you phone me when you hear something?"

"Yes, I'll do that."

"Thank you." I scrabbled around in my bag and found a scrap of paper and a pen. I wrote my name and mobile number.

"Here you are. Please ring. Anytime."

"Thank you." She took the paper and put it in a glass dish on the table. I finished my tea and put the mug on a coaster. I got up to leave.

"Thank you for coming," said Juliette, rising. "I appreciate it."

"No problem."

Rita, Joan and Justin were in the kitchen. Prudence was there too, and lunged for my feet.

"Any news?" asked Rita, looking anxious.

"No. Her uncle's a lawyer, and the family have put him on the case."

"Poor Geri. I wonder why they've gone for her and not one of us," pondered Joan.

"Maybe because she made Veronica's sandwiches," I said. I didn't share Juliette's theory with them. I turned to Justin, as Prudence nibbled my Kicker lace. "Any news of Dwayne?" I asked.

"He's in custody. That's all I know. Makes my life easier. Guess I shouldn't be saying that," he said. "How about you? Hear you had quite a bang on the head."

"I'm ok."

"Was it Dwayne?"

"I don't know. But it was his voice leaving the threat on my ansaphone. And I still don't know how he got my number."

"What happened at SoLCEC?" asked Rita.

"Nigel Bentley was there. Lawrence and Derek too."

"Hah! That doesn't surprise me," said Rita.

"And Felicity's husband, and a woman called Maria de Souza."

"Maria's good," commented Rita. Joan was quiet. I gave them the highlights of the meeting, finishing with the challenges about selling off properties.

"So that's what's going on," said Rita, looking at Joan.

"We thought it might be that," said Joan.

"But why?" asked Justin. "Why close down all the neighbourhood schemes? They'll only have to find somewhere else to run them from."

"They've kept the council tax down to get the votes," said Rita. "The money from central government's gone down. They've got to get the money from somewhere."

"But what's all this got to do with Veronica, or *Action in Caring*?" I asked.

"Maybe she knew what was going on," said Rita.

"But it's not rocket science. We've all figured it out. It's politics. People don't usually die over local government politics," I said. Prudence gnawed at my bootlace, oblivious to our pondering.

"Who stood to gain?" asked Joan.

"What do you mean?" asked Justin.

"I mean, who stood to gain from the community centres closing down, from the sale of the property, from the development of SoLCEC. We're the losers, that much is clear. Who are the winners?"

We were all silent. No-one knew the answer.

"When we've worked that one out, the rest will become clear," said Joan. "Now, there's an art class starting in half an hour, and I need to prepare. Justin, I'm going to want an heroic pose from you today."

"What?" He looked horrified.

"Heroic. Like …oh, I don't know: Richard the Lionheart, or a gladiator."

"Oh! I thought you said erotic!" He looked both relieved and disappointed.

"Heroic. This is a class for genteel people in their third age."

I went back to the reception desk having wrestled my shoe away from Prudence. I thought about what Joan had said. Winners and losers. What did Veronica know, and who lost out by her knowing?

"D'you want to call it a day?" I asked Iris, who had held the fort for the best part of the day.

"Yes. Better get home and sort out the tea," she said, putting on her jacket.

"Thanks," I said. "It's been a real help having you here. You in tomorrow?"

"No, can't do tomorrow. I can do Wednesday morning, though."

"Great. See you then."

I wanted to follow up my contact with Maria de Souza, and I still had Suresh's camera. I fished Maria's card from my pocket. As I was picking up the phone to ring her, the front doorbell rang. I buzzed in a woman in her late twenties and knew she had to be Geri's sister. Same nose, same eyes. Uncanny.

"Gina?" I said.

"Yeah. Have we met?"

"No, but you're the image of your sister."

She smiled. "And you must be Nikki the new girl."

"That's me. Any news?"

"They've let her go without charge, but they've told her not to leave the country."

"How is she?"

"Shaken. Exhausted. Scared."

"Is she at home?"

"Yeah, I took her home to Mum. She was going to try to sleep for a couple of hours. They were bastards, you know? Pretty much accused her of bumping off her boss."

"That's crazy. Why would she want to, even if she could?"

"That's what her lawyer argued. He's our uncle. If it hadn't been for him, she'd still be sweating it out in that cell."

"She's got an interview for another job on Wednesday. A second interview. I hope this doesn't knock her off track."

"Me too. I want her out of this place."

"Did you manage to find anything in the computer files?"

"Not yet. That's why I've come back. See what I can find."

"Want some tea?"

"Coffee'd be great. Milk, one sugar."

"I'll go and tell the others that Geri's at home."

Joan, Rita and Justin were upstairs getting ready for the art class. Justin looked ridiculous in a towelling dressing gown, hairy legs poking out at the bottom.

"Geri's out," I said. "Her sister's just come by. She's ok, but it was rough."

"I wonder when they'll come for us?" said Rita. I didn't want to think about that one.

226

I made Gina her coffee and left her hunched over Geri's keyboard. Eager artists started arriving and chatted their way to the art room. Justin definitely needed to think about a career change, judging by the way the class filled up when he was modelling. When the last one had trotted up the stairs, I rang Maria's number.

"Maria de Souza," she answered.

"Hi. This is Nikki Elliot. We met today…"

"I remember. Action in Caring worker masquerading as photographer."

"I can take pictures, too."

"I'm sure. What can I do for you?"

"Any chance of meeting up? You know what happened to Veronica Stein?"

"I heard she'd died."

"The police think it was suspicious. So do we. I mean, the staff and some of the management committee."

"And what if it is? What's it got to do with me?"

"Nothing. It's just that we're thinking it could be connected to some of the things that are going on in the council. You seem to know all the people involved."

"You're a friend of Suresh, right?"

"Yeah. We were at uni together."

"I've got half an hour tomorrow lunchtime if that's any good."

"Perfect. Where are you?" I scribbled down the address.

"This is interesting." Gina had emerged from Geri's office with an empty coffee cup.

"What?"

"Well, a whole load of files was deleted the day before Veronica died."

"Do you know what sort of files?"

"Mostly e-mails. It's normal in a well-run organisation. You clear the server periodically. Good housekeeping says you should delete unwanted e-mails regularly. So it might just have been routine. Some Word and Excel files have gone too. Whole folders of documents.

"Can you retrieve them?"

"Only if I can find a recent back-up, and that's the problem."

"What is?"

"Whoever was cleaning up also deleted the last twelve months' back-ups."

"Aren't they kept on separate tapes?"

"They should be, and there are tapes; but they're empty."

"You mean they've been wiped?"

"Yup. Someone was covering their traces."

"Who would have done that?"

"Whoever had administration rights on the system."

"What do you mean?"

"Whoever was authorised to take care of the system. You couldn't do it, for instance. You were only given access to your own files and the office diary."

"So who had rights?"

"Geri had limited rights, but only one person had full access to everything. Gordon Smedley."

The art class had finished, and everyone had left except for Gina and me. She was still digging around the computer system. I rang Suresh.

"How did the interview go?"

"Good. I've got a story. Don't know if the editor will run it. Could be dynamite."

I told Suresh what Gina had found.

"Let me know if she turns anything else up," he said.

228

Gina came out of her sister's office and closed the door behind her.

"I've done what I can," she said. "I need to figure out how to get some of the documents back. I don't know if I can with no back-ups. Depends on how they wiped stuff."

"Well, thanks for doing what you could. We know more now than we did."

"I'll try and get back tomorrow."

"Thanks. And give my love to Geri."

I closed up the centre and cycled to the South London Press offices off Streatham High Road. I locked up my bike and went into the garishly lit reception area.

"I've come to see Suresh Shah," I said to the man sitting behind the counter.

"Who shall I say is here?"

"Nikki."

He looked down a list of extension numbers, picked up the phone and pushed some buttons.

"Hi. Is Suresh there? Oh. Can you tell him there's someone called Nikki for him? Ok. Yup, will do." He put the phone down and turned to me. "He's in a meeting, but he should be out in the next few minutes. You can sit there and wait."

"Thanks." I sat down. The last edition of the paper was on a small table. There was an interview with the mother of the boy who'd been killed on the fifty-nine bus. His funeral had taken place. The picture of his grieving mother shocked me. She looked younger than me. I opened the paper. More bad news and a page full of letters about speed bumps and inadequate rubbish collections. A half page advert advertised Derek Ramsay's Stop Smoking Clinic. There was a smiling photo of a dapper man. I recognised him straight away: it was Derek from the management committee. I had thought he was an accountant, not a hypnotist. Well, it just went to show you never could tell. As I was getting to the classified section, Suresh burst through a door leading to the humming office behind the reception desk.

"Sorry Nik," he said. "Emergency meeting. This stuff is shit hot. Reckon we'll be front page tomorrow. You brought the camera?"

"Yeah."

"Come on up then."

He led me into a noisy, open plan office and settled at a workstation. I stood behind him – there wasn't room for a second chair. With impressive speed, he linked up the camera to the computer and uploaded the pictures I'd taken.

"Right, let's see what we've got," he said, doing some intricate moves with mouse and keyboard. "Ok, here we go." Suddenly, like déjà vu, scenes of that morning appeared on the screen. There was my first picture of Bentley and Standing. Shots of the mayor and the chief executive, which I guessed would not grab the readership's imagination. I'd got a great picture of Maria de Souza, and a series of pictures capturing the protest that changed the direction of the meeting. Best of all was the shot of the man in the green anorak facing up to Nigel Bentley. I could see the headline. I could write it: *Fists Fly at Celebration Feast*. I ran it by Suresh. He gave me a withering look.

"Don't give up the day job, Nik," he said.

We continued to scroll through. I'd taken a couple outside the centre as we'd left. Suddenly, I couldn't believe what I was looking at.

"Go back to that one," I said, as Suresh moved on to the next photo. He clicked the mouse.

"What have you seen?"

"Look."

"It's the group I interviewed before we went to the pub. Can't use it. Doesn't tell you anything."

"Oh yes it does," I said. "Look beyond the group. What's happening behind Leo Balmforth?"

He squinted at the screen. "I can't…oh yes, it's Nigel Bentley. But he's just talking to someone."

"Not just anyone. That's Nigel Bentley talking to Gordon Smedley."

"Are you sure?"

"Absolutely."

"But wasn't he arrested?"

"They must have let him out on bail."

"So what's his connection with Bentley?"

"I think you'd better find out."

I was only five minutes from home, so I picked up food that didn't need me to do much to it in the way of cooking from the Greek/Turkish/Polish grocery and headed back to the flat. Benjamin's bike was under the stairs. I parked mine and knocked on his door.

"Who's there?" he called. He'd be disappointed that it was me and not some muscle-bound clone looking for a good time.

"Only me," I said.

"Oh, Nik," he said, and I could hear that I was right. He fumbled with the lock and opened the door. "How you doing?" Even if I wasn't the man of his dreams, he still looked pleased to see me and gave me a hug.

"I'm fine now," I said, "but boy! What a day. You up for a glass of wine?"

"How could I refuse?"

"Ok, let me shove my supper in the oven and I'll bring a bottle down."

"I've got wine – and it's a damned sight better than the stuff you usually have! Just bring your lovely self."

I ran upstairs and put a potato in the oven. You couldn't go wrong with jacket potatoes. Well, not very wrong. I went back down where Ben's door was still open.

"Come in and tell me all about it," he said bringing out an expensive looking bottle of red wine, two designer glasses and a corkscrew so trendy that I couldn't see how it worked. Benjamin managed to open the wine and poured it out as I settled onto his sofa.

"I don't know whether to start with Wendy Baggott or the shenanigans at work today," I said.

"Ooh, start with Wendy."

I told Benjamin about Wendy and the dancing and still being sore about Ruth and not really knowing what to do about any of it.

"Have some more wine," he said, and I did. There wasn't really much more to say. I told him about my work experience as a press photographer. He looked almost impressed.

"So it looks like there's some kind of corruption to do with selling property, and Gordon Smedley wiped a year's worth of back-ups from *AiC's* computer system."

"Well, all I can say is that girl at the Jobcentre has a lot to answer for," said Benjamin. "Look, I'm sorry to be a party pooper, but I'm due to meet Rick Landor in Old Compton Street in a couple of hours. I don't want to be late."

"Who's Rick Landor?"

"*Who's Rick Landor??*"

"Should I have heard of him?"

"Darling, he only runs *the* most exciting gallery in the West End!"

"Oh." So Ben would be mugging up on modern art instead of building up his thighs for the leader of the cycling pack. He didn't hang around, that was for sure.

"So I need to get ready," he said. I thought he looked fine, but then my standards of how to dress for an evening out fell way below Benjamin's.

"I'll go and eat my solitary potato," I said. "Have fun!"

I'd got some phone messages. I sighed as I picked them up. Another call from the bank: *Ms Elliot, your credit rating is at risk if you do not make immediate contact and we may have to freeze your account.* Great! One from Wendy: *Uh..not sure if you got my last message. Hope you're ok. Um, maybe…look, just give me a ring sometime.* Why had I delayed getting back to her? *Hi Nikki,* said Ruth's voice. *Just wanted to say…you know…I hope you're ok…and …I'm sorry it didn't work out, and I still care about you, I hope we can stay in touch…* I pushed three to delete Ruth's message. I ferreted around in my bag for Wendy's number. She'd think I didn't like her, and I did, I definitely did. I punched in the number.

"Hello?"

"Hi. Is that Wendy?"

"Nikki?" Her voice brightened.

"Yeah. Look, Wendy, sorry I didn't get back earlier. Just lots of stuff, you know."

"Oh, that's ok. So, how are you?"

"Good. I'm fine now. Thank you. So…how about that drink?"

"I'd love to. When's good for you?"

"Thursday's ok."

"It's good for me. I'm on days this week."

God! If I dated a policewoman, I'd have to fit in with her day and night shifts! I hadn't thought about that. And she'd be working some weekends too. Bummer!

"*Sappho?* Half six?"

"Perfect. See you there."

I heated up some baked beans to put on my potato and ate my simple but satisfying supper starting a new book. I'd borrowed a Sarah Dunant from Carla, which she'd raved about. I was hooked after the first page. I drank half a bottle of wine, read a quarter of the book, which was set in renaissance Florence. Not my usual sort of read. Carla was right about the book and Benjamin was right about wine: mine was definitely inferior to his, but it warmed a space inside. I got ready for bed and was asleep by eleven. The phone woke me when it was still dark. I peered at my clock. It was six o'clock. I stumbled out to the living room and picked up the phone.

"Nik, it's Suresh. Sorry to wake you, but thought you'd want to know."

"Know what?"

"Our story's been shunted back to page three."

"For that you woke me up before dawn?"

"Our story's been taken off the front page because there's a bigger story."

"Well, doesn't that happen all the time? You need counselling or something?" My head was thick from last night's wine.

"Nikki, there's been another murder on Clapham Common."

"That's awful." Thugs on the Common had murdered a gay man last year. There was always the fear that it would happen again. And the law didn't protect gay people from hate crimes.

"Don't you want to know who the victim is?"

"Do I?"

"Yes, I think so."

"Oh, for God's sake, Suresh, put me out of my misery. Who died?"

"Gordon Smedley. Gordon Smedley was found battered to death in undergrowth just a little after ten."

Chapter 22

"Nikki? Nik? You still there?"

"Yeah. Yeah, Suresh, I'm still here. Just stunned is all. What else do you know?"

"A witness saw someone running away, but they didn't get a description beyond medium height, probably male, wearing a hoodie."

"D'you think that photo means anything? The one with him and Bentley? Maybe we should let the police have it."

"Our guys are onto it."

"I think I should be scared."

"I'd throw a month long sickie if I were you."

"D'you think it was connected to what's going on? I mean, it could have been random. You know, someone might have assumed he was gay and battered him just because of that."

"It's possible. Or he'd arranged to meet someone. Or maybe he really was out cruising."

"I don't think he was gay. I'm sure he wasn't."

"It's not just gay guys who cruise on the Common. And it wouldn't be the first time someone had arranged a meet-up in the bushes to clinch a shady deal."

"Tell me if you hear anything?"

"Yeah, I'll try."

"Thanks. I'd better start letting people know."

It was only six fifteen. Too early to call anyone, even with news this disturbing. I didn't know where to put myself, what to do. My mind was in turmoil. Veronica, Tanya, now Gordon. A box full of dirty tricks. Politics that had become deadly and that I didn't understand. I wandered into the kitchen, filled the kettle, switched it on. I was too wired and jumpy for coffee, so I made a pot of jasmine tea. It was too hot to drink. I showered and put on a black T-shirt and my Dockers. I didn't think

Veronica's smart casual dress code applied to *Action in Caring* any more. I wasn't even sure why I was thinking of going in. I combed my hair. I wanted to talk to someone. Carla, Wendy and Benjamin in that order. It was six thirty. They'd have to be at least thinking about getting up and going to work. I couldn't hear any movement from Benjamin's flat downstairs. Maybe he'd stayed out with Rick Landor, maybe he'd brought him home. Probably not, though. Streatham might be a bit down-market for a gallery owner. Brixton was cool. Streatham was…well, the only famous people associated with Streatham are saucy Cynthia Payne, a brothel owner famous before my time, and Naomi Campbell. Ben would have spent the night somewhere cool like Fulham or Hoxton. Carla liked to leave getting up until the last minute. She'd have at least another hour of sleep ahead of her, and I didn't want to ruin her day by depriving her of dreamtime and talking about murder. I didn't know anything about Wendy's sleep patterns. Was she an early to bed, sex in the morning type of girl? Or a night owl who prowled chat rooms and drank whisky at two in the morning? One way to find out. I rummaged for her card, picked up the phone, punched in the number.

"Yeah?" said a voice thick with sleep. Not an early riser, then.

"Wendy?"

"Yeah? Who's this?"

"Nikki."

"Nikki? What's up? It's still dark!"

Definitely not a morning person. "I'm sorry Wendy. I thought you might be up. It's just that Suresh called…"

"Who?"

"Suresh. Writes for the South London Press."

"Oh. What'd he want?"

"Gordon Smedley's dead."

"What?"

"Gordon Smedley. *Action in Caring's* finance manager. Arrested for molesting young boys."

"Yeah, Yeah, I remember who he is. Was. What's the story?"

"Battered to death on Clapham Common. That's all I know. But I'd seen him yesterday, I'd inadvertently taken a photo of him deep in conversation with Nigel Bentley."

"As in Councillor Bentley?"

"Yup."

"Hmm. Well, I guess the night shift copped it and someone will be dealing with it. Why don't you go back to bed?"

"'Cos I'm up and dressed and wired. This is death number three, Wendy!"

"Yeah. Yeah, s'pose it is. Hmm."

"I mean, I'm not feeling very safe right now."

"No. Look, Nikki, just take it easy for now and let me wake up. I'll be able to think when I've had some coffee. Then I'll come over. Ok?"

"I'm ok really..."

"I know, but it'd be good to see you."

"About an hour?"

"Half."

I think that's when I started to fall in love with Wendy Baggott.

Twenty-five minutes later, my doorbell rang. I sprang up, straightened my T-shirt, smoothed my hair, opened the door. Wendy stood on the mat, hair still wet from the shower. Her cheeks were rosy. Her skin glistened. She wore a navy tracksuit and trainers. She seemed slightly out of breath and was making little on the spot jogging movements.

"Did you run over?"

"Yeah. I'm training for a half marathon. You gave me a good excuse for a work-out."

"Where do you live?"

"D'you think I could come in?"

I stepped aside and she jogged into my living room. She did some stretches by the window, looking out at the view over glorious Streatham. Everything in me was in meltdown.

"What can I get you?"

"Coffee?"

"Ok. Breakfast?" It was the one meal I could produce that was usually more or less edible.

"Oh, let's see. I'll start with porridge, then go for the full Scottish with black pudding and scrambled eggs…"

"No black pudding! Sorry, I'm a vegetarian. Leave now if that's too much to cope with…"

"I'm disappointed in you, Nikki!" Her eyes twinkled. I wanted to kiss her.

"I think I'm out of porridge," I said.

"Well that's it, I'm out of here. The service is terrible!"

And then we were both laughing, and she sank into my sofa and she looked as if she belonged there. We glanced at each other for a moment, and the eye contact was electric. I backed into the kitchen.

"Coffee, then," I said, putting on the kettle. "I've got muesli. And there's bread if you want toast. And a mango. Have a mango."

"Heaven. I'll have it all," she said.

I set about creating a breakfast fit for a queen – or at least for a highly desirable police sergeant. I poured muesli into my best pottery bowl. I didn't make anything for myself. How could I eat with Wendy on my sofa and another murder to figure out? I handed her the tray.

"This is wonderful!" she said, tucking into the muesli.

I poured the coffee. I gave her my best mug, the blue one that Carla had brought me back from Skye.

"Shall I peel the mango for you?"

"Will you share it with me?"

"Yes." I peeled it carefully, slicing it into two bowls. Its juices dripped slowly, stickily. My hands were orange and wet. I sucked at my fingers and she gave me an unfathomable look. Then she picked up her bowl and spooned the fruit into her gorgeous mouth. I ate mine, my tongue lingering over the silky soft fruit. It was sweet and fragrant, with the slightest hint of pepper. We were silent. I didn't know what was meant to happen next.

"So Gordon Smedley's dead, then?" she said, as she placed her empty bowl on the tray. The spell was broken.

"Uh…yes, that's what Suresh rang to tell me," I said.

"And you think it's all connected?"

"I don't know. I think so." *Oh glorious Wendy, solve this dreadful puzzle, find the bad guys, lock them up for good, and then come away with me.*

"I'll find out more when I get to the station," she said, looking at her watch. "I'll need to go home and change, though."

"Where's home?"

"Tooting Bec."

"What time do you start work?"

"Nine. It's ok, I've got time."

It wasn't yet seven thirty.

"This is all getting a bit scary, Wendy," I ventured.

"Uh huh," she said. "I can see it would. I'll see if Ginny's making any headway and ring you later."

"They picked up Geri yesterday," I said. "You know? Geri who's the administrator."

"I remember her. Did they let her go?"

"Only after her lawyer intervened. So…are we still on for Thursday?"

"I hope so. Want me to pick you up from work?"

"What? And have my very own police escort?"

"We could pretend I was arresting you, and I could lead you off in handcuffs…"

"Wendy! It's not a joke, you know? Geri being arrested."

"I know, I know, I'm sorry. It's just…"

"You see murders and monstrous deeds every day?"

"Something like that."

To be honest, the thought of Wendy leading me away from my desk in handcuffs was thrilling.

"Maybe we'd better just meet at *Sappho*."

"Ok."

She got up. "Will you be all right?"

"I think so. I just wish it was all over."

Wendy helped me to take the dishes out to the kitchen. I walked her to the front door. She opened her arms to me, and we held each other softly. There was that lovely citrus cedar scent.

"You take care, now," she said. "And if you're worried, or if anything else happens, you just ring me, ok?"

I nodded. "Thank you."

"That was the best breakfast ever," she called, turning back as she skipped down the stairs.

"See you."

There was still no sound from Benjamin's flat. He must have got lucky with the gallery owner. It was just about late enough for me to ring Carla. I'd do the dishes first, give her time to surface. I squeezed the last of my bottle of Ecover into the sink, scrubbed at the dried baked beans, lovingly wiped clean Wendy's bowls and mug. Had I felt this way about Ruth? I was pondering the mysteries of love and lust and drying the suds from my hands when the phone rang, making me jump.

"Hello?"

Silence.

"Hello?"

Breathing.

"I'm going to hang up."

240

"We're onto you, bitch. That little tap on the head was just a warning."

Click.

Shit. Wendy was somewhere between Tooting Bec and me. I didn't know who else to call. It had been a different voice. Older. Whispering, a sinister rasp. I'd ring Ginny Lancaster. My hands were shaking, but I found her number amongst the dishevelled scraps of paper around the phone.

"DCI Lancaster," she said, picking up on the second ring.

"Hi. This is Nikki Elliot. Um, *Action in Caring?*"

"Yeah, I remember. How can I help?"

"I've just had a threatening call. Different voice, same sort of message. I thought you ought to know."

"Dwayne Robbins is still in custody, so he's out of the picture."

"It wasn't Dwayne. I'd have recognised his voice."

"Can you describe it?"

I described the voice, told her what he'd said, gave her the exact time, omitted to say that one of her officers had just left.

"Did you try one four seven one?"

"No, I didn't think of that."

"You never know. Give it a try, and if there's a number, call me back. Otherwise, take it easy and try not to go out more than you need to."

So that was it. No police protection, no promise of an early arrest. Just another weary detective at the early start of what she knew would be a long and difficult day. I guessed that if she didn't have a headache already, she would by the end of the morning. And as for me, well I was supposed to go on as usual. I dialled one four seven one to see who had last called me. I expected to get the automated message saying that the caller had withheld their number, and of course I wasn't disappointed.

I wheeled my bike out of the front door cautiously. Looked around. There was the neighbourhood Goth walking her Jack Russell and sucking at a red lollypop. A man in a suit, his head bowed, marched towards the High Road. No-one around who looked dangerous or like they were waiting to kill me. I pushed off towards the common and made it to work in record time. There was no-one there. I looked at my watch. No wonder: it was only eight fifteen. I didn't fancy being in the building on my own, so I continued down Tanners Lane, past the kebab shop, to the café that Geri had taken me to on my first day. It was open and serving breakfast. I chained my bike to the railings outside, and found a table near the window so that I could keep an eye on it. The mango I'd shared with Wendy felt more like sex than food, so I ordered coffee and a croissant with jam. There was a collection of newspapers, and I rummaged through them until I found the South London Press. It led with the story of Gordon's murder, and the by-line read Suresh Shah. *Suspect beaten to death on common* read the inspiring headlines. Suresh must have sweated buckets over that one. It went on:

Charity worker Gordon Smedley, recently questioned about a series of offences involving boys, was found battered to death on Clapham Common on Monday evening. Smedley, 46, worked for Action in Caring, the charity whose director, Veronica Stein, died in suspicious circumstances earlier this month. Smedley, who was single, was out on bail at the time of his death. He previously worked for the Guild for London Amateur Drama (GfLAD), which went into liquidation in 2005.

"Coffee?"

"Thanks." I closed the paper so that there was room on the table for the waitress to put down my cup.

"I bring croissant." She shimmied back to the counter, and came back with a giant croissant on a small plate.

"Thank you."

"You ok? Want something more?"

"No, that's fine. Thanks." I buttered the croissant and struggled to open the small pot of jam that came with it. At the point where I was about to give up, or at least find someone more butch than me, it gave way with a vacuum releasing pop. Raspberry. Not as good as strawberry, but better than marmalade. I spread it on my croissant, which was warm and flaky. The coffee was hot. I liked this café. When I stopped working at *Action in Caring* I'd carry on coming here. I turned to the inside pages of the paper. Page three carried the story about the SoLCEC meeting, and there was my picture of green anorak man about to sock it to Nigel Bentley. They'd credited the photo to N. Elliot. Fame at last. Next time I found myself the other side of Chantelle's desk I'd show her this, show her that I was a talented professional, not someone to be shoved into dead-end meat slicing or receptionist jobs. It was Suresh's by-line again:

Kennington: enterprise at any price?

Angry community activists heckled councillors and EU officials at Monday's official opening of the South London Community and Enterprise Centre. Representatives of the borough's community groups accused the council of closing down neighbourhood centres in order to sell off the properties. "You have to ask yourself who profits," said Maria de Souza, Co-ordinator of Young Futures. "Someone is making a killing, and it's not us," she added. Eurobuild Construction, the company that won the contract to build the centre, went £1.5 million over budget. SoLCEC cost £3.5 million and has been developed in conjunction with similar centres in three other EU countries. "This is the future," commented Nigel Bentley, leader of the Council. "Old style neighbourhood centres went out in the eighties. This centre will help to generate wealth and opportunities in south London." Last night, questions were being asked about the identity of the directors of Eurobuild. We can reveal that Nigel Bentley has links to a subsidiary company. It remains to be seen whether he declared a conflict of interest, and questions must be asked about whether he personally profited from the deal. Mr Bentley refused to comment. With local elections due to be held next month, a corruption scandal could result in a dramatic shift in power at the Town Hall.

Dynamite! Suresh was back on form. I was pissed that he hadn't told me first about the property link, but everything was happening so fast.

I folded the paper back together and sipped my coffee. It all seemed to come back to Nigel Bentley. What was the link between him and Gordon? And had Veronica been planning to meet him? I reached into my bag for my phone. Carla would surely be up and awake by now. I pressed the fast dial key and heard her phone ringing. Her voicemail answered. *Hi Carla, there's been another death. Have a look at the front page of the SLP and then go to page three. Would be good to see you. Ring me later. Love you.* I drew my finger around the plate, picking up the last of the croissant crumbs. I licked them off my finger. The waitress was watching me. She smiled. I went over to the counter to pay.

"Everything all right?" she said, her rich Polish accent rolling luxuriantly over the "r"s.

"Fine. Thanks." I said.

"Have a good day," she said, popping the tip I'd left into a communal dish.

"You too."

When I arrived at *AiC* Geri was already there. It was good to see her.

"Hi, how are you doing?" I went to hug her. She stiffened. "Hey, what's up?"

"Nothing. I'm fine. Yesterday was a real picnic."

"Yeah. Sorry. What happened?"

"Oh, you know. Usual police stuff. Where was I, what was I doing, didn't I hate my boss, that sort of thing."

"We were really worried. I met your mum."

"Yes, she said."

"How long did they hold you?"

"Long enough. Look, Nikki, to be honest I'm not in the mood for chatting. There's loads of stuff to be getting on with, so I'll make a start."

I wanted to tell her that I was her friend, but I didn't know where to start.

"Did you hear that Gordon's dead?"

"What?" She stopped and turned to face me.

"Last night. On the common. Someone killed him. It's in the SLP."

"Gordon's dead?"

I let her question hang.

"I don't know what's happening here. This is all so crazy. I'm getting out. I've got that other interview tomorrow. I just have to hope they don't make the connection between this place and me. So do you know what happened?"

"Suresh – my friend on the SLP – rang this morning first thing to say they'd found Gordon beaten to death on the common. And I got another threatening phone call. And while you were being interrogated yesterday, it was all happening at SoLCEC. I think it's all linked, but I can't figure out how."

"You know what? If I were you, I'd get the hell out. Go back to Charmaine or whatever her name is and get that job in Tesco. "

"Chantelle. I wish it were that easy. And you know, I really want this place to work, and the SoLCEC project stinks, if you ask me. I'm going to ring Maria de Souza and see what she makes of it all."

"Up to you. I'm going to sort out the bills, let the management committee know we're another one down, check on some bookings."

"Geri?"

"What?"

"I'm sorry. I'm so sorry they put you through all that. I wish they'd taken me as well."

"Thanks. Look, none of this is your fault. We've just got to get through it, ok?"

"Yeah. Take you to lunch?"

"Maybe."

"Cool."

The phone rang as I settled behind the reception desk.

"*Action in Caring,* Nikki speaking," I said.

"Hi Nikki, it's Chantelle."

"Oh. Hi Chantelle," I said. "Problem?"

"I read about Gordon Smedley in the SLP. You ok?"

"Thanks for asking. Yeah, I'm just getting threatening phone calls and hanging in here," I said.

"Look, I can find you something else."

"Thanks. I may take you up on that. But no meat counters."

"No meat counters. Just let me know when you need to move on."

Finally, a lifeline.

Justin arrived an hour or so later, and as he arranged his room, his boys struggled in. They looked more hopeless than ever. Dwayne wasn't amongst them. The guy who reminded me of South Park Kenny looked thin and scared. The skin around his nose and mouth was raw and scabby. He was alternately sniffing and wiping his sleeve across his face.

"Got a cold?" I asked.

"Nah."

"Guys, let's go," called Justin, and they trooped through to the meeting room.

There was a ring at the door. I glanced up at the CCTV and saw Suresh standing outside. I was surprised to see him there, to see him out of context; but then of course he'd come to see us. This was where the story began, or at least where a significant part of it was played out. I buzzed him in.

"How you doing?" he asked.

"Oh, well, you know…"

"Yeah. You know this is hot, don't you?"

"How hot?"

"Corruption in the council, people in high places linked to dirty dealings and murder, that sort of hot." He looked almost gleeful.

"You're enjoying this, aren't you?"

"Beats writing up a report on the local Cats Protection League jumble sale."

"People are dead. I'm getting threatening phone calls. Centres are closing and people are losing services. How can you be so flippant?"

"Comes with the job. Anyway, if I can be part of uncovering it all, I'm doing my bit for the community, fighting for right, that sort of thing. And I'd like to see this lot lose all their seats in the local elections."

"Yeah, you're a right Robin Hood!"

"Don't knock it. And you're the one who took the photo with the perv and Nasty Nigel."

"Do I get royalties?"

"You've got fame. You want fortune as well?"

"Just trying to earn a living. So what's Bentley doing?"

"Lying low. No-one's seen him today."

"What do you think was going on between him and Smedley?"

"We know Smedley's not short of a few bob."

"Smart riverside location?"

"Exactly. And we know there were questions about how he managed things at GfLAD."

"And we know that Bentley's into wheeling and dealing with property."

"I've asked the juniors at the paper to do some more digging."

"You know I got a dodgy phone call this morning?"

"No. What happened?"

"Some bloke rang to threaten me. Different voice to the last one."

"Go on," he said, fishing out his notebook. I reprised the call for him. He scribbled. "You told the police?"

"Yeah. I rang Ginny Lancaster."

"Ring me if anything else happens."

"Freaks me out."

"Yeah." He was frowning and flicking through pages in his notebook.

"What are you thinking?"

"Oh, nothing. Just wondering how it all ties up. Who your mystery caller could be. Listen, d'you need to come over and stay with Meena and me?"

"Thanks. That's a really nice offer. Can I think about it?"

"Sure. Look, I'd better head off. I'll let you know if there are developments."

"Thanks." I was touched at his offer. If it wasn't for his and Meena's toddler going through the terrible twos, I'd be tempted. And Meena had never really liked me. I don't know why. It couldn't just be my cooking.

I sifted through the post. Bills and promotional fliers, nothing interesting. My mobile rang. I looked at the number on the screen.

"Hi Ben, what's up?"

"Nik! You'll never believe what happened last night!"

"Let me guess: Rick whatshisname is the hottest dude since Mr Lycra Pants and you spent a hot and pornographically steamy night in his loft in Hoxton?"

"How did you guess?"

"Really?"

"Yes! You're amazing!"

I didn't want to burst his bubble and tell him that he was very predictable.

"Have you seen the SLP?"

"No. What's in it?"

"A bloke from the community centre got beaten to death on the Common last night. And they printed one of my photos. It's got my name on it." I told Benjamin about my stint as a snapper for the paper. I'd even started using the jargon.

"Hold on a minute…I've got a copy right here…yup, here it is. What page?"

"Three." I could hear him rustling the paper.

"Got it. Hey, that's not bad! Hang on…that bloke who's about to get hit…I've seen him before."

"He's a councillor. You've probably seen his picture in the paper before."

"No, it's somewhere else. What's his name?"

"Bentley. Nigel Bentley."

"I remember! He's a nasty piece of work. I've seen him trying to score with the young guys. He's bad news. I'm sure it was him who beat up a rent boy a couple of months ago. Round the back of Old Compton Street. I knew the kid."

"What happened?"

"I was out with Jon and Phil. We heard a scuffle. Sounded like someone was in trouble. This kid – his name's Sam – he was fighting off this bloke. I'm sure it was the same one. We went in and broke it up. He ran off and we checked that Sam was ok. He was shaken up, we took him for a drink, then he went back to some hostel he was dossing in."

"How old is Sam?"

"Looks young. Not more than sixteen."

"Would you talk with Suresh?"

"Your journo pal?"

"Yeah."

"I dunno…"

"Are you with the good guys?"

"You don't have to ask that, Nik."

"Then speak to Suresh. Help to join up the dots."

"You think it means something?"

"I'm sure it does."

This was a link between Bentley and Smedley that we hadn't thought of. Not property. Boys. Maybe both.

Chapter 23

I was wondering whether to call Suresh or Ginny first with this new information when my mobile rang again. It was Carla.

"How's the arm?"

"Mending slowly. I checked out the SLP. What's going on, Nik?"

I told Carla about Benjamin recognising Bentley's photo.

"Could Ben have got it wrong?"

"He sounded very certain. I'm going to get Suresh to do some more digging."

"You seen your sexy sergeant?"

"Carla!"

"Well?"

"It just so happens…" and I told Carla about the creepy phone call and Wendy's mercy dash, and breakfast.

"Bloody hell, Nik! Run the bit about the mango by me again…and what about Ruth?"

"Ruth's pregnant. That hasn't changed. She's going to marry a man. It was just a…I don't know, it was just a short, wonderful, terrible thing, fling, affair, I don't know what to call it."

"You're amazing, you know?"

"What do you mean?"

"Well, only a couple of weeks ago – if that – that you were wondering if you were in love with her. I s'pose you *weren't*, then."

"I'm not going to waste my energy on someone who doesn't care enough to let me know they're back in the country and who leaps from my bed into some bloke's."

"You know what worries me?"

"What?"

"I'm worried that you're covering up your hurt and burying it in Wendy-lust, and I'm worried that you're not letting yourself grieve and that you might hurt someone who sounds like they're really decent."

"So when did you become my therapist?"

"Don't get scratchy with me, Nik. Just think about it. Ok?"

"Sure. When I've stopped thinking about all the people who seem to be dropping dead around me and pondering why and wondering how quickly Chantelle can get me another job or if I'll be killed before I escape…"

"Oh, stop being such a drama queen, Nik."

"Yeah, well, there is quite a lot going on right now. And I really do like Wendy. I don't know her very well yet, but I like everything I've seen so far."

"Take it slowly."

I heard a door open behind me, and the sniffing and scuffing of Justin's group as they headed for the front door and freedom.

"Gotta go, Carla. Fancy a drink tonight?"

"*Sappho?*"

"Six thirty?"

"See you there."

The last of the boys had left and Justin was looking thoughtful.

"Penny for them," I said.

"Eh?"

"Penny for them. Your thoughts. Quaint English saying."

"Oh. Nah, it's nothing. Just a bit worried about one of the lads."

"Which one?"

"Leon. Kid in orange hoodie."

"He was sniffing a lot. I asked him if he had a cold. He said not."

"It's not a cold making him sniff, worse luck. I think he's snorting coke."

"How can a kid like him afford a coke habit?"

"He'll shove anything in his body to give him a high. And he'll do anything to pay for it. I thought I was getting through, he seemed to have cleaned up pretty good. But this last week, there's been something going on and he's using again."

"What's his family like?"

"Dad took off when he was seven. Mum struggles with her own habit. Oldest brother got sent down for GBH."

"Poor kid."

"You wouldn't say that if you were one of the people he'd mugged."

"Guess not."

"He's tight with Dwayne. Keeps asking what's happening with him."

"What is happening?"

"Dunno. In some secure unit, I s'pose."

"You modelling this afternoon?"

"Yeah! Seems like I'm a hit with the oldies. Think I'll get some air for a couple of hours. See ya."

Justin headed out through the front door. I was almost getting to like him. It would be quiet until the afternoon art class and I needed to talk with Suresh. I called his mobile.

"Hi Nik. What's up?"

I told him about Benjamin's revelations.

"I'll get someone onto it. Thanks."

I delved in my bag for Ginny Lancaster's number. She answered on third ring.

"Hi Ginny, it's Nikki Elliot again."

"No news on your anonymous caller, I'm afraid."

"I've got more news." I relayed Benjamin's story.

"Could be interesting. Would your friend be willing to make a statement?"

"I think so." I gave Ginny Benjamin's number. "Will you let me know if there are any developments?" Developments. That's what the police talk about, isn't it?

"I'll do that. Thank you for your help." I wished it were Wendy carrying out the investigation rather than this brusque ice queen.

The doorbell rang and I saw Rita on the CCTV. Great. She could cover for me while I went to see Maria. But first I had to see if she'd heard about Gordon.

"I can't believe it," she said. "Couldn't stand the man; but no-one deserves to die like that. What the hell's going on? We never used to have deaths and killings and whatnot. Only between the gangs."

"I had another threatening call this morning," I said.

"You'd better watch yourself, love," said Rita. "We don't want anything happening to you."

"Could you do me a favour?" I asked her if she'd cover the desk while I went to meet Maria.

"Yes, you get off then," she said. "Good woman, Maria de Souza. You send my best regards. Tell her my Scott's doing well for himself."

"Did he go to her project, then?"

"Yes. He used to do sports and things there. He's always said if it wasn't for *Action in Caring* and Maria de Souza, he'd be in the nick."

"I'll tell her. I won't be long," I said. "She said she could only spare half an hour. And then I promised to take Geri out to lunch. Can you cover me for both?"

"'Course I can, love. You get off, then."

"Thanks, Rita." I grabbed my bag and slipped my jacket on. I'd already checked out the location of Maria's project, and figured it would only take me ten minutes on the bike.

Young Hearts was run from a squat concrete building that had maybe started life as an industrial unit. There was heavy wire meshing across its windows. The walls were bright with murals depicting young people playing, making music, bonding. There were rainbows and gardens, a silver river, the impossible dreams of urban kids. The door was red and looked as if it had been freshly painted. WELCOME was spelled across the top in canary yellow. I pushed the bell.

"Who is it?" asked a cheery voice from the other side.

"Nikki Elliot. I've come to see Maria." ·

"Push the door."

I entered into a bright, clean corridor. The walls were painted white but they were covered with paintings and textile hangings. There were skylights in the ceiling, and the sunlight poured through, lighting up the place. A young woman stepped out from behind a counter to greet me.

"Maria's been a bit held up, but she'll be out in a minute," said the owner of the cheery voice. "Can I get you a drink while you wait?"

"Coffee please. One sugar, no milk."

"Ok. Have a seat." She gestured towards an orange sofa that sported cobalt blue cushions. I sank my body onto it. I heard laughter from a distant room. Two boys tore down the corridor and crashed through a set of swing doors.

"Late for class again," said Cheery Voice as she gave me my coffee.

"What's the class?"

"Literacy. Teacher's dynamite. The kids can't bear to miss it."

"Wow!" I thought of the reluctance with which Justin's lads shuffled into his sessions.

"Yeah, I know. But this place changes kids around. It's because of Maria. I'm Beth, by the way."

"How long have you been open?"

"Nine years now. Took a while to really get going."

"You been here long?"

"Nearly five years. Hard to believe!"

"You like it then?"

"Yeah, I love it. Don't get me wrong, some days are hell; but we offer a safe space for kids and we help them to grow up into decent human beings. That's reason enough for staying for me. So what do you do?"

"I'm the admin person at *Action in Caring*. Just been there a couple of weeks, but it's been like a nightmare."

"Didn't your director die?"

"Yeah. My first day."

"And wasn't there something in the paper about someone else?"

"The finance manager. He got killed on the Common."

"Shit! Wasn't he the one….?"

"Yeah, had up for molesting kids."

"So…not an easy place to work then?"

"You could say that. There's some good stuff too, but with all the council shenanigans…"

"Tell me about it! We have to fight every inch of the way just to stay open and pull in enough money to pay the rent. But we're supposed to be some sort of centre of excellence!"

"We *are* a centre of excellence, Beth." Maria had come out of one of the doors leading off the corridor. "Hello Nikki. Sorry to have kept you waiting."

"It's fine. I'm just grateful to you for seeing me." She was wearing black trousers with a long lime green tunic over the top. Her hair was dark with chestnut highlights and swung below her ears. A large red pendant dangled between her breasts. She was big and beautiful and didn't wear a trace of make-up.

"Would you like to come in?"

I picked up my coffee, waved goodbye to Beth, and followed Maria into her office.

"So, what do you think I can help you with?"

"Just some background, really. I think someone killed Veronica, and the police are looking into it. They picked on the woman who was Veronica's PA and I know she didn't do it. Gordon Smedley was killed. I'm being warned off. And what's happening to other community centres?"

"Why does it bother you? How long have you worked for *Action in Caring?*"

"A couple of weeks."

"So why not just get out?"

"Maybe because I saw Veronica die. Maybe because I like the people involved. And I don't like dirty politics."

Maria was looking at me curiously. She'd propped her elbows on the desk and was resting her chin in her hands.

"I like you, Nikki. And I'm sick of dirty politics too. So I'm going to try to help you."

"Thanks."

"But I don't know whether what I know will be of any use."

"What do you know about Nigel Bentley?"

"Nasty piece of work. Into making money out of council house sales. Wouldn't trust him as far as I could throw him."

"Is there anything apart from the property scams with him?"

"How do you mean?"

"I think there was a connection between him and Gordon Smedley. Smedley was rumoured to be into sex with young boys. Friend of mine saw Bentley assault a young guy in Soho. He recognised him from my photo from the SoLCEC opening."

"I've not heard anything, but I can ask around."

"Do you think there *is* some kind of scheme to sell off the neighbourhood centres?"

"It's looking that way."

"And it's because the council needs the money?"

"They're in deep trouble, so it's likely. Look, I'll ask around. See what the word is on the street. That's the best I can do for now."

"Thanks. It's a start."

"I didn't like her, you know."

"Who?"

"Veronica. Cold fish. Odd."

"Yeah, she seemed very cold to me. Angry. And both she and Gordon Smedley seem to have a history of working for organisations that closed down."

"I'd heard as much."

"He probably made thousands out of it. Leo Balmforth worked for him once."

"Ah. That would explain a few things. Listen, Nikki, I have a meeting now. I'll let you know if I hear anything."

"I'll do the same. Oh, by the way, Rita Bourne said to tell you that her Scott's doing all right for himself. He's working as a plumber."

"Thanks. That's wonderful news. I'm sorry, but I really must get on."

"Thanks for your time." I got up to leave. "Good meeting you. This seems like a great centre."

"Maybe you should come and work for us."

I thought about it. "Yeah, that'd be cool. Let me know if there's anything going." I liked the light in this place, the colour and the sense that something meaningful was happening. Maria held out her hand, I shook it and then left.

"Bye Beth," I said as I headed for the front door.

"Take care," said Beth.

Geri emerged from her office, rubbing at her eyes wearily. Her hair was frizzing out of its band just as it had been on the first day I'd met her. She looked tired and vulnerable. She'd lost weight, and her black skirt was loose around her small waist. I hoped she'd revive in time for tomorrow's interview.

"Lunch?"

"Yeah. Why not? Can't do much more here today."

"I thought we'd have heard from some of the management committee."

"Maybe they haven't read the paper. I've rung and left messages. Got through to Joan, and she sounded shocked, but she's coming in later. Can't get Bernard."

"Maybe his wife's sick?"

"Maybe. And Derek's gone off the radar."

"Lawrence was at the SoLCEC event yesterday. So was Derek, come to think of it, but he left before I could talk to him."

"Hmm. I'm not surprised Lawrence is lying low. Without Gordon to tell him what to do he's useless. Never could figure Derek out."

"Where d'you fancy going?"

"Don't much mind. I don't think I could eat, but it'd be good to get some air."

"How about the café on the Common?"

"Yeah, fine."

We put on coats, locked up the centre, strolled up to the Common. It was a glorious day, one of those spring days that make you feel that there is hope for the world. It seemed at odds with the death and dirty deeds that were facing us on all fronts. It was warm enough to sit outside. Au pairs were gossiping in a Babel of languages while their little charges either ran around or snoozed in deluxe buggies.

"What do you fancy?"

"Just a fruit juice."

"Sandwich?"

"I couldn't eat anything."

"You've got to keep your strength up."

"What for?"

"Tomorrow. You're going to get that job."

"Don't know if I'll bother going."

"You're going. I'll never speak to you again if you blow this chance."

"Who's going to want someone who's been questioned over the suspicious death of her boss?"

"They won't know."

"It's a small world, Nikki."

"But the point is, you're innocent. You didn't do anything to Veronica. None of this is about you, and none of it is because of you."

"I know that." A small girl with dark curls and a pink romper suit ran up to us and smiled at Geri. I got dogs, she got kids.

"So you leave work early, get your hair done, have an early night. Tomorrow you put on that snazzy interview outfit and you go and show them just what a catch you'd be."

She gave a small, rueful smile. "Ten out of ten for effort," she said.

"I mean it, Geri. God knows, I've seen good people dragged down by stuff that wasn't their fault, and I don't want you to be another victim."

"What do you mean?"

"You know I started to tell you about my last boss? The one at the hospice?"

"Yeah. You said he'd died."

"He killed himself."

"What happened?"

"Brent and I were the only gay people working at the hospice. Mostly that was fine. But then this guy joined as a project manager and he was seriously homophobic. He hated both of us, but mostly he hated Brent. He started to spread rumours."

"What sort of rumours?"

"About Brent having affairs with young male nurses. Even though no-one liked this guy much, and Brent had been doing a good job for a few years, people started to look at him in an odd way. It wasn't anything really obvious, just small things. Brent was senior to Jonah, this project manager, but he'd always undermine Brent. Guys wouldn't go into Brent's office on their own. He'd come across a group of people chatting, and then they'd stop. It got to the point where he thought they must have been talking about him. He started to make mistakes. I thought he was drinking more than he should. He talked about moving on and finding another job. And then Jonah left. He'd been there just over a year. With all the damage he'd done, no-one really liked him and most people were glad to see him go. We thought that was it. Brent started to get himself back together. Gradually things started to get back to where they were. Then a couple of months later, Brent was called into the Director's office. Jonah was taking the hospice to employment tribunal for constructive dismissal. He claimed that he'd been sexually harassed by Brent and that he'd been forced to leave because the senior managers wouldn't do anything about it. He said that his rights as a straight man had been infringed. The Director knew none of it was true, but the board of trustees said he had to suspend Brent until the case had been heard. The next day, I got to work and found Brent dead in his office. He'd hanged himself."

Geri looked at me, speechless.

"I don't know what to say," she said. "How can anyone do that to another human being?"

"I've been asking myself that question ever since."

"Why are you telling me this now?"

"Because someone will be very happy to see you taking the rap for Veronica's death. And because I'm still pissed with Brent for killing himself when he could have fought and won and most of us would have backed him all the way."

"Who do you think killed Veronica?"

"Gordon's still top of my list. I can't think who else around that table could have done it."

Geri nodded.

"So are you ready for a sandwich?"

"Share one?"

"Only if it's toasted cheese and onion."

"Ok"

"And you have to have a Mars Bar for pudding."

"A whole one?"

"A whole one."

Chapter 24

We walked back briskly to *Action in Caring*. The sky had clouded over, and there was a new chill in the air, reminding me that we hadn't quite seen the last of winter. Rita was sorting through the post at my desk.

"Anything good?"

"Bills and junk mail, mostly," she said. "But here's an interesting one: it's addressed to Lewis Fairclough."

"Who, as far as we know, doesn't exist."

"What's in it?"

She pulled out the papers and skim read them. "Junk mail from the bank where Gordon opened the second account. There's an identical envelope for Gordon, so they must have been doing a mail shot."

The doorbell rang, and Joan came in looking worried.

"I can't believe it," she said. "That horrible little man is dead. But what an awful way to go!"

"Makes you wonder who's next," said Rita.

No-one replied. The doorbell rang again, and Justin strode in.

"G'day ladies," he said.

His cheeriness seemed out of kilter.

"Shall we go upstairs?" asked Joan, glancing at her model. "Maybe you'd be kind enough to help me to set up the room?"

"Sure. No probs."

"I need to take the dogs for a walk," said Rita, heaving herself up from her seat. "You all right to take over now?"

"Yes," I said. "Thank you."

My phone rang. I scrabbled around in my bag until I found it. Suresh's name was flashing on its little screen.

"Hi Suresh. What you got?"

"Maybe something, maybe nothing. Gordon Smedley lived in the same block as Nigel Bentley."

"Weird! What does that mean?"

"Could mean anything. First of all, it tells you that either Gordon was loaded, or he was living way beyond his means. Guys who work for sad little community centres can't usually afford that kind of pad."

"Hey! Less of the *sad little community centre,* thank you very much!"

"Yeah, sorry. But I'm right."

"Yeah, I know you are. Either he was on the fiddle or he'd come into some serious money, then."

"Or he and Bentley are – were – an item and Bentley's keeping him – kept him – on a short leash."

"That it?"

"Not bad for a morning's digging. Did you see Maria?"

"I did. Great place she's got."

"Yeah, it would be. She's a classy one."

"Nice too. I liked her. But she couldn't tell me much. Said she'd keep her ear to the ground."

I started to type up the minutes from the last management committee meeting. Heaven knew when that motley bunch would next get together. My mobile rang again. It was Wendy.

"Just wanted to check you were ok," she said.

"Yes, I'm fine," I said. "Any developments in the case?"

"I'm not the best person to ask," she said, "but I did hear on the grapevine that Ginny's copped the Smedley murder."

"See you Thursday?"

"As planned."

Geri came out from her office. "What are you grinning about?" she asked.

"Am I?"

"Now you're blushing."

"Oh…it's nothing. Just a joke someone told me…"

"Nikki?"

She was in that arms folded across chest position again, and that meant she wouldn't go away until I'd told her why I was smiling.

"Wendy Baggott just called," I said. "Ginny Lancaster's looking into Gordon's murder."

"And for that you're grinning like the proverbial cream licking cat?"

"No…it's just…" but I was spared further explanation by the arrival of Joan's art students. Damart woman was first, closely followed by the tall willowy one with the artificial suntan. Brian, the solitary man, was the last through the door. He hovered by the reception desk as the others headed for the art room.

"Everything ok, Brian?" I asked

"Yes…no…well, I was just wondering…"

"Yes?"

"Well…it's just…"

"Something wrong with the art class?"

"No…well…would it be…no, it probably wouldn't…"

"What wouldn't?"

"Well, we've had the same model now for several sessions…"

"Is there something wrong with Justin?"

"No, no, he's very…well, he's very…male."

"Yes. Yes, he's certainly that."

"And I was wondering…will we have a…well, a…female model?" He was blushing. "It's not what you're thinking," he said. "It's just that we need to explore the human form in all its…well, in all its…"

"Diversity?"

"Yes, diversity. That's the word."

"I'll see what we can do," I said.

"Thank you. Well, I'd better…"

"Yes, you'd better…"

He scurried towards the stairs. Was he making a valid artistic point, or was he a tacky little voyeur? That was one too many things for me to worry about. My phone rang. I looked at the screen. Benjamin's number flashed at me.

"Nikki? You'll never guess," he started.

"No, you're right. I probably never will. Not unless you tell me, that is," I said.

"Rick's asked me to go for a weekend to Paris with him."

"Wow! He's a fast worker."

"He's the one, Nikki, I'm sure of it."

Just like Lycra Pants and Josh WASP had been before.

"That's great, Ben."

"So I just wanted to check that you'd be ok if I wasn't around next weekend."

I was touched: in the lusty midst of his new love, Benjamin was thinking about my well-being.

"I'll be fine. Thanks for thinking of me."

"Don't be in the house on your own," he said.

"I don't know what I'll be doing; but I can always stay with Carla."

"Maybe your new girly will come over?"

"I don't think so, but it's a nice thought."

"He's got a flat in La Défence," bragged Benjamin.

"Cool."

"There's an opening at the Musée d'Orsay," he added.

"Sounds great," I said, wondering how Ginny was getting on with her investigations.

"We're going first class Eurostar," he added.

"Can't get better than that," I said, thinking how good it would be if Benjamin and Rick lasted more than a fortnight. "Look, Ben, have a great time and let me know all about it when you get back. But I've got to get on with stuff."

"Thanks Nik. You take care now," and he rang off.

There wasn't much for me to do. Rita had tidied the desk. The monthly Grannies for Peace meeting was due to take place in half an hour, so I could arrange the chairs in the meeting room. I still felt nervous going into that room, despite the many good vibes that Felicity and her yoga classes had poured into it. I opened the door. Just a room. Just a room with chairs and tables and shelves of out of date books. I arranged the chairs in a circle, picked up a dirty mug that was growing something scientists might want to know about. I felt antsy. Apart from having some murders to solve, this job was boring for much of the time. I needed a good workout. If we closed up after Grannies for Peace, I just had time for a session at the gym before going to meet Carla.

The art class filed out at three thirty. Damart woman had a smudge of charcoal on her nose. Brian looked happier.

"I had a word with Joan," he said. "She said we'd get to work with a range of models."

"That's great," I said.

Joan stayed behind. "I'll stay for the Grannies for Peace meeting," she said.

"I got the room ready. Want some teas and coffees?"

"That would be lovely, if it's not too much trouble."

"Glad of something to do, to be honest. Joan, what's going to happen to this centre?"

"I don't know, dear. So much has gone into the SoLCEC centre, and the council doesn't seem interested in keeping its older community centres going."

The doorbell rang and a woman in her seventies with rosy cheeks and a friendly smile came in. She nodded to me, and gave a hug to Joan. Three more women and two men arrived shortly after. I took in a tray of tea and coffee and some biscuits I'd found in the pantry. Then I took to sorting out the inbox on my mobile. I erased most of my stored messages and deleted Ruth's number. Then I turned to the computer. I won two games of solitaire, lost one. I logged onto the BBC website to see what was happening in the world. More grief in Iraq, more idiocy from the demented moron who inhabited the White House. I checked my Hotmail account, read a cheery message from an old school friend, and then deleted two offers of penis enlargements and an invitation to join an online poker game. Geri was sorting out some admin in the office. At last, the grannies for peace finished their meeting and left.

"Let's shut up shop," I called to Geri.

"Let's do that. You know, it's really odd that none of the management committee – apart from Rita and Joan – have been in touch. I left messages with them all."

"I think I'll worry about that tomorrow." I was shrugging on my green corduroy jacket, a favourite almost as old as the red Kickers. "Big day tomorrow for you," I added.

"Yeah. My mum says go for it. Gina said the same. I don't know…"

"You were dead keen last week. Your mum's right. You need a fresh start."

"You're right. I'll go and get some pampering."

"See you afterwards?"

"Yeah. I should be in around midday." She locked the door behind us and I mounted my bike.

"Good luck, Geri."

"Thanks."

It was only four thirty so I had time to go to the gym before meeting up with Carla. I cycled across the Common and then down through Streatham towards Gunn's. I travelled six kilometres on the cross-trainer and then did my weights, my body easing into the work.

Once my t-shirt was wet with sweat, I headed for the sauna. Just me and a black woman looking spooky and alien in a white face pack. All it needed was for me to slap on a mud pack we'd look like a parody of the Black and White Minstrels. I stretched out on the hot top bench and felt the heat seep into my muscles. I tried to relax, but my mind was reeling with death and conspiracy. A couple of women came in complaining noisily about the Body Pump instructor, so I headed for the showers and let cold water shock my body into submission. I dried myself, got dressed, and cycled back towards London to meet Carla at *Sappho*.

"You look great!" said Carla, wrapping me in a big hug. "All rosy and smelling of night air!"

"Gym, sauna, and bike ride," I said.

"Share a bottle?"

"Why not?"

We ordered a bottle of the house Merlot and settled onto a sofa near the fire.

"So what's happening?"

I caught Carla up with my adventures and gave her an update about Gordon's untimely demise.

"Shit! D'you think his death is connected to all the other stuff that's going on?"

"It might be random. Another man killed because someone thinks he's gay. But it could all be linked. That's the problem. I don't know."

"And what about the threatening call you got?"

"Nothing's happened, but it feels scary."

"What does Wendy think?"

"I don't know. I mean, she was great this morning. But I don't know what she makes of it all."

"My life seems so simple."

"How's Siobhan?"

"She's lovely. Why did we ever break up?"

"I don't know. I thought you were mad at the time."

"Well, we seem to be getting it back together."

"Best news I've heard all week."

"I'm worried about you, Nik."

"I'm ok."

"But what if these psychos come after you?"

I thought about it. "There's one thing you could do."

"Name it."

"Benjamin's going away at the weekend. Could I stay with you?"

"Nik, you don't even have to ask! Of course you can!"

I hugged her. "Thanks, Carla. That means a lot."

"So what about Ruth?"

"History."

We finished the bottle of wine, and put the world to rights. Carla and I, we could sort out Iraq; reform the government; liberate Guantanamo Bay; end child labour; win worldwide human rights for women; halt global warming. It was just that the world wasn't ready to listen to us. Yet.

"Want me to drop you home?"

"I've got the bike. I'll be fine. Are you ok to drive?"

"Yeah, as long as I take the sling off. You sure?"

"Yeah. I'll walk you to your car."

As I walked Carla towards the side street where she'd parked, I had the strangest feeling. It was as if I was being watched. I glanced behind me. Nothing out of the ordinary. She gave me one last hug and a kiss on the mouth before she disappeared into the subway. I turned the bike around and started off towards Streatham. The night was clear, cold, and bright. There was that feeling again. I checked around me. Too much imagination. But I needed to be indoors, safe, and with the chain in place. I cycled towards Brixton, and then up the hill towards home. There wasn't too much traffic, and there was a slight wind behind me. I rode fast, and was by the front door in under twenty minutes. Benjamin's light was on. I propped by bike against the fence. As I delved in my bag for my key, I heard a noise behind me. This time it wasn't my imagination. I whirled round in time to see a figure lunge at me wielding something long and thick. I dodged out of the way and then dived forward, yelling as I went, to grab at my assailant. As they and I plunged to the ground, more lights went on around us. I was lying on top of someone smaller than me. Someone hardly adult. I pinned their arms behind them as I knelt astride them. I moved my right knee to their groin area, digging in hard.

"Ow!" cried a young male voice.

I straightened my back, not loosening my grip. I recognised my assailant immediately. The orange hoodie was a give away.

"Lemme go!" Leon whimpered.

"Not until I get some answers," I said, prodding him where it would most hurt with my knee."

"Ow! That hurt!"

"Just what do you think you're doing?" I shouted.

The door opened behind me.

"What's going on?" asked Benjamin.

"Trouble," I panted. "Call the police."

"Who's that?"

"Name's Leon. Don't know his surname. Go, Ben. Just call the police."

"What d'you think you're doing, you little shit?" I yelled, picking up his wrists and banging them back down on the path.

"Stop! Please stop," Leon wept, trying in vain to twist away from me. I could smell his fear.

"Not until I know why you followed me, who sent you, what you're up to," I said.

Benjamin had pulled his mobile from his pocket and was talking to the police.

"Yes, this is an emergency. My friend's been attacked. No, I don't think she's hurt. Yes, we've got the guy who attacked her. I don't know if he's hurt."

He gave our address.

"D'you know him?" he asked.

"One of the kids from the young offenders' group," I said. "His name's Leon. Snorts coke."

"Oi! You watch what you're saying!" wheezed Leon.

I knelt harder.

"Ow!"

"Well, it's true, you little piece of scum, isn't it? You do coke and whatever else you can lay your grubby little hands on."

"Fuck off!"

"When the cops come. Then I'll fuck off. And they may be a while. So why don't you tell me who put you up to this?"

"No-one, innit."

"I don't believe you."

"No-one, cunt."

I jabbed my knee into his groin and leaned my elbows into the soft tissue between his shoulders and elbows."

"Stop!" He was almost crying.

"Tell me."

"He told me. He said I was to…"

"Who? Who told you?"

"He'll kill me!"

"*I'll* kill you. Who told you?"

"The man, innit. He told me. He said to scare you. Hurt you."

"Which man?"

"Leave me alone!"

"Not until you tell me."

I could hear sirens heading our way.

"Who is he?"

"Council man. He told me."

"Council man? What's his name?"

"Dunno. Dwayne know him, innit."

"He put Dwayne up to attacking me?"

"Dunno. Lemme go!"

The sirens were getting closer.

"Not until you tell me."

"Want me to take over?" asked Benjamin.

"I'm doing fine," I said. "So, Leon, you little prick, who's the man?"

But the police had drawn up, two cars, blue lights flashing. Four uniforms jumped out and charged towards us.

"Here, officer," said Ben, trying to be helpful.

"All right miss," said the first on the scene. "We'll take it from here."

He'd got handcuffs at the ready. I eased off Leon, who went limp. He seemed so small and skinny.

"He'd been set up," I said.

"Leave it to us, now," said a second policeman.

"He says it was someone from the Council. I need to speak with DCI Lancaster."

"We'll see what we can do. Well, well, if it isn't Leon Dodd!" he exclaimed as he pulled Leon to his feet. "Can't stay away from trouble, can you son?" He yanked Leon's wrists behind him and cuffed him. "I should caution you that you don't need to say anything, but anything you say may be…"

Two of the policemen bundled the hapless Leon into a car and drove him off. His abandoned bike slumped against next door's hedge. The other two got out their notepads and prepared to interview Ben and me. Adrenalin was coursing through my body. I was wired up and freaked out. We all trooped into my flat and I told them what had happened.

"Talk to DCI Lancaster," I finished. "She knows what's been happening. Phone calls. Threats."

"Will do, miss," said the older of the two. "This your boyfriend? Sir, you need to look after your young lady tonight."

Benjamin's look was unfathomable.

"Ben always looks after me, don't you darling?" I said.

After the police left, I sank into my sofa. Ben had followed me in.

"Darling?!" he said.

"Well, what else was I to do? God, Ben, things just go from bad to worse. What was that little bastard doing? You know what, I think the man from the council is Nigel Bentley. I'm going to ring Suresh."

"You've got no proof. Let the police get it out of him."

"Who else? It always seems to go back to Nigel Bentley. He's dirty, Ben. I know it."

"Want me to call your police sergeant for you?"

"No. I'll be ok. Oh shit, no I won't."

"Want to stay with me?"

"Could you bear it?"

"I've got some good weed."

"Sold."

I locked up my flat and followed Benjamin downstairs.

"You were brilliant," he said as he closed his front door behind us.

"Really?"

"Yeah. He didn't stand a chance."

"What was he holding?"

"What do you mean?"

"He was going to attack me with something. What was it?"

Benjamin hesitated. "Didn't you see?" he asked.

"I was too busy pinning the little shit down."

"Looked like a knife. One of those long ones. The second policeman picked it up and bagged it."

I shivered. "Roll that spliff, then," I said.

"The Producers?"

"I don't think it'll work. Not tonight. Not after all this."

"Cuddle?"

I let him put his arms around me.

"Shall I tell you all about Rick?"

I sighed. It would certainly take my mind off being nearly killed by a teenaged coke addict.

"Go on then," I said. Ben had rolled us a spliff and he gave it to me to light up. I inhaled deeply. He'd only got as far as telling me about the tattoo on Rick's chest before I was asleep.

Chapter 25

I woke up in Benjamin's spare bed. The smell of coffee and something baking was seeping seductively under the door. I could hear music punctuated by talk. He had the radio on. I had slept in some of my clothes. Underwear, socks, t-shirt. My eyes were itchy. I must have gone to bed with my contact lenses in. My trousers were draped neatly over his one chair. I felt drowsy. I turned over and curled into myself. It was safe and warm here. Maybe I could just stay. Throw a sickie. Have a duvet day. The bedroom door opened.

"Rise and shine," said Benjamin.

I groaned.

"I've brought you coffee, croissants, juice. Is there anything else that Madame desires?"

"Oh, Ben, you're wonderful!" I said, stretching.

"I know," he said, setting down a tray beside the bed. "How are you doing?"

I sat up. My head was clearing. I was doing ok.

"I'll live," I said. "Weren't you telling me something about Rick before I crashed?"

"Well, I was telling you that he was hung like..."

"Enough! Too much information!"

"You're no fun."

I drank some coffee. It was hot and rich and sweet. Perfect.

"I just like to leave some things to imagination," I said, although the layout of Rick's genitals was not something I wanted to ponder.

I bit into a warm croissant and showered crumbs all over Benjamin's pristine black sheets.

"Sorry," I mumbled.

"You going to work today?"

"I'd better. And the police might want to talk to me."

"Your lovely sergeant?"

"No, the ice queen DCI."

"Ah."

I finished my breakfast and while Ben was showering I got up, put on my jeans and stripped his sheets. It was the least I could do.

"I'm off," I called

"Ok," called Benjamin through the splash of his shower.

I went upstairs into my quiet, cold flat. I took out my lenses, put aside the clothes I'd been sleeping in, and showered. The hot water and lemony shower gel felt good. I was stiff after the exertions of the day before. As I was drying myself, the phone rang. I padded out from the bathroom to answer it.

"Ginny Lancaster here," said the DCI, brusquely morningish. "I need you to come down to answer some questions."

"What time?"

"Soon as you like."

"Is Leon still in custody?"

"We've let him out on bail."

"Great. I feel really safe."

"He's on a curfew. I don't think you'll find he's a threat."

"Well, excuse me if I have a different view; but he did follow me home, he knows where I work and where I live; and last night he pulled a knife on me and would have killed me if I hadn't have been stronger and less spaced out than him."

"I understand your concerns, but Leon isn't the real problem."

"Oh. Well, sorry if I'm being a bit thick, but he was the one who came after me."

"Look. I understand your concerns. Please come into the station and we'll take it from there."

"I have to open up at work. Geri's got an interview. Someone has to let people in."

"Does it help if we come to you?"

"Yeah. Yeah, it does." She'd taken me aback with this helpful suggestion.

"We'll be there at ten."

There was a knock at the door.

"Who's there?"

"Me," said Benjamin. "Just wondered if you wanted me to ride to work with you?"

"Yeah. I'd like that."

"Meet you downstairs in ten."

I had to work hard to keep up with Benjamin. No pausing to enjoy the budding daffodils or chuckle at unruly dogs. We streaked down the High Road and across the Common in record time. I arrived at work just after nine.

"Thanks, Ben," I said, puffing out cold morning air.

"Pleasure," he said, hugging me before taking off towards the City.

I unlocked the door and waited for Felicity and her stressed out yoga group to arrive. The place looked grubby. I never had understood how the cleaning worked: seemed like we all did a bit as and when it was needed. I decided to clean the surfaces and mop the floor. Coffee first, though. I headed for the kitchen and filled the kettle. The doorbell rang, so I ran back to the front door, glancing at the monitor before letting anyone in. To my surprise, it was Bernard. I opened the door.

"Hello Bernard," I said. "We'd been wondering what had happened to the management committee. You ok?"

"Hello," said Bernard. There was a tremor in his voice. His hands looked almost blue with cold.

278

"Can I get you some coffee?"

"Yes. Thank you. If it's not too much trouble," he said.

"I was about to make one for myself." He followed me out to the kitchen and I pulled out a stool for him to perch on. "So, how's life treating you, Bernard?"

"Not very well, I'm afraid."

"Sorry to hear that. Milk and sugar?"

"Yes please. Just the one sugar."

He thanked me as I handed him the steaming mug. I'd managed to find one that wasn't chipped.

"So…have you been ill?"

"No, no. Nothing like that. It's my wife, you see." I remembered that he had a wife with Alzheimer's.

"Has she got worse?"

"Yes. We lost her last week."

"Oh, I'm so sorry! Was it very sudden?"

"No, I don't mean she passed away. We lost her. She went for a walk and got lost."

"Oh!" I felt stupid and clumsy. "Did you find her?"

"Eventually she was found crying in a café in Croydon. She'd got on a bus and forgotten where she was going or where she lived. She couldn't remember my name, and she'd gone out without any identification, just her bus pass in her pocket and a little loose change."

"How long was she missing?"

"Two days. She must have slept out somewhere. She was in a dreadful state and her shoes were worn to shreds."

"She must have been relieved to see you," I said.

"She might have been if she had recognised me. But she didn't. She thought I was a stranger who meant her harm and she kept asking for her mother, who died twenty five years ago."

"Oh, that's awful. I'm really sorry."

"Yes," he said. There were tears in his eyes. "So, you see, I couldn't do much until I'd got her settled. I'm sorry I haven't been very helpful. I saw the news about Gordon. Dreadful."

"Yeah. Well, not much you could have done in the circumstances, and we've managed. But the committee will have to make some decisions about where we go from here. We haven't heard from Derek, and someone's going to have to sort out all the finance stuff. But you can't worry about that now, Bernard. Is your wife back at home?"

"No," he sighed. "No, I had to find somewhere safer for her. She's in a nice little home where they keep an eye on her."

"Does she mind?"

"I'm not sure she's noticed."

"And you?"

"I'm...well, I'm..." his voice faltered. "The truth is," he said, trying to steady it, "I'm lonely. Don't know what to do with myself."

We drank our coffee without saying anything else. I washed up our mugs and found the cloths and cleaning liquid. I wasn't sure what to do about Bernard and thought the best thing was to let him be.

"I thought I'd clean up a bit before the yoga group arrives," I said. "Then we've got the young offenders."

"Can I help?"

"No, no, you just make yourself comfortable," I said.

"I'd like to do something," he said. "Would it help if I looked at the books and bank statements?"

"Yes, that would be great," I said.

"We'll need to see how long we can keep going, how to get back on track," he said. I was impressed that even in the midst of all the other problems he was facing, he could consider *Action in Caring*.

"Do you have any children?" I asked.

"Two," he said. "Dinah's in Orkney. Doesn't get back as often as she'd like. Our son, Keith, lives in a community in Sussex. He has learning difficulties, you see."

Not much support for Bernard, then.

"Shall I find you the latest statements and let you loose in the office?"

"Yes, why don't you do that?"

An hour later, Bernard was whistling to himself as he sifted through and sorted the jumble of papers that had been waiting for Gordon. I had cleaned the floors, got rid of the dead palm, wiped over all the surfaces. The centre smelled cleaner and looked brighter. The doorbell rang, and I expected to see Felicity; but Iris and Pete were there. I buzzed them in.

"Morning," said Iris, plonking a shopping bag down on the floor. "Come to see what we can do."

"Great!" I said, wondering what exactly they *could* do.

"There's some light bulbs need changing and one of the door handles needs fixing," said Pete, who was carrying a tool box.

"Brilliant!" I said. As he trundled off to fix things, the doorbell rang. In the monitor I saw Ginny Lancaster and her sidekick Darren Lowe. I let them in.

"Iris, could you cover reception for me?" I asked. "Felicity should be turning up any time now." Iris nodded and moved into my place behind the reception desk. I led Ginny and Darren into Geri's office.

"So, what's the latest?" I asked.

"Tell us about last night," sidestepped Ginny.

"I told the uniforms," I said. "What else do you want to know?"

"How do you know this boy, Leon Dodd?"

"I don't. He comes to the young offenders' group here most days," I said. Justin says he's a friend of Dwayne Robbins."

Darren was writing everything down.

"Anything else you can tell us?" asked Ginny.

"Not really, " I said. "Just what you know. I've had a couple of threatening phone calls. Don't suppose you've managed to trace them?"

"We're looking into it," said Ginny. Why did she never give me a straight answer? "Where's Miss Francis today?"

"She had an appointment," I said. "She'll be in this afternoon."

"I see."

"So do you know who's threatening me? Who put Leon up to trying to kill me?"

"There are several possibilities and we're looking into them all."

Did that mean that they didn't have a clue but didn't want to admit to it?

"So what does that mean?" I tapped at the floor with my left Kicker.

"It means we're looking into it," said Ginny. "What can you tell us about Gordon Smedley?"

"Apart from that he's dead?"

"Nikki, this is serious."

"Tell me about it! I've been attacked twice and you're no clearer as to who put the boys up to it."

"Gordon Smedley."

I sighed. "I'd only met him a few times. He seemed pretty cold. He lived in a flat that may have been beyond his means. He's connected with Nigel Bentley. He probably roughed up young guys in Soho on a regular basis. The last organisations he worked for folded." Darren was scribbling my words of wisdom into his too small notebook. "Look, if you want to know more, why don't you speak to Suresh Shah at the SLP?"

Ginny glanced up and gave me a look I couldn't fathom.

"How do you know Mr Shah?"

"Old college friends. We shared a flat in Mile End."

"What was Geraldine Francis's relationship with Gordon Smedley?"

"They worked together. She was junior to him. That's all."

"Did she get on with him?"

"I don't know. I haven't been here long enough."

"But what were your first impressions?"

"First impressions were that they both took their jobs seriously, he was bossy, she did what she was told and more. That do?"

"Did she have any cause to resent him?"

"I don't think so. I told you, I haven't been here that long. Veronica died on my first day. We didn't see much of Gordon after that." What was Ginny doing? Trying to build a case against Geri? Well, I wouldn't be helping her.

"So, Nikki, do you want to run through what happened last night?"

I repeated the story I'd told the uniformed officers last night.

"Thank you. Oh, and by the way, does your employer know that you're moonlighting as a press photographer?"

"Who is my employer? My boss dropped dead on my first day, the second in command was killed in my second week. So whoever is technically my employer, I shouldn't think they'd mind about my taking a couple of hours to snap the action at the SoLCEC. I wanted to find out what the new place was like, and Suresh needed a photographer. Anything wrong in that?"

"I don't know. You tell me," said Ginny. I didn't say anything. "Mind if we have another look around?"

"Help yourself. There's a group in the meeting room. Bernard from the management committee is working through some papers in Gordon's office."

"I don't think we'll be long."

Darren had snapped shut his notebook and tucked his biro into an inside pocket. They went out and headed for Veronica's office. I went back to the reception desk. There was a low hum coming from the yoga group.

283

"Someone called Suresh called," said Iris, handing me a note. She'd printed Suresh's number out in a clear hand. She was better at my job than I was.

"Thanks. Anything else?"

"No." She moved closer to me and whispered, "What are they up to?"

"Having a look around," I whispered back. "Don't know what they're hoping to find."

Pete came through from the kitchen.

"Needs a good spring clean," he said. "I've done the odd jobs. Think I'll come back and give it all a lick of paint."

"Don't you think we should see if we stay open?" I asked.

"Might help people to make up their minds if the place looks good," he said pragmatically. My mobile rang.

"Excuse me," I said, fishing it out of my desk drawer and almost knocking Iris off her chair in the process. Carla's number flashed up.

"Hi Carla," I said.

"Hi Nik. You ok? I bumped into Benjamin earlier on, and he said there'd been some kind of attack on you."

"Yeah. I'll tell you about it later."

"But are you ok?"

"I'm fine. Pissed off. What is it about me that makes these losers want to kill me?"

"Why don't you come and stay with me?"

"I will when Benjamin goes away. I'm ok with him there."

"I might have to change my mind about him."

"I wish you would. Listen, Carla, gotta go. Ring you later."

"Take care."

Felicity and her group of stressed students emerged from their class. The group seemed looser, more relaxed than they had been last week. Felicity bade them all goodbye and then turned to me.

"Leo wants to meet with you and the journalist," she said.

"Suresh?"

"Whoever he was talking with the other day. He thinks he can help. I don't know what that means. Will you call him?"

"Yeah. Can you write down his number?"

Felicity scribbled some numbers on the back of a leaflet advertising free legal advice. She handed it to me.

"I'll phone him later on."

Justin's group were working on some teambuilding.

"We're doing trust games," he said. I didn't like to tell him I wouldn't trust one of his lads if you paid me.

"That's nice," I said.

I phoned Suresh. He picked up on the third ring.

"Wassup Nik?"

"Leo Balmforth wants to speak to us both. Thinks he might have some information. And you rang me and left a message to call."

"Yeah, something interesting turned up. I'm on a story right now. Call you later?"

"When later?"

"Dunno. Look, gotta go now. Cheers."

"But…" He'd hung up.

Ginny and Darren emerged from upstairs. Darren was holding a clear plastic bag. His hand concealed whatever was in it.

"Found something, then?"

"Might have done," said Ginny. I was beginning to wonder if Darren ever spoke.

"Cup of tea, Darren?" I asked. He glanced up.

"We've got to be off," said Ginny. "Another time. Thanks for your help."

"Did you talk to Bernard? He's going through the bills and stuff."

"He was very helpful," said Ginny, heading for the door. "We'll be in touch." The two detectives exited in a cloud of something earnest and businesslike.

I was curious about what Bernard might have discovered, so I put the phone onto ansaphone and walked up the stairs to Gordon's office.

"How you doing, Bernard?" I asked as I went into the room that I still felt was more chilled than the rest of the building.

"Who's Lewis Fairclough?" asked Bernard, turning from the desk and lifting his reading glasses up over his head.

"We don't think he exists. We think it's a name Gordon used in order to fiddle the books."

"Ah. The family silver," said Bernard.

"What do you mean?" I asked.

"You've heard the phrase, no doubt: making off with the family silver."

"Yes…"

"Well, I had my worries that Mr Smedley was not what he might seem."

"I remember you saying something,"

"Yes. Well, I hadn't wanted to employ him. I knew something about his past, and the tendency of organisations to take him on and then soon fold. But Lawrence insisted, and Veronica was keen to get him on board. And of course, he did have a good grasp of finance."

"Why do you think Veronica and Lawrence were so keen to have him?"

"I always wondered that."

"Veronica worked for organisations that folded, too. Could they have been running a similar scam?"

"She seemed committed to *Action in Caring*. Worked hard."

I remembered how she'd described the centre to me during my interview. She hadn't come across as someone who was trying to run the centre into the ground. But neither was she a team builder, a leader who could inspire and carry her staff to bigger and better things.

"Did you find anything in the papers?"

"Mostly bills. And a paper authorising Lewis Fairclough to sign cheques. It was in a folder on the shelf. I was being nosy."

That would explain why Geri hadn't spotted it. He'd filed it in one of his pristine Lever Arch files. "Who were the other signatories?"

"Gordon Smedley and Derek Ramsay."

"Could they have got this Lewis person signed up without Veronica knowing?"

"Possible. But unlikely, I would have thought."

"Could Gordon and Veronica have been fiddling the books together?"

"I can't believe that of her. And I'd have thought Derek would have noticed."

"Maybe they kept stuff from Derek. Or maybe he was in on it. Maybe Veronica didn't have a choice?"

"There's always a choice."

"But suppose Gordon had something on her…"

Bernard gave me a look that said, *get real* only I didn't think Bernard would ever put it quite like that. But it seemed to me that there was one possibility, and that was that Gordon was blackmailing Veronica. Or maybe everything was as it seemed: the two senior people at *Action in Caring* were robbing its coffers and steadily demolishing it. And the treasurer hadn't been paying close enough attention. Or maybe he had.

The doorbell rang. I went to see who was coming to delight us with their presence. Iris had already buzzed Dora Popp in.

"Fucking cold out there," said Dora.

"Not summer yet," I said.

"Fucking aint," agreed Dora. She was wearing red tartan slippers and a sludge green beret.

"Cup of tea?" I asked.

"Four sugars," she said. She shuffled after me as I went towards the kitchen.

"They caught 'im yet?"

"Who?"

"Cops. Caught that bent toff?"

"What bent toff?"

"Bloke whose picture's always in the paper."

"Why's he need catching?"

"Put them lads up to it, didn't he?"

"Up to what?" This was beginning to feel like twenty questions.

"Beating you up, stupid."

"Dora, don't call me stupid if you want me to make you tea." The kettle had boiled so I poured it over a teabag, added milk and the hideous mountain of sugar. Dora grabbed the mug from me and slurped. "Could you point him out?"

She sniffed and wiped her nose with her sleeve. "Might do," she said.

"Ok, I'm going to get the paper. You tell me if his picture's in it." I ran out to reception, pulled the South London Press from under the counter and took it into the kitchen. I handed it to Dora.

"Here. Look through this. Tell me if you see him."

Dora Popp looked at me slyly. "Where's the biscuits then?"

"Start looking." She squinted at the first page of the paper. I opened cupboards and drawers until I found a packet of malted milk biscuits in the art class cupboard. Joan would forgive me. Dora turned the pages of the paper. She didn't have to go very far.

"'Ere," she cried. "This is 'im!". She was jabbing a filthy finger at the grainy reproduction of my photo of Nigel Bentley under attack.

Chapter 26

"Are you sure?"

"'Course I'm sure," said Dora. "Know 'im anywhere. Shifty little bastard."

I couldn't have put it better myself. "How do you mean?"

"I seen 'im give them boys stuff."

"What stuff?"

"You born yesterday? What d'you mean *what stuff*? You blind?"

"Maybe I'm not a genius like you, Dora. Humour me. What did you see?"

"Stuff in packets. I see 'im give 'em packets on the Common."

"Big packets?"

"Small ones."

"What's that got to do with me getting beaten up?"

"You're a nosy bitch, in't ya?"

"I'm going off you, Dora."

"'E said, *now go and finish off that nosy bitch*. That's what 'e said. 'E never seen me. I've gone into the bushes for a piss. I 'ear 'im say, *she's getting too nosy, that new one. Finish her off and there's more where this came from*"

I felt cold. So Nigel Bentley had wanted me dead. Not just injured, not frightened off, dead.

"When did this happen?"

"Dunno. Few days ago. Last week."

"Shit." My legs were shaking.

"'E said, *do her like you done that other bitch*."

What other bitch? What had he been talking about?

"Dora, you've got to tell the police," I said.

She sniffed. "Don't get on with cops."

"Yeah, well, sometimes you've got to try."

"Think they'll believe old Dora, do ya?"

She had a point. "Did you see or hear anything else?"

"Might've done."

"What else do you know?"

She sniffed and lifted her beret to scratch her head. She raised her mug to her mouth, and put it down again. "I'll 'ave more tea," she said.

"Yeah, I'll make you more tea; but only when you've told me what you know."

"Tea." She thrust the mug at me. My hands were trembling and I almost dropped it. I took a deep breath and switched on the kettle.

I'd put my mobile in my pocket and it startled me by ringing as I was adding the sugar to Dora's tea. Spoon clattered against cheap china. I fumbled for the phone and looked to see who was calling me. It was Suresh.

"Hi Suresh, you able to talk now?"

"Yeah. Sorry about earlier. Listen, I might have something interesting on Bentley and his companies. It looks as if he was definitely on the take over the SoLCEC contract."

"I've got more than that," I said. "How quickly can you get here?"

"Leo Balmforth can wait, Nikki. He's only going to want to share his conspiracy theory."

"This isn't about Leo. Can you get here?"

He must have heard the urgency in my voice. "I'll be over in ten," he said.

I handed Dora her tea. "I want you to talk to a friend of mine," I said.

"Who says I want to talk to anyone?"

"I do. Look…if you talk to him, I'll take you for dinner."

"Where?"

"Where do you want to go?"

"Kebab place on the corner. Fancy a nice shish kebab."

"Deal. You just need to stay here for a few minutes, drink your tea, and talk with my friend. Ok?"

She looked at me in her sly way. "I seen you too," she said.

"What do you mean?"

"I seen ya sneak in on a Sunday. 'E was 'ere too. And that other bloke."

My Ben Sherman shirt was soaked in nervous sweat. "Who else was here, Dora?"

"Bloke from the paper and the one what used to work 'ere."

"Gordon?"

"If you say so."

I should ring Ginny Lancaster. This information was dynamite. The puzzle was almost complete. But Nigel Bentley couldn't have killed Veronica. That had to have been Gordon. But why, if they were both on the take?

"Hey you two. How's it going?" Geri had come in without my hearing her. She looked flushed and excited.

"How'd it go?" I asked, although her face told me the answer.

"I got it," she said. "Nikki, I really got it!"

I put my arms around her and we danced a funny polka around the little kitchen. Dora squinted at us through puzzled, rheumy eyes.

"It's brilliant," I said, but I could hear the quaver in my voice. "When d'you start?"

"I need to give in a month's notice here, so I'll probably start second week of May."

I'd have left by then. Good. I wouldn't want to work here without Geri to keep me sane. "It's what you need," I said.

"That's what Mum said. Gina, too."

"Gina get anywhere with those computer files?"

"She had to come back for the hard disk. She's sent it off somewhere, mate of hers, and she's waiting for it to come back. Said that the disk hadn't been reformatted."

"What does that mean?"

"I don't know, but she said it was good news."

I heard the doorbell ring. Iris would let in whoever was there. I peered around the door and saw Suresh coming in looking windswept.

"Chilly today," I heard him say to Iris.

"Kitchen's that way," said Iris.

"In here," I called. "Tea?"

"Coffee please, Nik. So, what's going on?"

I filled the kettle and switched it on. "Suresh, this is Dora," I said, pointing at the sly, dishevelled little woman. Suresh nodded at Dora. Dora wiped her sleeve across her nose and looked askance at Suresh.

"What's going on?" asked Geri.

"You'll find out," I said. "Dora, Suresh works for the South London Press. Can you tell him what you told me?"

"What's it worth?" she asked.

"Lunch. Remember? I'm taking you for a kebab."

"What's 'e gonna give me?" She jabbed a grimy finger at Suresh.

"Front page splash," said Suresh. Dora didn't look convinced.

"Forget it," said Dora, and got up.

"Ok, wait," I said. "What do you want?"

"A new bed," she said. "I want a bed 'n' a telly."

I looked at Suresh. "How much do you pay for a good story these days?"

"I'm not Rupert effing Murdoch!" he spluttered.

"How much do you want to nail Bentley?"

He rubbed his nose and looked from Dora to me. "What's she got?"

"Dynamite," I said. "Bribery, corruption of minors, drugs…that do?"

"I want me telly 'n' a bed," said Dora.

"Ok, ok, I'll get you your bed and telly," said Suresh.

"One of them big ones like at the pictures," said Dora. "Digital."

"Yeah, whatever. Just tell me what you've got," he said. "And you," he added, turning to me, "You'd better be sure that this is good."

"I'm sure," I said. "Look, Dora, you tell Suresh about the boys and the packets. Tell him what you told me. I've got to make a call."

I made Dora's tea and Suresh's coffee and ushered an open-mouthed Geri out of the kitchen.

"Good Lord!" She said. "I can't even go to an interview without it all happening here!"

"She saw him," I said, as soon as we were out of earshot of the kitchen. "She saw Nigel Bentley bribe Dwayne and Leon with drugs. He's the one who set them after me."

Geri stared at me. "Who's going to believe a batty old woman like Dora?"

"She was there when I came to dig around the weekend after Veronica's death," I said. "She saw Bentley and Gordon. They were the two fighting upstairs."

"But who will believe her?"

"I'm going to ring Ginny Lancaster. Can I use your office?"

"Yes. Go ahead."

I shut the door behind me and sat at Geri's desk. Ginny's number was stored in my phone. I punched the fast dial. Ginny picked up after two rings.

"Ginny, I've got a witness. Someone who saw Nigel Bentley bribe two of the lads to beat me up. He bribed them with drugs. She's here now, the witness, talking to Suresh Shah. Can you get here?"

"Who is the witness?"

"Her name's Dora Popp. She comes to the centre a lot. She lives nearby."

"Dora Popp? That crazy old woman in the coat like a dressing gown?"

"She knows what she saw. And that Sunday that I came in to …er…find my book? She saw Bentley and Gordon Smedley. Can you come over?"

"I'll send a uniform to take a statement."

"But…"

"Look, Nikki, Miss Popp's well known to us, and she's usually got some wild story to tell. I wouldn't get too excited if I were you."

"She's no reason to lie. She was pissing in the bushes when she overheard him telling them to get me. She saw him hand them packets of stuff."

"She could be making it up. I'll send whoever's on duty."

"But…"

"Nikki, I'm very busy right now."

"Send Wendy, then. Send Wendy Baggott."

"I'll put out the call and whoever's on duty will be with you within the hour."

"It may be too late, she might have gone."

"Then find a way of keeping her. Sweet tea and food usually keeps her quiet."

"But…"

She'd hung up. I punched in Wendy's number.

"Hi Nikki, how's it going?"

"I need you to get over here," I said. "There's a witness here says she saw Nigel Bentley set up two boys to kill me. They'd already hurt someone else. I don't know who."

"You need to let Ginny Lancaster know."

"I did. She's not interested. Said she'd send uniforms round. I want it to be you, Wendy."

"I'm in the area. I'll try to pick up the call. Who's the witness?"

"Dora Popp."

"Oh God, Nikki, not smelly Dora!"

"Look, she saw it all. Please, Wendy, please get here. She's talking with Suresh Shah."

I heard her sigh. "Ok, I'll see what I can do."

Suresh emerged from the kitchen. I'd told Iris to go home and resumed my seat at the reception desk. Dora was shuffling towards the toilets.

"How'd you get on?"

"Well, she told me what I presume she told you. Nik, do you think there's any connection between Bentley, these thugs and Tanya Middleton dying?"

"Yeah, that's what I've been thinking."

"Because when she said that Bentley referred to them sorting out some other bitch, I wondered whether they meant Tanya. Could they have found their way to Manchester?"

"But Tanya died," I said. "She was killed. Or it might have been an accident."

"Someone was seen leaving the scene."

"Shit."

"Look, Nikki, I have to play this one carefully. If I put the story out before it's all been checked out, Bentley will sue for libel, and your fragrant little friend out there will be in danger. Not to mention you."

"I've told the police. Uniforms are on their way."

"Dora says you're taking her to lunch."

"She wants a kebab. I can't take her out of the centre in case the police come!"

"Ask Geri to tell them where you are. Simple."

"Ok. It's probably the best way of making sure she doesn't do a runner. What about Leo Balmforth?"

"I'll ring him. Probably nothing important."

I heard a toilet flush and Dora emerged. "You ready for that kebab after all your hard work?"

"Yeah."

We'd beaten the lunchtime rush of school kids. The man with the kind eyes, whom I hadn't seen to talk to since the day of my interview, was carving grey meat from the reconstituted mess that was gyrating before the heater.

"Hello ladies," said the man, wiping his hands on a stained white tunic. "What I can do for you?"

"Shish kebab. Big one. Chips. None of that hot stuff," ordered Dora.

"No problem, madam. And for you?" He looked over to me. "Ah! I remember you! You go for interview at funny centre, innit? How things? I hear lady boss die."

"Er, yes. She died," I said. "I got the job. I mean, I got the job I went for, not her job."

"And you not come for Ozzie's kebab? Why not?" He'd taken out a skewer of dull red meat and slapped it on the grill. "I say, you come, I give you free."

"Yeah, I know. Thanks. That was kind. I...uh...I don't eat meat."

"So you come for falafel, I make nice salad. You want eat now? You with this pretty lady?"

I could have sworn that Dora simpered. And because he'd probably said the kindest – if least honest – thing to Dora that she'd heard in years, I decided to risk a falafel.

"You eat in or take away?"

"Eat in, please."

"Go find table. I bring. I bring drinks, free. What you want?"

"I'll 'ave tea," said Dora.

"Coffee. Black, please," I said. We found ourselves a table in the middle of the café. It was clean, with a shiny orange top. The metal chairs looked oddly dainty for a kebab café, and their green padded seats were spotless.

"D'you come here often?" I asked Dora.

"Nah. Sometimes when they pay me pension early," she said.

"Is there anything else I need to know?"

"About me pension?"

"No, about Nigel Bentley and what's been going on."

"I told that darkie what works on the paper. I told him what I know."

"Suresh."

Ozzie brought over the kebab and the falafel. The pita breads were warm and yeasty and he'd stuffed them with salad. I hadn't thought I could eat, but the smell of the bread and tangy tomatoes made me realise that I was quite hungry.

"I bring drinks." He placed steaming mugs of tea and coffee in front of Dora and me and went back to serve the kids who had started to drift in.

"Dora, I called the police," I said, as she bit into her kebab.

She glared at me and chewed. "Thought you would," she said.

"They'll want to come and talk to you."

She snorted. "They won't believe me," she said, picking out bits of tomato and laying them on the side of her plate. "Nah, they won't believe old Dora."

The door opened. I glanced up. There, in all her glory, was Wendy. I waved at her.

"Over here," I called. She was with Geoff Newsome, as she had been the first time we'd met. She smiled at me. Geoff nodded. They both looked warily at Dora.

"D'you know Dora Popp?" I said, as they sat down.

"We've met before, haven't we, Dora?" said Geoff. It sounded more like a threat than an introduction.

"If you say so," said Dora, who was cramming kebab into her mouth.

"I think we came to see you when your flat was broken into," said Wendy.

"Fat lot of good you did me," muttered Dora. "Never got me telly back."

"I'm sorry," said Wendy. "So, Nikki says you've got something to tell us. She says that you saw something on the Common."

They winkled Dora's story out of her, Wendy doing the winkling, Geoff writing everything down. They looked as if they were taking her seriously.

"Any idea what they meant when they talked about *the other bitch?*" asked Wendy.

"Nope. S'pose it was some other twat what got in 'is way."

"Thank you, Dora, you've been most helpful," said Wendy. I loved her soft, Scottish accent. Tomorrow we'd be out together. Tomorrow that mellifluous voice, those hazel eyes, would be all mine. Mellifluous? Where the hell did I get a word like that? This was getting serious. I got up to pay Ozzie.

"Everything ok?" he asked.

"Fine. It was really good. Thank you. I must come by again," I said, and meant it.

"You welcome. Always welcome."

I went back to the table. Wendy was talking to Dora.

"Now, don't be telling this to anyone else, will you?"

"Like who?"

"Anyone. Just keep it between you and us for now. And if you think of anything else, give me a call." She handed over a card to Dora, who stuffed it into her battered bucket bag.

I got back to *Action in Caring* as Justin's group was leaving. No Dwayne, no Leon. Just the rest of the motley bunch slinking away from the centre. Justin was tidying up the meeting room.

"Go all right?" I asked.

"Yeah. Not too bad. Nobody got dropped in the trust games. Tell you the truth, they're all freaked out about Dwayne being inside and Leon back in trouble. It's put them all on their best behaviour."

"Best not complain, then."

"No, I s'pose not."

"They ever leave London, your boys?"

"Dunno. I think Dwayne went to Jamaica once. Why?"

"Just wondered. They ever mention Manchester?"

"As in up north?"

"Yeah."

Justin scratched his head and frowned. "Not as far as I know. Dwayne disappeared for a few days a while back, but he never said where he went. They don't usually move far out of their patch, these guys."

"When did he disappear?"

"I'd have to check the register. Why? What's this all about?"

"Your lads are in Nigel Bentley's pocket. He paid them with dope to scare me off. He paid them to do the same to someone else. I'm wondering if it was Tanya Middleton."

"Tanya? Girl who used to work here?"

"Yeah. She died in Manchester just over a week ago."

"Jesus! That's sad, really sad. What happened?"

"She fell – or was pushed – under a tram."

"You can't think one of the lads did it. They wouldn't know how to get to Manchester, let alone find a girl they'd only seen a few times."

"When did Dwayne go walkabout?"

"Just a couple of weeks ago – if that. Shit, it might have been the same time."

"You'd better tell the police, Justin."

"Shit." He opened his flip-top phone and started to punch in a number.

I went home early. My head hurt and exhaustion was kicking in. Rita had come by, but even Prudence salivating over my shoes wasn't enough to revive my spirits. It's tough knowing that someone wants you dead. Geri was high on knowing that she would soon be moving on.

"Go home, Nikki. I'll take care of things here. You need some rest."

The flat was quiet. Benjamin was still at work. I ran a bath, and poured in a generous amount of rose and geranium bath oil. I poured a tumbler of whisky and found the Jackie Kay book. The bathroom misted up like a steam room and I sank into the soothing hot water. The whisky sent rivers of warmth through my body. Jackie's stories made me forget my own bizarre tale for a blissful half hour, and I laughed and cried at their bitter sweetness.

The phone rang as I was wrapping myself up in a towel that I'd warmed on the radiator. I padded into the living room and picked up the receiver.

"Nikki?" It was Ruth, but she sounded odd.

"Ruth." My stomach had been invaded by whirling dervishes. "What's up?"

"Nikki? I...I need to talk to you. To someone..."

"Why? What's wrong?"

"It's Tawfiq."

"What about him?" What did I care about the man who'd taken my place in her heart and her bed?

"He's…" I heard her gulp back a sob.

"What's happened?" Probably the bastard had left her and married a nice Palestinian girl like his mother always said he should.

"He's dead, Nikki."

"Dead?" How should I react to hearing that someone I'd never met, couldn't picture, had died? But I hated to hear Ruth distressed, despite everything. "What happened Ruth?"

"There was a bomb. It went off too soon. And now he's gone." Her sobs put paid to any further conversation.

Chapter 27

"Where are you Ruth?"

"Home. I can't stay here."

"Why don't you come over?"

"Can I?"

"Yes. Just get yourself here."

What was I doing? I dried my hair and put on some clean jeans and a white denim shirt. I had enough problems of my own, God knew; but she'd sounded so desperate and the truth was, I still cared. I wasn't one of those who could just switch off and ignore the call of old tenderness. When the doorbell rang, I expected to find Ruth standing on the mat; but it was Benjamin, brandishing a bottle of wine.

"Hey, Nik. Just thought I'd pop up and see how you're doing. You look like you're ready to go out. Nice smell! Geranium?"

"And rose. No, I'm not going out." I told him about Ruth's call.

"Shit, Nik. You've just got the woman out of your life. Last thing you need is for her to wriggle her way back in and fuck you up even more."

"She won't, but thanks for the marriage guidance. I couldn't tell her to sod off, could I?"

"Don't see why not. She was a bitch to you."

"We were over. I just hadn't come to terms with it."

"So why are you letting her back in?"

"She hasn't got many friends in London. The father of her kid's been killed. What do you expect me to do?"

"What does *she* expect you to do? That's what worries me." He was heading for the kitchen."

"Where you going?"

"Looking for your corkscrew."

"Ben, you can't stay."

"You need me."

"Probably. But you can't be here when she comes."

"She's not here yet."

"She will be. Benjamin, I need to do this on my own."

He sighed. "You sure?"

"Yeah. Keep the wine for later. I'll come down when she's gone. You staying in?"

"Yes. Rick's gone to Edinburgh for some auction or other. He won't be back until Friday."

"You must be pining."

"Desperately."

"So it's going well?"

"He's the one, Nik."

"Today was crazy," I said, and told him about Dora Popp's revelations.

"So the wicked old councillor done it, then?"

"He's certainly done something; but he couldn't have killed Veronica. Not directly, anyway."

"What's Suresh turned up?"

"More stuff about dodgy property deals. He's still digging. And there may be evidence on the computer files that Geri's sister's looking at."

"Shouldn't the police be doing that?"

"Probably. They never asked for them, though."

"You want to watch that you're not charged with tampering with evidence."

"I hadn't thought of that."

"You should be ashamed of yourself, especially with all those cop books you read."

"Maybe I should talk with Ginny Lancaster again."

"When are you seeing wonderful Wendy?"

"Tomorrow."

The doorbell rang.

"You'd better go," I said to Benjamin, wishing he didn't have to. I opened the door. Ruth's face was ashen, her eyes red and swollen from crying.

"Hi," I said. "Benjamin's just going."

"Sorry," said Ruth. "I should have thought you'd have plans."

"I don't. Ben just popped up to see if I was ok."

"All right, Ruth?" said Benjamin, although she clearly wasn't.

"Hasn't Nikki told you?"

"Er…yes. I'm…er… sorry. Look, gotta go. See you later, Nik. Bye Ruth." He slipped past her and scooted down the stairs.

"Some things don't change," said Ruth.

"Yeah, but plenty does," I said. "Come and sit down. What do you want to drink?"

"I don't know. Anything. Oh, Nikki, what am I going to do?"

"I don't know, Ruth," I said, and because she looked so small and lost, I put my arms around her and just held her.

Two hours later, Ruth had cried herself out and I'd made her up a bed on the sofa. Yes, I could have taken her into my bed; but I wasn't going to.

"So, how's the new job?"

"My boss died on my first day. The finance manager was bashed to death on Clapham Common. Two kids are in the pay of a high profile councillor with instructions to get rid of me. There's a very orange yoga teacher, a buxom dog walker, an eccentric art teacher who also runs Grannies for Peace. Oh, and there's a mad old woman who drinks too much tea, wets herself, and is a key witness to some of the dodgy deals."

But Ruth didn't hear any of it. When I turned to look at her, she was asleep. She was right: some things didn't change. I covered her up and crept downstairs to take Benjamin up on his offer of wine.

"She gone?" he said as he let me in.

"No. I've left her snoring on the sofa."

"Fancy watching a movie?"

"Got any popcorn?"

"No, but there's a jar of pickled cucumbers in the fridge."

"God, Benjamin! When are you going to realise that people need real food, like popcorn and crisps and chocolate when they drop by?"

"So what are we going to watch?"

"*Local Hero*?"

"Again?"

"I haven't seen it for at least a month."

He sighed and rummaged through his alphabetically ordered DVDs. "The things I do for you," he said.

"How about I go and find something to munch while you get the film started?"

"Deal."

Two hours later I went back to my flat, which was in darkness. I could hear low snoring sounds from the sofa. Ruth was still out cold. I could smell her familiar sleepy scent. I cleaned my teeth, undressed in the dark, and shut my bedroom door behind me. My bed felt big and cold. Would Wendy ever warm it up for me? I suddenly felt exhausted. It had been a long, hard day, although watching the film with Benjamin had been a good way to end it. I pulled the covers over my head, and fell into a deep sleep. I dreamt of beautiful beaches and northern lights; of an old woman dangling a key in front of my face; of trying to run from a faceless assassin, only to find that I was wearing stiletto heels and kept falling over, and he was closing in on me, but there was a boat I could swim to and there on the prow was Ruth, and Wendy had her hand on the tiller. I woke up with a start to hear noises in my kitchen. A bolt of fear flashed through me until I remembered that Ruth had stayed over. I got up and wrapped myself in an ancient dressing gown. Ruth was dressed in T-shirt and knickers. She had her back to me as she poured water from the kettle into the women hold up half the world mug that I'd always thought of as hers. I'd forgotten how thin her legs were. You couldn't tell from her back that she was pregnant.

"How did you sleep?"

"Oh, hi Nik. Ok. Sorry, I must have just crashed."

"You needed it. No bad dreams I hope."

"Only the same one. Tawfiq's standing there holding his arms out to me – and then there's a bang and he disappears and there's just …" She clasped her head in her hands. "Oh, Nikki, I can't bear to think about it. About how he…how he…died." She sobbed. I didn't say anything. I didn't know what to say. Part of me wished I'd never suggested she come round. I didn't feel that I could hold her pain as well as deal with everything else. And she'd hurt me badly over the past months, backing off, phasing out contact, not telling me she was back in London, and then the bombshell about Tawfiq.

"I'm sorry. Look, hang out if you need to, but I have to get ready to go to work. Mind if I have the first shower?"

"No. No, you do what you need to do. I'll…er, I'll …just go."

"You don't need to, but I need to see what's happening at work, so I'll go and get ready." I didn't recognise this person. Someone who sets boundaries and has to go to work. Me. It was almost funny. I was almost funny. I headed for the bathroom, but the doorbell rang. I padded to the front door.

"Who is it?"

"Wendy. Got any breakfast going?"

Shit! The woman I was nuts about was outside my front door and my ex-lover was making herself at home in my kitchen dressed wearing next to nothing.

"Yeah. Yeah, I can knock you up some breakfast. Someone's here, though."

"Oh. Sorry. Am I interrupting?" The change in her tone from bright and hopeful to embarrassed pulled at my heart. I opened the door.

"No, no. You're not interrupting anything." She'd been jogging and was dancing her little warm down on the doormat. "Ruth's had some awful news. Her boyfriend just died. Got killed in Gaza. She stayed on the sofa last night."

Wendy's face said she was wondering whether to believe me or not. She stepped in, looked around, and her eyes rested on the messy bedding on the sofa.

"Sorry," she said. "I don't know why I came round. I was out for a run and found myself five minutes away and just came on impulse."

"I'm glad you did," I said, giving her a kiss, just a light one, on the lips. "Look, I have to shower, then I'll knock up some breakfast. Help yourself to coffee."

Ruth came out of the kitchen. Wendy's face tightened up again.

"Wendy, this is Ruth. Ruth, Wendy," I said, like some hostess at a party.

"Have we met?" asked Ruth.

"I don't think so," said Wendy.

"Wendy's a police officer," I said. "She came to the centre when Veronica died, and she was first on the scene when I got attacked the first time."

"Oh, I see," said Ruth.

"I think I saw you outside the Bedford the night Nikki was attacked," said Wendy.

"We're going out," I said. "We're going out tonight."

"Oh, I see," said Ruth, and this time she did see. "Um...listen, I'll be out of here in just a minute. Just need to..."

"You're ok," I said. "Have a shower, have some breakfast."

"No, no, I'd better go. I have to check in with the office."

"Don't go on my account," said Wendy. "I was just passing by. Nikki makes a great breakfast."

Ruth's face was a picture. "Yes, I remember," was all she said before diving behind the sofa to retrieve her jeans, which she struggled into, displaying clumsiness I'd never seen in her before.

"Sorry about your boyfriend," said Wendy, trying to understand what was going on. "Was he…I mean, how…?"

"He was killed by a suicide bomb that went off too soon," said Ruth. "It was in Gaza. He's – was –Palestinian."

"Was it his bomb?" Wendy's voice had risen. "I mean, was he going to blow himself up?"

"No. Why does everyone assume that every Arab is about to blow themselves up? He was just a lovely man in the wrong place at the wrong time." Ruth was crying again.

"I'm sorry. It's just…"

"I know. You just thought. You just heard the words Gaza and bomb and assumed. That's what everyone does, just assumes."

"Look, Ruth, cool it, ok? Wendy's just asking, that's all. She doesn't know anything about you or whatshisname…"

"Tawfiq! His name is Tawfiq. What's wrong with you?"

"There's nothing wrong with me, and of course I should have engraved on my brain the name of the man who knocked up my ex-girlfriend."

Wendy's mouth had fallen open as she looked first at Ruth, then at me. "So…you two…?"

"It's been over a while," I said, looking at Ruth.

"I'd better go," said Ruth. You two have obviously got things to talk about, and I wouldn't want a member of Her Majesty's finest to go without her breakfast."

At that moment, I almost hated Ruth; but Wendy was heading for the door.

"No, you stay. I'd best go," she said. "Leave you two to sort things out."

"No, don't," I said. "I'll make you porridge."

"Another day," said Wendy, her hand on the door handle.

"Where shall we meet tonight?"

"How about I call you later?"

"We can decide now," I said, panic rising.

"I'll call later." And she'd gone.

"Did I say something?" asked Ruth.

"Yeah, you could say that," I said. "Ruth, I'm sorry about Tawfiq, and I'm sorry that things are so shit for you; but you opted out of my life and I'm trying to get on with it."

"Don't worry, I'm off," she said. "Hope things go well with your policewoman. God, Nikki, I never thought I'd see the day when you were screwing a pig."

Fury flashed through me. "Don't you dare, ever, talk about Wendy like that," I yelled. "Or me, for that matter. You don't know anything. She saved my life, that woman." That was probably an exaggeration, but Wendy had certainly shown more care in two weeks than Ruth had in forty. And I realised that the old battle lines didn't matter any more. I'd changed. I took people for who they were and how they acted, not on the basis of whether or not they wore a uniform or voted the right way. And I also realised that Ruth only ever took from me. She took my time and space and love and gave precious little back. "I think you'd better go. I hope things work out for you and the baby. And I *am* sorry about Tawfiq."

Ruth gathered her jacket and bag. She didn't offer to tidy up the sofa.

"See you then," she said, and banged the front door behind her.

I pushed aside the covers that she'd slept in and slumped onto the sofa. Things were getting heavy and complicated. I had to shower and get to work. I wanted to go back to bed and sleep until it was time to watch Richard and Judy, and then sleep some more. My doorbell rang. I didn't think I could face a soul-searching session with Ruth, and who knew what was going on in Wendy's head. I rose wearily and moved towards the front door.

"Yeah?"

"Nik? It's me, Ben."

"Oh." I opened the door.

"What's up?"

"Everything."

"I thought you might want me to ride to work with you again."

"That'd be nice. I need a shower, though."

"Can you be ready in fifteen?"

"Yeah."

"Want to tell me what happened?"

I sighed. "It's kind of complicated," I began.

"You didn't...."

"No! Nothing like that."

I gave Ben the short version.

"Phew! What happened to Ruth?"

"She went."

"Coming back?"

"Doubt it."

"I'll be back in fifteen. Ok?"

"Thanks."

Geri was already at work when I arrived. I gave Ben a hug, sent him on his way, and set about making myself some coffee.

"I don't know who to write to about my resignation," said Geri with a new lightness in her voice.

"Lawrence, I s'pose," I said.

"He seems to have disappeared," said Geri. "Derek too, although he flitted in to have a quick look at the books and bank statements first thing. He was only here for about half an hour."

"Who is he, anyway?"

"What do you mean?"

"I mean, I know why Rita's a trustee. And I think I understand why Bernard is. And Joan has a stake in the centre, and Maryam did at one point, and I suppose even Lawrence does in a way; but what's in it for Derek? How did he get involved?"

"I'm not sure. I never thought to ask. Just assumed he was a local business person who wanted to do some voluntary work. He's some sort of business man, but I couldn't tell you exactly what he does."

"I saw an advert in the paper with his name and picture. It looked like he ran some sort of hypnosis clinic for people wanting to stop smoking."

"So maybe he knew Veronica. She was having hypnosis."

"You think it could have been with him?"

"Maybe. She never said. She kept it all a bit hush-hush, like she was embarrassed about it."

"Weird if she was seeing Derek for hypnosis."

"Everything feels weird at the moment."

I couldn't disagree. But we needed to focus on keeping things as normal as we could. "So, what's on for today?"

"The art class. That's about it."

"And we've got a while before they all turn up."

"I'm thinking we should advertise the space here, see if we can drum up some more business now that Gordon's out of the picture."

"What did you have in mind?"

"A few adverts, some ringing around. The refugee advice sessions were going well until a few weeks ago, and I'm guessing that the SoLCEC isn't really their sort of place. I know the project worker, I'll give her a ring. Then there's the Tai Chi class. We can undercut SoLCEC and tempt them back in. And a woman I know who runs a Portuguese Women's group wants to use this place for a community café."

"Sounds like a plan."

"I shouldn't care really. I'll be out of here in a month."

"It's good that you do still care."

"How about you sort out the post and see if you can get the management committee, or what's left of it, to agree to meet again?"

"Ok."

By lunchtime, Geri had got the refugee advice project to agree to come back by offering a tempting discount. They'd be holding twice weekly sessions.

"Luisa said that there'd been all sorts of problems at the new place," said Geri, sounding triumphant. "She said they'd missed the friendliness of *Action in Caring.*"

"How'd you get on with the Tai Chi group?"

"I made the guy who runs it a deal, and he's coming back from next week."

"Brilliant! Does that mean we're solvent?"

"Not quite, but getting there. And with no salary for Veronica or Gordon, there are savings, but it means more work for us."

"I can live with that."

"How'd you get on with the management committee?"

"Ansaphones for everyone except Bernard. He said he could come in tomorrow, and he'd try to get hold of Rita."

"Joan should be in by now. She's not normally this late."

"She didn't answer when I rang."

"Odd."

"Fancy some lunch?"

"We've got time for a quick break."

"The kebab shop does a good falafel."

"I fancy a kebab."

"Shall I go and get a takeaway?"

"Better had, so there's someone to let Joan in."

I put my jacket on and sprinted down the road to Ozzie's kebab shop.

Ozzie was stuffing meat and salad into a toasted pitta bread. He laid a fat pickled chilli across the top with a flourish, wrapped the sandwich in white paper and handed it to a spotty boy whose shirt was hanging down below his blazer.

"Cheers," said the boy. He had already bitten off half the kebab as he opened the door. Ozzie glanced up. He saw me and smiled.

"You come for free falafel, innit!" he said

"Happy to pay for it. And a kebab for my friend," I added.

"How you doing, then?"

"Ok. We're getting the centre back together. You might be getting new customers."

"That's good, innit."

"Yeah. It's good." I didn't want to think about all the other stuff we had to sort out, all the questions that were still waiting for answers.

"You want chips?"

"No thanks, just falafel and a kebab."

He busied himself grilling a skewer of meat and pepper and dropped the falafel balls into hot oil.

"How about you and I work out the new timetable?" said Geri, after we'd eaten lunch. "Then we can start to get some publicity materials together." Getting the new job seemed to have given her a new lease of life, and I liked seeing this positive side to her.

My mobile rang as I was designing a poster for the refugee advice sessions and wondering how many languages it needed to be in. It was Wendy.

"Hi Wendy. Listen, I'm really sorry about this morning."

314

"That's ok. I shouldn't have just turned up."

"No, it's nice that you did. And I'm sorry about Ruth. She was bang out of order, but I suppose it's understandable given what had happened."

"So how long were you two…"

"Not long really. And it was over. She'd only come to me because she didn't have anywhere else to go."

"I see."

I wondered if she did. "So, what are we doing tonight?"

"Are you sure you want to?"

"Of course I am! Are you?"

"I think so. I mean if you and Ruth are really…"

"It's been over for ages, Wendy."

"It's just that…"

"What?"

"Well, you seemed…it felt like there was unfinished business."

"Maybe. But I really want to see you."

"Are you sure?"

"Yeah. More than I've been about anything for a long time." There was a pause. Please, Wendy, don't pull away. The pause seemed to last forever.

"How about meeting for a drink, then?"

There was a god. "*Sappho?*"

"Seven thirty?"

"See you then, Nikki."

Chapter 28

I was in the toilet contemplating my good luck when my mobile rang. I pulled it out of my pocket and saw Suresh's name flashing on the screen.

"Got some stuff on Bentley's property company that'll interest you," he said. "Where are you speaking from? There's a weird kind of echo."

"I'm in the loo." It smelled of old shit, was down to the last few sheets of loo roll, and the toilet seat hung off one of its hinges.

"You're not…"

"No, of course I'm not. What did you find on Bentley?"

"He's a partner in Cityscape, one of the organisations that's behind Eurobuild Construction. It's a shadowy connection; we had to do quite a bit of digging. But here's the killer."

"What?"

"Gordon Smedley's name came up too."

"How?"

"He was company secretary of Cityscape."

"So they were in it together?"

"Looks like it. At least their accounts need to be scrutinised. We've referred it to the Serious Fraud Office."

"I'm finding it difficult to get my head around all of this."

"It's simple, really."

"No it's not. None of it makes sense."

"Ok, let's see. Smedley and Bentley are creaming off profits from a property development company that's got a major contract funded by public money to develop a new community centre. Bentley's hidden his involvement in the company, but he wheels and deals so that Eurobuild get the contract. Smedley's involved in the subsidiary company, so he gets his cut."

"But why run down *Action in Caring* and all the other neighbourhood centres?"

"We'd already figured that one out. They're sitting on valuable land. They have to get rid of the tenants so that they can sell it off for development. And you can guess which property company's lined up to put in the winning bid."

"Eurobuild?"

"Who else?"

Someone rapped on the toilet door.

"Nikki? You ok?" It was Geri. "Who you talking to?"

"Yeah, yeah I'm ok. Just talking to Suresh."

"You going to be long?"

"No."

"Only, I've got to…"

"Ok, just give me a minute and I'll be out." I heard her footsteps walk away. "You still there Suresh?"

"Yeah."

"So why did Smedley die?"

"Maybe he got too greedy? Maybe he was planning to spill the beans? Maybe it was a random killing."

"Not likely. The random killing theory."

"No, you're probably right."

"You going to talk to the police?"

"No choice. I'm talking with my editor, but I think we'll be calling it in soon."

"Nikki…" Geri was back.

"Coming. Suresh, can we talk later?"

"Call me in a couple of hours. I should know more then."

I unlocked the door and went to the basin to wash my hands. I glanced at my watch. I'd been half an hour, and my date with Wendy was just over an hour away, allowing for travel time. I went back to Geri's office. She was doing something with her PC.

"Loo's free."

"Thank God!" she said, leaping up from her chair, clicking with the mouse and making her screen go blank.

Geri was tidying her desk and logging off. She'd got her jacket half on.

"Ready to lock up?" I asked.

"Yes. But what did your friend ring about?"

I gave her the short version of Suresh's story.

"Why am I not surprised? I never liked those two," she said.

I just about had time to go home and change before heading off to meet Wendy. Benjamin was just opening his front door as I bowled into our shared hallway.

"Hey, Ben, how's it going?"

"Oh. Hello Nik. Well, you know…"

"No, that's why I'm asking."

"Not so good, as it happens."

"Why? What's wrong?" I hoped it wouldn't take him long to tell me – I had to be at the Elephant and Castle in half an hour and I wanted to shower and change.

"The weekend in Paris is off," he said, looking glum.

"Bummer. What happened?"

"He just said he couldn't take me, that it would be all work and no fun."

"Maybe he has a point."

"I was looking forward to it. What if he's taking someone else?"

"Then you're best off without him."

"But Nik, he's the one!"

"Look, Ben, I'm really sorry, but I'm meeting Wendy in under half an hour and I need to go and wash and change. Can we talk later?" I knew where Ben's he's-the-one moods led him.

"You might not come back tonight."

"I'll be back." I made it a rule never to sleep with someone on a first date, however hot they were. Call me old-fashioned, but I'd never woken up with regrets. I ran up to my flat, kicked aside a pile of post and flung off my clothes. I had the quickest shower ever and then, hardly dry, dressed in black chinos and a loose cheesecloth shirt. I added a jasper and silver pendant that Carla had given me, dabbed some soft musk scented essence onto my neck. I combed a side parting into my damp hair: it would end up spiky whatever I did. For once my socks matched. I might not have any intention of sleeping with Wendy, but I liked to know that I looked my best at every level. I slipped back into my red Kickers, shrugged on my khaki bomber jacket, and exited. I had ten minutes to get to Kennington. I'd left the bike outside. Caution made me glance around as I opened the front door, but there was nothing to arouse suspicion. I switched on the lights, mounted the bike, and rode north to *Sappho*. It was downhill all the way, and I made it in just over ten minutes.

Eva greeted me at the door. "Good to see you! How're you doing?"

I signed the members' book, paid my fee and told Eva that I was ok. I looked around the bar. Not many punters tonight. The light was dim. I squinted to see if I could spot Wendy. I couldn't. I glanced down the list of women who'd signed in for the evening. Her name wasn't there.

"Meeting someone?" asked Eva.

"Yeah. Wendy. She was here on the karaoke night."

"Doesn't ring a bell. What does she look like?"

I described Wendy, and Eva nodded. "I remember. She was with a red headed woman. Scottish."

"Yup."

"There's time yet. Get you a drink?"

"I'll have a Jamesons. It's been that sort of day," I said.

"Coming up."

Two women poring over the latest Carol Ann Duffy collection of poems occupied the sofa by the fire. I found a pair of easy chairs and a table and settled down to wait for Wendy. After ten minutes, I dug my mobile out of my bag in case I'd missed a call. No messages waiting, no missed calls. I went to the bar for another drink. The barmaid measured out the whiskey and I took it back to my seat. I waited another ten minutes, then I sent a text to Wendy: *I at Sappho: you still on?* And waited. It was past eight o'clock. The door opened and a group of giggly women came in. I thought about going home and ministering to Benjamin. I felt numb with disappointment. She could have told me she'd got cold feet. The door opened again and Wendy breezed through. I saw her before she saw me. I didn't know whether to feel relief or panic. Maybe I should have left when I still had the chance. I watched her sign in and look around until she saw me. She grinned and waved. Maybe it would be ok after all. I waved back.

"Nikki, I'm so sorry," she said as she landed in the chair beside me. "I couldn't get away from work, and then the Northern Line went down on me."

"That's ok. You're here now," I said, not a trace of my panic leaking through. "What do you want to drink?"

"Wine," she said. "Red – if that's ok with you."

"I'll get us a bottle. Merlot ok?"

"Perfect. God! What a day!"

I went to the bar, a new lightness in my step, ordered a bottle of Merlot with two glasses, and took them back to our table.

"So what happened?"

"Oh, you don't want to know. Just a call out that took longer than we'd thought. Some bloke who thought he wanted to kill himself and his girlfriend and we had to talk him out of it."

"What happened?"

"We got the kids out, then the girlfriend, and then he threw down the gun and we got him out too. He's under section at the Maudsley."

We sat in silence for a few moments, savouring the wine and reflecting on our strange and eventful days. Wendy spoke first.

"Hey, Nikki. What was going on in your flat this morning?"

"What, with Ruth?"

"Uh-huh."

"She'd rung me up last night in pieces because of her boyfriend being killed. She didn't have anywhere else to go, so I told her to come round. We talked. She slept on the sofa. That's it."

"So are you still in love with her?"

Her question took be aback. Had I ever been? Probably. Was I now? I wouldn't be feeling like this about Wendy if I were. "No. It was just...you know..."

"No, tell me."

"Well...it was kind of intense for a while. But it wasn't ever going to go anywhere."

"Why?"

"Wendy, can we talk about you?"

"No, I want to know."

"Well...most of her life she was on some kind of front line in a war zone, and that was how it was with her. Don't get me wrong, she's amazing. What she does...I mean, I could never do that, never take the risks she does. Afghanistan – helping to run those schools for girls, supporting the most oppressed women in the world, knowing that she could be shot, or worse. Knowing that if she took one wrong step, women and girls would die. I couldn't have done that."

"You take your own kind of risks."

"Nothing like hers; but Ruth and me, well, in a way I think I was relieved when she told me about Tawfiq and the baby. I didn't realise it, but I was. And then I met you."

"You like women who take risks, then?"

I thought about it. Wendy's job was risky. Today she'd had to deal with a man armed with a gun, his, hers and others' lives in the balance. I smiled. "Looks like it," I said. "So how about you? How come there's no special someone in your life?"

"There was, but the job got in the way," she said in a matter of fact tone of voice.

"Oh?"

"Back home. Susan. She worked for a marketing company. We were worlds apart."

"When did it...you know, when did you..."

"Split up?"

"Yeah."

"Almost two years ago. It's taken me a while to get back into circulation."

"So, here we are," I said, for want of anything better to say. There was another long silence while we both peered intently into our wine glasses. "How long have you been running?" I asked.

She gave a short laugh. "All my life! You mean as in marathons? That sort of running?"

"Yeah."

Before she could answer, my phone rang. Suresh's number flashed on the screen. I looked at Wendy. She nodded. I pressed the green button.

"Hey, Suresh. What's up?"

"Nikki? I don't know for sure, but something's going on. Incident at the block of flats where Nigel Bentley lives. Want to come along for the ride?"

"Really?"

"My snapper's still sick."

"I'm ...out. With someone." Wendy was looking at me curiously.

"Oh well, if it's more important than seeing what's going on chez Bentley…"

"No! I mean it is…but…"

"Pick you up at your place in twenty minutes."

"Ok…" Why did I say that? I could blow my chances with Wendy forever. "But… " I was talking to dead air. Suresh had hung up.

"Something wrong?" asked Wendy.

"A friend. Wendy, I've got to go home. Can we do this another time?" I didn't know her well enough to read her face. Disappointment? Resignation?

"Must be someone special. Is it Ruth?"

"No! No, it's nothing like that, just something I've got to do. Work…sort of. Wendy, I really like you," I said as shrugged on my jacket, "and please, please, can we meet later or tomorrow, and I'll make you breakfast whenever you want, but this is an emergency and I've got to go."

"Call me?" She looked bewildered.

"Yeah. I'll call you later. Thanks, Wendy, I'm so sorry…" and with Eva watching the proceedings, hands on hips, head shaking in amazement, I bolted out of the club, fumbled open the lock on my bike, and belted back through Kennington, then Brixton, dodging the red traffic lights at Streatham Hill, skimming sluggish buses, dozy learners and bolshy white vans until finally, breathless, I arrived home. Suresh was waiting outside in a nippy looking silver Mazda. He flashed the lights as I screeched to a halt.

"What took you so long?"

"Just let me put my bike away…"

"No time!"

"I'm not leaving it out here."

Benjamin peered out of his window to see what was going on. "You ok, Nik?"

"Can you take my bike in? Cheers! I owe you!" I left the bike propped against the gatepost and leapt into Suresh's car. He'd pulled away before I'd shut the door."

"Seat belt," he barked.

"Give us a chance!" I yanked the belt around me and clipped it in place as Suresh shot through an amber light. "Where we going?"

"Battersea. If that phone goes, answer it." He pointed towards a Nokia in the well in front of the gear stick. His grip on the steering wheel had turned his knuckles white. "Your kit's in the back. Get it ready to shoot."

"Is it to do with Bentley?"

"With any luck."

His phone rang. I answered it. A woman's voice said, "Suresh there?"

"Yeah. He's driving."

"Who are you?"

"The snapper."

"Cool. Tell him they're heading for Cityscape Towers. Check he knows where it is."

I relayed the message to Suresh. "Need me to check in the A-Z?"

"Where you been, Nik? We've got sat nav now. Ask if she knows the postcode."

"He says have you got the postcode?"

"SW11 9FZ. Number 48. Got that?"

"Yeah. Got it."

"Tell him they're in unmarked saloons but they've got the blue lights on. There's an ambulance too. Good luck." There was a click as she rang off. I gave Suresh the address. We'd stopped at a red light and he tapped at keys on a little box that was propped on the console. I jumped as a posh woman's voice said, *in two hundred yards turn left.*

"What's that?"

"Sat nav, I told you," said Suresh.

For half a mile continue straight.

"It talks to you?"

"If you're lucky it takes you right to where you want to go."

"And if you're not?"

"You end up in Essex."

"So what happens when we get there?"

"We watch. We get ready to jump out and take pictures. We turn on the tape recorder and ask everyone questions. Then we sit up for the rest of the night and write the story."

In three hundred yards turn right.

"What if the police don't want us there?"

Right turn coming up.

"They're used to us, we're used to them."

"I'm not used to any of it."

"Get the camera ready. Set the flash."

I reached into the back seat and found the camera bag. I checked that the battery was charged, set the flash to auto and put the strap round my neck.

"Were you on a hot date, then?"

Left turn coming up..

"Potentially. First one. Maybe last."

"How'd you meet?"

I started to tell Suresh about Wendy coming to *Action in Caring* the night of Veronica's death, and then about her being first on the scene when I'd been attacked outside the Bedford.

"You're dating a cop?"

"Yeah. Maybe. So?"

"You? Nikki Elliot of poll tax marches and eco warrior fame?"

Continue straight for half a mile..

"So what? I like her."

"Does your mother know?"

"Look, we've only been on one date, and that got cut short after ten minutes when you phoned."

"Only asking."

Carla wouldn't believe how tonight was turning out. I pulled my mobile out of my pocket to call her.

"What are you doing?"

"Ringing Carla." I hit the quick dial keys.

"Can't it wait? We're nearly there."

"Your friend said it was half a mile." *And anyway, she won't be there,* I could have added. Sure enough, Carla's ansaphone answered. I listened for the beep after her message. *Hi Carla, it's me. I'm out on a job with Suresh. Something going down near Bentley's apartment block, and you'll never guess…*and she'd never guess what she'd never guess because her ansaphone gave a long rude beep and kicked me off line.

Left turn coming up..

Ahead of us I saw a blue light flashing. Two blue lights. Shooting across the red traffic lights were two dark saloon cars. An ambulance, yellow and green with seizure inducing flashing blue scissored in. My heart was beating faster and my mouth had gone dry. I could feel Suresh's adrenalin as if it were my own as he held the car in first gear, willing the lights to change.

"Come on, come on," he murmured between clenched teeth, urgent fingers drumming the steering wheel. The lights turned to amber and Suresh pulled away with a screech. My phone rang.

"Leave it! We're nearly there," cried Suresh as we tried to catch up with the vanishing blue lights. Carla's name showed on my screen.

"Hi Carla, can't really talk right now."

"You just called *me*! What's going on? Where are you?"

"Chasing cars. Police cars. Battersea. With Suresh. You in later?"

In one hundred yards turn right..

"Be careful, Nik."

Right turn coming up.

"Yeah.." We had nearly caught them up. I hung up on Carla.

You have arrived at your destination.

Chapter 29

"No fucking parking spaces!" said Suresh as we looked for a place to stop. Police cars blocked the way ahead, and men were stretching blue and white tape across the road. We were near the river on reclaimed land. Derelict warehouses had given way to light brick and glass tower blocks and expensive looking restaurants. There was a small development of business units on the other side of the road. We pulled in and parked in front of someone's unit on a double yellow line.

"No-one's going to ticket us this time of night," said Suresh pulling on the handbrake. "Let's go."

We slammed the doors shut and Suresh clicked the remote on the car key to lock it. The car winked at us as we sprinted towards the action. Ginny Lancaster was talking to a pair of uniformed officers. She gesticulated towards the tower block and they nodded. A bald man in a mac stood smoking a little apart from Ginny. He was looking up at the building. Three more uniforms guarded the tape cordon. Paramedics crouched over a figure on the pavement. We'd reached the cordon.

"DCI Lancaster, can you tell us what's happening?" called Suresh. I hoisted my camera into place and snapped as Ginny turned to see who was asking.

"This is a crime scene, please stay back," said a burly uniform in a stab proof vest.

"Suresh Shah, South London Press. DCI Lancaster, has this got anything to do with Nigel Bentley?"

Ginny muttered something to the uniforms and strode over to us. She didn't look happy.

"Mr Shah, do you want to sabotage yet another case? And what's Ms Elliot doing here? She's a possible witness to a serious crime."

"Just doing my job, Ginny," said Suresh. "Nikki's here as my snapper. Usual man's off sick."

"Well, get her out and do without the photos."

"Public interest, Ginny," said Suresh, though I thought she probably had a point about me being a witness, and I wondered what she'd meant about his sabotaging other cases. I'd ask him later."

"I'm warning you, Mr Shah. I'll be making a formal complaint to your editor. I want her out – now."

"I'd better go," I said, starting to step back. Just then there were sounds of shouting from in front of the building. We all turned to look.

"Ginny, we need you here," called the bald man. Uniformed officers were emerging from the flats. There was an urgent conference between Ginny, bald man and the uniforms. The paramedics manoeuvred a stretcher onto the ambulance.

"I'm going back," I said. "You'll never get anything with me here. Take the camera." I handed it to Suresh. "You just point and click. See you at the car."

Suresh grabbed the camera, lips set into a thin line of frustration. As I jogged back to the car, I heard him call out again:

"What's happening Ginny?"

I waited by the car wondering what was happening. It was a cold, clear night, and I shivered. After ten minutes I saw Suresh walking back. He didn't look happy.

"What's up?"

"A kid's been killed. A jogger found him outside the foyer of the apartment block and called it in. Kid was badly injured. Stab wound. He didn't make it."

"Shit. Was there a fight?"

"No-one seems to have seen anything. Probably some sort of gang thing, or a drugs deal gone wrong; but you expect that on the sink estates, not on the ones where a two bed flat costs a million."

"Is Bentley around?"

"No sign of him." Suresh unlocked the car. "Sorry Nik, I shouldn't have called you out."

"Screwed up a hot date," I said.

"Yeah, sorry about that."

"I might never see Wendy Baggott again."

"You will if she's worth it," he said, starting up the engine. Before setting off he took out his mobile and tapped a couple of keys. "Jude? Suresh here… Kid stabbed. No, no sign of Bentley. No, he didn't make it. Yeah, I'm coming back."

"Can you drop me off at home?"

"Yeah, no problem." We backed out of the business park. The cordon was still across the road ahead and police were standing in huddles talking into walkie-talkies. We turned the other way and went back the way we'd come.

"What did Ginny mean about you sabotaging other cases?"

"What? Oh, that. Old history. We got wind of an arrest, hit the scene before the police and the perps saw us, figured out the cops wouldn't be far behind, and scarpered. Gang stuff."

"You going to be in trouble?"

"Probably."

"Know the way back?"

"Yeah."

There was a pile of CDs in the slot beneath the radio. I rummaged through them and chose Clapton's *Unplugged*. It took me back to student days, our finals year. The year my dad died. I'd played *Tears in Heaven* over and over.

"Nice one," said Suresh.

We didn't talk until we reached my house. Suresh said, "Hope you sort it with Wendy."

"Yeah, well…let me know if you hear anything about Bentley."

Benjamin's light was on. I tapped on his door.

"What on earth was all that about earlier?" was his greeting to me.

"Long story. Can I come in?"

"Yes, come and help me drown my sorrows. I should be packing to go to Paris, but now I'll be here all alone."

"Bummer. And *we* didn't see any bad guys getting caught."

"Eh?"

I filled him in on my evening, the aborted date with Wendy, Ginny's fury at seeing me on the job with Suresh.

"Wine?"

"Need you ask?"

He went out to his sterile, foodless kitchen and came back with a corkscrew and a bottle of Sicilian red.

"Thing is," he began, "Rick might be on the level. He might just want to focus on work. I might be too much of a distraction."

"Yeah, that's probably it," I said.

"But then again, suppose he's got someone in Paris? Or he's shagging one of the crew?"

"Have you asked him?"

"Not if he's shagging one of the crew."

"When's he back?"

"Tuesday or Wednesday. Wants to take me to The Ivy next Friday. He's booked the table. They're gold dust. Think he had to twist a few arms."

"There you go. If that isn't love, what is?"

"But what if he meets someone in Paris?"

"Try trusting him and see what happens. At least you haven't just blown your first date with someone really incredible who may never want to see you again."

"Wendy?"

"Yeah. I got Suresh's call and left. Didn't tell her why. I s'pose I thought she'd disapprove and try to stop me going."

"You could ring her."

"It's a bit late now. Maybe I'll ring tomorrow."

"Ring her now. It's not ten yet. She's probably crying into her cocoa."

I gulped a mouthful of wine and reached in my pocket for my phone. Punched in Wendy's number. After five rings, the ubiquitous Orange Ansaphone woman came on line telling me the person I wanted to speak to wasn't available. *Why the fuck not?* I wanted to scream. The beep told me I could leave a message. *Hi Wendy, It's Nikki. I'm really sorry about earlier – Suresh got a scoop and needed a cameraman. Woman. Come for breakfast. Ring me.*

"Wanna watch *Sex in the City*?"

I sighed. "Why not?"

I went upstairs to my flat at ten thirty and rang Carla. She picked up: wonders would never cease.

"What's going on? I've been really worried!"

I filled her in on my eventful evening.

"You broke a date with Wendy to go out with that stupid git Suresh?"

"He was doing me a favour."

"Oh yeah! He fucks up a date with a really classy woman and lands you in it with the detective who's investigating the suspicious death of your former boss!"

"He thought something might be going down with Bentley. There might have been an arrest."

"And you didn't even get that!"

"You've never liked Suresh."

"And you wonder why? Get real, Nik, the guy's a liability. He's probably fucked his own job too."

Carla only swore when she was really angry.

"How's the arm?"

She sighed. "Aching. Itching. And the bus company are denying liability. I've had a letter from someone whose level of grammar is that of a six year old. Worse. Look, sorry Nik, I'm not good company and it's been a shitty day. It'd be nice to see you – you around tomorrow?"

"Want me to cook for you?"

"No, no, don't cook. Let's have a take away."

"I could rustle up…"

"No, it's ok, I really fancy an Indian. Or we could go to *Wholemeal.*"

We hadn't been to our favourite veggie restaurant, a cosy little Streatham institution, since before Christmas.

"Ok," I sighed. My cooking would never get better if I didn't have the chance to practise. "*Wholemeal* seven thirty?"

"And don't you dare stand me up for one of that journo's harebrained schemes!"

I was in bed by eleven. Wendy hadn't called back. Not even a text. I read a bittersweet Jackie Kay story and then switched off the light. Sirens screamed up and down Streatham High Road like demented foxes. South London lullaby. I'd set the alarm clock for an hour earlier, just in case Wendy took me up on my offer of breakfast. She didn't. She didn't phone either. Shit. I thought about sending flowers to the police station but decided against it: she might not be out at work. I sent her a text: *Sorry again. U ok? Ring me.* Then I set off for work.

I rode across the common, dodging the usual packs of dogs, nodding a greeting to the early morning strollers who were now becoming familiar. A skinny woman scooped up poo deposited by her sleek whippet. I'd hate to have to do that. I got to work early, but Geri was already there.

"I'm putting the new timetable together and working out some costs. If the council gives us back our grant, we're just about in business."

"But we've no manager, no finance person, most of the management committee have buggered off, and you'll be gone in three weeks," I said.

"Mmm. Well, there's a challenge for you. Rita'll help."

"You've got to be joking!"

"And there's Iris and Pete, maybe Jade. There's a real chance we could pull this place together. Maybe do something a bit different with it."

"Not if the council wants the land. There's still that little problem. And I think they're going to want to centre everything at SoLCEC, whether or not people like it."

"You might be right. How was your evening?"

"Not what I'd planned."

"You didn't get stood up?"

"No." I told Geri about Suresh's call and our abortive mission to Battersea-sur-Thames.

"He the one that promised Dora a bed and telly?"

"The same."

"He'd better deliver. She'll be in today, wait and see. She'll be wondering why her furniture hasn't turned up."

"He's probably forgotten about it."

"Better remind him, then. You don't want to be in Dora's bad books!"

The doorbell rang. I looked up at the monitor. Dora Popp was standing in the sunshine wearing a lime green knitted hat, a brown raincoat with its buttons missing, a red moth-eaten jumper and a skirt of indeterminate, slushy colour. On her feet she wore white trainers. I pushed the release button and opened the door.

"Hello Dora," I said.

"What you doing 'ere?"

"I work here. Remember? My name's Nikki."

"I've run out of money and I want tea. I 'aven't 'ad no breakfast today. Nor no supper yesterday."

"Come on then, I'll put the kettle on."

She shuffled after me and waited as I filled the kettle.

"You got any family, Dora?"

"Nah."

"You grow up around here?"

"Not far. Four sugars."

"I know. You ever marry? Have kids?"

She sniffed. "They didn't let you," she said.

"Who?"

"Them. At the 'ospital."

"How long were you in hospital?"

"Forty one years."

"How old were you when you went in?"

"Fifteen. 'Ere, why you asking all these questions? Gimme that
tea."

"Why'd you go to hospital when you were fifteen?"

"Nosy cow, aint ya?"

"Sorry. I didn't mean to…"

"Fuck off. You're just like all them other social workers and
nurses. Fucking useless the lot of you." She stomped off towards the
little café area splashing tea before I could reply, or before I could offer
her breakfast. I'd heard about women – girls, really – being locked away
for having sex before marriage. Mentally defective, they were called. I
wondered if that was what had happened to Dora. I headed back to the
reception desk. The phone rang as I was settling into my chair. It was
Maria de Souza.

"I wondered if we could meet," she said. There was an urgency
to her voice.

"Well…yes," I said, taken aback. "What for?"

"Something's happened. And I think I've found out something.
I want to run it by you. Keep it to yourself for now."

"When d'you want to meet?"

"Are you free this afternoon?"

"I can be."

"Good. Can you come over to *Young Hearts*?"

"Yeah."

"See you later, then Nikki." She put the phone down before I could ask any questions. It all felt very clandestine. I was thrilled and fearful. What could Maria want to talk to me about?

Felicity was splendid in gold and emerald green. She'd piled her auburn curls on top of her head revealing a long neck lightly dappled with freckles. Silver and peridot earrings dangled from her pendulous ear lobes.

"Glorious morning!" she said as she swept in.

"Yes, I suppose it is," I said. I'd hardly noticed, what with wondering whether there was a connection between Nigel Bentley and the stabbing by his home, and if Dwayne and Leon were out and about.

"Any news? Are we any nearer to solving the mystery of Veronica's premature flight to her next incarnation?" I didn't know whether Felicity was being ironic or this was how she spoke all the time.

"Not that I know of," I said. "A kid was stabbed last night. Right by Bentley's block of flats."

"You know, your journalist friend really should talk to Leo," said Felicity

"I'll remind him," I said.

Felicity's class came in with their mats and foam blocks, all loose tops and baggy trousers. The women all wore drop earrings and meaningful pendants. The men who weren't bald had plentiful tangly hair and wore clothes in natural fibres, comfortable shoes on their long feet. They left after an hour and a half chatting softly to one another and looking relaxed.

"Mind if I stay for a cup of tea?" asked Felicity. "Geri said she wanted to go over my timetable with me."

"Of course not," I said. "There's some herb tea in the cupboard over the microwave."

"Perfect," she said, and headed for the kitchen.

Geri emerged from her office. "Felicity still here?" she said.

"Making tea." I pointed towards the kitchen.

"Great," said Geri.

Dora scuffed her feet across the floor, the trainers squeaking unpleasantly.

"What can we do for you, Dora?" asked Geri.

"I want me lunch and some money. It's all gone 'til Tuesday."

"I can make you some toast. Will that do?"

"S'pose. What about me money?"

"Ok, I'll lend you a tenner," sighed Geri. This clearly happened on a regular basis.

The doorbell rang. I glanced at the monitor and saw Rita and Prudence. I buzzed them in."

"Ooh, it's nippy out there," said Rita, stamping her feet as if to warm them. Prudence leapt up at me, tongue hanging out. How could I resist?

"Tea?" I asked.

"Not 'alf!" said Rita. "Don't move, I'll get it. Make one for you?"

"Coffee please. Black. One sugar."

Rita and Geri headed off towards the kitchen. Dora shuffled back to keep vigil until her toast was ready. The doorbell rang. I glanced up at the monitor. Justin was standing there, his gelled hair unmoving in the breeze. I pressed the button and he pushed the door open and stepped inside.

"G'day Nikki," he said.

"To what do we owe this pleasure?" I asked. "You haven't got a group with your lads, have you?"

"Nah. Just wanted to talk about some timetable changes with you guys."

"Geri and Rita are making tea if you want one."

"Cool." He strode towards the now overcrowded kitchen.

I opened up the Outlook calendar on my PC and started to input some of the activities that Geri had jotted down on a sheet of A4. The week was looking busier. There were activities planned for most days and some were getting decidedly crowded. Things were looking up for *Action in Caring*. All we needed to do now was pull it all together and get someone to manage it all.

The doorbell rang. Today was the busiest I'd known it to be. I looked up at the monitor. Gina, Geri's sister, was standing there. I buzzed her in.

"Hi," I said. "Any joy with the computer files?" But I didn't really need to ask: Gina's face said everything. She had the broadest grin I'd seen since starting this job.

"What've you found?" I asked.

"Is Geri here?"

"I'll get her." I went back to the kitchen. "Geri, your sister's here. She's found something on the computer files." We both went back to the reception area where Gina was pacing. She and Geri hugged. Gina was rounder and a couple of inches shorter than Geri.

"So?" asked Geri.

"Can we go into your office?"

"Yes, just tell us what you found!"

"I will but I need to show you on your PC."

Everyone else was gathered in the kitchen. Dora was slurping tea and interrogating Justin about Australia.

338

"Ok," said Gina, as we settled around Geri's PC. "What you have to understand is that getting rid of files isn't as straightforward as most people think."

"You just delete stuff, don't you?" I said.

"No, you have to empty the recycle bin," said Geri.

"And it still hasn't gone. Not really," said Gina.

"How do you mean?" I asked.

"When you empty the recycle bin or delete a file some other way, the file isn't really deleted. The file name is removed from the list of names in the folder or the Recycle Bin, and the space occupied by the file is made available to Windows for reuse. But Windows does not reuse the space straight away, so the data contained in that file will remain intact for some time to come, which means that you can recover it. Of course, the longer you leave it, the less likely it is that you'll be able to get it back, because the computer will reuse all or part of the file's disk space for something else."

"So Gordon or whoever thought they'd deleted a load of stuff hadn't really?" said Geri.

"That's right. If they'd defragmented the hard drive since the file was deleted, then the chances would have been much slimmer for successfully recovering the files, and even using the software tools that can undelete deleted files wouldn't have brought them back."

"So they hadn't done that?" I asked

"No. I took the disk away to see what there was. The software I used understands the internals of the system used to store files on a disk and can locate clues to the whereabouts of the disk space a lost file occupied. It can also read the unallocated disk space, the space the deleted files formerly occupied and which is available for reuse."

"That's amazing! I never knew you could do that," I said.

"You need the special software to do it," said Gina. "Standard programs can't read the space in that way. Whoever deleted all those files on your system didn't know all this. They deleted files and emptied the recycle bin. And they wiped the backup tapes. But they didn't reformat or defragment the hard disk, so I've gone through and recovered a load of files, including e-mail folders."

"I knew you'd sort it," said Geri.

"I've put the documents I thought you'd want to see on this USB stick. Want to see?"

Geri was already grabbing at the little device and plugging it into her machine. "Ok, where do I go now?"

"There's a list of folders you might want to start with. And then there're the e-mails. I skimmed through them and most looked pretty boring, but have a look and see what you think. You know what you're looking for." She moved aside and Geri and I took her place in front of the PC.

"Look," Geri said, "There's a folder called NB."

"Nigel Bentley?" I said.

"Elementary, my dear Elliot." She tapped at some keys and a list of folders unfurled. They were e-mails. Geri clicked on the first one.

N: Tracks covered. G.

"What's that about, then?" asked Geri.

"What does the next one say?"

G: I don't want any mess. Make sure nothing's traceable. N

"I'll leave you two to it and go and get some tea," said Gina. Geri double clicked the next document.

N: it's taken care of.

"What does that mean?"

"Let's see what Gordon was replying to." Geri scrolled down:

G: You're getting careless. Sort it. N

"Go down to the one before," I urged. Geri spun the mouse wheel until she reached the start of the thread.

"Ok, here's where it starts," she said.

N: the girl who works here saw the transfer and thinks something's up. Could be a problem.

"Shit! What are the dates on those?"

"Let's see…" Geri moved the cursor to field that told us when the message was sent.

"Last month…"

"They're talking about Tanya, aren't they?"

"Nikki, you don't…"

"They must be! She was a girl, she worked here, she saw the bank statement. Look at the date! You know what this means, don't you?"

"I think it means we call the police."

"Yeah. How stupid were they to put all this in writing?"

"People don't think. They use e-mail when they would have spoken or written letters. Then they think they've erased it all, only they haven't."

"What else is there?"

We scrolled through some messages that were pretty banal. Confirmation of meetings, a crude joke. Then we came across one from Gordon that chilled me and caused Geri to draw in her breath sharply:

N: New girl too nosy. Need the usual. See you later. G

Bentley had replied:

G: Supplies short. Need a few days. Talk later. N

"They were talking about me, weren't they?" I said.

"Look, I've moved into the documents folder. Here's one telling the bank that Lewis Fairclough is a signatory," said Geri, sidestepping my panic.

"We need to talk with Ginny Lancaster."

"You're right."

There was a whiff of old pee and Dora shuffled through the door.

"'Ere. You got some money for me, or what?"

"We're kind of busy right now, Dora," said Geri.

"I've come for me money." She stood with her feet planted firmly, hands on hips. I guessed she wasn't going anywhere without her sub.

"Geri'll get it for you in a couple of minutes," I said. I was desperate to know what else was in the files.

"I want it now."

"Look, I need to make a phone call," I pleaded.

"I ain't stopping yer," she said. "That coloured one can give me me money." I looked at Geri, who raised her eyes to heaven.

"I'll get your money, Dora, on condition you call me Geri, not *that coloured one*," said Geri. "Nikki, make the call."

"Ok," I said. I'd ring Ginny and I wanted to tell Wendy too. "I'll phone from my desk." I went back out to reception while Geri unlocked the cabinet that held the petty cash tin. The others were in the kitchen, oblivious to our drama. I pulled my mobile from my bag. *Bentley and Gordon were in it together. We've got proof.* I sent the text to Wendy and Carla. Then I forwarded it to Benjamin and Suresh for good measure. I pressed the quick dial button for Ginny Lancaster. The phone rang three times before someone picked it up.

"DCI Lancaster's phone," said a man's voice.

"Is that Darren?" I asked.

"No, can I help?"

"I need to speak to Ginny. DCI Lancaster. It's urgent," I said.

"She's out on a case at the moment. Can I take a message?"

"This is Nikki Elliot from Action in Caring," I said. "We've recovered some computer files that have evidence relating to the deaths of Veronica Stein and Tanya Middleton and the attacks on me. Can you get someone over here?"

"I'll tell DCI Lancaster you called," said the voice.

"Look, this is really urgent," I said. "She needs to know what we've found."

"I'll try to get the message to her," said the voice. "Does she have your number?"

"Yeah. Just tell her to ring Nikki," I said. The voice hung up. I still hadn't heard from Wendy. I rang her number, and then hung up when it went straight onto the ansaphone. I remembered Maria's call. I needed to get over to Young Hearts. I went back into Geri's office.

342

"Maria de Souza wants to talk to me," I said. "Says she want to run something by me. I've left messages all over the place – Wendy Baggott, DCI Lancaster. Can you hold the fort?"

"Yeah, but get back soon," said Geri.

Chapter 30

I cycled through the back streets until I reached the *Young Hearts* building. The cheerful murals looked surreal in the context of the violence and corruption that was unfolding. I rang the bell and the door, heard Beth asking who was there.

"Nikki Elliot," I said. "Maria asked me to come."

"Come in," said Beth's disembodied voice.

I followed the corridor through to the reception area. Beth was sitting behind her desk.

"How you doing?" she asked.

Before I could answer, Maria appeared. "Thank you for coming, Nikki," she said. "Please come in."

I followed her into her office. Today she was wearing a lime green shift dress that reached to her ankles. Her hair was bound back in a fuchsia bandana and round her neck she wore a matching string of oversized glass beads.

"What have you found?" I asked.

"I've been asking around," she began, "and talking to the boys. Some of our boys go to Justin's group at *Action in Caring*. I knew something was wrong, but I didn't know how bad it was." She looked pale. Worry lines had etched deep grooves across her forehead.

"Tell me," I urged, my belly knotting in fear of what she might reveal.

"First of all, no-one had anything to say about Gordon Smedley being arrested for molesting boys. No-one knew anything about it. Most didn't know he existed. No-one had heard of a man of his description being into boys."

"Would they tell you?"

"Someone would say something. There'd be talk. But there's nothing. The kids don't know who he is. He hasn't hurt anyone, or not that we know of."

"What does that mean? Has he been preying on kids who don't use our centres?"

"That doesn't make sense. The story was about him abusing boys he had access to through his work. Has anyone said anything to you?"

"No, but I'm new. They don't know me well enough. But I don't think anyone said anything to Geri. Or Justin, for that matter. But Gordon was arrested. What does it all mean?"

"It could mean – and I have to stress *could* mean that he'd been set up."

"Why would anyone do that?"

"He was definitely involved in the other stuff, the corruption. Our friend Suresh found connections between Smedley and Bentley."

"Maybe things went wrong. Maybe Gordon got too greedy and Bentley wanted to lose him."

"It's possible. And Bentley's dirty. Really dirty. One of the boys told me that he likes to hang around and see what he can get from them. Sex in return for drugs. Other favours too, is what he said."

"Shit."

"There's something else, Nikki." She drew her hands across her face in a weary gesture. "Another man, someone close to Bentley, is seriously interested in boys. And the younger they are, the better. And this man could have some involvement with *Action in Caring*."

"How do you know all this? Who told you? And who's the other man?"

"Leon Dodd talked. He came in yesterday afternoon."

"Leon Dodd? And you believed him?" I almost shouted at Maria. "That little piece of scum tried to kill me. He does coke and whatever else he can cram into his skinny little system. He'd probably say anything if there was a fix at the end of it." I paused for breath. Maria looked at me and I couldn't read her face. "What?" I said.

She looked down and rearranged the pens on her desk. Then she looked up at me. "How well do you know Leon?" she asked, finally.

"Not very well," I admitted. "He tried to kill me. Said a man from the Council put him up to it – I presumed it was Bentley. Before that, I noticed his nose was always running. Justin said it was coke. Justin said his mother was a user."

"I've known Leon since he was ten years old. His older sister brought him here one day, said that she was worried about leaving him at home and could we look after him. He couldn't read or write, but he could roll spliffs and had stealing from the local offie down to a fine art. We helped him for a while. I really thought he'd turn out ok. I still think he could if he had a chance. He talks to me and that means there's hope; but he's fallen in with a bad crowd."

"Dwayne?"

"Dwayne and others from the gang that runs the Goodbody estate."

"So you believe him?"

"One of the other lads backed his story. Damien's one of our successes, tries to look out for the younger kids. He knew about the sex for drugs and he saw Bentley with Leon. He told me this morning. He mentioned the other man, but he didn't know who he was."

"Do the police know?"

"I called it in as soon as Damien told me. Leon's in care, or that's what Social Services told me. I'm expecting the child protection guys to arrive any time now. So…" but she was interrupted by her mobile ringing. She'd got the ring tone set to something sleek and jazzy. "Excuse me…" She picked up the handset. "Hello, Maria de Souza…Bradley? Where are you?… Yes, of course …Yes, I know it…Bit out of your usual patch, isn't it?…Oh, I see… Can't you come here?…Well, I'm sure that's not true…Yes, I understand…Of course…Give me half an hour…Yes, I've got your number…No, I won't bring anyone…Just keep breathing…I'm on my way." She hung up with a sigh, shaking her head.

"Problem?"

"One of the kids. Says he's in trouble and needs to talk to me." She was wrapping a turquoise pashmina around her shoulders. "Said he didn't want to come here in case he was followed. This gang business is getting beyond a joke."

"Where are you meeting him?"

"Streatham Common. The Rookery. Odd, it's right out of his patch. I'm surprised he even knows about it. Nice place. I used to go there for Sunday walks with my parents."

"How are you going to get there?"

"I'll take the car. It'll take too long otherwise."

"D'you want me to come with you?" Something didn't feel right.

Maria groped in a shapeless Hessian bag and pulled out a set of car keys. "No, it'll be fine. Bradley's always getting into trouble of one sort or another. We'll talk later. I'll call you." She was already half way through her door and I followed behind.

"Ok. I want to know who this other man is. There's really only Justin and the guys on the management committee."

"Beth, can you hold the fort? I've just got to go out and rescue Bradley Brown."

"Again?"

"Again!"

"Are we expecting anyone?"

"Police and social services are likely to come by to talk about Leon. I shouldn't be too long. Nikki, speak to you later." And she was gone.

"Did you catch where she's going?" asked Beth.

"The Rookery, Streatham Common," I said.

"Why there?"

"I don't know. She said it was off his usual patch."

"Yeah. And you know, these kids don't travel far, they tend to stay in their own territories." The phone rang, and Beth answered it and started making notes. It sounded as if something bad had happened. Beth quizzed the person on the other end of the phone.

"I can't believe it… He was here yesterday afternoon! Yes… Yes, I'll tell Maria when she comes back. Thank you for letting us know." She placed the handset back into the cradle of the phone.

"Trouble?" I asked.

"One of the kids has been stabbed. Last night, in Battersea. He was here just yesterday. Leon, his name was. Leon Dodds. Maria'll be devastated."

I made my decision.

You can ride from Clapham to Streatham almost entirely off road if you ignore the *no cycling* signs on the Common footpaths. The South Circular was at a standstill anyway, so I cut through the back streets of Balham, across Tooting Common and then followed the railway line until I was riding parallel to Streatham High Road. It had started to rain, a fine grey drizzle, and I didn't have my waterproofs. I cut through to the top of Greyhound Lane and then across the High Road to the Common. Streatham Common rises from the A23 up to the ridge that links Norwood to Croydon. At the top of the grassy expanse is woodland and the Rookery, a park made up of a number of individual gardens. There are little streams, big old cedar trees, lawns on which to sprawl or roll, a rose garden, seasonal borders, places to sit, and plenty of places in which to hide. I rode up the path that runs along the side of the Common until I reached the top. Breathing hard, I locked my bike outside the little café that beckons like a reward to those who have made it up the steep incline. Maria and Bradley weren't amongst the few hardy souls who were sitting smoking at the outside tables. A tot with a snotty nose tried to make friends with a frisky spaniel. I peered inside the café. An elderly couple in raincoats nursed cups of tea and ate Battenburg cake. No sign of Maria or a boy in distress. Maybe I'd got here before them.

I walked to the entrance to the Rookery. At one level I felt stupid: what would Maria think if she saw me? But somewhere in my gut, warning lights were flashing and I wondered if the call out had anything to do with what she'd found out about Bentley. Still, I was here now. Geri would wonder where I was, but she could cope without me for another half hour. I turned down the path to the left of the entrance. There were few people around because of the rain, which now was coming down hard and heavy. A slight woman in a burkha scurried towards the exit, pushing a pram, a toddler holding on to the handle and trying to keep up with her. I crossed a lawn area bordered by a dense shrubbery. I heard Maria before I saw her. She was talking to someone. Her voice was low and measured, as if she were trying to calm the other person down. I crept quietly towards the sound. Then I saw a flash of fuchsia pink. I edged round until I could see better. She was inside a clump of bushes, in the sort of place where children play hide and seek and make dens. She was kneeling and holding both hands up. She was looking at someone in front of her and talking. I couldn't see whom she was talking to or hear what she was saying, but something was very wrong. I crept forward and slipped behind an azalea. I was now only a metre or so away from Maria and whoever else was there.

"It doesn't make sense for you to kill me, Nigel. Bradley won't keep quiet and people know I'm here."

"And you think I can't take care of a little loser like Bradley Brown, Maria? He's probably history as we speak. Another victim of south London gang warfare. A statistic. And his prints are all over this knife. As far as the police go, yours will be an open and shut case. Patron saint of disaffected youth knifed by kid with grudge."

"My staff know I'm here. They'll raise the alarm if I don't call in or get back. You're putting yourself in danger for no good reason, Nigel."

"Your staff won't be around to notice whether you're there or not, Maria. In fact, there's probably not much left of that youth club of yours by now. Nasty spate of arson attacks. Someone's got it in for community groups. *Young Hearts*, *Action in Caring*. Probably one of those nasty little yobs you keep taking in. Timed devices. Crude but effective. Such a tragedy. Still, something for that Suresh Shah to get his pen around."

I didn't know what to do first: try to cause a commotion and get Maria out or phone the centres to warn them. She was keeping him talking, playing for time.

"Tell me, Nigel, when you've got rid of me and liberated the land my centre's on, what next?"

Silently, I pulled my mobile from my pocket. Damn! I didn't have Geri's mobile number, and if I tried to call, Bentley would hear. I'd send a text to Wendy. Copy it to Suresh and Carla, anyone just so that the alarm was raised. They'd need to try to get to Bradley Brown before whomever Bentley had paid to silence him, as well as evacuate our buildings. My hands were shaking so much I could hardly tap in the message. I kept it short and clear. I finished by saying *this is for real* because they might think I was having them on. Who would believe this was really happening?

Bentley laughed a short, humourless sort of laugh. "SoLCEC will change the face of south London and I'll get credit for the vision and drive to make it happen. They'll name sports arenas and shopping centres after me. When the maggots are feasting on you, Maria, I'll be campaigning to be next Mayor of London. And I'll win. You'll see, I'll be London's next Mayor."

"I can see that happening, Nigel," she said, "you'd make a powerful Mayor, a real match for Ken Livingstone; but tell me, why the rumours about Gordon Smedley? And why did he have to die?"

I remembered that my phone had a Dictaphone function. I wondered if it would be powerful enough to record the conversation. It would be evidence that might survive even if Maria and I didn't. How did it work? I scrolled through the menu. Office, open, recorder, open, options, record sound clip. I pointed the phone towards Bentley and Maria. A blue bar inched across the screen as my phone recorded Bentley's confession – or so I hoped.

"Gordon? Oh Maria, you're not as bright as I thought you were, are you? Haven't you done your research? Or did you leave that all to the nosy new girl at *Action in Caring?*"

"Humour me, Nigel. We've known each other a long time."

She was cool, so cool. Establishing rapport. Doing what you're supposed to do in hostage situations. I sent the sound-clip to Wendy and reset the voice recorder: it could only record a minute at a time. Record.

"Gordon was getting greedy. He'd got too pally with Veronica Stein. They had some history. Something to do with amateur dramatics and that outfit he used to work for until he managed to run them down.

Stupid bastard told her about Cityscape and Eurobuild, said he'd cut her in."

"I still don't know why he had to die. Didn't that just mean he'd get less from the deals?"

I sent that clip to Wendy and started the process of recording again.

"He thought they could screw me if they worked together. Stupid bastard. They tried to blackmail me. Said they'd tell the EU or whatever. How dumb is that? They stood to lose as much as me. Concocted some story about a sting operation. So they had to go. I'd got things running just the way I wanted them, and I wasn't having some pathetic losers fuck it all up."

I sent the sound-clip to Wendy. I hoped to God she was getting them, otherwise we'd run out of time. I started the next one.

"So you killed Veronica Stein as well?" asked Maria.

"Veronica? Someone got to her before me. I don't care. They're both out of the way. That's good news as far as I'm concerned."

So Nigel Bentley hadn't killed Veronica. Had Gordon? But from what Bentley had just said, Gordon and Veronica were working together. He'd have no reason to kill her.

"But they'll never pin Gordon's death on you, will they?" continued Maria. "You've been far too clever for that. You'll have got away with that girl who went to Manchester too, won't you?"

He gave a nasty little chuckle. "And that Leon Dodds. Stinking little dick sucker. I was getting well sick of him always hanging round, always wanting something, fucking everything up."

"Leon? What's happened to him?" asked Maria. There was a shake in her voice. *Don't lose your cool! Not now!*

"You mean you don't know? Well, well. You would have found out soon enough. But they'll never pin it on me. Tragic, I'll say. Tragic waste of promising young life, and they'll quote that in the paper."

I saved the sound-clip, sent it to Wendy, started to record the next one. Damn! My memory was full. Just then, the familiar

Eurhythmics song blared telling the world that someone was trying to phone me. Benjamin! His timing was the worst in the world. Why hadn't I thought to turn the phone to silent? As I rammed it in my pocket, fumbling at the off button, I could hear his disembodied voice: *Nikki? Nik? You there? That bastard Rick...*

"What's that?" snarled Bentley, turning unseeing towards me. The sudden movement after so long in the same position knocked him off kilter. As he tottered sideways, he stretched out his arm to balance and the knife fell from his hand. Maria seized her moment and rolled out from under the bushes, bellowing for help. I leapt forward to help her, but Bentley had righted himself. He grabbed at the knife and hurled himself towards us. I could hear sirens in the distance. Bentley lunged at me, but Maria dived between us. Then we all seemed to freeze for a moment that was long as a lifetime, until Bentley pulled back, Maria fell to the ground, and Bentley lunged again. I swung my body away from him, old judo lessons unlocking themselves from the archives of my memory, and he fell staggering onto the grass. The camber meant that he was unable to stop himself rolling away from us. I glanced at Maria. A red stain was spreading across the lime green dress like some ghastly tie-dye mistake. She wasn't moving.

"Maria!" I yelled, one eye still on Bentley, who had stopped rolling and was trying to pick himself up. The sirens sounded nearer. Much nearer. Someone screamed. Two teenagers in school uniform, ties loosened, skirt waistbands rolled up, had rounded the corner and stared at the scene in horror.

"Call the police!" I watched as the taller girl grabbed for her mobile.

"Wassa number?" she called.

"999!"

I reached a hand out to Maria and felt her move. "It's ok," I said, "you'll be ok."

Bentley had staggered up and was coming at me, knife slashing the air between us.

"It's over, Bentley," I said, trying hard to mimic Maria's calmness and ducking neatly away from his thrusting right arm. "I've heard everything. Recorded it." He thrust again, teeth bared like some demented dog. I dived down and rolled away from him. The sirens stopped. "I've sent it to the police," I said as he lunged towards me, panting with the effort. I sensed Maria move, but right now I had to focus on Bentley and staying alive. I sidestepped Bentley and he lost his footing on the grass, now slippery with rain. The school kids had vanished. I felt the vibrations of running feet before I saw anyone. Bentley was struggling to stand, but he didn't seem able to take weight on his left leg. Still, he raised the hand clinging to the knife and hurled it in my direction. I swerved, and the knife fell into the shrubbery.

"Stop!" someone yelled from behind me.

"You're surrounded, Bentley. Put your hands in the air," said someone else. As Bentley's face registered that the fight was over, and that he'd lost, he crumpled like a punctured zeppelin. I watched as uniformed police in padded vests ran towards him, handcuffs at the ready. I turned towards Maria.

"Call an ambulance," I cried. "She's bleeding!" I crouched down beside her, felt for the pulse in her neck. It was beating, but weakly. The stain of blood had spread and was pooling beneath her belly.

"Nikki, are you ok?" Wendy was here.

"Yeah, I'm fine, but Maria's hurt. Did you get my texts?"

"Yes, yes, I got them. You're brilliant Nikki."

A man and woman in green overalls marched towards us bearing a stretcher and emergency kit.

"Did you warn *Action in Caring* and *Young Hearts?*" I could hear the panic rising in my voice: what I'd heard was finally hitting home.

"Yeah, we've got police at both places."

"Bradley Brown? He was the bait."

"I don't know."

"Bentley killed Leon Dodds. And Tanya. And Gordon."

"I know."

The paramedics had looked at Maria and assessed her injury. "Is she going to be ok?" I asked as they manoeuvred her onto the stretcher.

"Hope so," said the woman. "Can you tell us what happened?"

"Nigel Bentley stabbed her," I said. "He'd lured her here. I followed her. They were in the bushes. She tried to get away and he went for her with a knife."

"Ok Maria, we're going to get you to hospital," said the paramedic as her partner did something intricate with gauze and an oxygen mask.

"I'm so glad you're ok," murmured Wendy, as her colleagues read Bentley his rights.

"How can anyone be so evil?"

"Some people just are."

"What now?"

"The detectives will want to talk with you. Want to come along with me?"

"I want to know that Maria's going to be ok."

"Wanna go with her?"

"Yeah."

"I have to clean up here. I'll call you later."

"Thanks." I glanced at her face and it was full of concern.

"Sorry about…"

"Yeah, well, we'll sort it out later."

I rode with Maria to Mayday Hospital in Croydon. They said it was the nearest. The accident and emergency ward was a shambles of beds and nurses, overtired doctors, distraught relatives, patients in pain. Maria's gurney was wheeled to centre stage and a young doctor examined her. The paramedics had managed to stop the bleeding, but she hadn't regained consciousness.

"Will she be ok?"

"Are you her next of kin?" The nurse was small, fine dark hair coiled neatly into a bun. Philippino I guessed.

"No. But I was there."

"Sorry, we only can give information to next of kin."

"But I was there."

"Sorry, we need to speak to next of kin."

"I don't know who…"

"Is there anyone you can call?"

"I don't…" and then I thought about Beth. She'd know what to do.

I left the ward as they were wheeling Maria into another room. I stood outside the entrance next to the huddle of smokers. I rang *AIC*. Geri picked up the phone.

"Nikki! What's going on? We've had police combing this place, and they evacuated us all, and then they let us back in, but left a couple of officers by the front gate. What's happening?"

"It's a long story. I'll tell you later; but can you give me the number for *Young Hearts*? I need to speak to Beth. Maria's hurt."

"God! Badly?"

"Bentley stabbed her. There was a lot of blood. She's in casualty."

"Are you ok?"

"Yeah, but I need Beth's number."

"Ok…" I could hear her tapping on a keyboard. "This is it. Got a pen?" I fumbled in my bag, found pen and notepad.

"Go ahead." Geri reeled off the number. "Thanks. I'll be in later." I ended the call and rang Beth, told her what had happened.

"Oh, shit," she said. "Oh, fuck. I always worried that he'd hurt her. Bastard. Oh, shit. How bad is it?"

"I don't know. And they'll only say anything useful to the next of kin. Do you know who to contact?"

"Her daughter Helena. I've got her number. Jesus, she'll be frantic."

"If you can get her to come to the hospital I'll wait for her."

"I'll ring now."

"Take my number. Just in case. How are things your end?"

"Crawling with police. They found some homemade firebomb or something tucked under the front step. Someone wanted rid of us."

"You're ok?"

"Yeah. I'll ring Helena."

I knew the young woman running towards the doors was Maria's daughter without her saying anything. Same dark wavy hair, same bone structure, same liking for bold colours.

"Helena?"

"Nikki?"

"She's this way." I led her into the ward and over to the nurses' station. The nurse I'd spoken to earlier was filling in some forms. "This is Maria de Souza's daughter," I said.

"Next of kin?"

"Yes. Helena de Souza. Next of kin. How's my mother?"

"Ok, let me check…" the nurse rifled through a stack of files. "This one, I think. De Souza?"

"Yes, yes. Just tell me, please, is my mum going to be ok?"

"Let's see…oh yes. She was stabbed. She's lost quite a bit of blood, but the knife missed her heart. She's in theatre now."

"Is she going to be ok?"

"I can't tell you. We have to wait and see."

"When will she be out?"

"Depends if any organs were damaged. Why don't you get some tea? I'll let you know as soon as there's any news."

"I'll get you a drink," I said to Helena, as she prepared to give her mother's details to the nurse. "What do you want?"

"Coffee. With sugar. Thanks."

I was queuing at the *Upper Crust* for coffee when I felt a hand on my shoulder.

"Does trouble follow you, or you it?"

I turned to see Ginny Lancaster. She was wearing yet another smartly tailored trouser suit and a stylish grey striped shirt.

"Seems to be following me at the moment. Get you a coffee?"

"No, thanks, I'm getting one for my partner too. So how come you were at the park when Bentley went for Ms de Souza?"

"I was with Maria when she got the call to meet some kid at the Rookery. I don't know, Ginny, call it instinct. I just got on my bike and headed for the Rookery." It was my turn to be served.

"I'll need to interview you formally," said Ginny.

"Ok, just let me know when's good," I said. "Look, Maria's daughter's here – that's who the coffee's for – and I really need to know that Maria's ok. Do you mind if I…?"

"I'll come with you."

Darren had caught us up.

I led them back to the Accident and Emergency ward. Helena was sitting in the waiting area. I handed her the coffee.

"Thanks."

"Any news?"

"Yeah, they think she's going to be ok."

"Thank God! Helena, this is DCI Ginny Lancaster, and her partner Darren Lowe."

Helena stood up and held out a hand. She had the same dignity as her mother. "Helena de Souza. I'm a barrister at New Circle Chambers."

"Good to meet you." Ginny was at least being civil. "Is there anything you can tell us?"

"This Nigel Bentley, the one who attacked her. She talked to me about him recently. Isn't he the council leader?"

"Yeah, he is," I said.

"She'd told me she thought there was a lot of corruption going on. I remember hearing his name. She'd talked about blowing the whistle on him, thought she'd nearly got enough to go on."

The little nurse came out of a side room. "Ms de Souza?"

"Yes. How's my mum?"

"She's going to be ok."

"Oh, thank you!" Helena looked as if she were about to hug the nurse. "Thank you!"

"Bradley Brown," I said to Ginny. "Have you managed to pick him up?"

"We picked him up an hour ago. He's in detention."

"He's ok?"

"As ok as a kid like him is ever going to be."

I felt absurdly triumphant that we'd managed to stop Bentley from killing another young person.

I'd been to the police station, given my statement. I'd been driven there in style, in a squad car. It was almost half past five. I'd left my bike chained up outside the café on Streatham Common. I needed to get back to *Action in Caring*, tell Geri and the others the latest, then retrace my steps and reclaim my bike. I was supposed to be going out to dinner with Carla. My quick thinking with the recorded sound bites had put me in the police good books, and they offered me a lift to retrieve my bike and go back to work. When I went outside to the car, Wendy was standing there holding open the passenger door.

"Quite a day, then," she said.

"Yeah, you could say that. What's happened to Bentley?"

"He's in custody. I don't think he'll be out for a long time, thanks to the confession you taped."

"What makes someone do stuff like that?" I mused out loud.

"Power. Money. Greed."

"Guess you see a lot of it."

"Fair bit."

We were driving through Brixton towards Streatham.

"Wendy, you know the other night…well, I'm sorry."

"Yeah, me too."

"It's just that…well, Suresh's call made it sound like something big was going down, and he needed a snapper…"

"Yeah, I can see the attraction."

"Hey, don't be like that!"

"Sorry. It just felt a bit like you'd set up a get-out. And knowing that the thing with Ruth was still so fresh…"

"No! I wanted the evening with you. I did, Wendy. Look, can we try again?"

"I'll be on nights next week."

"How about tomorrow?"

"Maybe."

"Maybe yes, or maybe no?"

"Maybe maybe. Do I go left here?"

"Yeah. Left here. All the way to the top. Ok, you know what? I'm going to be at home tomorrow. If you want to see me, I'll be there."

"Maybe."

Wendy helped me to load my bike in the back of the car and then she dropped me and it off at *AiC*. We parted on the promise that I'd be at home and she might, or might not, come round. Everyone was still at

AiC even though Geri would normally have gone home by now, and so would Justin.

"Emergency management committee meeting planned for Monday," said Geri.

"I didn't have much else planned," I said. "I'd have thought you'd have all gone home by now."

"We wanted to see that you were ok."

"Thanks. I'm meant to be going out tonight. Think I'll have to go home and change first."

I rang Carla's number. The ansaphone picked up, as I knew it would. *Just me. Crazy day. Bentley's in custody. Need to meet you a bit later. Wholemeal eight-ish.*

"So what happened love?" Rita had come out of the kitchen, drying her hands on a grubby tea towel. Justin came out behind her. I told them about the drama at the Rookery. And then I realised that someone would need to tell Justin about Leon.

"Justin, I've got some bad news," I started.

"What, worse than Maria de Souza being stabbed?"

"Yeah."

Justin crumpled when I told him. All that Aussie brashness left him and his bright shiny face seemed to fold in on itself into sad, dull, deflated creases.

"I'm so sorry," I said.

"He was only fifteen," said Justin. "I thought I was getting somewhere with him. He could have turned himself around. Oh shit, he didn't have to die!" He thumped his knees with his fists. "What kind of fucking country is this?" he cried. "It's bad enough with the gangs and drugs; but where do these fucking fat cats get off from fucking up young kids' lives? Like they haven't got enough to deal with with their fucking awful families. Fuck it, I've had enough. See ya." He leapt up, and before I could say anything or hold him back, he'd stormed through the front door and slammed it behind him. I got the feeling I wouldn't ever see him again.

Chapter 31

We locked up and went our separate ways. I headed for home. The free paper was rammed in the letter box along with a letter from the bank that I shoved under the phone onto the ever growing pile of mail that I really should deal with, but was avoiding. Too much else going on. There was a phone message from Ruby. She was having a party on Saturday, maybe I'd like to go. Maybe I would. I stripped off my clothes and hoped that the grass stains would wash out of my chinos. I showered, relishing the comforting flow of the hot water, soaping away some of the cares of this most crazy of days. I'd towelled dry briskly and was stepping into clean cargo pants when the doorbell rang.

"Who is it?"

"It's me, Ben. You ok?"

"Yeah. Hang on…" I pulled on a dusky pink, brushed cotton shirt that didn't need ironing. I padded to the door and opened it to let Ben through.

"Jesus, Nik, don't you ever open your post?"

"Not if I can help it."

"You don't answer your phone, either. Why did you hang up on me? I really needed a friend this afternoon."

"Your call nearly got me killed," I said. I told him about Bentley, Maria, and me in the Rookery.

"Oh," he said, looking almost sorry, almost humble. "God, that's awful! Is she going to be ok, this Maria?"

"Think so. He'd just missed her heart, according to the nurse."

"And you? Are you ok?"

"Yeah, yeah, I'm fine. Just a bit shaken. And sad. He killed a kid. The kid who attacked me on Tuesday."

"So why are you sad? The kid tried to kill you!"

"I know. He was fucked up. Crap family. Drugs. Probably marked out as a loser from the day he was born. But he was still a kid, Ben, he was just fifteen. Justin thought he was getting somewhere with him. Maybe he would have come good, but he just didn't have a chance. Maybe he'd never had a chance." I thought of Justin, of his despair. I wished I had a way of contacting him. After these weeks of seeing him as vain, a bit shallow, out of his depth with the kids, I now knew that he was more than that. I hoped he wasn't having to hold all that sorrow on his own.

"So don't you want to know why I phoned you?"

"Yeah. Yeah, go on, tell me." I dragged myself back to the present, put thoughts of Justin aside.

"Rick. He's a bastard. All that time he was in Paris, he was shagging some skinny young assistant. Honestly, Nik, I really thought..."

"...he was the one?"

"Well, maybe. Different from the rest."

"I'm sorry Ben. You deserve better."

"Fancy keeping me company?"

"Not tonight, Ben. Sorry, I'm meeting Carla and Siobhan. You're welcome to come along too."

"No, I'll pass. Thanks, though."

I wished Carla and Benjamin liked each other more. "I'm around tomorrow. Cook you lunch?"

"No – let's go out. My treat."

"Ok." Why did everyone suddenly come up with other plans whenever I mentioned cooking for them? How bad could my cooking be?

I arrived at the little vegetarian café just after eight. Carla and Siobhan were already there, tucking into hummous and olives. I realised I was starving.

"So, what happened? You sounded very mysterious on the phone," said Carla. "More gruesome goings on at *Action in Caring?*"

"You could say that," I said. "Let's order first."

Carla and I chose homity pie and salad, a house speciality, and Siobhan decided on a spicy red bean casserole. The waitress looked as wholesome as the food. We opted for a bottle of organic red wine so as not to seem too puritanical.

"So?" Carla had that look that said, tell me now or we won't be friends. Siobhan, next to her, was armed back-up. I relayed my tale once more, this time giving my sheltering azalea a starring role.

"So then we were all at the hospital, waiting to see if Maria would be ok," I finished.

"Shit, Nikki, it just gets worse!"

"Yeah, but at least we know Bentley's behind bars."

"But if he didn't kill Veronica," said Siobhan, "then who on earth did?"

I was pondering that one when my homity pie arrived and at the same time my phone rang. Damn! I should have switched it to silent. Suresh's name flashed from my screen. I pressed the green button.

"Hi Suresh. What's up?"

"Wanna be my snapper tomorrow?"

"What's happening tomorrow?"

"Haven't you heard? Bentley's been arrested. Ginny Lancaster's giving a press conference tomorrow."

"Oh, that. Yeah, I was there."

"What?"

"I was there. Bentley had Maria in the bushes at the Rookery. I taped his confession on my mobile. Sent it to Wendy Baggott."

"And you didn't think to call me?"

"Kind of busy wondering if Maria would live, Suresh. Sorry. But yeah, I'll be your snapper tomorrow."

"I might have changed my mind."

"I was going to call you after my dinner."

"Yeah, and the rest, Nik."

"Look, you don't need me to tell you what's going down. And I had a date with Carla and Siobhan. And Benjamin called round just as I was getting ready…"

"Ok, ok. Pick you up 9.30 tomorrow. Be ready."

"Yessir. Don't forget the camera."

"Cheeky bitch."

"Don't forget, Meena doesn't, but I know about…"

"Yeah, ok, ok. Let's not go there, Nik. Pick you up tomorrow."

"'Bye."

"So what was that all about?" asked Carla.

"Suresh is my passport to the press conference Ginny Lancaster's giving tomorrow," I said. I went back to enjoying my dinner.

"That man's nothing but trouble," grumbled Carla.

"So, shall we finish off the evening at *Sappho?*" asked Siobhan. "I think there's a band or some kind of music," she said. "Anyway, it should be good craic."

Sappho was filling up nicely. The last time I'd been here had been with Wendy. I wondered if she'd be in tonight.

"What was going on with you the other night?" asked Eva when I went to the bar to put in our order. "Looked like you just walked out on that gorgeous girl."

"Yeah, I know. I got an urgent call. To do with work and stuff."

"Work and stuff? You stand up a beautiful woman like that for *work and stuff?*"

"It was just one of those calls I couldn't ignore." Now I wished I hadn't bothered, had stayed put. I didn't know if she'd give me another chance.

I carried the drinks over to the table that Carla and Siobhan had commandeered. It was open mic night, and a buxom black woman was singing an R and B number. She was good. Siobhan was talking about something that had happened to her at work. It was hard to hear above the music and after a while I stopped trying. I couldn't keep my eyes away from the door, looking to see if Wendy arrived.

"Are you listening?" said Carla.

"What? Oh, yeah, well, trying to, but it's hard…"

"Siobhan was just saying that they're being taken over by some American firm. She doesn't know if she'll still have a job."

"She's good at what she does, they'd be mad to lose her."

"That's what I said, but…hey, isn't that…?"

"Yeah! Look, I'll catch up when it's quieter, I've just got to say hi to Wendy." As I leapt up, I knocked over Carla's glass of wine.

"Oh, God, our Nikki's in love," teased Siobhan.

"I'll get you another," I said. Wendy was taking off her jacket. She looked even more gorgeous out of uniform. A black t-shirt clung to her lean top, her legs looked long and slim in well-cut jeans. She'd come in alone. Maybe there was hope. I went over to her.

"Hi Wendy, can I get you a drink?" I gabbled.

"Hey, Nikki. I thought you'd be in bed sleeping off your afternoon. You're not answering your phone."

"Did you ring?"

"About half an hour ago."

"It's noisy. I probably didn't hear it."

"Well, you're here."

"Would you like…I mean, I don't know if you're meeting someone…but if you want to join Carla and Siobhan and me…"

"Well at least tonight you won't hear your phone if it goes off." She was grinning.

"So, can I get you a drink?"

"I'll have a pint of Stella."

"We're just over there." I pointed at our table. Carla waved.

"Ok, if you're sure your friends won't mind."

"You're one lucky girl," said Eva as she pulled Wendy's pint. "She's either mad or nuts about you."

Carla and Siobhan were smooching to a slow bluesy number being crooned in Spanish by a slinky Latino woman

"So why were you ringing me?" I asked, settling into the chair next to Wendy's.

"Thought you'd want to know what I'd been doing at work after I left you," she said.

"Why?"

"I got to sit in on Ginny's questioning of Nigel Bentley."

"No!"

"Uh-huh. And although he didn't say much, he's going to find it very hard to refute all the evidence."

"So what'd he say?"

"This is between us? You won't tell your pal on the paper?"

"He'll want to know."

"He'll get the official version soon enough. There's to be a press conference tomorrow morning."

"Ok, I won't say anything. He's asked me to be his snapper at the press conference."

"Ok. So Bentley called his lawyer straight off. He admitted to attacking Maria and being involved in some company called Eurobuild."

"The company that won the contract for SoLCEC."

"You knew about that?"

"Yeah, and Gordon Smedley was company secretary for a subsidiary company, Cityscape."

"You have been doing your homework!"

"So what about the killings? And setting those boys up? And killing Leon Dodds?"

"He denied it all, of course, but there's evidence that he was at the Common on the night that Gordon Smedley died, and of course there's the evidence that you phoned in. That'll clinch it. Sound quality's not brilliant, but his words are clear enough. And there's some forensic evidence, but I don't have all the details. And one of the lads is being questioned."

"What about Veronica?"

"He denied all knowledge, but Ginny seems to think he might be connected. It's to do with trying to get all the centres closed down."

"Yeah, we'd worked that one out."

"So, that's what happened. It doesn't look too good for him. Magistrate turned down his lawyer's request for bail."

"All that harm and death, just because some man's power crazy. Did you get that bit about him wanting to be mayor of London?"

"Yeah. Pathetic, isn't it?"

"More than that." We sipped at our drinks in silence for a while. Carla and Siobhan were still dancing.

"So, how about a dance?" suggested Wendy. The R and B woman was holding centre stage again and singing the old Carole King number, *Will You Still Love Me Tomorrow?* How could I refuse?

I woke late on Saturday. I'd come home alone. I could still smell Wendy, and my skin still tingled from where she'd held me. But I needed to take things slowly, and I felt that she did too. I'd asked her if she wanted to come to Ruby's party with me, and she'd said, *why not?* I'd crashed into bed and slept through my alarm clock a deep and dreamless sleep. No time now for breakfast. I showered and dressed and was ready to go when Suresh called at nine. I followed him down my stairs and into the car. Sat-nav woman was having a day off.

"I spoke to Leo Balmforth yesterday," said Suresh, as he pulled away from the kerb.

"He's been trying to get hold of you for ages."

"It may be something or nothing."

"What did he say?"

"He said someone should look into senior appointments being made at SoLCEC."

"What did he mean?"

"The top jobs went out to advert last month. Chief Executive, Director of Finance, Director of Enterprise, Director of Marketing and Communications. CEO's going for ninety thousand, and the others for sixty. He said I should look into how the appointments were made and who got the jobs."

"Can you do that?"

"Not until Monday, I shouldn't think."

"Why does he want you to look into it?"

"Says there's been massive corruption and hinted at backhanders."

"How would he know?"

"That's what I asked him. He got cagey then. Said he'd got inside information but couldn't disclose his source."

"Sounds like he's been reading too many bad crime novels."

"I'll look into it on Monday. They only did the interviews this week. They haven't issued the press release with the names of the lucky candidates."

"So it could be something or nothing."

"Guess so."

The press conference started at ten, which I thought was pretty early for a Saturday morning. Suresh parked the car.

"Let's go," he said, thrusting the now familiar camera at me.

I checked my camera to make sure the battery was charged and there was space on the card. Suresh had to do his routine about the regular cameraman being off sick in order to get me in; and then there we were in a room full of skinny women and paunchy men with tape recorders, cameras, and shorthand pads. The TV crews with their bulky cameras stood in the aisles. I thought I recognised a blonde woman in smart khaki from breakfast TV news. We squeezed past a couple of guys, who knew Suresh and greeted him with "aright?", into the middle of the third row. There was a long table and a line of chairs on a stage. We'd just settled ourselves when a familiar figure came out and took the centre chair on the platform. Ginny Lancaster's hair was neatly tied back and she was wearing the usual sharp suit. She glowed as if she'd just come out of the gym, not like someone who'd spent the night grilling scummy councillors in subterranean interview rooms. Ginny was flanked by an officer in uniform and a well built black man in a suit.

"Good morning ladies and gentlemen," she began, and the room went quiet. "Most of you know me. I'm DCI Ginny Lancaster. On my right is Detective Jim Caper who has been helping to piece together the evidence for this case. On my left is our communications officer, Errol Johnson. Yesterday we arrested Councillor Nigel Bentley on suspicion of being involved in the deaths of Veronica Stein, Gordon Smedley, Leon Dodds, and Tanya Middleton. All the deceased had a connection with local charity *Action in Caring*. We charged Mr Bentley with the murder of Mr Smedley, and conspiracy to murder Tanya Middleton, in the early hours of this morning. We also charged him with grievous bodily harm in relation to an attack on local community leader, Maria de Souza. Who's got the first question?"

Cameras were flashing and hands shot up. Ginny pointed at someone in a row behind us.

"Yes?"

"Kate Leeming of the Telegraph. Can you tell us, Ms Lancaster, what evidence you have against Mr Bentley?"

"Confessional, foresensic, and circumstantial. We're still evaluating evidence. Yes?" Ginny stretched and pointed towards the back of the room.

"Laurie Griffin, London in Focus. Can you tell us what motive the suspect had in killing the three victims?"

"There would appear to be links to fraudulent business dealings. I'm afraid I can't tell you any more at the moment."

"Des Sherman, The Sun. Is it true that Bentley and Smedley shared a love nest and that the killings had S and M aspects?"

"There is no truth in those assertions, Mr Sherman," replied Ginny.

"Lyn Newman, Daily Mail. Can you comment on the rumour that Councillor Bentley was claiming disability benefits for himself and child benefits for the illegitimate child he'd had with Tanya Middleton?"

"The Department for Work and Pensions has not made any allegations about fraudulent benefit claims in this case, and Tanya Middleton had no children. There is no evidence that she ever met, let alone had a relationship, with Councillor Bentley." She pointed at a tall thin man in the front row.

"Chris Keen, The Guardian. Detective Lanchester, can you tell us whether there's any truth in the speculation that Councillor Bentley was orchestrating a deliberate campaign to close down small community centres in order to sell off the land and that Graham Smedley was about to blow the whistle?"

"I'm afraid I can't comment, Mr Crane," said Ginny.

Suresh had been pushing his hand up from the start of the proceedings. Ginny looked at him reluctantly. I took her photo, and she squinted at the unexpected flash.

"Mr Shah?"

"Suresh Shah, South London Press. Ginny, what evidence do the police have so far that Councillor Bentley was profiting through his connections with Eurobuild in the development of South London Community and Enterprise Centre, and that Gordon Smedley was also profiting through his role as company secretary with Cityscape, Eurobuild's subsidiary?"

I thought I saw the trace of an admiring smile flit across Ginny's face.

"The investigation is in its early stages, Mr Shah," she said. "I'm not in a position to comment on your questions at this point, but we will let you know as soon as there are developments."

"Bingo!" whispered Suresh, as he scribbled shorthand onto his pad.

"This press conference is now ended. Thank you, ladies and gentlemen. We will let you know as events unfold." Ginny rose and strode off the stage, accompanied by the two silent men who had flanked her and the flashes of cameras.

"So, where does that leave us?" I asked Suresh between mouthfuls of scrambled egg at the little Portuguese café round the corner from the hall that had just hosted the press conference.

"It means that we're going along the right lines," said Suresh, buttering his croissant. "It means that the Mail is likely to face a libel

371

suit if it publishes the stuff about benefits and bastards; The Sun will sub-edit with its usual skill, but headlines alluding to deviant sex will boost sales; and The Guardian will get everyone's name wrong so no-one will be any the wiser as to who did what to whom."

"So you're chasing the elusive scoop," I said.

"Of course!" he said, and slurped at his cappuccino. When he put the cup down, he'd got a foam moustache.

Suresh drove me home. I felt so tired, I just wanted to go back to bed; but Ruby had invited me to her party, and Wendy was coming round. There was something nice about weekend afternoon parties. And I'd promised Benjamin lunch. I felt safe now that Bentley was in custody. Maybe we could start getting back to whatever normal was and *Action in Caring* could get on with the business of doing good things for the community. I kicked off my shoes and slumped onto the sofa. I rang Carla. She picked up before the ansaphone: a miracle. Maybe today was going to turn out ok.

"Hey Nik, how'd it go?"

I replayed the press conference for Carla. She laughed when I got to the bit about the reporter from The Sun.

"So it's all over?"

"Just about. Looks that way. Except I don't see where Veronica's death fits in. Bentley says he didn't do it. Gordon could've done, only he's not around to say. Well, it'll have to wait until Monday. Wanna come with Wendy and me to Ruby's party?"

"No. Siobhan and I thought we'd hang out for a while. You free Tuesday?"

"Yeah, should be."

"Glass Bar?"

"Sounds good. Half six?"

"See you there."

"Have fun."

"You too."

Benjamin came up at 12.30. "You ready to go, Nik?"

"Yeah. Where do you fancy?"

"Noodle place?"

"Cool. I need to be back by three."

We walked down the High Road until we reached the noodle bar which described its cuisine as *fusion,* which meant that it didn't know if it was Chinese, Japanese or Thai. Or possibly Indonesian or Vietnamese. It was the same place I'd been to with Chantelle, what felt like a lifetime ago.

"People think I Japanese, but I not Japanese," proclaimed the waiter as he plonked the menus down.

"Oh," I said, not sure how I was supposed to react.

"Where you think I from?"

"I don't know," I said. "Definitely not Japanese."

"Where you think I from?" he demanded of Benjamin.

"Um…Vietnam?"

The waiter snorted. "Huh! Vietnam? *Vietnam?* No way."

At that point I knew that our lunch was unlikely to be edible, at least if our waiter had anything to do with it.

"Please tell us," I said, trying to get the waiter back on our side.

He stood, hands on hips, frowning as if trying to decide whether to tell or not. "I part Chinese, part Thai, part Philippino," he said.

"That's nice," said Benjamin with an ingratiating smile.

"I hate Philippinos," he said. "What you want drink?"

Our food was fine. Benjamin told me about Rick Landor's betrayal of his trust and how his heart was broken. He didn't think he'd ever be able to go to an art gallery again. I said I hoped that wasn't true. I told him about bumping into Wendy last night, and about our plans to go to Ruby's party. Benjamin said he thought he'd go to *Edge* and see who was there. At least he wasn't as desolate as when lycra man dumped him. We paid the bill and left the waiter a good tip. It must be tough to hate a third of your genetic make-up. We walked back up the High Road.

"Want a beer and a spliff?" Benjamin asked.

"No, I'll pass. Thanks, though," I said. "I need some quiet time before I meet Wendy." Yesterday's drama and today's early start had begun to hit me and I felt tired and limp.

I had a couple of hours before Wendy was due. I could chill out, catch up on my reading. Finish the Jackie Kay. I made a cup of jasmine tea and curled up on the sofa with my book. The next thing I knew, the doorbell was ringing. I'd fallen into a deep sleep and it took me a few seconds to uncurl my leaden body and stumble to the door.

"Who is it?"

"It's Wendy. Are you ok?"

"Yeah. I'll let you in." I pressed the button to open the door to the street and then opened my front door. Wendy bounded up the stairs looking fresh and ready to party. She was wearing tight black jeans and a khaki t-shirt that hugged her pert round breasts. I felt like shit. I must have looked dreadful. I hated her seeing me like this, but then Wendy had seen me in various states of awfulness, so maybe she thought this was my natural state. "Sorry. I fell asleep," I said.

"We don't have to be there yet, do we?"

"No, I think it was any time from three. D'you mind if I have a shower?"

"Go ahead. I'll just browse your bookshelf."

"Want something to drink?"

"I can do it. Can I get something for you?"

"Coffee. Black and strong." I liked that Wendy felt at home in my flat. The shower felt good and I started to feel more like a woman about to go on a date with someone really hot and less like something scraped from the gutter. I heard the door open, and through the shower curtain saw Wendy come in bearing a steaming mug.

"Will I scrub your back for you?" she asked, placing the coffee on top of the toilet cistern.

"Oh…well…I don't know…" but she'd opened the curtain, gently prised the bath sponge from my hand and was poised waiting for me to turn around. "Ok then," I said. Mum had taught me all about passive resistance to police pressure when she'd taken me on marches. Somehow I don't think this was the kind of scenario she had in mind.

"Wait," said Wendy, "I'll get soaked. I'll just take off my t-shirt."

I surrendered to Wendy's sensual soaping. She reached up to my shoulders. She moved the sponge in circles that became more and more like caresses, and then she moved up and down my spine, until she found the base and circled, moving more and more slowly, until I moaned.

Later, much later, Wendy and I lay in a tangle on my bed. Every cliché I'd ever heard or read ran around my head: died and gone to heaven; blown my mind; it must be love.

"We going to your niece's party, then?" she crooned, a kiss glancing my neck.

"Mmm."

"I'm going to put my clothes on…"

"Don't!"

By the time we staggered into Ruby's, the party was buzzing. Everyone looked impossibly young. Ruby disentangled herself from the arms of a sinuous young man with long hair and came to hug me. She was holding a long, fat spliff.

"Hey Auntie Nik, how you doing?"

"Oh, I'm just great," I said, wondering how much longer my legs would hold me up. "This is Wendy."

"Hi Wendy," said Ruby, scrutinising the glowing woman whose hand rested lightly and deliciously on the small of my back. "What do you do, then?"

"I go to parties with your aunt," said Wendy with a mischievous smile.

"What else?"

"Oh, I'm in law," said Wendy.

"Cool," said Ruby.

"We've brought some wine," I said.

"Great," said Ruby. "The drink and food's through there…" she pointed towards a kitchen. I was famished.

"What's the party for?" I asked. "It's not your birthday for a couple of months."

"We just thought we'd have one," said Ruby, dragging at the spliff. "A sort of happy- Sunday-it's- nearly-summer type of party." For once, I was relieved that she hadn't offered me a smoke.

Wendy and I headed for the kitchen and grabbed some French bread and hummous. The music was loud. Some people were dancing, young women a glorious whirl of colour and grace, the men darker, mostly stiffer, although Ruby's man moved like a Brazilian dancer. Other groups of people sat in intense groups, debating life and death topics. Yet others were standing, talking and laughing, knocking back the wine, cider, beer. Once we'd eaten, Wendy and I joined the dancers until night fell and we headed back, wrapped in each other, to my flat.

"Do you want to stay?" I asked.

"D'you think you could stop me?" she replied.

Chapter 32

I woke early, feeling stronger and clearer than I had in months. Wendy was asleep and I turned into her, kissing her back until she stretched and turned, kissing me hard on the mouth.

"Tea? Coffee?" I asked, thinking that I'd give anything not to have to get out of this bed, and wondering how I could endure an hour, let alone a day, without this woman in my arms.

"Wassatime?"

"Seven."

"Shit! Oh Nik, I've got to go home." She sat up and brushed her hand through her hair. "I'm on duty at nine, and my uniform's at home."

"Coffee? You must have time for some breakfast. Then you can run home."

She grinned at me. "You and your breakfasts! You're a porridge temptress."

I tore myself away from her and headed for the kitchen. I made us both coffee and porridge and took it all on a tray back to bed.

"I can't believe this," said Wendy, sipping at the coffee.

"What, that I can cook porridge?"

"No, silly; I'm sure you're a wonderful cook. No, I can't believe that you and I are here, in your bed, and that yesterday happened."

"Me too." I wouldn't disillusion her about my cooking. Not yet.

Wendy left, and my flat had never felt quieter. I made more coffee and thought about dealing with my post; but why spoil a perfect morning? I switched on the radio, but it was the morning service from some happy clappy congregation in Guildford, so I turned it off again and read another short story. At ten o'clock, I decided to spring clean the flat. I put the radio on again: it was time I caught up with *The*

Archers to give myself something to talk about with Mum. Radio's great: you can listen while doing all manner of things. I cleaned out the fridge, scrubbed the top of the cooker, mopped kitchen and bathroom floors, thought about changing my sheets, but decided not to because they smelled of Wendy. I weeded out the junk mail from the pile under the phone and shoved it into the recycling box. I stopped short of opening the bank statements or looking at the bills. Not a bad morning's work. I sank back into bed to listen to the end of the everyday tale of country folk. Phil and Jill were still going strong, David and Ruth a bit rocky, and the Grundys had retained their crown as the most dysfunctional family in Borsetshire. The closing tune bounced its way across the airwaves. The time had come, I knew, to face my demons. It was time to deal with my bills and open my bank statements. Now that I'd been paid, I had just enough to cover the bills without going over my overdraft limit. After I'd written the cheques, I decided to celebrate by taking Benjamin out for Sunday lunch.

"So how was last night?" he asked, with uncharacteristic delicacy. We'd gone to Soho and were noshing falafels at Ma Oz in Old Compton Street.

"The best," I said.

"And Ruth?"

"History. You're dripping tahina sauce down your shirt."

Monday morning came round too soon. I'd spent an hour on the phone on Sunday telling Carla about Wendy, and I'd rung Helena de Souza to see how Maria was doing. She was recovering well and had been interviewed by the police. Benjamin had come up with a bottle of wine and a DVD of *Priscilla, Queen of the Desert* part way through the evening. Wendy and I had texted each other at least ten times, much to Benjamin's annoyance as the phone ringing interrupted his viewing. I had almost forgotten about the mayhem of the previous week by the time I flopped into bed; but Monday morning meant going to work, and going to work meant facing again the terrible things that had happened. And I couldn't forget that part of the puzzle was still missing: who killed Veronica?

I arrived at *Action in Caring* just after Geri.

"Good weekend?" she said.

"Yes," I answered. Then I decided to take a risk and tell her about Wendy.

"Well, I don't know what to say!" she said. "I mean, are congratulations in order?"

"Maybe," I said with a grin. I was floating. Today I could do anything.

"How was yours?"

"Not as exciting as yours! Listen, I know it's hard and you'll not be thinking about much other than when you can next see Wendy, but we've got a couple of new things happening today, so we'd better be on our toes."

And so the day passed, with Felicity's class for pregnant mums, a Tai Chi class; and a refugee advice session. Someone phoned through to say that the young offenders' group had been cancelled for the week, and I guessed that Justin really had thrown in the towel. I felt sad. His boys needed someone who believed in their capacity to change and make something of themselves. Still, the place felt lively for once. I enjoyed showing new people around, helping them to feel at home. If word got around that this was a friendly and welcoming place, maybe other groups would start to use the centre.

"You look like a new woman," said Geri, catching me humming as I tidied the fliers on the reception desk.

"I've *got* a new woman," I said.

"Maybe that's where I've been going wrong," said Geri, grinning. "You haven't forgotten it's the management committee meeting tonight, have you?"

"The papers are all ready. Shall I make the sandwiches?"

"We'll do them together. I'll pop out and get the bread."

"No Mighty White!"

While Geri was out, my mobile rang. It was Suresh.

"Nik, I've got something. It's dynamite. I think I know who killed Veronica and why."

"Are you serious? So who…"

"I can't do this on the phone. I'm coming over."

"But we're having a management committee meeting. It's due to start in under an hour."

"All the better. Make sure you're not on your own at any time."

"Shit, Suresh, can't you just…"

"No, just need to check a couple of details. See you in an hour."

Rita was the first to arrive, Prudence wagging her tail and leaping up in joy to see me again. I ruffled her head. She dived for a shoelace.

"Well, what a turn up," said Rita. "I always knew there was something dodgy about that Nigel Bentley." I didn't say anything, but it sounded as if she was in for another revelation this evening.

Bernard came in next. He looked happier than he had done last time I saw him. Surely Bernard couldn't be a threat to anyone.

"How's your wife?" I asked, as I made him a cup of tea.

"She's settled down in her new place. Still doesn't know me most of the time," he said. "But Dinah's been down to stay, and she's invited me to go for a holiday to Orkney, and I think I might just do that. It would be good to have some time with the grandchildren."

Lawrence came through the door looking more dishevelled than ever. I didn't see him as a threat, either. Weak, self-absorbed maybe; but a killer? Yet Suresh's warning suggested that someone here was responsible for killing Veronica.

"Are we all here?" asked Lawrence.

"Just waiting for Derek and Joan," said Geri. As if on cue, the doorbell rang. I buzzed it open, and there was Joan.

"We'll just go and get the tea and sandwiches," I said, grabbing Geri's elbow and steering her towards the kitchen.

"What's up, Nikki?" she said, as I shoved her through the door.

"Suresh is coming," I said, "my friend the journalist. He says he thinks he knows who killed Veronica. Listen, I need to let Wendy know. Maybe Ginny too. He may have involved them, but you never know with blokes. Especially blokes who think they're Streatham's answer to Hercule Poirot."

"Jesus, Nikki. Things were pretty quiet around here until you came to work with us."

"Yeah, well, blame the Job Centre. Blame Tony Blair and Europe and Welfare to Work."

I rang Wendy, but her voicemail picked up. I sent her a text. I did the same to Ginny. Then I helped Geri to take the sandwiches and tea into the meeting room.

Everyone filed in and took their places around the table. As I got my pad ready to take the minutes, the doorbell rang, and I went to open it, checking the monitor first. Derek was standing there, so I buzzed him in.

"We're about to start," I said. He just nodded at me and headed for the meeting room. He sat at the table in the same place he'd occupied at that first meeting. He unzipped his case, took out the slender laptop, and placed it on the table in front of him.

"Well, I think we're all here now," said Lawrence. "There's a lot been happening and we need to…er, we need to…" he paused while he bit into a sandwich.

"…decide how to keep *Action in Caring* going?" suggested Rita.

"Yes. We need to think about whether we can do that or whether it would be better to join up with SoLCEC."

"I don't think we should be considering that," cried Rita, red with indignation. "It's our job to keep *Action in Caring* open for all the groups that use it. Geri and Nikki have done splendid work in bringing in new business. Derek, what's the latest on the cash flow?"

Derek tapped at some keys on the laptop. "From what I can see," he said, "there's not much improvement. Lawrence is right that we should be looking to merge with a more viable centre."

"I hope I'm not speaking out of turn," said Geri, "but I've done some projections based on the new work that we've brought in and some hopeful leads. There've been some developments since you were last here, Derek." She passed a slim set of papers around the table. The doorbell rang.

"I'll get it," I said, as people were looking at Geri's tables. I ran back out to reception, checked on the monitor, buzzed in Suresh.

"So what's going on?" I demanded as I closed the door behind him.

"It's so fucking pathetic," said Suresh. Then he outlined what he'd found.

"How'd you put it all together?"

"Leo Balmforth. One of Maria de Souza's kids. Asking around. And the police were just about there."

"I've let Ginny Lancaster and Wendy Baggott know that you're onto something."

"Yeah, I've left messages for Ginny and the Child Exploitation and Online Protection Team, and I put one into the Child Abuse Investigation Command for good measure."

"Let's go."

We joined the meeting as Geri was talking the committee through her projections. Either no-one noticed that a stranger had joined the proceedings, or they were beyond caring.

"You'll see that things are really tight, but if the tai chi group and refugee advice sessions carry on, and if we can bring back some of the mums and toddlers groups, we should just about break even. Pete, one of the new volunteers, has offered to do odd jobs for free and to give the centre a lick of paint."

"That's brilliant news," said Rita.

"Yes, well done," said Bernard.

"But it's not what you want to hear, is it Derek?" I said.

Derek frowned at me. "I'm not sure what you're getting at," he said.

"You'd like to see the back of this centre, wouldn't you?" I said. Everyone looked at me as if I'd gone mad.

"Why would he want that?" asked Rita.

"Veronica wasn't coming to you for hypnosis any more, was she?" I continued. "She was blackmailing you. She'd found out about your fondness for young boys, and she knew that if it got out, you'd be finished."

"I'm sorry, Vicky, but I don't know what you mean," said Derek.

"Is this relevant to the agenda?" asked Lawrence

"My name's *Nikki*," I said, "and Lawrence, in the circumstances, fuck your agenda." Lawrence started to protest, but Joan said,

"Oh, do shut up, Lawrence."

"Go on, Nikki," said Bernard.

"Bentley and you had a nice little set-up, didn't you? You used your connections to get boys for him, and he shoehorned you into the Finance Director post at SoLCEC. Suresh, tell them the rest."

"Gordon Smedley found out," said Suresh, "and even he couldn't stomach what you were doing. He told Veronica, but instead of siding with Gordon and reporting you to the police, she saw her chance to make some money. But you were running out, weren't you? You didn't have enough to keep her quiet."

"This is outrageous!" cried Derek, snapping down the lid of his laptop and starting to stand. "I don't have to stay here and listen to this craziness!" Beads of sweat had broken out on his forehead, and damp patches were spreading under the arms of his smart striped shirt.

"I think you do," said Joan.

The doorbell rang. "I'll get it," said Geri, and slipped out.

"I'm not standing for this!" said Derek, packing away the laptop. His hands were shaking.

"Leo Balmforth works for the London Development Agency, and they'd been overseeing the recruitment to the SoLCEC posts. He knew that the senior appointments were a fix," said Suresh. "That's why he's been trying to talk to me for days. Gordon was becoming a liability, so he had to go. Nigel Bentley thought that by appointing you as Director of Finance, he'd have an accomplice in place, someone who owed him enough to be prepared to keep the lid on some of the dirtier deals."

"Prove it!" yelled Derek, lunging across the table at Suresh.

"Sit down," commanded Bernard.

"Can we bring this meeting to order?" said Lawrence.

Derek started to move towards the door. Prudence, who had been sitting quietly under the table, growled and leapt out to block his exit.

"This is madness!" cried Derek, cringing back from the dog.

"I don't think so," said Ginny Lancaster, who, together with Darren Lowe, and two uniformed officers had come into the room. "I'll have that laptop, please. We've already got enough evidence to charge you with possession of child pornography, the abuse of a minor, and the unlawful killing of Veronica Stein."

"You haven't got anything," said Derek.

"We've got a USB stick with your prints all over it, traces of peanut oil on the casing, and indecent images in its memory."

The room was silent. Derek crumpled. I suddenly flashed back to Darren Lowe on that Wednesday, emerging from Veronica's and Gordon's offices carrying a little plastic evidence bag. Derek had come into the fateful management committee meeting with Veronica. They must have been talking in her office beforehand. I remembered they'd both come out of the kitchen. He could have contaminated the sandwich in an instant, even in front of Veronica if one of their backs were turned.

"Derek Ramsay, I'm arresting you for the murder of Veronica Stein. You do not have to say anything, but anything you do say…" Ginny continued to read Derek his rights, while the guys in uniform cuffed him.

"I'll be in touch, Mr Shah," said Ginny, nodding at Suresh. "Sorry for the interruption. Do go on with your meeting," she said before turning and following Derek, Darren and the uniforms out.

"I'll be off then. Got a deadline to meet," said Suresh. "Good luck with whatever you decide to do next. I'll be in touch for some quotes tomorrow."

"Thanks Suresh," I said. "Catch you later."

No-one spoke for a while. Bernard broke the silence. "It's always the quiet ones," he said. "I didn't like Gordon – I'd met his type before; but I thought Derek was all right. Just goes to show."

"But *how* did he do it?" asked Rita. "I mean, how could he have doctored her sandwiches without one of us knowing?"

"You all knew that Veronica had a separate plate," said Geri. "It would have been quite easy to squirt or drop the nut oil on a sandwich, replace the cling film. No-one would know anything was wrong."

"They were both in the kitchen just before the meeting," I said. "Maybe they went in for a glass of water, who knows. But all he needed to do was go to the fridge on some pretence or other. He'd know that the smaller plate was hers. He'd know that the cheese sandwiches were for everyone else."

"He was a hypnotist," said Joan. "Not a very good one, but he could have put Veronica in a light trance, so that she did not register what he was doing."

"How dreadful, to be that desperate, to want something so badly you'd kill for it," said Geri.

"We'd better get on with the meeting," said Lawrence. "It's obvious that with no director and no treasurer we'll have to merge with SoLCEC."

"No, it isn't obvious at all," said Joan. "What's obvious is that we need a new chairperson."

"Couldn't agree more," said Bernard.

"Allefuckingluia!" said Rita. "You standing, Joan?"

"Well…"

"You'd be the best person, if I might say so," added Bernard.

"Very well," said Joan. "Thank you. I accept. But I'll need a first rate treasurer. Bernard?"

"It would be my pleasure," said Bernard.

"This isn't constitutional," said Lawrence. "We need an AGM."

"No, we don't," said Joan. "As members of the management committee, we can decide to appoint – or remove – the officers. You should consider yourself removed. Nikki, would you be so kind as to minute that the management committee decided to appoint a new Chair and Treasurer?"

There was something wonderfully Miss Marplesque about Joan tonight.

"Then I'll go," sniffed Lawrence. "At least there's a future with SoLCEC." He scraped back his chair, gathered his papers and left. Amazingly there was a half eaten sandwich on his plate and he'd not touched the chocolate biscuits.

"We'll need to recruit a new director and finance manager," I said, having noted down all the new appointments. "Do we need to put out an advert? And with Geri moving on, we'll need to bring in an administrator."

"Nikki and Geri, would you mind going to make some more tea?" said Joan, and it was clear that she wanted to talk with the others without our being there.

"Yeah, no problem." Geri and I left the room and went into her office.

"What do you think all that's about?" I asked.

"Could be that they can't afford to keep both of our posts going. Maybe they're going to try to do without a manager or downsize the director post. We'll know soon enough. Shall we make that tea?"

We took our time in the kitchen and then walked slowly back to the meeting. We handed round the fresh tea and resumed our places.

"This has been an extraordinary month," began Joan. "Our centre has been hit by tragedy, and at a time when it's harder than ever for small grass roots groups to keep going, we need a strong team to manage *Action in Caring*. Nikki, you've been with us for less than a month, and yet you've played a major role in keeping things going. Geri, you've shown calm, vision, and we think you have great leadership skills."

"Thank you," we said together. Ok, I thought, now tell us we're fired. Chantelle, here I come.

"So we want to make a proposition," said Joan. "Geri, we know you've been offered a good job at LOTUS with more money and a promotion. But we'd like to offer you an even better one. We'd like to offer you the post of director of *Action in Caring*."

"Me? But I'm just an administrator." said Geri

"You've got great organisational skills, you're competent with money, you've got a vision for this centre. We think that with you in charge, *Action in Caring* has the best chance of survival it's going to get."

"I don't know what…"

"Just say yes, love," said Rita. "Anyway, you're the only one who can handle Dora Popp."

"Can I think about it? Let you know tomorrow?"

"Of course," said Joan. "And Nikki, we've been impressed by your skills. We think that you and Geri make a great team. We'd like you to be her deputy and take over the administration."

I think my mouth dropped open. No words came out. No going back to Chantelle, then. Not for now, at least.

"What do you say?" asked Rita

"Well," I said, "If Geri says yes, then I do too."

"There'll be some changes," said Joan. "We can't pay for a finance person too – Geri, you'd need to look after the money side of things, and Nikki, we'd want you to be out and about and drumming up new business."

"Sounds ok," I said. "And maybe we could join forces with the other small groups. Organisations like *Young Hearts*. Share resources. It's happening more and more."

"Yeah, I could go for that," said Geri, and I think I knew then what her answer would be. Joan was right. We'd be a great team. We'd revive *Action in Caring*, we'd harness the good will of people like Iris, Pete, Jade, and we'd turn our little centre into something that belonged to the community. Maybe we could even track down Justin and persuade him to give the job one more go.

"Here's to the future!" said Bernard, raising his teacup. Prudence gave my shoelace an extra tug.

I'd been to see Maria. She was at home now, and Helena had sent me a text with her address. Maria had asked to see me, and anyway I wanted to let her know how things had turned out.

"So, how are you doing?"

"Better every day. Thank you. Thank you for following your instinct. You saved my life, you know." She reached out for my hand. She looked so vulnerable without the bright colours and flowing clothes to protect her. But she was safe now.

"I'm glad I was there," I said. "There've been changes in the management committee at *AiC*," I said, and then told Maria about the offers that had been made to Geri and me.

"You should go for it," she said.

I told her about the suggestion that we band together as independent community groups. "We could share resources, order stuff in bulk, that sort of thing. It'd keep costs down, help us to stay viable."

"It's the best way forward," she said. "Let's talk when I'm properly better."

I left Maria and went to *Sappho*. Carla was already there, puzzling over the Guardian crossword. Wendy was trying to help. They both got up to hug me.

"So, tell us what happened?" said Carla. I described my day. "Wow! So Nigel Bentley killed Gordon Smedley, arranged for Tanya Middleton's death, and then killed the boys he'd set up?"

"And it was Derek Ramsay who spiked Veronica's sandwich," added Wendy.

"What happened when they questioned him?" I asked. I was still curious about one or two things.

"He cracked. Admitted to working with Smedley to defraud *Action in Caring*. Denied deliberately killing Veronica, saying that one of the peanuts that you'd put out must have got into her sandwich; but we had the USB stick which we'd found in Veronica's office. It had fallen under the desk. Eventually he admitted to having been in her office, to having taken her keys the night she died, and to coming into the building on the Saturday. He'd watched whoever set the alarm so he'd even been able to punch in the right code. She'd been blackmailing him and he wanted to see if she had anything on him on paper. Of course she *had* kept a record, but it was on her computer at home, not at work. She was looking to see what she could get from him and Bentley. If Ramsay hadn't killed Veronica, Bentley would have done. She had enough to send both of them down for years."

I told them about Joan's offer to Geri and me. "What do you think?"

"About time," said Carla. "You'll be brilliant."

"I've been really impressed by Geri," said Wendy.

"What about me?"

"I hadn't finished! And as for you, Ms Elliot, lifesaver extraordinaire…"

The next evening I sent a text to Carla, Benjamin, Geri, Suresh and Wendy: *Be at my flat 2nite 8pm or else.* I cycled home, stopping at the Greek/Turkish/Polish shop to pick up some vital ingredients on the way. I put away the clean dishes and washed up the dirty ones. Then I got to work. Benjamin was the first to arrive.

"Hi Nik, what's going on?" he said, frowning at my floury hands. "You're not cooking, are you?"

"Yup. Tonight's a really special occasion, so I've asked my best mates round and my new girlfriend, and my new work partner, and I'm trying out a recipe I saw in the paper for hassle free chocolate brownies."

"Oh God, Nik, you know you really shouldn't be let loose in a kitchen."

"Just shut up, Ben. Help me out by opening these bottles of wine." The doorbell rang, and I went to open it. Carla bounded in, arms open, but then recoiled at the sight of my hands.

"Is that talcum powder?"

"No, it's flour."

"You're doing some kind of art work with flour and water paste?"

"I'm baking chocolate brownies."

"Oh no."

"That's what I said," chipped in Benjamin.

"She can't cook," said Carla."

"Have you tried telling her?"

"Oh, many, many times."

"Me too."

At last, these two most important people in my life had managed to establish rapport. I should have been pleased, had I not felt that it had been entirely at my expense. I went back into the kitchen to add some salt – or was it sugar? – to the batter and give it a stir. I threw in some rum for good measure, even though it wasn't in the recipe. The doorbell rang, and I welcomed in Suresh.

"We'd better make the front page," I said.

"Can't think of a story to top this one," he said. "And the editor's talking about promotion. What's that all over your hands?"

"Flour. And cocoa. Maybe some salt or sugar," I said.

"Not brownies?"

"A new recipe, it'll be fine."

"I don't think I'll risk them – not after the last time."

"What can go wrong with chocolate brownies?"

"You tell me!"

Geri was the next to arrive, and she was carrying a huge flat pizza box and a carrier bag.

"Hey! Real food!" cried Benjamin. "Come in and be my friend!"

"I've brought ingredients for rum punch seeing as this is a party," said Geri.

"I love you already," said Benjamin.

Geri mixed the punch and Benjamin made sure everyone had a drink, while I stirred the batter some more. It had a strange consistency. There seemed to be little islands of goo swimming in pools of egg white. Maybe I'd missed out a stage with all the doorbell interruptions. I was about to spoon it into a baking tin when Benjamin came in.

"Look, if you're cooking brownies, at least put some of this in the mix so that there's some compensation for eating them!" And he tipped a handful of brown powder that looked like dark brown sugar but smelt like very good hash into the bowl. "Give it a good stir," he said. I'd forgotten to turn on the oven, but it would heat up soon enough if I turned it to its highest temperature, and the cake would cook sooner. I lit the oven and shoved in the baking tin. The doorbell rang. I ran to answer the door: it could only be Wendy, and there she was, more beautiful than I'd remembered.

"Any developments?" I asked, once we'd stopped kissing.

"Nigel Bentley's been formally charged with conspiracy to murder Tanya Middleton and with the murders of Gordon Smedley and Leon Dodds. Derek Ramsay's still not admitted to killing Veronica, but the evidence against him says it all. And CEOP are unpicking his computer files. We've got enough evidence and witnesses to put him away for years. How about you?"

"Geri and I said yes."

"Oh, Nikki, that's brilliant." She grabbed me again. Once we started kissing, we just didn't seem able to stop.

"Something smells good," she said, when she paused for breath, and she was looking at the kitchen, not at me.

Carla and Benjamin were sitting on the sofa, chatting like old friends when I brought out the cake. Geri had helped me to cut it up.

Suresh and Wendy were comparing dodgy south London crooks they'd investigated in their different roles.

"Cake's up!" I announced.

"Brilliant!" said Wendy. No-one else said anything.

I prised squares of flat and gooey brown stuff out of the tin and handed them around on pieces of kitchen towel. Each stared at their portion of my latest culinary sensation. Carla and Benjamin looked at each other and nibbled a corner. Suresh crumbled his and picked at the little lumps of dough. Eventually he put one in his mouth. Wendy made love eyes at me and ate half of hers in one go.

"Well, shame to waste such good ingredients," said Benjamin, and ate a large piece, chewing hard and closing his eyes in an effort to swallow.

Twenty minutes later, Benjamin and Wendy were giggling like a pair of ten-year-old schoolgirls. Suresh was communing with his Blackberry, checking the status of his story. Carla and I were sitting on the sofa.

"What a weird couple of weeks," she said. "So you're definitely going to give the new job a go?"

"Yeah. Why not? I think Geri and I can make *Action in Caring* work. See if we can help build it back up. We're going to start by decorating and making the centre somewhere that people want to hang out."

"We're a good team," said Geri, joining us on the sofa. "And there are all those great guys queuing up to help – Iris, Pete, Jade. Maybe we should give Dora Nikki's old job!" and Geri collapsed into helpless giggles

"There's still part of me would just like to move on. Part of me thinks that even with Derek and Bentley safely put away, we'll still not survive against the new way of doing things. You know, everything being seen as a business, all that professional glossiness that seems to be taking over everywhere. I don't know how much longer little players like *AiC* can keep going."

"Girl, you just stop that negative talk!" said Geri, wagging an index finger in my face. "Things are gonna change!"

"You tell her," said Carla.

And suddenly I felt that maybe things *were* going to change. I felt an arm go around my shoulders, a kiss on my neck.

"Nikki Elliot," said Wendy, "I just want to tell you: I don't know what you put into your cake, but it's the best brownie I've ever eaten."

"At least she can say honestly that she never inhaled," muttered Benjamin to Carla.

"We can always blame it on the rum punch," murmured Carla. Wendy didn't hear: she was heading for the bedroom.

"Guys, I love you all," I said, "but we've all got work tomorrow..."

"...and you and Wendy have got some serious business to see to," said Geri.

"Yeah, well," I said.

"Ok! Ok! We get the message," said Carla, putting on her jacket. "Tomorrow, *Sappho*, 6.00pm. I want to know everything!" she whispered as she hugged me goodnight.

"See you tomorrow," said Geri.

"Let me know how it goes," said Suresh.

"Sleep tight," said Benjamin, blowing an air kiss.

At last it was quiet. I took the plates and glasses into the kitchen. I thought back to the person who'd sat across the desk from Chantelle, not yet a month ago. These weeks had changed me. I wasn't so frightened of everything. I'd made new friends, was holding down a job. I was proud of what I'd managed to do. I felt taller, more sure of myself. Happier. For the first time in months, I felt that I had things to look forward to. And I had a warm, sexy, woman waiting for me in the next room. I threw off my red Kickers and headed for bed.

The End.